BEFORE
HE KILLS
AGAIN

An unputdownable crime thriller full of twists

MARGARET MURPHY

Detective Cassie Rowan Book 1

JOFFE
BOOKS

First published 2020
Joffe Books, London
www.joffebooks.com

**Join our mailing list for free Kindle books
and new releases.**

ISBN 978-1-78931-462-5

For Murf

ACKNOWLEDGEMENTS

I've long been fascinated by psychology, and in particular the psychopathology of the criminal mind. Book research is one of my great pleasures in being a writer, and I am grateful to all the authors whose writing has shaped my thinking and influenced my own work. There are a few research texts, however, that I've returned to again and again, and they deserve a special mention: *The Anatomy of Human Destructiveness* and *To Have or To Be?* by Erich Fromm; *Children's Minds* by Margaret Donaldson; *An Unquiet Mind* by Kay Redfield Jamison, *Hallucinations* by Oliver Sacks; and *Psychoanalytic Psychotherapy in the Independent Tradition* by Sue Johnson and Stanley Ruszczynski (eds). In a career creating fictional psychopaths and victims, I feel privileged and humbled to have been taken into the confidence of people whose lives have been shattered by violence. Professionals, it must be said, can sometimes be less willing to 'share', so I've also been threatened with arrest when I asked to talk about procedure with a senior police officer, and was once accused of spying at a British Psychological Society meeting! I am deeply appreciative therefore that an invitation to speak about my research at the Tavistock and Portman NHS Trust in London introduced me to Stan Ruszczynski, who was then Clinical Director at the Portman Clinic. He generously agreed to read an outline of this novel and commented in detail on its psychological and psychoanalytic elements. His insights informed and enriched my attempts to create a credible, tormented and frightening narcissist, and I am indebted to him for his invaluable advice and deeply grateful for his patience and forbearance in answering what must often have seemed outrageous questions. I've almost certainly misinterpreted or misunderstood some aspects of Stan's detailed and informative notes and suggestions — for which I apologise, and I claim those errors as mine alone.

Thanks, too, to DCI Dave Griffin (retd.) — a professional who was an enthusiastic facilitator and supporter from our first meeting, and has become a friend over the years. I tip my hat to Daniel Sellers, whose forensic eye helped to unravel a couple of knotty problems before I submitted the novel. I will always be grateful to the Royal Literary Fund for the RLF Fellowship Scheme which gave me time to write, and to the Society of Authors for their invaluable advice over many years. Finally, my deepest gratitude to Murf, whose endless patience is frankly astonishing.

The late, great Reginald (Reg) Hill, praised an earlier draft of *Before He Kills Again*, and it's partly because of his encouragement that this novel is now being published. Lastly, thank you, Joffe Books, for being so receptive to a speculative and unsolicited author pitch!

PROLOGUE

The first time I see her is in the minimart — one of those places with the prefix 'Metro' or 'Central' to make it sound cosmopolitan and sexy. Go to a city centre minimart around lunchtime and you'll find it's just humming with hotties.

She's stand-out gorgeous. Nice hair — touchable hair. Blonde. Skirt suit in a girly colour — lilac or mauve. She's wearing a blouse with a wavy chiffon edge in a vee. God, I want to ruffle that chiffon! She bends over the freezer and I stand to her left, looking down the vee. She is a looker — I mean Playboy *centrefold — the real deal.*

Now I have her all to myself. She looks at me with her big Bambi eyes. She's even sexier by candlelight — I've got the place rigged out like a Meatloaf video — "I Would Do Anything for Love" — and there's nothing she won't do for me. Maybe she's a bit woozy from the bump on the head, because she doesn't struggle against the restraints — doesn't even look all that scared, yet. I've been following her for so long I feel she should know me, and knowing me, she should be very scared. We've shared train carriages and supermarket queues, I've been with her in bars and restaurants, trailed her walks through the park and sat for long nights with her, reading by lamplight. I know her cat is named Oscar, she visits her mother in Stockport every Sunday, she dates occasionally, but isn't desperate to share her bed or her bathroom with a man on a permanent basis.

1

I tell her this, see a glimmer of fear, like the dip and flare of a candle flame. Then I pick up the taser and she begins to understand just how much trouble she's in. It's fully charged, but I'm not ready to use it, yet, so I set it down and switch to the knife, holding it lightly to her throat, applying just enough pressure so she can feel the bite. She holds her breath, leans back, trying to avoid the blade, but she's bound tight to the pillar — there's nowhere to go. A tear brims on her lower lid and I see the whites of her eyes. This is more like it.

A wisp of hair trembles over her eye — her whole body is shaking.

Now she's exactly where I want her — I own her — body, soul and mind. I am her worst nightmare.

I lean in close and whisper, 'This game has endless possibilities, doesn't it?'

CHAPTER 1

October

Tasha McCorkindale liked her corner pitch. For flagging down a taxi or catching passing custom, the corner was the strategic place to be. The massive sandstone cathedral opposite her was built on an outcrop above the sheer face of what was first a quarry, then a cemetery, but was now a garden, tenanted by the wealthy dead of the Victorian age, and haunted at night by drug addicts and prostitutes looking to score according to their individual needs.

When a storm blew in off the Mersey, the wind would scream up Duke Street and scramble over the quarry wall — slice you two ways to the bone. But tonight was one of those rare October nights in Liverpool when the air was so warm it seemed to curl up like a cat and purr sweetly at your feet. It was still and soft, loaded with the fragrance of leaf mulch and salty ships at anchor.

Hayley, ten yards down the terrace from Tasha, straightened up from her slouch and called out, 'Got the time, lad?'

A man swerved, stepping into the road to avoid her. *Aw, a shy guy.* He was wearing sunglasses, although it was dark as sin under the privet hedge and the canopy of trees in front of Gambier Terrace.

Tasha fluffed the fur of her stole and sighed to attract his attention. He hesitated and she stepped into the light.

'Too hot to sleep, isn't it?' she said, her voice low and husky. She dipped her head and lifted a long hank of hair from her neck.

He grunted and she heard the animal ecstasy of lust in it.

'How much?' he said, and she smiled, moving to slip her arm through his. He tensed and she reached across and patted his chest to soothe him.

He paid her — less than she was worth, but evidently more than he'd expected — and they walked on.

I might paint him. In sepia tones, or Lucozade-orange and tar-black. I'll call it Shades of Night, or Blind Lust.

'Where's your car, hon?' They had already crossed the main road, into the continuation of Hope Street, and were heading towards the Catholic cathedral.

'This way.' He turned right into Back Canning Street.

It was little more than an alleyway, but money had been spent on the Georgian houses in recent years, so the perimeter walls were solid and neatly pointed. At the corner of Back Hope Street, one of the business properties had carved a car park out of a section of garden, and three cars stood on the gravel.

'Here?' she said.

He indicated the narrower alley, just wide enough for one car to trundle along its stone setts. Even the back streets in this part of town had undergone the heritage treatment, and a single faux-Victorian lamp post cast a pinkish glow onto a saloon car parked beneath it.

'There,' he said, taking out a key fob.

She quirked an eyebrow. *Not so very shy, then?*

He walked fast, clamping his left elbow close to his side to trap her arm, as if afraid she might change her mind. Tasha's heel caught in an uneven paving sett and her ankle twisted under her. He took her weight easily, and grabbed her right wrist with his free hand, saving her from a fall. They were facing each other now.

'Eager to get on your knees are you, love?'

Something in his tone made her heart jump sideways in her chest and she said, 'You can let go of me, now.'

He frowned, startled by the emergence of rounded vowels, and a slight plumminess in her accent: her street persona had slipped.

'You taking the piss?'

She eased free of him. This was a man who would be quick to take offence, and Tasha knew from experience that kind was the most dangerous. 'Look,' she said, reverting to her street voice. 'It's late. My feller'll be wondering where I've got to. Let's say I give you your money back and we call it quits?' She felt in her pocket for the money and offered it to him.

He stared at the notes as if she'd spat on them. 'And the rest.'

Her heart did that sideways jump again. *Not good. This is not good.* 'That's all of it.' She held out the money.

'I've been watching you,' he said. 'You've had five punters at sixty quid a dip. That makes three hundred, plus my original stake.'

They were thirty yards from Hope Street. Another twenty from where the other girls were working. No way could she run in three-inch stilettos. Scream? *Yeah, and who's going to gallop to your rescue, Tasha?* Not a single window was lit in the houses around her. The locals had long since stopped noticing the sounds of night-time rut in this part of the city. Feeling the pulse in her throat, Tasha opened her clutch bag and drew out the notes. Her hand shook slightly but her voice sounded steady enough. 'You can have the cash,' she said. 'Just don't hurt me.'

He smiled. 'Aw . . . but that's the best part.'

He moved fast. Took the money with his left hand, clamped her wrist with his right and slammed her backwards against the car. She cracked her head against the rear windscreen and the screech of his car alarm reverberated with the booming in her skull. She rolled and fell, clutching the back of her head.

He hauled her to her feet and propped her against the side of the car while he popped the boot.

Sick pain throbbed in her skull and the stone setts seemed to ripple under her feet. Her legs buckled, but he caught her stole and twisted it, holding her up.

Can't breathe! She fought wildly. Tugging at the ligature, his hands. Desperate, she scrabbled for purchase, her fingers tangled in the lapel of his suit jacket.

'Let go,' he said.

'*You* let go,' she hissed.

He raised his fist and delivered a punch that exploded white hot pain behind her eyes. Tasha crumpled. He hoisted her up, and she reached into her bag a second time; his face was so close to hers she was afraid he might bite her. As he heaved her towards the back of the car, she brought up a canister of pepper spray and squirted chili-hot liquid into his eyes.

CHAPTER 2

Alan Palmer walked the two miles from his office to the NHS clinic. Fog trickled inland from the waterfront, chafing at his heels, swirling around his ankles like an incoming tide. It overtook him as he began the steep climb up Duke Street, creeping over and around and under and through the traffic, until even the monumental sandstone structure of the Anglican cathedral was obscured. Traffic streamed past him, tearing through the vapour, vehicles trailing tendrils of grey mist in their wake which immediately closed behind them. It grew denser by the minute until, at three in the afternoon, every street was shrouded in murk, so that even the buttery halos of street lamps turned sickly yellow.

The junction with Rodney Street came into view as a smudge of red from the traffic lights and Palmer turned left. Dr William Duncan, the first appointed British Medical Health Officer, had lived on this street in the mid-nineteenth century; now Palmer walked on fifty yards or so, to the three-storey Georgian building that housed Merseyside's NHS Forensic Psychiatry Service outpatients' department.

The fog had sunk into the basement; it lapped at the rim of the wall and trailed through the railings. Palmer mounted the steps up to the wide front door and pressed the buzzer for entry, tilting his face to the security camera for identification.

* * *

The consultation room was not that different from any of the serviced offices on the street, except that the furniture was perhaps more worn and the windows on the upper floors were all fitted with metal grilles. There was no couch — Dylan Corbie was not undergoing full psychoanalytic therapy. He was registered as a psychiatric patient with Palmer's friend and one-time teacher, Karl Atherton. Dr Atherton thought that Dylan might benefit from a more psychoanalytic approach than was the norm, and Palmer had seen him three times a week for the past three months.

Dylan arrived and nodded in recognition of Palmer's greeting. He then checked the pictures, the position of the chairs around the coffee table, the hooks on the wall. Palmer's overcoat and scarf were in their usual place on the far-left hook, and this seemed to reassure him. He retrieved a mobile phone from his pocket and began manipulating the keys with both thumbs.

'Eight Wi-Fi networks enabled,' he muttered. 'One unsecured access.' He switched off the phone and took a slim green notebook and biro from the inner pocket of his hooded jacket, then sat in the chair adjacent to Palmer.

In their early sessions, Dylan had experimented with the other, more distant chair, but this required sitting opposite Palmer, confronting him with the unpleasantness of increased eye contact, and Dylan Corbie did not cope well with eye contact.

'How are you, Dylan?' Palmer asked.

He answered by opening his notebook and writing in a small, crabbed script.

A long silence followed, then a lorry rumbled past in the street below and Palmer caught a flash of Dylan's bright green eyes as he glanced towards the window, then flinched and looked away, as though he had seen something beyond the steel mesh and the glass. But it was fully dark, and anyway, the consultation room was on the second floor: all Dylan would be able to see was his own reflection.

'Why are you concerned about unsecured networks, Dylan?'

'They can sneak in and change things,' Dylan said. 'Like here. It's unsecure — open access.' He cast wildly about the room, as if he might find one of the previous occupants hiding behind the furniture. 'Why can't I come and see you at your other place?' he pleaded.

'We discussed this during our first session,' Palmer said.

'Yeah,' Dylan's lip curled. 'The freak's too high-risk to be out in public.'

'This *is* a public place, Dylan,' Palmer said.

'I can pay. I'm loaded since she died.' Dylan's mother had been killed in a holiday boating accident in April, leaving him an orphan. Rich, and completely alone.

'This clinic is less isolated,' Palmer said. 'It has trained staff other than me around. Which protects us.'

'Protects *you*, you mean.'

'You, too.'

Dylan looked Palmer in the eye. 'I didn't threaten to kill *myself*.'

'No,' Palmer said, keeping his voice matter-of-fact, unemotional. 'You threatened to kill a playground full of seven-year-old boys.' Dylan lost eye contact, and Palmer added, 'Your father died when you were seven, Dylan.' He wasn't checking the detail but drawing his patient's attention to it.

In fact, Dylan's father had committed suicide — but in recent months, Palmer had found that word hard to say.

Dylan glared at him. 'You think I went for the kids so I could chicken out of killing *myself*?'

It seemed that Dylan was more willing to question the projections and defences of his unconscious than Palmer was.

Maybe Karl Atherton is right, Palmer thought. *Maybe I'm not ready for this.*

CHAPTER 3

Cassie Rowan tore through the twilight gloom, arms pumping, her fists punching holes in a thickening fog. She screamed for assistance, but none came.

He's so close! Her stupid shoes didn't have enough grip and he gained crucial yards. Her fake-fur shrug slipped from her shoulders, pinning her arms, and she threw it off, losing a few more paces.

She screamed again into her body mic, 'Officer in pursuit of suspect. On Jamaica Street heading north. Have eyeball Furman. Repeat — in pursuit! Request assistance.' Then, abandoning codenames and protocols, 'Wicksie, get your lazy arse over here!'

They pelted past warehouses and lock-ups, her quarry's feet thudding heavily on the pavement. He darted left without warning and sprinted across the street.

'He's ducked into—' She swore softly. 'No road name — Watkinson, maybe, or Bridgewater Street. Where the hell *are* you, Wicksie?'

A car turned the corner, the headlights throwing long shadows into a gathering mist, grille lights flashing blue and red.

DC Roy Wicks leaned out of the window and yelled, 'Go get him, tiger!'

The fleeing man skittered off the pavement and pounded across a tussocky strip of grass. His way was barred by a grey zinc alloy fence. DC Rowan eased back, keeping a few yards' distance between them. He was well over her fighting weight and, once cornered, she knew this man would not hesitate to use his fists against a woman.

But he didn't even slow down. He charged the fence, and it vibrated like a tuning fork. For a moment she thought he was trying to shoulder his way through, then he swung two of the spiked palings sideways and squeezed through the gap.

Rowan's eyes widened. 'Police!' she yelled. 'Stop!'

To hell with it — she wasn't going to lose the bastard now. She ran forward and he tripped over the lower batten of the fence. She dived for his trailing leg, wrapping both arms around his calf. He kicked out, forcing the air from her chest, and Rowan loosened her grip. One more vicious flick of his foot, grazing her cheekbone, and he broke free, but the heel snagged on the batten and he lost his shoe.

Rowan groaned. She was caked in freezing mud, her cheek oozed blood and her lungs creaked with the effort of every breath. She heard car doors open and slam — the two tossers in the unmarked car had finally got moving — but she didn't wait to see if they followed: she rolled onto her elbows and scrambled head-first through the gap in the fence.

The air stung the raw skin of her cheek and scoured her lungs like wire wool, but she ran on. She was in a freight yard. The fog lay thicker so near the river, and the vans and trucks parked in bays on the litter-strewn concrete were no more than ill-defined smudges.

The man loped on, imbalanced by the loss of his shoe. Rowan heard shouts behind her — *Wicksie and his useless oppo*. Ahead, a starter motor whined, coughed and caught, and she heard the throaty roar of an HGV engine. The Furman's shape was a fuzzy grey blur, ten or fifteen yards away. If he got to that truck, the driver wouldn't know what hit him.

She forced her aching limbs into action, but he was way ahead of her, and she was losing ground. 'Sod it.' She stooped to pick up a stray beer bottle and managed a few more steps — enough to close the distance and bring him back into view. The thrum of the truck was louder. Rowan pulled her arm back and lobbed the bottle in a high arc over the Furman's head, heard it smash, then launched herself into the fog.

The Furman's shadow was huge, magnified by the fog and the headlights of the oncoming truck. He took two more lurching steps and cried out. Rowan didn't stop to think; she threw herself in a flying tackle, catching him in the small of the back. He crashed to the ground and she heard glass crunch under his weight. He screamed as shards drove hard into his flesh.

Rowan was on her feet in an instant. With both hands she seized one of the Furman's arms and twisted it. He bellowed, fighting her, and she stamped on the small of his back, gaining more leverage.

The thrum of the engine grew louder and the twin headlights of the truck lit Rowan and her prisoner. The driver hit the brakes, and the truck came to a bouncing stop with a surprised yelp and a hiss of air from the pneumatic system.

The man writhed and screamed, cursing and bucking under her foot. Her sweat mingled with the clammy cold of the fog and she felt her grip on his wrist slip. She was losing him. She yelled, leaning with all her weight on his hand, summoning that last ounce of strength — for Tasha, for Jade, for all the girls he had hurt.

'*Wicksie!*'

A dull thud-thud-thud, then Wicksie, barrel-shaped and panting, appeared out of the fog, trailing wisps of vapour behind him.

He stopped five yards short and burst out laughing. 'Ride 'im, cowgirl!'

'Wicksie — for God's sake, do something *useful*,' Rowan gasped.

The Furman bellowed with rage, and she felt him turn, breaking the lock on his wrist. Next, she was in the air, thrown three feet into the grille of the truck. She dropped to the ground, winded, and heard Wicks curse, then a scuffing as the Furman got to his feet.

No air! Three agonizing attempts, then her diaphragm relaxed and Cassie sucked in river mist and diesel fumes.

The Furman had already reached the truck. Rowan heard a yell of dismay and fear, then the sound of flesh hitting concrete. A second later, the truck's engine roared. *He's thrown the driver out of the cab — Oh God, he's in the truck!*

Wicks screamed an order to stop.

The gears crunched and the truck's cab seemed to bounce on its axle. *Got to move.*

Rowan willed herself to her hands and knees as the gears ground again.

For God's sake, MOVE!

She pushed forward with her fingertips, like a sprinter ready for the starter pistol. Her shoes lost traction on loose grit and beads of glass. The truck lurched forward in a hiss of hydraulics and grinding metal. Rowan threw herself a yard further. The bumper clipped her heel, sending her spinning. She curled into a ball, waiting for the impact, and felt the ground vibrate under her as the truck's massive wheels rolled past within a millimetre of her.

The truck swerved, smashing two vans out of its path. Rowan unclasped her hands from around her head and struggled unsteadily to her feet. A grey blur came panting through the fog: the new guy, Finch, carrying Rowan's fake-fur shrug. The truck was almost on him. Rowan yelled, but her voice was drowned out by the howl of the engine. Finch darted left, then right, and finally leapt out of its path. It ploughed on, clipping another van and tearing through the fencing as though it was as insubstantial as the mist.

* * *

The CID office set up a cacophony of catcalls and ironic applause when DC Rowan appeared, still wearing her sex-worker outfit. She flipped two fingers at them; it was Wicksie's oppo she'd come looking for. She spied him near the photocopier. He was a slender twenty-four-year-old with fine blond hair and the look of an eager spaniel.

'I want a word with you,' she said.

Finch froze as all eyes turned to him.

Wicks spoke up: 'Keep your hand on your tackle, Finch lad — she's liable to rip them off with her bare teeth!'

More laughter. Rowan scowled at them until they were shamed into silence.

Finch picked up his photocopies, nearly dropped them, recovered, took a step towards her, then turned back to retrieve the original from the copier. It was a miracle he made it across the room without knocking over the furniture.

She waited just outside the doorway — there were things she wanted to say out of Roy Wicks's earshot.

'Finch, is it?'

'Fincham,' he said. 'They call me Finch.'

'What kept you?'

'The fog?' Finch avoided her eye.

'Are you asking me or telling me?'

She glared at him while he stared at his boots.

'Wicks laid bets I could take the Furman, didn't he?' she demanded.

Finch didn't need to reply, she knew from the guilty look on his face it was true.

'You should've been watching my back,' she said.

'Cassie, I'm really—'

'Don't apologise,' she said. 'Just don't take your lead from the class clown, okay?'

He nodded, his boyish face dark with shame. 'I *am* sorry, though.' She turned to go. 'Cassie—' He hesitated, anxious. 'Are you going to tell the boss what happened?'

'It depends what kind of mood she's in,' Rowan said. 'I've already had one kicking tonight; I'm not up for another.'

'Fair enough,' he said. 'I've got your shrug. It's on my desk.'

She went to her own workstation to find her locker keys; she needed to shower and change.

Finch carried the ratty fur to her like it was a fine mink stole.

Wicks wolf-whistled and Finch's colouring deepened to cherry red.

Rowan glared at him with vengeance in her heart. It was only a small consolation he'd lost his bet — she wanted much more if she was going to take an ear-bashing from old Warhorse. Then Wicks turned to the crowd and tipped his hand in the universal gesture that means 'fancy a pint?', and Rowan had an idea that brought a smile to her face.

She snatched up a teaspoon and tapped it against a Merseyside Police issue mug till it rang like a dinner gong. When she had everyone's attention again, she said, 'The Baltic Fleet. Wicksie's buying.' She beamed at Wicks. 'Nice one, Roy!'

DC Wicks's protests were drowned out by the cheers of his colleagues.

Keys in hand, Rowan turned to leave and came up against her boss. If Rowan thought that Detective Chief Inspector Pat Warman had gone to the trouble of walking from her office to check on her well-being, she dismissed the notion in a microsecond.

Pat Warman's face was not made for smiling; in fact, the skin over her cheekbones was stretched so tight it looked like a smile might cause actual physical pain.

The cheers and words of appreciation for Wicks's generosity died down under the arctic glare of the DCI.

'Someone from Scientific Support is waiting for you in the custody suite,' she said, as if Rowan had deliberately kept him waiting. 'When you've finished there, make yourself decent and report to my office.'

* * *

Rowan was relieved to find that the representative from Scientific Support was Ian Chan. Chan was twenty-five, gay, and angry that his parents couldn't accept his sexuality. He had a wicked disregard for others' feelings and an almost magical way with all things technological. Rowan had met him on a forensic awareness training course three years previously and they had been friends ever since.

'Sweetheart!' he cried. 'What *have* they been doing to you?' It wasn't a particularly sincere exclamation of concern, and Rowan knew that she was safe from a comforting hug, but it made her smile, all the same. Chan handed her a mirror — its presence in his kit was a hangover from his commercial photography days — before he'd moved to forensic work, he had specialized in family portraits.

The worst damage was to her face: the skin over her left cheekbone had started to scab and the flesh under her eye was swollen and purple.

'Well, I knew the applause was ironic, but . . .'

'Who applauded?' Chan said.

'The entire CID room.'

'Charmers, all. Mind you, you haven't looked this bad since the disaster of the blonde experiment, last summer.'

Rowan narrowed her eyes.

'Well, don't look at me like that — at least I had the heart to *tell* you.' He fitted a close-up lens to his camera and invited her to sit. 'I mean, with your skin tone, what *were* you thinking?'

Rowan's chest ached where she'd been kicked; it felt tender to touch, and a dull brown oval of bruising had already started to form.

His gaze flitted over her face and hair and she knew he was sizing up the best angle to make her look her worst. She fingered her hair; it was stiff with mud.

Chan slapped her hand away. 'Leave it alone. I want every festering spatter of slime intact,' he said, plucking the mirror from her fingers. 'It'll make a wonderful victim-shot for the jury.'

'Yeah, well, good luck with that.' Rowan sat still while Chan zapped off a few shots, but refused to look pitiful for the camera.

After a minute or so, he exclaimed, 'Don't move! Do not even *blink*.' The shutter clicked a few more times. 'Perfect. Just the mood of despondency I need. Now tell me what you were thinking about — it *was* her, wasn't it?'

He meant Warman.

'I knew you were in trouble. That *tone* — all gruff and dominatrix. Is she very cross?'

'I wasn't the only one on this op,' Rowan grumbled. 'I don't know why she's so pissed off with me.'

'Warman's permanently pissed off,' he said, clicking off a few more for the album. 'But credit where it's due — you do have a talent for bringing out her inner Grinch.'

'This is not helping, Ian.'

'Okay, then, look at it this way: she puts you on shit detail to teach you a lesson in humility — and what do you do? You go and collar yourself a big bad criminal, that's what.'

'The big bad criminal got away, remember?'

'Which, technically, gives her another excuse to be pissed off — see how it works? But she can't even blame you for it, cos *you* did your job. I mean, where was your backup?'

'Don't ask,' Rowan said.

Chan stopped clicking off shots for a moment and gave her another appraising look.

'Your photo-session is complete. Unless there's any . . . unseen damage.' He gave her a theatrical once-over. 'And from where I'm standing, there's not a lot I could have missed.'

He set the camera down carefully and offered his hand in one of his unthinking chivalrous gestures, and Rowan was so stunned that she took it.

He helped her on with her shrug, wincing with her as she caught her breath.

She smiled, tilted her head in a gesture that was supposed to convey, *It's no big deal*, but his look of concern brought humiliating tears to her eyes.

For the first time since she walked through the door, Ian Chan looked serious. He smoothed the matted fur over her shoulders and gave her a gentle squeeze. 'Sweetheart, you did just fine — it's those two who've got some explaining to do.'

This was why Cassie Rowan loved The Evil Chan — just when you despaired of him, he said something that made you feel wonderful.

* * *

DCI Warman stood with her back to the window, her fingertips just brushing the surface of her desk. She wore no make-up and her skin, sallow and lined, had the papery thinness of a heavy smoker, though Rowan had never seen her with a cigarette. Her hair, ash-blonde fading to grey, was cut short and neat. Her grey-blue eyes were flat and expressionless, but the room hummed with her sanctimonious disapproval. Finch stood to the left of the desk, looking fidgety and unhappy.

'You should have waited for backup,' Warman's voice had a harsh edge — a consequence, no doubt, of having spent a career trying to make her voice heard over alpha males.

Rowan ground her teeth and said nothing. If she landed Wicks in the shit, Finch would be right in it with him, and even worse, it would make her look like a whining snitch.

Warman frowned, annoyed by her silence. 'You broke protocol.'

'I heard a scream,' Rowan said. 'I went to check it out. The Furman had Tiffany by the hair. His fist was drawn back, ready to punch her in the face. If I'd abided by protocol, he'd've—'

'He'd've what?' Warman raised her eyebrows. 'Got away? He *did* get away, Cassie. And caused fifty thousand pounds-worth of damage making good his escape.'

'I was going to say he'd've smashed the girl's face in.' Rowan's mind flashed to Tasha McCorkindale after the Furman's failed attempt to bundle her into his car.

Warman looked mildly chastened, but rallied after a moment. 'My understanding is that you can't provide a useful description.'

19

'He was ten yards away from me when I identified myself,' Rowan said. 'He wore a hooded jacket and a scarf. You can hardly see your hand in front of your face out there.'

Rowan had showered and changed, rubbing shower gel into stinging grazes and cuts, but Warman looked at her like she'd missed a spot of crud on her face.

'So, we're looking at a substantial insurance pay-out to the haulage company — and for what?' Warman said. 'God help us if the driver of the truck makes a compensation claim.'

'We've got a lot more on the Furman than we had before,' Rowan said, hearing the belligerence in her own voice, but powerless to do anything about it.

'Oh, of course — how could I forget — we do have his *shoe*,' Warman said, sarcasm oozing from her pores. 'Perhaps we should go knocking on doors.'

'Um . . .' Finch had finally roused himself. 'I could find out where it retails,' he suggested, timidly. 'If it was a credit card purchase, it could take us straight to him.'

Warman considered. 'Worth a try. Well done, Finch.'

He flushed with pleasure.

'We also have his DNA,' Rowan said, lifting her chin, and looking Warman in the eye.

The Chief Inspector's gaze was cold and grey. 'Well, we'll just have to hope the scientists know how to do *their* jobs, won't we?'

Rowan felt a surge of hot anger at the injustice of it. She hoped that Wicks had lost a sack-load of dosh on his bet. And she fervently hoped that every off-duty CID turned up at the pub to take him up on his offer of free ale.

CHAPTER 4

It was just after ten p.m., her injuries documented and report written, that Rowan was given the all-clear by the police surgeon. She headed straight for the Baltic Fleet. The pub was an inconvenient distance from the Albert Dock for the tourist trade, and it prided itself on an absence of slot machines and juke boxes. A refurb and the addition of outside seating had brought it into the twenty-first century, but the clientele didn't come for the hipster vibe. It had a reputation for keeping a range of local craft ales, so the Baltic was a magnet for serious beer drinkers.

Rowan inched down Wapping at ten miles an hour. The pub's bow-shaped westerly frontage rose out of the fog like the prow of a ship, and she half-expected to hear a foghorn blast from its bows. Then it slipped back into the greyness, and she almost missed her turning into a side street.

Her mobile rang as she locked up. It was Tasha McCorkindale.

'Hey,' Tasha said, her tone warm and full of concern. 'I heard you had some trouble — are you okay?'

Of course, the girls on the street would have let Tasha know — although she'd quit street work since her near-miss with the Furman in October, she'd stayed in touch with the working girls.

'I'm *fine*,' Rowan said, but despite the bravado she heard a wobble in her voice. 'He came off worse.'

'Want to come over, compare battle scars, share a bottle of wine?'

Rowan dithered on the foggy pavement; it was tempting. Then a shout of laughter went up in the pub, and Rowan realised she didn't really have a choice.

'There's free ale going at the Baltic Fleet,' she said. 'If I don't show up, I'll look like a wuss.'

'Nuff said. But we're still on for Friday?'

Rowan groaned.

'Hey!' Tasha laughed.

'Sorry, Tasha,' Rowan said. 'It's not you — it's the thought of dragging around town looking for frocks.'

'Clothes shopping is supposed to be *fun*, missy.'

Under other circumstances, it might be. It was the reason why she had to go clothes shopping that was the problem: a family wedding. And in the Rowan household, family weddings were especially complicated.

'Friday it is,' she said, knowing that she sounded like a doomed woman.

* * *

The bar was crammed and noisy — it seemed her wish had come true — the place was heaving with off-duty police. Rowan was welcomed and the crowd parted for her. She had tied her hair back from her face, and even in the mellow light of the bar she knew that the bruises and grazes must look painful. That attracted a few comments from the older men, and their avuncular expressions of concern surprised a tug of emotion in her which she quickly reined in.

Tomorrow, she would try to cover the worst with make-up. For now, she was too sore. And if it caused Wicks some embarrassment, even better.

He was standing at the bar; Rowan saw a gap to his right and plunged in. Wicks exchanged a word with the man next to him, then looked over his shoulder at her. 'You here for the free ale?'

'Well, it's not for the pleasure of your company, Roy,' she said. Stan, the barman, gave her the nod and poured her a vodka tonic. 'Anyway, I earned this.'

Wicks raised his glass. 'To near-misses.'

'To *teamwork*,' Rowan countered.

He took a breath, then let it go. Was he scared she might've told Warman what really happened? *Good.*

His gaze flickered to her eyes and mouth, trying to gauge her mood, maybe trying to estimate how much he could get away with. But Rowan had perfected her poker face at the age of eighteen. Getting away with telling lies to professionals who were lied to every day took work — and a certain amount of natural talent.

In the end, he caved. 'You shot off like a rabbit, Cass,' he said.

'You were in a *car*, Roy.'

'The fog . . .'

'The fog, your two flat feet — and a bet you lost.'

'How did you know—' Wicks's mouth quirked into a smile. 'Finch . . .'

'Finch didn't tell me,' she said, taking a sip of her drink. 'You just did, just now.'

He shook his head, even managed a chuckle. 'Cassie Rowan, you sly fox.'

The man standing the other side of Wicks paused mid-sip and leaned forward to get a look at her.

Rowan met his gaze and something contracted inside her. It felt like a cramp — a spasm of fleeting anxiety, perhaps. Or anger. After what she'd just been through, those two emotions had got hopelessly churned up. 'Do I know you?' she said.

The man looked away, staring ahead at the bottles ranged above the bar, and the anxiety, or anger — whatever it was — faded. He took an unhurried sip of his beer and placed the glass squarely on the mat without looking at her. 'Apparently not,' he said.

The doors opened and another gang of off-duty police came in, the grey air wrapped around them like a shroud. A shout went up and Wicks jogged her elbow.

'Bloody hell, Cass — this lot'll beggar me!' he complained.

When Rowan turned back, Wicks's friend was gone.

CHAPTER 5

Tuesday, 18 November, evening

Watching them sets my senses alight. It sears like acid through my veins, drawing me to the quiet backwaters, the shortcuts and alleyways that reek of excitement and danger and sex.

* * *

Forecasters had predicted a change in the weather, but for the second day the fog rose from the sumps and hollows, the river exhaling it like ectoplasm. For an hour or two after midday it looked like it might lift, but by three in the afternoon the sun was no more than a bloody thumbprint near the horizon. Now, all over the university campus, students were emptying out of lecture theatres and seminar rooms as groups came together to chat and make plans for the evening.

Emma Hammond peered into the murky air.

Vinnie materialised from the gloom, waving her arms as if to bat away the thickening fog. 'Two days running,' she grumbled. 'Bloody vapers — we didn't have to contend with all this till they made them take it outdoors.'

Vinnie was a plump Asian girl, an extrovert Mancunian who bounced from group to group; she was given to sarcasm, but her infectious sense of the absurd meant she rarely gave offence. They walked together, finding their way across campus by a kind of homing instinct, their landmarks — the stark modernity of the arts library and the prim elegance of the Georgian terrace at Abercromby Square — having vanished in the fog.

Emma felt happiness like a warm glow in her breast; she was eighteen and in her first semester at university, yet she had already made friendships she was certain would last the rest of her life. They crossed Oxford Street and took a shortcut through one of the car parks, chatting all the way. Emma was on her way to a biological sciences faculty open lecture. The guest speaker was a leading exponent of adult human stem cell research.

A half-dozen buses rumbled outside the Students' Union Building, parked crookedly to accommodate the curve of the road. Students were piling on to them or forming untidy queues, their breath intensifying the mist.

Emma said, 'You're sure you won't come?'

'Well, let's see . . .' Vinnie drummed her fingers against her chin as if seriously considering the proposition. 'Is it compulsory?'

'No.'

'Hm . . . Is it likely to come up on our next exam paper?'

'No.'

'I see. Will there be beer?'

Emma sighed. 'No, Vinnie, no free beer.'

'Then I'm sure.'

'Vinnie, it's *Michael Clarke* — it's the scientific equivalent of Adele visiting Mountford Hall for an "unplugged" session.'

Vinnie put her arm around Emma. 'Here's the thing: Adele hasn't toured since 2017, so the chances of her fetching up at Liverpool Students' Union are minus ten to the power of a trillion. However, we are agreed — she is the definition of cool. Michael Clarke, god among the geeks though he may be, is not — and *can never be* — cool. Anyway, what kind of unplugged session could it be without beer?'

Emma played the injured party, detaching herself with haughty disdain, taking Vinnie's hand by the index finger and brushing it from her like a troublesome fly. 'You don't know what you're missing.'

'Um . . . I think I do.'

Emma grinned and hugged her friend. 'Later, philistine.'

* * *

The lecture was perfect. It was held in the Hartley Building, in a small, Victorian lecture theatre with narrow bench seats and acres of polished wood, newly waxed and gleaming. Emma came out into the foggy night, her head full of technical jargon, buzzing with the dizzying notion that science would soon be capable of repairing damaged neurologies — of literally making the lame walk and the deaf hear.

The others quickly dispersed, heading left for London Road or vanishing like sprites into the murk. Alone, in the dark, she felt almost that the fog shrouding the buildings and deadening the thrum of traffic was laid on for her. This was a night she was supposed to remember always — a pivotal moment that would shape the rest of her life.

She would dodge Vinnie and the others for another half hour when she got back to halls, so that she could write up the alchemy of words while their impression was strong in her mind: *blastocyst, pluripotent, master regulators, therapeutic cloning*, and the sweet, simple, most powerful word of all: *cure*. Her fascination with the subject owed a lot to the slow fall into silence she had seen in her Nanna Hammond. She was only eight when her quick, clever, uncompromising paternal grandmother died of Parkinson's disease.

Emma rounded the corner near the Quadrangle, just behind the Victoria Building with its ornate clock tower, where cars still jostled to park in the narrow space between the huddled buildings and the small patch of green. This was the oldest part of the university and, as the traffic noise faded still further to a dull swish, it was possible to imagine herself back in the nineteenth century, when the place was first opened, its redbrick facade and gleaming clock a new landmark and a symbol of prosperity and hope for the city.

The lowing of foghorns on the Mersey a mile distant, and the rapid clip-clip of her boot heels on the pavement thrilled her so that she wanted to hug herself with secret joy. She almost held her breath, waiting for something to happen — something wonderful and mysterious and exciting.

At the quad, she edged past a couple of cars parked nose to tail and made for the Victoria Building where an archway led through to the main road. If she was lucky, the tall iron gates would be unlocked and she would save the couple of minutes she needed to catch the next shuttle bus to the halls of residence. Ten yards from the opening, the archway remained invisible, though she could hear the traffic noise on Brownlow Hill echoing as though through a tunnel, and she thought that the dense vapour glowed a more lurid orange in that direction.

A *creak-thud, creak-thud* from up ahead sent a trickle of anxiety down her spine. A dark form, huge, troll-like, loomed in the curve of the archway. Emma froze, the hairs rising on her arms and the back of her neck. Light chased right to left and the shadow seemed to slide forward, expanding, flowing up and over the concavity of the arch.

All her instincts told her to run — run fast and not look back.

Then the shadow seemed to shrink and took human form. It was a man on crutches, the monstrousness of his shadow caused by the combined magnifying effects of tiny water droplets in the air and the headlamps of a passing vehicle. Emma choked back a laugh of relief.

He swung a couple more steps, his head down, panting, concentrating on the uneven surface ahead. The creak of his crutches and thud of his plaster cast set up a weary rhythm.

Emma moved left to let him pass, but he glanced up, startled, tried to manoeuvre around her, misjudged the direction, and dropped the books clamped under his right arm. They apologised simultaneously, accepted blame, and reached for the books. Emma, unencumbered by crutches, was more agile and got there before him.

'I'm not usually such a klutz.' He spoke softly, smiling at her. 'Which is probably hard to believe, what with the broken leg as evidence and all.'

Was he flirting? He was bit old — maybe mid-twenties? But he had a nice smile and he wasn't bad-looking, either — what she could see of him in the fog, with his beanie hat pulled down over his brow and the English Soc. scarf wrapped twice around his neck.

'Well, I'd better . . .' She jerked her head, indicating the direction he had just come from, and offered him the bundle of texts.

'Oh! Right. Sorry.' Flustered, he made space under one arm for the books and she wedged them back in place. 'It's really very good of you.'

She felt a pang of guilt at leaving him to struggle. But the fog was getting worse and if she missed this bus, she'd have to wait in the freezing cold for twenty minutes or more.

A few steps later, she heard a flutter of pages, followed by three thuds in quick succession, and he cursed mildly. He really was rather sweet — 'Blast it,' indeed! Even her *dad* used stronger language than that.

Emma sighed and told herself that twenty minutes wasn't long to wait. She caught up with him as he was bending down, left leg out in front of him, like a trained horse attempting a bow. He had both crutches in one hand. The look of comical embarrassment on his face when he saw her made her laugh out loud.

* * *

He told her his name was Andy; he was a fourth-year medical student, and he wanted to specialize in virology. He'd taken a gap year in South America, volunteering on a project to research vaccine strategies to control the Zika virus, then the professor who led the study invited him to work in his lab in Brazil for a year, developing a new vaccine. 'Which accounts for my extreme old age,' he said.

She felt her cheeks flush, thinking, *God, did I make it that obvious I thought he was old?*

He wanted to know about her course and the stem cell lecture and listened closely to her answers, agreeing with her in a way that made her blush again with pleasure.

The hypnotic *creak-thud* of his crutches now took on a jauntier rhythm and she flattered herself that she was the cause. They walked easily together, despite his injury, their breath steaming before them, mingling with the milky vapour. Emma became less concerned about getting back to halls and was even building up to asking him out for a drink.

She didn't think to question why he had been walking through the Victoria Building archway when he had just come from the science library. Didn't think to suggest that a shortcut through the arch of the Industrial Sciences Building back onto Ashton Street would save them five minutes' walk and an unnecessary detour to reach the car park. She was happy to retrace her steps, taking a long loop past the Foresight Centre and the Old Royal Infirmary, simply glad to be in Andy's company. She clasped his books to her and thought she would like to be seen with him, so that she could keep her girlfriends agog.

She fell quiet for a moment and sensed him looking down at her. Her heart quickened, but she couldn't think of anything to say.

'Isn't this fabulous?' he said, and she knew he meant the fog and the night and being young and not knowing what might happen next but knowing — just *knowing* — that it would be something wonderful.

'Yes, yes!' she wanted to exclaim, but felt suddenly shy that he seemed able to read her thoughts and could only nod her agreement.

The car park was almost empty, and she could barely make out the shapes of the few remaining cars.

'This is me.' A set of keys appeared in his hand and a car a few feet away gave a flash of indicator lights and a surprised *cluck*, as if it had been goosed. Emma didn't know cars, but this one looked expensive even to her undiscerning eye. Big and voracious. The beading of moisture on the paintwork seemed to make it glow with a pearly depth. She couldn't make out the colour in the Irn Bru orange of the car park lighting.

'Stick them on the passenger seat,' he said. 'Door's open.'

He shot the crutches into the passenger well and, dismayed, it occurred to her that he would have to drive with a broken leg. Again, he seemed to anticipate her thoughts.

'It's automatic,' he said. 'I won't need the left leg.'

He reached down and for a surreal moment she thought he would unstrap the leg like a prosthetic. She covered her gasp of alarm by opening the passenger door and placing his texts on the empty seat.

He lifted his left leg into the seat well and followed after with a groan of pain or relief. 'Well — come on then.'

She flushed, confused.

'Get in — I'll give you a lift.'

'I'm fine.' She smiled, feeling herself blush more deeply.

'It's the least I can do after you went to all that trouble.'

'I only carried your books.'

'And believe me, not many would.'

'I can catch a bus just across the road.'

He rolled his eyes. 'I rode those buses for a year — it'll take an hour in this weather. And what if it breaks down? You could end up having to walk those lonely Mossley Hill roads all alone.' He stopped. 'Sorry. Didn't mean to scare the whatsit out of you. Curse of a vivid imagination,' he said, smiling at himself. 'Let me give you a lift,' he said. '*Please?*'

31

Emma bit her lip, and he shoved the books unceremoniously onto the back seat. It *would* be fun to take him to meet Vinnie and the others. A smile twitched at the corner of her mouth as Vinnie's voice popped into her head, *'So, who's the hamstrung hunk?'* But reason fought with impulse.

You're mad, she told herself. *You're all alone. You just met the guy and you're actually getting into his car?* She stood uncertainly, holding the door open. The upholstery smelled of new leather; the fog had begun to swirl inside the car, tinted pearl grey by the interior light.

'Come on then, if you're coming.' He looked up at her, an amused expression on his face, and she took her decision.

She swivelled her shoulder bag around and slid into the seat.

'Seatbelt,' he said, like it was a rehearsed cockpit routine.

When she was safely harnessed, Andy grinned, slid the key in the ignition and turned.

Nothing happened. He tried again.

Again, nothing.

'Fuck.' He squeezed the wheel in both hands then slammed the heel of his right hand into the dashboard. 'Fuck!'

She flinched. 'What's wrong?'

He reached across her and she jerked back involuntarily. He punched the button for the glove compartment and came out with a clean white cloth and a can of WD-40.

'Piece of shit Japanese fucking garbage,' he said, breathing hard. 'That, Emma, is the essence of what's *wrong*.' He pulled a lever near his seat and popped the bonnet, tore one of the crutches from her hand and shouldered the door open.

Emma winced as he put weight on his left leg, but he seemed not to notice.

'Slide over,' he said. 'Try the ignition when I tell you.'

The crutch formed a barrier between the seats and she got out instead, walked around to the driver's side. 'I warn you,' she joked, 'I don't have a licence.' Her voice sounded weak to her.

He didn't smile.

The first try, it turned over a few times, then cut out.

'Wait!' he yelled.

She began to bristle. Then, as if he had sensed her resentment, Andy's face appeared around the side of the bonnet, looking rueful. 'Sorry,' he said. 'It's been a hell of a day.' He had a smudge of grease at the side of his nose, which made him look boyish and vulnerable. 'One last try?' He fluttered his eyelashes and she clenched her jaw against a laugh — she didn't want him to think she was a pushover. 'One last try.' She turned the key, the engine whined, coughed, caught.

'Yes!' He lowered the bonnet and she got ready to switch places. Just at the last moment, she glanced up.

There was something in his look that stopped her dead. Triumph, certainly — that was there — but there was something more. Something feral and cold, that made her jump out of the car and take a step back.

'Hey,' he said, smiling again. 'I'm giving you a lift, remember?'

He stepped forward, closing the distance between them, trapping her against the side of the car. The wool hat, the crutch under his left arm, the smudge next to his nose now gave him a piratical look, sinister in the swirling mist.

'It's fine — I'm fine. N-no need.' She looked right and left, but the few remaining cars had vanished in the fog. It was just her and Andy the pirate, Andy the troll. 'I just remembered — I'm meeting a friend at the Union Bar. Two friends. A whole bunch of people. They're expecting me — they'll be wondering where I am.'

He laughed. '*Em*-ma . . .'

Suddenly, her name on his lips sounded obscene. She tried to squeeze past him, but he seized her arm. 'Next you'll be trying to convince me they'll send out a search party.'

'Let *go* of me!'

Startled, he let his hand drop, and jammed it in his pocket. 'I just wanted to give you a lift,' he mumbled, staring at his feet. But he didn't back off.

'Sure,' she said, trying to conjure up Vinnie's sarcastic sneer. 'Whatever.'

She edged past, but her foot somehow got tangled with his crutch and she fell headlong.

'You okay?' He was bending over her, his face full of concern. He took his hand from his pocket and Emma thought he was going to help her up. But she saw he was holding something. She heard a crackle and the fog seemed to flare blue-white for an instant. *Ozone?* Did she smell ozone?

Then he touched her neck lightly and her brain caught fire.

CHAPTER 6

The fog thickened as Palmer approached Karl Atherton's house. His friend occupied the top floor of a tall, narrow, late-Victorian property, standing in its own grounds. The rest of the house was in darkness, but the windows of Karl Atherton's top-floor flat were a milky blur through the fog, lit like a beacon to the weary traveller.

The flat was near Sefton Park, although the official area designation was Toxteth, which for many years had been synonymous with riots and looting. Palmer knew that Karl and Millie had bought the place at a time when national headlines frequently returned to the riots during the summer of 1981, when entire blocks were razed, destroying homes and family businesses and punching holes in the landscape.

Palmer knew that Atherton and his wife, Millie, had stuck it out through the rest of the grey eighties and the uneven recovery of the nineties, when the city's regeneration was dependent on European hand-outs. Now the area, with its proximity to parks and the city centre, was a prime location for executives and professionals. And, twenty years on, Atherton was still fearless, though Palmer thought his optimism had been struck a blow by his wife's death. Millie had been just sixty-eight, looking forward to a belated retirement, when she had her first attack. Gastric flu, they said, then gallstones. A week after that diagnosis she collapsed and was rushed into hospital where they performed a gastroscopy and found an inoperable tumour in her stomach. She died a few months later.

Cooking smells and the rising wail of an oboe wafted down from the kitchen like an invitation. Palmer mounted the stone steps and rang the bell.

He heard Atherton's voice from above. 'Come on up, the door's open.'

Palmer felt his way blindly around to the side of the house where a glossy fire escape scaled the wall, disappearing into the mist like a stairway into the clouds. The iron was damp to touch and freezing cold, even through his gloves. He reached the top breathing easily and stepped into the steamy heat of the kitchen. Pots bubbled on the stove and Palmer's host turned to greet him, a pan in his hand, sauce dripping from a spoon back into the pot.

Atherton was small, compact, his hair still sandy-fair despite his years. He wore a white shirt and maroon tie, with a maroon cardigan that Palmer recalled was a present from Millie for his last birthday. A tea towel was tucked into his belt as an improvised apron.

'It's an invitation to a burglar, leaving your door open like this,' Palmer chided, knowing he sounded fussy and overprotective.

'*At my great age*, you mean?' Atherton's mouth twitched in amusement. 'The old fire escape rings out louder than any burglar alarm.'

He stood with his feet neatly together and his head cocked to the side, a quizzical look on his face. 'I take it you left your mobile at home.'

'Mm,' Palmer said, refusing to fall into the trap of saying he had 'forgotten' it. Like many of their profession, Dr Atherton believed that forgetting had unconscious motivations. Palmer's wife, Elspeth, had cited his 'unavailability' as one of his major vices, and though he hated to admit it, she had a point: walking was his thinking time and he could not think if he anticipated the despotic interruptions of his mobile phone.

'I wanted to remind you that you undertook to provide the wine,' Atherton said, turning back to the stove. 'And since you walked here, it seems unfair to send you out again.'

Palmer narrowed his eyes; Karl enjoyed his Sherlockian challenges of deduction. He glanced down at his overcoat; a beading of moisture glowed opalescent in the kitchen downlights. 'The condensation on my overcoat,' he said. 'The moisture in my hair.'

Atherton smiled. 'Such perspicacity, and yet *still* we have no wine.'

'White or red?' Palmer asked, extracting one of each from his coat pockets.

He saw the slight wince at the generic terms — for Atherton, wine was known by region, grape, appellation, vintage — but his friend's face brightened when he saw the labels.

'The wine merchant was very helpful,' Palmer said.

Atherton took the red between right index finger and thumb, supporting the base in the palm of his left hand with as much tenderness as a father holding his newborn child. 'This will take a week to recover from the jostling you've given it,' he said with deep regret. 'Good wine should not be treated like cough medicine, Alan.' He set it to one side and accepted the white. 'Sauvignon — not a bad choice. And at the perfect drinking temperature. Shall we?'

Over dinner, they talked of Dr Atherton's planned lecture tour of America in the summer, and of Alan Palmer's marital problems.

'I'm still seeing Lucy on Thursday afternoons and alternate Saturdays,' Palmer said. 'We've already split the proceeds on the sale of the house.'

There had been no question of either one of them keeping the family home: after the events of late spring, they would not want their daughter to be faced with the prospect of entering it ever again.

'And Lucy,' Atherton asked. 'How is she?'

Palmer put down his knife and fork, suddenly sick. He forced the memory away, focused instead on the question. 'I don't know, Karl. She still has nightmares.' The image pushed back, searing, like a camera flash at the back of his eyes. He drew a hand across his forehead, and it came away damp.

'She's young, Alan,' Atherton said kindly. 'The memory will fade. And she has the support of two intelligent and vigilant parents.'

Not quite vigilant enough, Palmer thought.

Atherton squeezed his forearm. 'She'll be fine.'

Absurd, but these words from his former teacher did more to reassure Palmer than all his own rationalisation.

* * *

They turned to professional matters over coffee and brandy, seated in Atherton's library. The room took up a full third of the apartment's floor space — thirty feet by twenty of built-in bookshelves. It housed Atherton's collection of psychiatric texts, Millie's historical reference books, and a fiction section that encompassed British and American classics, a sizeable crime collection and a few science fiction and fantasy novels.

The room was furnished with three armchairs, two sofas and two desks. Atherton added a log to the wood burner and the two men took an armchair each, facing the fireplace.

'How are you finding the workload?' Atherton asked.

'It's fine,' Palmer said. 'In fact, I took on a new patient a week ago.' Atherton didn't comment, but Palmer added defensively, 'He was in a bind — his analyst withdrew suddenly — a personal crisis.'

'If you feel equal to the task . . .'

There were times recently when Palmer felt unequal to answering his damn phone — as Karl already knew — but Palmer didn't feel like tackling the reasons behind it; not now, not yet. So, he changed the subject: 'Dylan has been worrying me,' he said.

'He has been withdrawn, recently,' Atherton observed.

'He asked me for private sessions,' Palmer said.

'I take it you refused.'

Palmer nodded.

'How did he react?'

'He thinks I'm afraid of him.'

'And?'

'I think he's afraid of himself.'

They sipped their brandy for a few moments, listening to the logs crackle and hiss in the grate. 'Did Dylan ever tell you why he started keeping his notebooks?' Palmer asked at length.

'No,' Atherton said. 'Why do you ask?'

'I think he uses them to keep him anchored to reality.'

'Proof of experience?' Atherton frowned, thinking. 'You know we tested his memory?'

Palmer nodded. 'I gather he's close to eidetic.'

'Hmm . . .' Atherton rotated the brandy in his glass, supporting the goblet in his small neat hand, peering into the tawny liquid like a fortune teller into a crystal ball. 'Puzzling, isn't it? Why would a person who has almost perfect recall need to make a written record of the tiniest details of his day?'

'Because he doesn't trust what he sees,' Palmer said. 'Or because he feels that others will question his memory of the facts.' He shrugged. 'But this is mere speculation.'

'Yes,' Atherton said. 'Even after all these months, Dylan remains an enigma.' He paused for some moments. 'Imagine how it would be if you have the ability to summon at will sights, sounds, feelings — *entire conversations*, including gestures and inflections. And yet to feel that your memory is faulty — that it can't be trusted.'

Palmer worked his thumbnail at one of the raised diamonds in the cut glass, pinging it like an alarm bell. 'That,' he said quietly, 'would be enough to drive you insane.'

CHAPTER 7

Well, this is nice.

The place is damp; it stinks of rot and rat-piss, and there's not nearly enough candles. I should be disappointed, but I'm not.

I do love the thrill of the hunt, the — what do they call it? — the deferred gratification of letting them go home safe one night, only to snatch them out of their lives on another.

She's blindfolded. Which, again, is not ideal. But I can work within the limitations, for now. She moves her head from side to side, trying to sense where I am. 'What's the worst?' I ask.

She startles. Begins panting with terror.

'Shh . . .' I don't want her to hyperventilate and pass out.

She gives a little squeak, clamps her mouth tight to stop the noise.

She's a quick learner — I like that in a girl.

I've tethered her arms behind her. I tilt her head back with the palm of my hand. The pulse in her throat flutters, then picks up pace, hammering like a piston. Can a person truly die of fright? The idea excites me almost more than I can stand.

I lean close to her, whisper in her ear: 'I want you to imagine your worst nightmare.'

She's a good girl — she does as she's told.

'That's what I'm going to do to you, little Emma.'

Tears seep from under the blindfold and trickle down to her neck. I wish I could see the fear in her eyes.

I want to see every nerve and muscle in her body vibrate with fear. She tries to swallow, but with the tether, and my hand flat against her forehead, her neck is stretched so tight all she can manage is a kind of spasm in her throat.

'And when your worst nightmare has been outdone by a factor of a thousand, what will happen then?'

I feel a tiny movement of her head under my hand: she really doesn't know.

'Em-ma . . . I thought you were so bright.' I pause, giving her time to think. 'Then it will happen all over again. And again. And again.' Now I can smell her fear.

She sobs. Her blouse is fluttering with the force of her heartbeat, hammering so hard, you'd think her heart would burst.

I touch the pulse in her neck with the tip of my tongue and she cries out.

This is going to be even more fun than I thought.

CHAPTER 8

Wednesday, 19 November, night

Cassie Rowan hugged herself, hopping from one foot to the other. The cold had seeped into her, numbing her face, stiffening her muscles and sinking into the very marrow of her bones. She had stopped shivering, which somewhere in the back of her mind she knew was not a good sign. For the first hour, she had felt like she was balancing on frozen golf balls, but for half an hour since, her feet had been painless, solid blocks of ice. The fog was so thick that she couldn't even see the lights on the cathedral concourse, and the spotlights intended to highlight the towering sandstone edifice only created a slightly brighter patch in the milky swirl of freezing moisture. The city had gone to ground. Only an occasional taxi rattled past, parting the fog like a curtain and vanishing again in seconds. Sounds were deadened.

The problem with slow nights was they gave you too much time to think. Rowan had been fretting about her younger brother since she started her shift: he'd been unusually solicitous that morning. He wondered if she should take time off to allow her injuries to heal. And when he got home from school that evening, he'd helped with dinner, then washed up, without having to be told. Since when did Neil wash dishes without being asked?

'God, Cassie, you are so naive . . .' she muttered. She heard the drone of a diesel engine and expected to see another taxi approaching, its 'for hire' sign a blur of orange light. But the vehicle decelerated fast, and a white van pulled in to the kerb.

The door slid open and Rowan stepped forward and peered inside.

'Sorry, lads, I don't do group rates,' she said.

'For God's sake, stop arsing about and get yourself in here, girl — it's bloody freezing.'

'You think?' Rowan said, climbing inside and hauling the door shut after her.

There were just three in the van: Kirkhof, Finch and the techie. It reeked of Chinese takeaways, flatulence, and the indefinable chemical odour of a chain smoker: everyone called Kirkhof 'Hoff', or — when he was well out of earshot — 'Hoff the Koff' — forty years of smoking thirty a day had taken its toll on his lungs.

'Bloody hell, Cass, you wanna get a few more clothes on, this weather.'

Rowan was wearing gold shorts with thick tights to cover the grazes on her knees, a fluffy pink sweater that was cut way too low to be of any practical use, a tiny gold cross-body evening bag, just about big enough to take her warrant card, and the ratty fur stole that Finch had rescued the previous day. 'I did think of wearing my duffle coat, but it just doesn't work as an off-the-shoulder number,' she said.

Hoff grunted and shoved a blanket at her. 'I don't know what the boss is on — I mean, who's gonna come looking for business on a night like this?' Hoff had been brought up in the Vauxhall area of the city centre and had stayed there all his life. His accent was undiluted Scouse — a mongrel mix of the languages and accents of all the seafarers and immigrants that had washed up on the shores of the Mersey since the eighteenth century. It was nasal and harsh and the tar in his lungs seemed to rattle in sympathy with the catarrh in his throat, so that every 'c' and 'k' caught like phlegm on his soft palate.

'Not that there's any chance of hooking him anytime soon,' Rowan said. 'The amount of blood he lost, I'd be surprised if he can even walk on that foot — and he'll stay well clear of his usual pick-up points for a while. Warhorse is punishing me for letting him get away.'

Finch shifted uncomfortably on the bench seat opposite. 'It wasn't your fault, Cass.'

Rowan raised an eyebrow. 'No shit, Sherlock? So, are you going to tell her what really went down?'

Finch shuffled his feet and avoided her eye.

After a while Hoff glanced at Rowan and shook his head. 'You should've took a few days off, Cass.'

'I look that bad, do I?'

Hoff frowned. 'No, nothing like that. It's just — you're entitled.'

Entitled? Maybe she was. But anyone taking time off for injuries risked office gossip. By the time she got back, she could be labelled a hysteric who flipped out as soon as the Furman cut up rough. And no doubt had to be rescued, sobbing, by the manly intervention of Finch and Wicks.

'Everyone's *so* worried about my health,' she said. Hoff opened his mouth to say something more, but she interrupted. 'I'm *fine*, Hoff.'

He wheezed a sigh. 'Best chance we've got of catching that toerag is DNA,' he said. The Furman had wiped the lorry clean of prints when he'd dumped it, but he'd left plenty of blood on the glass at the transport depot.

'Well let's hope the labs aren't too busy,' Rowan said. ''Cos I can't stand much more of this.' Her shiver reflex had returned with a vengeance and her teeth were chattering so hard she was in danger of cracking a tooth.

'Pass the thermos, lad,' Hoff said.

Finch hung his head, guiltily. 'I finished the last of it ten minutes ago.'

Hoff shot him a withering look. 'Why don't we whip round to Subway and get a fill-up? I'm gasping for a smoke.'

Using his weakness for nicotine to cover for the fact he was worried about her: Rowan was touched. 'I've got a better idea. My place is just up the road.' It was an exaggeration — Rowan lived in the unfashionable north end of the city, near Walton — but she couldn't shift the niggling suspicion that her brother's uncharacteristic concern that evening was a cover for one of his escapades.

'It's a straight run — this time of night, we could make it in ten minutes — fifteen at the outside.'

Finch looked doubtful. 'If the boss finds out . . .'

'Who's going to tell her, Finch? Not me. Not Hoff. And we both know you can keep your mouth buttoned when it suits you.' It was a cruel sideswipe, but her feet had woken up in screaming agony. 'Come on . . . I'll make us a fresh brew and some toast. How's that?'

Finch shrugged, miserably. 'Fine. I'll drive.'

中 中 中

The house was lit up like Blackpool Illuminations and the walls pulsed with the bass rhythm of angry metal rock.

Rowan slid the van door back like she was racking a pistol slide. 'I'll kill him.'

Hoff tried to catch her arm, snagging a few nylon fibres from her fake fur. 'Hold on, Cass. You can't—'

She couldn't hear the rest for the screaming of the band and the roar of blood in her ears. The front door opened directly onto the street; it stood ajar and she shoved it so hard it bounced off the wall.

The place was heaving: boys, mostly — a few girls — all wearing black or combat green, most with gelled hair and *fuck you* sneers on their faces. Rowan ploughed through the mass of bodies, jostling elbows and spilling drinks. Shouts of protest followed her, a few wolf whistles.

Neil was in the front room, leaning against the fireplace, a plastic beer glass in one hand. He was dark-haired and slim, like Rowan, but give him a year or two, her little brother would have a rugby player's build. The girl standing next to him saw his potential, and so did three or four others — Rowan clocked them, eyeing him up at a distance — though she doubted if Neil had any notion of his physical appeal. At that moment, he noticed her and blanched, lowered the glass as if he meant to conceal it, then seemed to realise there was a hell of a lot more he couldn't hide, and blushed frantically.

'What are you doing here?' he yelled over the music. 'You're supposed to be working.'

'And you're supposed to be in bed.'

A chorus of catcalls went up, and Rowan saw that the crowd had pushed back, leaving a semicircle of space around them. A vodka bottle passed from one girl to another. They hissed refusals at each other, neither one wanting to be caught with the evidence. Twenty kids crammed into her tiny front room, staring at her, slack-mouthed, their eyes glazed with drink and God knew what else, and not one of them over sixteen. She moved to the music system and turned it off.

'Party's over,' she said. The silence throbbed in her ears. A few started to grumble, but most of the kids began edging to the door.

'No!' Neil lunged forward, pulled at sleeves, trying to turn back the tide. 'This isn't just *your* house, you know. I can invite who I like.'

'It's eleven o'clock at night, it's a school night. And you're underage. You follow my rules.'

'*Your* rules? You're not my *mother*, Cass.'

Rowan gritted her teeth. *Not now, Neil.* He had challenged her before — so many times she'd lost count. But never like this. Never in front of his friends.

She stared him full in the face, willing him not to take it further.

A ruckus in the hall was followed by shouts of complaint. 'Who's killed the music?' Rowan heard. 'I'll kick his arse from here to Birkenhead!'

Fifteen stones of testosterone-charged bulk bulldozed through the press of exiting teens. Seeing Rowan, the big lad stopped dead in the doorway. A couple of kids bounced off him, but he seemed not to notice.

Gary Miller — school dropout, steroid junky and supplier to half the gym jockeys in the city centre. She must have arrested him half a dozen times. He wore a black T-shirt that bulged with pumped muscle, and black cargo pants. His flies were open.

He looked her up and down. 'Hey, Neil, you never said there was a stripper.'

Rowan was thrown for a moment. Then she remembered that she was still in full sex-worker get-up. Neil tilted his head and challenged her with a look.

'Don't push it, Gary,' Rowan said. 'I want you out of here.'

Miller grinned, opening his arms wide. 'Constable Rowan . . . I've never seen you look so go-oood.' His eyes darted rapidly right and left; his pupils were mere pinpoints.

Great, he's off his head on something.

'Come on, Cassie — let's part-*ay*!' He shimmied his hips, and one of the remaining teens sniggered. That did it. Rowan went straight at him. He eyed her with bland curiosity, as if she was an ant making an assault on a steel door.

Looking him dead in the eye, she scooped her right leg behind his and flicked the back of his knee with hers. He buckled. Simultaneously, she brought her right arm up and round to the side of his neck, taking him off balance. Shouts of dismay went up as a few laggers tried to avoid ending up under him. He toppled backwards into the hallway and sagged against the stair rail. It gave an ominous *crack*.

Next moment, Hoff was between the two of them, one hand on Miller's chest, the other gripping Rowan's upper arm.

'What the hell are you doing?' he hissed.

'I'm about to arrest this scum.'

'For what?'

'He's stoned, Hoff, and he's in my house.' She tried to force past him, but he manoeuvred her into the now empty front room, out of earshot of the partygoers.

'You want us to search him? Search the bedrooms an' all? You know how that's gonna look on the charge sheet? Like you said, Cassie — it's your house. And your brother hosted this little get-together.'

She closed her eyes briefly. *Hell* . . .

Hoff eased the pressure on her upper arms and looked into her face. 'Okay now?' he said.

She nodded, and he looked over his shoulder to the hall-way, where Miller was straightening his clothing.

'On your bike,' Hoff said. 'And do up your flies before you go out on the street, or I'll have you for gross indecency.'

Miller took his time about it, and as he passed Neil, he leaned in. 'Later,' he said.

CHAPTER 9

The wind had whipped up another squall, spattering the students and academics hurrying to and from lectures with hard, cold rain. Dylan struggled against the torrent, alternately tugged and shoved by savage gusts.

A van was parked on double yellows in Rodney Street and traffic backed up behind it, windscreens awash with rainwater, flanks streaming. Dylan darted through the stationary vehicles, edging sideways to avoid a cyclist who flashed across his path, riding on the pavement. The cyclist swore, kicking out at him, but he rode on, and Dylan took refuge in a small café across the street from the NHS psychiatric clinic.

The café was set up in a leased Georgian terrace. Small by the standards of some of the houses in Rodney Street, its front door stood open. Just inside the hallway, another door, and tacked to it a handwritten sign on a piece of card read, *Open*. The added message, *Just warming up!* was an oblique reminder to keep the inner door closed.

He pushed through and the wind shrieked after him, snatching a paper napkin from the nearest table and flapping it halfway across the room like a wounded bird. He shut the door quickly, putting his back against it. The floors, stripped and waxed to create a bohemian feel, had suffered under a sodden flow of customers.

Dylan ordered coffee and a sandwich. The only other customers were a rumpled-looking academic sipping tea, and a mother spooning orange-coloured mush from a glass jar into her infant's mouth.

He sat at the table by one of the windows, and delicately pushed the bowl of sugar packets away from him with the tip of one bony finger before taking out his notebook. It was warm and dry, protected by his jacket. While he waited, he turned the pages.

This notebook, like all his notebooks, contained a description of Mr Alan Palmer: Height, five feet eleven inches; hair, mid-brown; eyes, hazel; build, athletic. He also noted that his therapist dressed formally for work, though he carried a leather messenger bag instead of a briefcase — presumably to facilitate his walks from his home to his private office, and from there to the NHS clinic. Palmer walked most places.

Dylan knew Palmer's home address as well as his private office address. He had followed Palmer to Dr Atherton's home on Tuesday. Palmer did not live with his wife, though she lived nearby. They had one child — a daughter named Lucy who was quite young — perhaps three or four years old.

It was warm in the little café and the glass quickly fogged. He used a napkin to clear a porthole so that he could spy on the street.

He had finished his sandwich and was drinking his second coffee when he saw Alan Palmer, still buttoning his woollen overcoat, trotting down the steps of the clinic. A gap opened in the traffic and Dr Palmer sprinted across the road, his bag strapped over his left shoulder.

Dylan made a note of Palmer's time of departure, jammed the remainder of his sandwich into his mouth, and stuffed the notebook and pen into the inside pocket of his waterproof.

Practised in the art of stalking, he fell easily in step with the analyst, keeping close to the buildings, so that he could dodge off the street if his quarry glanced back.

Palmer had the long, fluid stride of a habitual walker. The rain slowed and stopped, though water continued to rush down the steep slope of Duke Street, gathering in the wells of cracked paving stones, rippling in the gusting wind.

At the end of Lower Duke Street, they parted company: Palmer was headed towards his private practice along Dock Road; Dylan knew he had two more patients to see before he finished for the evening. Which left Dylan free to explore the more exciting prospects on offer in the city centre.

CHAPTER 10

Late autumn and early winter are my favourite hunting seasons: long nights, short days, and the cold a perfect excuse for hoods and scarves.

My quarry today is Constable Cassie, hero of the hour. I hardly recognized her. Of course, her hair's a few shades darker than it was when we first met — that's taken some of the shine off her. And a boot in the face can shake a girl's confidence. I knew it was her as soon as I saw her in the Baltic — frigid bitch. But did she remember me, I wonder? She'll know me all right, by the time I've finished with her.

Well, well, well — look who she's with. When most girls are bundled like sacks of rags, you really notice the ones that shine. Like the lovely Tasha, darling of the local media, apparently none the worse for her little adventure in a dark alley last month. Look at her — dressed for attention — practically dancing along as if the sun came out especially for her. You'd think she'd have learned to be a little less flamboyant after that near-miss. But it's attention her sort wants, and she's certainly got mine. Legs right up to her assets, perfect skin, and a neck you could just about circle with one hand.

Tasha and Cassie — two for the price of one; it's a delightful prospect. Emma was sweet in her way, but she did lack sophistication. Tasha, though . . . Tasha is so shiny, she damned near sparkles! Makes you want to rub off the gilt, see what's underneath.

* * *

The last of the rain had swept eastwards, leaving a crystal blue sky, and the city centre twinkled in late autumn sunshine. The air smelled fresh and droplets of rain trembled on every bent twig and dormant bud, bejewelling the ornamental trees.

Tasha walked next to Rowan, matching her stride for confident stride. The two women turned heads amongst the afternoon shoppers: Rowan's dark brown hair and Tasha's honey-gold curls provided a pleasing contrast, as did their difference in style. Rowan was comfortably dressed in a short trench coat over slim-fit needle cords and Cuban heel boots. Tasha wore her favourite brown leather jacket over a flared wool skirt, cut to just above the knee. It swung and flirted as she kept easy pace with Rowan in her three-inch heels.

Rowan was glad to feel the sun on her face and to be with a friend who, although she'd only met her in the summer, she felt closer to than anyone since her mother had died.

'How long have we got?' Tasha said.

'My shift begins at five,' Rowan wasn't sure which she felt more glum about — dress-shopping or spending another freezing night on the streets.

'All the better to catch office drones, craving a quickie before they head home to the bosom of their families.'

Tasha talked like no other sex worker Rowan had ever met. She had shown up at the front desk in August, demanding to speak to a senior detective. Rowan had been passing through and heard the well-spoken woman wearing expensive urban chic say that she was representing girls who were being hounded by a violent sexual predator. The civilian on the front desk assumed she must be a lawyer and reiterated doggedly that she couldn't direct her to the 'relevant party' unless she gave the name of her client, or at least a case number.

Rowan had diverted to the desk and introduced herself. Tasha had been hostile, initially, but Rowan had given her word that she would listen and if she thought Tasha had a case, she would take it to her superintendent. So, they'd found an empty interview room, and Tasha had told her the story.

There were three victims at that point. The first was a mother of two whose husband thought she was working in a city centre pub three evenings a week — she hadn't even reported the assault. Two others had put in a complaint, but only after several days, and they hadn't been taken seriously. That was when Tasha had stepped in. The girls called him the Furman, because he seemed to have a fetish for it — made his victims wear a fur stole he had in the boot of his car. He left them naked, beaten and bound on wasteland many hours after he had abducted them, leaving no DNA or trace evidence. And none of the women were able to give a reliable description of the man. Warman had been assigned as SIO and Tasha had been brilliant at bringing the other girls on board, but the Furman went quiet and the investigation stalled.

Then, in October, Tasha herself had been attacked. Rowan stole a glance at her friend. Tasha's eye was almost healed, now, but a star-shaped scar on her right temple would remain — emergency surgery to repair a detached retina had restored her vision. She'd appeared on local TV news from her hospital bed for a police appeal and had tried to give a description of her attacker. But she'd suffered a concussion and anterograde amnesia, so the minutes up to the attack were muddled and only came to her in brief, frightening blasts. Still, she'd survived — and she hadn't been raped.

Finally, Warman had resorted to using Cassie Rowan as bait, fur stole and all. And to be fair, it would have worked — if Finch and Wicks had done their job.

But that kind of thinking wouldn't change the facts.

When she'd first met Tasha, Rowan had wondered at the collision of circumstances that had brought an intelligent, well-educated middle-class woman into street prostitution. Had even asked her, once, if she had considered another way of paying her tuition fees.

Tasha said, 'I tried waitressing — it didn't pay for the kind of light I need.' At the beginning of her second year of undergraduate study, Tasha had bought a studio apartment overlooking the river, where she had as much light as any artist could want.

'No drugs habit,' she'd said, by way of explanation. 'Don't even do coke.'

By now, they had reached the bottom of Church Street and Rowan was suddenly aware that she herself was under scrutiny. 'I can recommend an excellent foundation to cover that,' Tasha said.

'Cover what?' The bruising had begun to fade, and although the skin of her cheek still felt tight where the Furman had grazed her with the point of his shoe, Rowan had thought she'd done a good job of covering the worst of the damage.

A mirror appeared in Tasha's hand. She didn't even break stride.

Rowan took the proffered mirror and winced at what she saw. 'This light's brutal,' she muttered, shoving it back into her friend's hand.

Tasha smiled crookedly. 'Hey, I didn't mean to—'

'I know,' Rowan said. 'I just wish I'd held on to the bastard.'

'Did you get a good look at him?' Tasha asked.

'I heard Jade scream and he was off and running as soon as he saw me.' Rowan sighed. 'I only ever saw the back of him — and he was wearing a hoodie and scarf.'

Tasha shrugged. 'CCTV?'

'In that fog?' Rowan shook her head. 'All we got is blood DNA and a size ten shoe.'

'DNA — that's good, isn't it?'

'I've got all my hopes riding on it. I don't suppose you've remembered any more?'

Tasha shook her head. 'It's still a blank, I'm afraid.'

'Have any of the girls been in touch?' Tasha might have stopped working the streets, but they checked in with her regularly.

'Not since Tuesday.'

Which was when Rowan had got a face full of shoe leather.

'How about you — anyone been asking for you?' Rowan asked. When a girl went missing off the street, punters sometimes asked questions.

Tasha looked askance at her. 'Is this a friend's concern or professional curiosity?'

Rowan felt her cheeks flush. 'I just want to stop this bastard before he hurts somebody else, Tasha.'

After a moment, Tasha gave a brief nod. 'Kimmy said someone had asked after me, wanting a date. And the gallery's had a few callers who clearly weren't interested in art.'

'Tell them to ask for a number to call back,' Rowan said. 'I'll check them out.'

Tasha waved away her concern. 'Just weirdos seeking the thrill of proximity to violence.'

Rowan laughed. 'God, I wish I could have you tucked in my back pocket when I'm writing reports.'

Tasha tossed her head. 'You're such an inverted snob. Anyway, I've had a few commissions for paintings on the back of the press coverage — I wouldn't want you scaring away the genuine punters—'

She must have read Rowan's disapproval in her face, because she smiled. 'Cassie, you're so easy to shock!'

Rowan did find it hard to reconcile herself to Tasha's easiness with the concept of body as commodity.

'When you say "genuine punters" . . . ?'

'I mean people who want to buy my art along with my notoriety.'

Rowan took a breath and let it go. She didn't know exactly what to say to her friend: she was off the streets, and that had to be safer than the way she had been earning a living. But pandering to the fantasies of men who got a thrill out of reading that she'd narrowly escaped violent rape?

'Just be careful,' she said at last.

Tasha put an arm around her shoulder. 'I haven't been *near* the gallery since it happened. The staff come to me to pick up canvases. They don't pass on my number to *anyone* without checking with me, first.'

'You mean you have allowed them to pass on your number to *some* people?'

'Don't *worry*.' She tightened her grip and the bruising to Rowan's chest gave a shout of protest. She uttered an involuntary grunt of pain and Tasha let go.

'God, I'm sorry. Are you all right?'

Rowan searched her friend's face. 'Why do you take risks, Tasha?'

'What risks?'

Rowan held her gaze and she laughed.

'Oh, come now — I'm practically a recluse!'

Rowan knew she'd pushed it as far as Tasha would allow. 'All right,' she said. 'Okay. Let's shop.' She veered off in the direction of Next but Tasha dragged her back on course, pinching the sleeve of her jacket between thumb and forefinger.

'No-no-no-ooo . . .'

'Come on, Tasha,' Rowan wheedled, 'it can't hurt to look . . .'

'Hurt?' Tasha said. 'I'm getting a migraine at the very *thought*.' She continued tugging on Rowan's sleeve, keeping up the pace, moving implacably towards the designer boutiques and department stores at the more expensive end of town. 'You told me this was an *important* wedding.'

'It is,' Rowan had to agree. 'Why d'you think big brother is honouring us with his presence?'

'Neil mentioned that Alex is flying over from New York,' Tasha said.

Rowan had dragged Neil to Tasha's flat on the disastrous night of the party so that she could keep an eye on him. Tasha had taken in the rebellious teen without hesitation, even though she'd been dressed ready to go out.

Tasha's brow furrowed. 'I thought you didn't get on with the Scottish Rowans.'

'You thought right,' Rowan said.

'So, why are they descending on Merseyside?'

Rowan groaned. 'My second cousin, Stuart, is marrying a church-going Presbyterian girl from the Wirral, and *her* family want the wedding near home, so we're expected to be there.'

They ploughed on through throngs of shoppers and business types, dodging market surveyors and street performers.

'Ah . . . They don't know that Alex lives in the States?'

'Why else would he break with his busy schedule to come to Liverpool?' Rowan knew she sounded bitter. 'We need them to think he's still around. If they get to know he's living in the States, and me working shifts, they're guaranteed to meddle.' She felt a sudden wash of emotion, and Tasha, always sensitive to her moods, touched her arm lightly.

'You okay?'

Rowan blinked back a tear and forced a smile. 'Oh, you know, just worried about my next Visa card statement.'

They had reached the end of Church Street and, as a distraction, Rowan said, 'How about Hobbs?'

'My Aunty Peggy likes Hobbs.'

'You don't have an Aunty Peggy.'

'And *you* don't have the fashion gene, which is why you asked *me* to come with you. How about we take a look at Vivienne Westwood — she might have a cheeky little check that would scandalize the Scots?'

Alarmed, Rowan resisted Tasha's gentle pressure at her elbow. 'I don't want to be conspicuous — I just want to blend in.'

Tasha laughed. 'Honey, you're not *wallpaper*. If you could be bothered to take five minutes on a make-up routine, you'd be gorgeous.'

'I've a friend just like you,' Rowan said, thinking of Ian Chan. 'He delivers a compliment with one hand and a smack round the chops with the other.'

'Maybe you should've asked *him* to help you pick out a frock.'

Rowan stopped dead. 'Wait a minute — I didn't say anything about a frock.'

'If you showed your legs once in a while, you might be surprised by the positive effects on your social life.'

'I don't *have* a social life — and my legs have been on show every night for the past two month. If it's taught me anything, it's that too much exposure brings out the worst in men.'

Tasha got behind her and shoved her through the doors of Reiss.

Until Grosvenor Properties poured money into a massive demolition and reconstruction programme, the area from Paradise Street down to the docks was a jumble of slummy sixties low-rise in concrete and bile-coloured bricks. Known locally as 'The Big Dig', the transformation, completed in 2008, had involved excavating for underground parking, removing and reinstating a park, and creating new buildings over forty-two acres of the city centre. The friends covered most of it in the course of the next two hours. Tasha allowed a brief respite: coffee at a restaurant overlooking Chavasse Park, during which, with photographic recall and the ruthlessness of a military despot, she recapped the boutiques they had visited, stores they hadn't, the maybes, must-haves and still-to-be-tried among the dresses, suits, skirts and accessories they had seen.

'So,' Tasha said, eyeing Rowan over her cappuccino. 'How is Neil today?'

'Hard to tell. We're not on speaking terms,' Rowan said.

'You haven't spoken to him since the party?'

'Oh, there've been *words*. But not what you'd call a conversation.'

Tasha spooned some foam from her cup, savouring it like it was fresh cream. 'It *was* supposed to be an Xbox session and a few beers with his best mates. The rest of the year group found out.' She shrugged. 'You know how it goes.'

'He's fifteen years old,' Rowan said. 'I'm not even supposed to leave him alone overnight.'

'He's nearly sixteen.'

Which was Neil's same argument the day of the party. He'd flat out refused to sleep another night on their neighbour's couch, and Rowan had only caved in to his demands because she was too tired to face another teenage strop.

'Well, he isn't sixteen yet,' Rowan said. 'God, if social services found out he'd been *drinking*—'

'He seemed sober to me,' Tasha said

'That's not the point, Tasha. I trusted him, and he let a load of boozed-up kids — worse than that — he let a *drug dealer* into our house.'

'Ah, Gary Miller.'

Rowan glanced sharply at her friend. 'He really opened up to you, didn't he?'

'He told me you put Gary flat on his arse.'

Rowan suppressed a smile. 'Is that what he said?'

'Mm-hmm. Sounded incredibly proud of his big sister.'

* * *

They descended the steps to the shops as the sky began to shift from pale blue to a greenish haze. Tasha paused for a moment, transfixed, it seemed, by the chilly beauty of the department store ahead of her. On a clear day, if the lighting was right, it seemed to take on the blue-green light reflected from the Mersey a short distance away.

'It's beautiful,' Tasha breathed. 'I'm going to paint it as an ice palace.'

Rowan had little appreciation of architecture. She liked the modernity of the new buildings, and the fact that everything felt so much cleaner since they had rebuilt the city centre, but that's about as far as her interest went. Tasha, now only a semester away from graduating in Fine Art, spoke endlessly about colour and light and form and texture, but Rowan could never make any of it stick, and often couldn't see what it was that had sent her friend into raptures. So she gave a neutral 'Mm,' and trudged wearily towards the Met Quarter, the next designer mall on Tasha's mental tick list.

They were barely though the doors when Rowan's mobile rang. It was Finch. Rowan stopped and listened to

Finch explain the reason for interrupting her afternoon off, while shoppers and sightseers flowed around her.

She ended the call and turned to Tasha. 'I've got to go.'

'Oh, you don't expect me to fall for that old chestnut,' Tasha said, laughing. 'We've got another hour and a half.' She made a feint for Rowan's phone.

'Tasha,' Rowan said, and the smile faded from her friend's face.

'What?' She looked suddenly fragile and frightened.

'The Furman took another girl,' Rowan said. 'And it looks like he's upped the ante.'

CHAPTER 11

'Emma Hammond?'

Rowan had been shown to a room off the General Medical ward at the Royal Hospital.

A solid-looking Indian girl leapt from the chair by the bed. 'Who's asking?' Rowan took out her warrant card. 'Detective Constable Rowan.'

The girl looked ready to take her on, but Rowan avoided the confrontation by side-stepping to the foot of the bed. 'Miss Hammond, I'd like to ask you a few questions. Would that be all right?'

Emma Hammond lay propped up by pillows, her eyes, red-rimmed from crying, were open, but blank of any understanding. Her hands, in her lap, picked constantly at the cuticles of her nails.

'Can't you see she's not up to this?'

Rowan turned her attention to Emma's friend. Emma's parents had been informed, but they were travelling from York, and might not arrive for another hour. It seemed that this young woman had appointed herself as Emma's personal bodyguard. Rowan recognized the set of the jaw and the spark of fire in the friend's eye — she saw the same defiance reflected in the mirror every day.

'You must be Emma's friend — Vineeta, is it?'

'Vinnie,' the girl corrected, with an aggressive lift of her chin.

'Vinnie,' Rowan said, 'I'm here to help. I know it doesn't feel like that right now, and all you want to do is get between Emma and more hurt. But I know this man. He's hurt other women.'

Vinnie's attention flickered to the graze on Rowan's cheek, then away.

'I want to find him and put him away,' Rowan said. 'But I need Emma's help, okay?'

Vinnie looked uncertain whether she wanted to toss Rowan out on her ear, or dissolve into angry tears. 'She needs rest.' There was a note of desperation in her voice, as if she knew even as she said it that a lifetime's rest couldn't put Emma right.

Emma stirred and cleared her throat. 'Vinnie?' It seemed the words came from far away, as if she was trying to make herself heard from across the blasted landscape of her shattered illusions.

A tear trembled on Vinnie's lower lid. 'What, love?' she asked.

'I'll talk to her.'

Vinnie went to the chair on the far side of the bed and lowered herself into it, gingerly.

Emma's eyes were huge, the irises a pale, clear blue. She turned her gaze on Rowan and it felt like a cry of wild terror. Shocked, Rowan broke eye contact, and Emma fell to a distracted examination of her hands, watching herself pick the cuticles till they bled. Her face was unmarked, but Rowan couldn't shift the notion that she looked *raw*, as if a layer of skin had been peeled away.

She listened without interruption as Emma told her about the lecture, how excited she'd been, how thrilled to be alone in the fog afterwards. She explained that she had felt sorry for the injured student, that he had been funny and bright and interested in her. He was studying genetics and his name was Andy. She heard about Emma's growing unease, Andy's fury when the car wouldn't start, and the look of triumph on his face that made her want to run. 'I tried to get away,' she said, her eyes pleading with Rowan to believe her. 'I *did*. But he shocked me.'

Rowan looked to Vinnie.

'Shocked?'

'My neck.' Emma's hands fluttered and fell into her lap again, like a broken butterfly. 'I can't . . . Help me, Vin.'

Vinnie sighed and wiped her face with her hand. When she stood, she held onto the arms of the chair until the last moment, as if she feared to let go. She steadied herself, then gently lifted Emma's hair from her neck.

'He tied her hands behind her,' Vinnie explained. 'Her shoulders were almost dislocated. Turn your head a bit, hon,' she said softly.

At first Rowan didn't know what she was supposed to see. Bruises overlaid bruises in ugly black and purple ovals. She began to shake her head in confusion, then she saw, almost obscured by the bruising, two tiny red circles, perhaps three centimetres apart.

Her gaze shifted up to Vinnie. 'What caused this?' she asked.

Emma answered. 'A taser.'

'When she tried to get away, or fight him, he shocked her with a taser.' Vinnie let Emma's hair fall, smoothing it onto her friend's shoulders in a tender gesture.

Emma sank back into the pillows and closed her eyes.

'Could you—' Rowan's voice caught and she had to cough to loosen the tightness in her throat. 'Can you describe the man who did this?'

Emma shook her head tiredly. 'He was muffled up in a scarf and beanie.'

'What about his nose, his eyes?'

'His eyes—' Emma flinched. 'Blue, I think — I'm not sure — they kept changing.' Her breath came in short gasps. 'So much hate—'

'Okay,' Rowan soothed. 'It's all right . . . Don't worry, we can come back to that.'

Emma nodded, and Vinnie gave her a sip of water, eyeing Rowan angrily.

'How about his voice — was there anything distinctive about that?'

'I thought northern — maybe Liverpool — at first. But after . . . after I woke up, I . . . couldn't tell. I was blindfolded — I couldn't tell where he was.' She twisted her head to the side, as if trying to squirm away from her captor. I'm sorry — I really *can't* remember what he looked like.'

'That's perfectly normal,' Rowan said. 'What you went through was horrible. Sometimes the brain shuts down to protect itself.'

'The taser shocks *might* be a factor,' Vinnie said in a snarky tone that Rowan was beginning to think was a signature trait.

'I didn't know tasers could affect short-term memory,' Rowan said.

'Well, now you do. Fifty-thousand volts, direct to the skin, detective,' she added, bugging her eyes in a silent 'Duh!'

And Emma had been shocked many times over several days. Rowan didn't want to think too hard about the cumulative effects of all those jolts of electricity.

She turned back to Emma; she was staring at the bedclothes and mercifully didn't seem to have followed this last exchange.

'Things might start coming back to you,' Rowan said. 'And if they do, I'd like to hear from you. It doesn't matter how small or insignificant, or *odd* the details might seem, I want you to know that I'm here — *any time* — just phone me.' She placed a business card on the nightstand.

Emma's eyebrows twitched. 'His scarf,' she said. 'It was English Soc. — but he said he was studying medicine.' Her eyes widened. 'And his name was . . . was Andy!'

Rowan smiled warmly. 'That's great,' she said. 'You're doing great!'

But the student's eyes darkened as she recalled more of her ordeal. 'He kept asking if I *liked* it.'

She continued in a monotone: he had strangled her while he raped her, revived her and raped her and strangled her again, until she felt like one tortured bruise.

'He went away for a time. I don't know how long — I was drifting in and out by then,' Emma said. 'But he came back for a few hours before he let me go. Said he wanted to make the most of me.'

The flat emotionless delivery made Rowan more anxious for Emma than if she had been weeping and distraught. Because Rowan had seen it before — in witnesses and rape victims and assault victims — Emma was in shock. For now it protected her from the pain of what had been done to her, but the shock would fade, and when it left, she would be swept up in a firestorm of emotion and self-recrimination as every humiliating incident came back to her with camera-flash sharpness.

'Do you remember anything about the place where—' Rowan wasn't sure how to say it. 'Where he kept you?'

'He made me wash. I think . . .' She lifted her head as if listening. 'I think the water came from a bottle — I didn't hear a tap running. He wouldn't let me get dressed. I was so cold . . .' Emma shivered, remembering. 'He made me walk up some steps.'

'What type of steps? Wooden? Concrete?'

She frowned. 'Stone, I think.' She closed her eyes. 'I sensed a steep drop on one side, and open space, like a well, but bigger. He took me outside. It was raining. He made me get into the boot of his car.' Her words came out in jerky puffs. 'It was lined with plastic. I thought I'd suffocate. I . . . thought he . . . was going to—'

She's hyperventilating. 'Emma, it's okay. You're safe now.'

'Couldn't breathe—' Emma's hands flew up but fell heavily into her lap and she cried out in pain. Her breath came in asthmatic whistling gasps and her eyes bulged.

Rowan turned to the door to shout for help, but a nurse was already on the way in. Vinnie flattened herself against the wall as she barged past.

'What have you been saying to her?' she demanded, reaching across for the oxygen supply. She held the mask to Emma's face and the girl fought for a moment, her hands scrabbling weakly to protect herself, to beat the nurse off, but when the oxygen reached her lungs, she relaxed, gulping air gratefully.

Rowan backed away. 'I'm sorry,' she said. 'I'll come back when you're—' She stopped herself; it seemed heartless to say, 'when you're feeling better'.

She looked into Emma's eyes and saw again the rawness, and this time she understood that it was innocence and joy and hope that had been torn from the girl, strip by bloody strip.

CHAPTER 12

'Daddy!' Lucy Palmer hurtled up the pathway, arms flung wide. In her right hand, she held a fairy wand. The smile on his daughter's face sparked a warm and joyful surge in his chest.

He swept Lucy up and swung her high till she shrieked with laughter and his wife, frowning, admonished him. 'She's just eaten, Alan.'

Alan Palmer gave Lucy his pop-eyed guilty look and she imitated him, revelling in the naughtiness of a shared joke against Mummy. Then he swung her onto his shoulders and finished locking up.

'I was on my way round to you,' he said, lolloping down the path. 'I thought we'd arranged for me to pick her up.'

Elspeth Palmer waited by the gate, as if to underline the fact that she was here under sufferance.

'We were in Lark Lane anyway,' she explained. 'It was as quick to come here as go back home. I called your mobile, but I got your voicemail.'

'It's switched off,' he said apologetically.

Elspeth raised an eyebrow. 'I don't know why you waste your money on the contract.'

'Friday's my half-day. You know I turn my mobile off.'

'Giddy-up!' Lucy commanded. Palmer snorted and stag-gered a little, to placate her, while he drank in the contours of his wife's face, her russet skin tones, her eyes dark with mistrust.

Elspeth balanced the demands of her executive job against the rigours of single parenthood, and still managed to look fabulous. Her brown hair fell straight to her shoulders, her gloves, boots, scarf and handbag co-ordinated perfectly with her burnt-orange coat. Workwear for Elspeth was tai-lored skirt suits and shoes with impossible heels. For relax-ation, she wore soft wool trousers and cashmere, so Palmer knew at once that she had taken the afternoon off: this, for her, was casual dress.

'Fancy a walk?' he asked.

'Noooo!' Lucy exclaimed. 'No walking! Trot, Daddy! Trot!' She waved her wand to make the magic lights flash and the tinkle of magic notes sound. On the third pass, the wand caught Palmer just above the eye.

'Youch!'

His four-year-old daughter stretched forward over his shoulder to check for damage, and her face appeared, close enough to kiss, her cheeks flushed with cold, her hair smell-ing of lavender and camomile. She tried the pop-eyed guilty look on him, and he closed one eye.

'You've taken me eye out, you scurvy dog! I'll have to become a pirate, I will.'

'No!' Lucy shouted, jigging up and down to make him go faster. 'Horsey! Horsey!'

Elspeth sighed and he saw a fractional loosening of the tension in her shoulders, a minuscule relaxation of the tight-ness around her eyes. Not forgiveness — he would never have that — but slowly, over the months, he had sensed a less-ening of her fury against him. It came in small acceptances, little gestures: a smile, an hour extra allowed with Lucy — or in agreeing to walk a while with him.

She held the gate open while he trotted through, snort-ing and neighing for Lucy's entertainment, and trailed them to the kerbside.

Palmer's house was directly opposite Sefton Park. They crossed the road and stepped over the low wall on the perimeter, Palmer taking it at a canter, rearing up as though it was Becher's Brook at the Grand National. The last squalls of rain had blown eastwards, heading towards the Pennines, leaving a high, clear blue sky. The grass was still sodden, though, so they followed the gravel path in a slow curve downwards.

'Where we goin'?' Lucy demanded.

'Since you've got your wand, I thought we'd go to . . .'

'Fairy Glen!' Lucy swooshed the wand again, and then contented herself gazing around at the sweeping parkland from her high vantage point. A pair of joggers panted down the path towards the lake. A quarter of a mile away, a man threw a stick for his dog, but otherwise the park was empty.

'How are you?' The question sounded awkward — too formal for the woman who had shared his life and his heart, his home and his bed for the past seven years — but it characterised Palmer's conversations with his wife since last spring.

Elspeth allowed the silence to become uncomfortable, before saying, 'Business is booming. I've been asked to lead the audit team.'

Palmer noticed that she had avoided answering his question directly. 'That'll mean long hours, won't it?' Elspeth worked for a law firm with offices all over the north of England and as far south as Birmingham.

Elspeth looked across to a stand of hornbeams. Their lollipop heads, stripped of leaves, stood black and stark against the winter-blue of the sky. 'I've decided it's time Lucy had a nanny.'

'*You've* decided . . . ?' Palmer suppressed a spurt of anger.

'It's the only practical solution,' she said, a flush spreading along the sharp line of her cheekbone.

'Is it?'

Elspeth glanced at him. 'Don't try that with me, Alan. You're not the one who has to sit up with her when she can't sleep at night. You don't have to drag her out of bed in the morning when she's too exhausted to open her eyes.

You don't have to juggle work with the childminder and pre-school and dance club and still be one hundred per cent committed and on the ball at endless bloody meetings—' She broke off and he felt once more, as he had felt it a thousand times, the burden of what he had done.

'I've told you,' he said, trying not to make it sound like an accusation. 'I can do more. That's why I bought this house — so I'd be just around the corner. I can *be* there in the morning. I could be there at night, too — or she could come to me.'

'And what about your patients? Your practice?'

'I'll find a way. Even if it means cutting back my list—'

'That's ridiculous.' Elspeth hated any suggestion of a reduction in their means — even now, when they had lived apart for months. 'You've only just begun building it after—' She checked herself, took a breath, started again. 'You have to live.'

His guts twisted into a knot. He wanted to say, *This isn't living, Elspeth — it's existing.* But Elspeth despised hyperbole, no matter how deeply felt. So, he remained silent. Lucy had become quiet, too, and a moment later, he felt her little hand, cool against his forehead. She patted him gently and he felt his heart swell till it threatened to choke him.

His afternoons with Lucy were mere snapshots of the bigger story of her life. Their lunches and trips to the zoo were asides — her real life was the childminder and pre-school and dance club, breakfasts and teatime and dinner time and bath time and bedtime stories. There wasn't enough time — was *never* enough time — to see every season and shift of her nature in these brief, meaningless outings.

'I'll call you,' he said, when he had a better hold on himself. 'We can talk about it, can't we?'

Elspeth hesitated before giving a stiff nod, avoiding his eye, and he suspected that the matter was already settled.

They reached the tarmac pathways that skirted the smaller ponds and Lucy gave a gasp of delight. 'Step-in stones! Let me down — *let me down*! I want to go first.'

Palmer lifted her lightly down and she raced ahead, tripping in her excitement, almost falling.

'Careful!' her mother called. 'You haven't got your wellies on. Mind you don't get your feet wet.'

Palmer watched his daughter run to the brink of the stream which connected two ponds, feeling the warmth and the welcome weight of her still in his shoulders. She stood, barely three feet tall, watching the torrent tumble and twist. Her multicoloured gloves hung from a cord, threaded through the sleeves of her coat. Her hair, chestnut-brown like her mother's, escaped from the confines of her felt hat. She wore maroon shoes to match her coat, and cream woollen tights on her plump baby legs. Lucy spurned trousers.

She turned to them, her eyes wide with fear and excitement. *Look at me!* They said. *Look what I can do!* She jumped, landing on the first flat stone, sending water in a corona that almost reached her parents' feet.

'It's flooded,' Elspeth called, and Palmer heard the anxiety and strain of the last months in her voice. 'You'll get drenched.'

Palmer touched her arm. '*Shh* . . .' he soothed. 'She needs to do this.'

Lucy turned again, uncertain this time, and nearly lost her balance. Palmer smiled. 'You can do it,' he urged. 'Count the stones.'

Lucy drew her brows down, as Palmer had seen her mother do so many times, then faced forward with renewed determination apparent in every bone and sinew of her little body. She leapt from stone to stone. 'One, two, three!'

They both cheered and Lucy cheered herself, her confidence restored, and trotted ahead of them.

Palmer had told his daughter stories about Fairy Glen since she was a baby, repeating and embellishing the stories his mother had told him as a child. In summer it was crowded with children, this man-made ravine, carved deep, it seemed, into the sandstone bedrock underlying the city. Rhododendrons drenched the glen with colour and scent in

May and June, and even now, the dark waxy leaves lent a hint of the exotic.

Today, the miniature waterfall, usually a dainty trickle, was swollen with rain. It gushed and foamed and gurgled and splashed, cascading down to the pond below.

The place was deserted, and at the top of the steps into the grotto, Lucy stopped, transfixed.

'What is it, sweetie?' Elspeth asked.

Lucy pointed with her wand, a look of delight and wonder on her face. Drawing closer, Palmer caught a glimpse of colour, and guessed what his daughter had seen. He crouched beside her and motioned for Elspeth to do the same. Reluctantly, she complied, then gave a little laugh of pleasure that Palmer felt as a tug at his heart.

The sun glanced through a mist of fine droplets thrown up from one of the bigger rocks. Within it, the light split, dancing in an arc of bright colours — a tiny, shimmering rainbow.

'Magic . . .' Lucy whispered.

Palmer hugged her. '*Fairy* magic,' he agreed. 'Go carefully to the bottom of the steps, turn around three times, and make a wish. If the rainbow is still here when you get back to the top, your wish will come true.'

Elspeth glanced sharply at him.

He read irritation and impatience in that look, but he waited until Lucy had managed the first few steps and was absorbed in her task before saying. 'It's a *game*, Elspeth.'

'She needs to learn that toys and presents can't be magicked from thin air.'

Lucy was murmuring something under her breath. At first, he heard numbers — she was counting the steps to the bottom — but as she reached the last one, she raised her voice in triumph.

'*Down* the bloody steps to *darkness* and *death*.'

Palmer felt the hairs on the back of his neck prickle. 'Lucy?'

She turned, her eyes blank, and he felt a chill ripple down his spine. 'Lucy, darling . . .' He rose to his feet.

This time, Elspeth restrained him. 'Leave her,' she said, and Lucy turned again, and began a stately pirouette, eyes closed, making her wish.

'What else has she been saying?' he asked. 'Elspeth? What has she—'

His wife stood beside him, brushing her hands together, as if to dislodge dust or dirt from them. 'You can't help yourself, can you, Alan?' she said, her voice fastidious, filled with lofty contempt. 'Why do you have to constantly *analyse* her? This constant . . . *scrutiny* does more harm than good.'

That hurt.

They stared at each other, not as strangers, but as two people who knew each other too well, and who shared a horror that not even time could soften.

CHAPTER 13

The central plaza of the Student Union Building is packed with students between lectures; every table in the high-vaulted shopping square is taken. The ring of crockery and the clamour of voices, together with the mingled smells of coffee and food, conjure up the refectory din and fug of Dylan Corbie's public-school days.

Dylan sits alone, a cup of black coffee slowly cooling next to the crisp new notebook lying open on the table, its blank pages full of possibilities. His hand is hooked awkwardly over the top of the page. It's a habit of secrecy he developed as a child. For some moments the hand remains still, and he stares at it, appalled, but also thrilled at what it might do next.

'Hi.'

He jumps violently, spilling the remains of his coffee. Slams the notebook shut, his heart pounding.

The girl laughs, helping him to mop up. 'Sorry. I didn't mean to startle you.'

'No, it's . . .' He stuffs the notebook inside his hooded jacket and snatches some napkins from the dispenser. 'It's cool.'

'I've seen you in Victorian Literature,' she says, helping him with the mess. 'I'm Laura.'

Laura. He tries it out in his head. *Lovely, laughing Laura.*

She leaves the sodden napkins on the table. 'This is your cue to introduce yourself,' she says, still smiling. Laura has even, white teeth.

'Dylan,' he says. Dylan Corbie.'

'Corbie — the raven.' She tilts her head. 'Dark and mysterious. Mind if I join you, Dylan Corbie?'

He feels jostled by a tumult of emotions.

'Um . . . I've got this essay to finish. I promised my tutor I'd hand it in by three thirty.' Lies come so much easier than truth.

She looks at him as though trying to decide if she can believe him, then shrugs, like it doesn't matter either way. 'Later,' she says.

She walks away without looking back.

Dylan wipes the table down until no trace of coffee remains, then he takes out his notebook again.

He writes: *INTERRUPTION*. No gaps, no blank lines. Not even room for a single word that doesn't belong. He enters the time, day, date, location.

He notes precisely what she said to him, how she smiled, what she is wearing, that she stands talking to two other girls for a minute, that they leave together.

This and other notebooks have documented details: the lectures she has attended, where she takes her meals, descriptions of the girls she is friendly with. He has noted her use of the library. He knows that when she concentrates a frown line appears between her eyebrows. He has seen her blonde curls caress the page as she writes. Laura uses the computer suite at the Harold Cohen Library every day except Sunday. There's a coursework deadline coming up, so this might not be a regular pattern. She prefers the Students' Union bars to pubs in the city centre — but will occasionally drink in the Rose, which is close to the halls of residence. On weekdays, she always returns to her halls by eleven p.m.

He writes, *Her name is Laura*. He stares at the name inscribed neatly on the page. Immutable. Indelible. *Now I know everything about her.*

CHAPTER 14

Friday evening

Rowan's shift had started at five, as usual. She had spent the last two hours working through a list of people who had attended the open lecture with Emma Hammond on Tuesday. A few remembered the pretty blonde girl, but nobody had seen her talking to a man, or getting into his car.

'Cutting it fine, aren't you, Cass?' Hoff said. It was now seven forty-five, and Rowan was back on Operation Kerbwatch at eight.

'Waiting to hear what the DCI has to say,' Rowan said. DCI Warman had called a briefing, and even fifteen minutes of reprieve from her sex-worker gear was precious.

Neil still wasn't speaking to her, and he'd come home from school that afternoon with bruised knuckles and a red mark on the line of his jaw that would blacken by morning. She suspected that Gary Miller had taken his public humiliation out on Neil, but when she asked him, all she got was an angry, 'What do you care?'

Rowan sighed, and Hoff said, 'All right, Cass?'

Wicks, Finch, Hoff and Billy, the audio-tech, were all in the office.

'Just knackered,' she said, forcing a grin.

'D'you think the DNA results are in?' Finch asked.

'God, I hope so,' Wicks said. He closed his eyes and put his feet up on his desk.

He and Finch had been assigned to tracking down and interviewing recently released sex offenders, and Rowan guessed that two days away from his desk was eating into his sleeping time.

Warman swept into the room, carrying a document wallet in one hand and a mug of coffee in the other. 'The Furman is not on the DNA database,' she said, without preamble.

Wicks said, '*Shit . . .*' under his breath.

'Not on the database?' Rowan repeated. 'How can that be?'

'Maybe he's new to the game,' Wicks said.

'It's a sadistic attack, Wicks, not a game,' Rowan said, a bit more sharply than she'd intended. 'Anyway, pervs like him don't just start straight in with abduction and rape. You'd expect to have other offences recorded — which means he should be on the database.'

'Not if he's been abroad,' Warman said. 'Working in the Arab states or the armed services.' She tapped her chin with her pen. 'Roy, you and Finch can drop what you were doing and start checking with the military, embassies, the Passport Service.'

'What are we looking for?' Finch asked.

'Dishonourable discharges, foreign prosecutions and deportations for bad behaviour,' Wicks said.

'He called himself Andy,' Rowan said.

'Which might be an alias,' Warman said. 'But, yes, try the name by all means. Just follow Wicks's lead.'

Rowan rolled her eyes. Wicks held up as a role model was just too much.

Warman broke in on her thoughts. 'Cassie, you're on Kerbwatch.'

'He's long gone, boss,' she said.

'He does seem to have changed his stalking grounds, I'll grant you,' Warman said stiffly. 'But whose fault is that?'

Rowan shot a look at Wicks and Finch, but it was plain they weren't about to break down and make a sobbing confession, so she bit her tongue and gave Warman a blank stare.

Hoff cleared his throat wetly. 'She's got a point, boss,' he wheezed. 'The working girls are on guard. Like you said, he's probably moved on. Looking for softer targets like that poor student.'

'And how do you propose we protect these "softer targets"?' Warman said acidly. 'A description — of sorts — was issued to the press and media the day after Cassie was attacked, the public was warned to look out for a man with foot or leg injuries. But it didn't help Emma Hammond, did it? We know his MO: he strips the girls and makes them wash before he dumps them naked on waste ground. What *you* need to do, Cassie, is work your contacts.'

It made sense, which in her perverse mood only made Rowan resent it more. They stared at each other for a few charged moments, then Rowan stood up. 'Fine,' she said. 'I'll get out there right now.'

'You'll change, first,' Warman said.

The room went so quiet Rowan could hear her heart thumping.

'You have a rapport with the girls,' Warman said, her face unreadable. 'I wouldn't want you to break cover.'

* * *

Rowan caught a glimpse of herself in the locker room mirror and groaned. Her evening ensemble comprised a pelmet skirt and pink crossover sweater. The clear PVC mackintosh she wore over them would not keep out the cold, but at least it was waterproof — rain was expected later. Her hair was raked up in a tight ponytail that was known locally as a Kirkby facelift.

'"Description — of sorts",' she muttered, imitating Warman's grating croak. '"Rapport with the girls." Well, I don't give a toss if it "breaks cover", that duffle coat is definitely making an appearance tomorrow.'

Laughter zinged in her ear and she winced. 'Good to know the wire's working, lads,' she said. 'But I mean it — it's six degrees of frostbite out there, and I'm sick of it.'

'You can hop in the van for a warm any time you like, Cassie.' Hoff, worrying about her again.

Rowan mentally balanced the benefits of relative warmth against the disadvantages of breathing a toxic mix of McDonald's takeaway fumes and caged farts. Before she could think of a tactful answer, the door swung open and the DCI looked in. 'There's a hysterical woman in Interview Room One.'

Why is it that everything she says sounds like an accusation?

'I'm on my way out, ma'am.'

Warman held the door wide, as if being found with Rowan in a closed room might place her in a compromising position. 'You can deal with her before you leave.'

Rowan felt a shimmer of excitement: Warman wouldn't be giving her the chance of escape unless it was a possible lead. 'What's the story?'

Warman narrowed her eyes. 'I was hoping you would use your detective skills to find out.'

Sarcasm. Nice. She heard a muffled guffaw through her earphone, then Hoff said, 'Steady, Cass. Remember, she's just kicking your arse because her bosses are kicking *her* arse.'

'I'll do my best,' she said, answering her backup team and DCI Warman in the same breath.

Warman's flat gaze travelled over her street gear. 'You'll need to change, obviously.'

* * *

Rowan edged through the interview room door with a cup of tea in each hand. She even bought a Twix bar from the vending machine. Penny Kominski was an attractive twenty-something. She wore a good-quality business suit — probably with a designer label that Tasha would approve of. Her eyes were red from crying and she had a small bruise on her right cheekbone, which for now looked like overenthusiastic application of blusher, but the swelling under it told Rowan that it would deepen and probably give her a shiner by morning. Her fair hair was raised in tufts on the right side of her scalp, and her hands trembled as she took the polystyrene cup.

'You're sure you want to do this?' Rowan asked. The forensic medical examiner had checked Miss Kominski over and given her a mild sedative, but he wasn't overjoyed that she had insisted on making a statement against his advice.

She nodded wordlessly, and Rowan sat opposite, a block of lined paper in front of her.

Miss Kominski sipped her tea in silence, tears sliding down her cheeks.

'You were at the Albert Dock,' Rowan prompted.

This only made her cry harder, and Rowan touched her hand lightly, to get her attention. 'Maybe it'd be better if—'

'No.' Miss Kominski pulled her hand away. 'No.' She dashed a tear from her cheek and picked up her handbag. 'Shit,' she said, rattling through its contents. 'Shit, shit, *shit*.' She came up with a block of tissues and blew her nose. 'I'm not like this.' Her accent was crystal-cut Hampstead. 'I'm not this bloody *helpless*.' She threw a furious glance in Rowan's direction.

'I know what you mean,' Rowan said, and this time, Miss Kominski held her gaze. Her eyes were pale blue — the shade that seems to reflect light like a swimming pool. She scrutinized Rowan with unabashed curiosity.

Rowan hadn't had time to reapply make-up once she had wiped the street-worker gunk off her face, so the pinkish scar tissue and the last fading remnants of bruising on her own face were clearly visible under the harsh light of the neon strips in the interview room.

'Someone hit you?' Miss Kominski asked.

'Put the boot in. Criminal didn't want to be arrested.' She didn't add that the criminal could well be the same man who had assaulted Miss Kominski. 'I cried buckets when I got home.'

Miss Kominski gazed at her a little longer, then nodded. 'Men are such bastards.'

'Amen to that.' Rowan nudged the Twix bar towards her, and Miss Kominski slid one biscuit from the pack.

They sipped their tea in companionable silence for a while.

'Thing is,' Miss Kominski said, taking a clean tissue from the pack and dropping the damp one back into her handbag, 'I feel such a bloody idiot. I work in investment banking, for God's sake! I *know* liars and con men — I can see the bluffers and bullshitters fifty yards away with the sun in my eyes — I deal with them on a *daily bloody basis*. I just can't believe I—' She closed her eyes and Rowan realised that, more than anything, she was embarrassed.

'Why don't you just take it from the top?'

Miss Kominski took another sip of tea, visibly putting her thoughts in order. 'I'm attending a weekend conference,' she began. 'I thought I'd skip a session, do a bit of sightseeing. The Liverpool Tate was on my must-see list. I stopped in at the Pan-American Bar afterward, had a glass of wine, walked around the central dock — the Albert?'

Rowan nodded.

'It was freezing, but I needed to clear my head. Perhaps if I hadn't had a drink — you see I hadn't eaten since breakfast, and—'

'Miss Kominski—' Rowan said.

'Penny,' she corrected.

'Penny. You need to stop blaming yourself.'

She shrugged. 'I suppose. I'd booked a table at Gusto's with a view of the dock — I'm a bit of a water freak. Do you sail?' she asked, with the casual assumption of the rich that privilege is universal.

Rowan's mouth twitched. 'Sail-*board*.'

'Really?' Her shoulders sagged. 'God, I envy you — I haven't the coordination. My brothers despair of me.'

'How many?' Rowan asked.

'Brothers? Two.'

'Same as me.'

Penny Kominski rolled her eyes as if to say, *What can you do with 'em?* and Rowan found herself liking the woman.

'Okay.' She moved the empty cup to one side and placed her hands palm down on the table. 'Here's how it happened.'

This was better. Her face was less flushed, her eyes less swollen, and she was calm and lucid.

'I'd taken my seat, ordered a drink, and was looking at the menu. I heard someone say my name and looked up. I thought it was one of the waiters.'

'Why did you think that?'

'I don't know.' She frowned. 'I suppose because he was *dressed* like a waiter — you know, black shirt, black trousers, dress shoes. I think he even had a notebook.'

'Can you describe him?'

'Late twenties, maybe? Medium height, medium build. Brown hair . . . I *think*.' She shrugged. 'I'm sorry.'

'Don't worry — we can come back to that. So he came to your table . . .'

She nodded. 'He asked if my car was parked outside. I said yes and he said someone had tried to break into it — would I please come and check if it was all right?'

She slapped her forehead. 'I didn't *think*. Why would he ask me *if* my car was parked outside if he already knew someone had tried to break into it?'

'You were flustered,' Rowan said.

'I was bloody stupid . . .' She sighed. 'I thought *Christ, I left my laptop in there*, and I sort of panicked. He asked me to go with him and . . .' Her shoulders slumped as she remembered. 'I suppose I led him straight to it.'

'Had the alarm been triggered?'

'Not that I could tell. He asked me to unlock the doors and check. I did — everything was fine. The laptop was there

— nothing had been disturbed. I just locked up, thanked him and thought that was it. I started back towards the restaurant.'

'So what happened?' Rowan asked. 'Did he grab you?'

Penny sighed again. 'This is the *really* idiotic bit. He told me he needed to get my signature on a complaint form. I told him I didn't want to make a complaint — the car was untouched, dinner was waiting . . .' She paused, her blue eyes troubled. After a few moments she shook her head. 'He said he'd spent thirty minutes tracking me down. His boss would give him a bollocking if he went back to the office with nothing to show. He was shivering in his shirt sleeves — and I suppose I felt sorry for him . . .'

'So you agreed to go with him.' Rowan thought how cleverly manipulative this man had been: switching stories, embellishing, even thinking to use the wind off the Irish Sea as a means of gaining his victim's sympathy.

'He took me to a car parked in a bay a few up from where I'd left mine. Said it was a bit of a hike — quicker to drive, and it would save his bad leg.'

Rowan's skin prickled. 'He was injured?' she asked.

'Said he'd sprained an ankle chasing a kid who'd pinched something from one of the shops.'

'And you got into his car?'

She shrugged helplessly. 'He seemed so confident I would, and so damned *nice*.'

'D'you remember the make?'

'It was a Lexus IS,' she said, promptly.

Rowan raised her eyebrows. 'You seem very sure.'

'I've got my eye on one — the hybrids are exempt from the London congestion charge, you see.'

'I don't suppose you got the licence plate?'

She shook her head. 'Sorry.' She blinked, and her mouth fell open, realising what she had just said. 'A high-end executive car — what kind of security guard owns a car that costs thirty-five K?'

'He was persuasive,' Rowan said kindly, noting that Penny Kominski hadn't yet realised that her attacker had first given the impression that he was a waiter.

'He *was*. Persuasive and charming and rather sweet,' she agreed. 'Apologised for dragging me away from my meal, asked me was I here on business, told me he was looking forward to his own dinner — he was due to knock off and his wife was a stickler for timekeeping.'

All designed to put her mind at rest. The time factor, so she thought it wouldn't take long; mention of the wife, so she saw him as a family man, and therefore not a threat; and the notion of him as henpecked husband, playing on her sympathy.

'And then?'

'He drove past the big stadium—'

'The Echo Stadium?'

'That's it.' She stared past Rowan, as if visualising the route. 'He turned left and I thought there must be a security office near there. But he kept driving and driving, right along the waterfront — all I could see was black water on one side and security fencing on the other — and I started to feel nervous. But he said it was only a bit further. He turned left at a roundabout, and I thought, *We're heading back to the main road*.'

Her focus switched to Rowan's face. 'I told him to stop. I said I want to go back. He ' She was pale, her face still as she relived the moment. 'He looked at me, and it was as if every human emotion had gone out of him. His *eyes*.' She covered her own as if to block out the memory. 'I swear, I thought I was going to die.'

That's what he does, Rowan thought, remembering the horror on Emma Hammond's face when she recounted how he had forced her into the boot of his car.

Penny swallowed and Rowan heard a dry click.

'You've finished your tea,' Rowan said. 'I can get you a glass of water? Or maybe we should take a break.'

Penny sat up straight and raised her chin, determined. 'I'm fine.' Nevertheless, she had to take a few breaths before she went on. 'I reached for the door and he hit me in the face.' Her fingers went to her cheek, to the bruise, now livid against her pallor. 'I think I must have passed out for a few seconds, because the next thing I remember is he had hold of my right wrist and he was trying to clamp something on it. Handcuffs, I think. I couldn't see straight.'

'Was he still driving? Had he stopped the car?'

'He was driving — not fast, but yes — we were moving. I hit out at him. I tried to punch him with my left hand, but he pushed me away. I grabbed his hair—'

'And you think his hair was brown?'

'Yes. Maybe . . . I'm not sure . . .' Miss Kominski said, distractedly. 'The light, it was . . .' She seemed to lose the thread for a moment, then picked up from an earlier point: 'I pulled and pulled, but he was so *strong*.' She was losing control, panicky tears spilling down her face and she circled the bruised wrist with her left hand.

'But you did get away,' Rowan reminded her. 'Tell me how you did that, Penny.'

It was enough to break through her terror. She gave a little hiccup and rooted for another tissue. 'I'm sorry,' she said, 'It's just—'

'You've nothing to be sorry for,' Rowan assured her.

She dabbed at her eyes as if trying to salvage her ruined make-up. 'The car must have veered off-course. I felt a bump and our heads clashed. I don't remember getting the seatbelt off, but I do remember wrestling the door open. I fell out onto the pavement — I didn't even feel it. I got up and *ran*.' She had to stop for a moment.

'He . . . he came after me. He was screaming things — *horrible* things. We were near the junction and people heard. There was a pub opposite. Oh, God — I don't remember—' She stared frantically at Rowan as if her safety depended on remembering. 'I don't remember the name.'

'That's okay,' Rowan said. 'We'll find out.'

'They helped me. In the pub, they—' For a moment her distress seemed to overwhelm her, but then she frowned, and

Rowan got the impression that she was irritated with herself for giving in to her emotions again. 'Some of the men went looking for him, but he'd gone.'

'Penny, this injury — was he using any kind of walking aid?'

'What, like a stick, you mean?'

'Or a crutch.'

Penny frowned. 'No . . .' She stared at Rowan a moment, evidently puzzled by the question, then her eyes widened, and her hand flew up to her mouth. 'Oh God, you think it's him, don't you? You think it's the man who took that poor student.'

It seemed like she was about to lose it, and Rowan said, 'I'm just asking questions, trying to make connections.'

That seemed to calm her. She fell into a puzzled reflection and after a moment, Rowan said, 'Have you remembered something?'

'Yes,' she said. 'It's weird, really. I hadn't thought about it, but now you ask — when he came after me, he wasn't limping at all.'

CHAPTER 15

Friday night

It was November cold: a night to stay indoors and crank up the heating. But Tasha had made a promise to herself: no more hiding. She thought of these late-night forays as therapy.

The hotel bar was warm, just dim enough that she didn't feel exposed, but not so dark that she started staring into shadows, looking for the potential threat. She sat back in her leather chair and gazed out into the room, her eyes unfocused, but her senses super-sharp.

There were thirty or forty people in the room, she estimated. A few couples, a noisy party of ten, the rest mixed groups of four or five. Safe.

She passed over a man sitting at a table alone, then back to him. A nervous quiver began in her stomach and radiated out, notching her pulse up and sending a flush into her cheeks. She looked quickly away but forced herself to stay put. That was the point of the exercise: to prove that she could. She'd proved it to herself half a dozen times in the last two weeks, and every time she'd wanted to run away. But she had done it. And every time it got that little bit easier.

Her heart settled from a jittery canter to a slow trot and eventually found its normal rhythm.

Nothing to it, she told herself. Emboldened, she forced her gaze back to the man. He was staring frantically into his drink as if he might take a dive into it, just to escape her notice.

He took a sudden gulp of his whisky, choked, and was taken in a fit of coughing.

Safe . . .

She listened to the music for a while — jazz, rather than the usual tragic hotel compilation of pop arranged for a Big Band. The mellow sounds and the changing tableaux of clientele were soothing. For two hours, nothing bad happened.

She walked to the bar and ordered her second martini of the night. The place was full now, and she had to weave between the tables to return to her seat. Someone shoved their chair back, jostling her arm.

She gave an inarticulate yelp of protest and he turned to her, his eyes widening. 'Oh, God — I'm so sorry.' He grabbed a cocktail napkin from his table and raised it, then blanched in horror at what he had been about to do.

It was Shy Guy.

'Here,' he said, thrusting the napkin into her hand, his eyes darting everywhere but her face. 'I'm such a bloody *idiot*.'

He sounded so disgusted with himself that she said, 'Hey . . . no harm done. Look.' She stood back and opened her arms to prove to him that her dress was unharmed.

After a moment he seemed to regain his composure and said, 'Thank goodness. But I did spill your drink. At least let me buy you another.'

She considered, and the pleading look in his eyes decided her. She followed him to the bar — ostensibly to hand over her now empty glass, but actually to keep an eye on her drink — she wasn't ready to be *that* trusting.

He was medium height, good-looking. Young, which made a pleasant change. And he smelled . . . wholesome. Oddly, that was the word that popped into her head: wholesome.

'Business?' she asked, while they waited for their drinks.

'Sorry?'

'The suit,' she said.

He smiled weakly. 'Interview.'

'I'm guessing it didn't go well.'

'Is it that obvious?' he asked.

'You've been scowling into your drink for the past two hours,' she said, by way of explanation.

He slipped a couple of tenners over the bar and picked up their drinks. 'I didn't realise I was being watched,' he said stiffly.

She felt a little ashamed. 'Sorry. It's a habit of mine.'

He handed her drink to her.

'A *bad* habit,' she added with a smile.

He nodded, accepting her apology. 'D'you fancy . . . um . . . I mean, would you like to join me?'

She raised her glass. 'Well, you've paid for the privilege,' she said, just to see him blush.

'What about you?' he asked, when they were settled. 'Are you here for an interview?'

She gave him a quizzical smile. 'An interview . . . ?' She laughed softly. 'Of sorts.' She tilted her head, weighing him up. He seemed uncomfortable in a suit. He was gentle and courtly — an academic, maybe. She made up her mind.

She took a sip from her glass and eyed him over the rim. 'I come here occasionally, looking for company.'

His brow creased and she realised he hadn't understood.

'Not usually on a Friday, though — the businessmen mostly go home on Fridays. The demographic is definitely slanted towards tourist trade at the weekends, and they aren't so good at picking up on nuances.'

A puzzled smile started at the corner of his mouth. 'Why do you need to worry about nuances? Are you in advertising or something?'

She laughed again, low and soft, tilting her head back, to show the white perfection of her throat. 'You really don't get out much, do you?'

'You'd be surprised.' There was a sharpness behind his eyes that she hadn't noticed before, and she realised she had hurt his pride.

'Hey . . .' she soothed. 'Don't be offended — it's just *in these situations* . . . a girl has to be careful what she says.'

'Because?'

'*Because* . . . what I do,' she said, 'is notice who's with whom, who wants to be left alone — and who might be looking for company.' She trailed an exquisitely manicured fingernail over the smooth plane of his hand, finishing at the crease between his thumb and palm. His shudder of response told her that he was beginning to get the idea.

* * *

His car was the first surprise: a big, gleaming Lexus. Newish, sporty, and very high-spec. Tasha revised her estimation of him: he was too soft-spoken, too uncomfortable in his skin, to be a sales rep, and he lacked self-assurance, the easy badinage of her business clients. Computer type, musician, entrepreneur? Something that made him money, anyway.

He had paid upfront, no argument, and opened her door for her, held it while she got in. She thought he was actually going to fasten her seatbelt for her. Until she caught a glimpse of something in his hand.

Then her brain was alight, synapses overloaded, shorting out like fuses in a power surge, and in the moment before she passed out, she thought she caught a whiff of burning hair.

* * *

She woke in the pitch dark. He was holding her up. Her legs seemed unwilling to support her, and he coaxed her, encouraging her to try. 'Keep going,' he urged, 'not far now.'

Confused, groggy, she tried to speak, but her tongue felt thick in her mouth and he shushed her. *What's wrong with me? So dark . . . Did I pass out?*

She felt a charge of fear. *The drink?* No, she had been careful. She remembered him reaching into the car as she sat down. *Why is it so dark?* She felt cloth around her eyes and flashed back to a few months earlier, a hospital bed, her eyes bandaged, a doctor's warning that she might have a detached retina.

Panicked, she tried to raise her hands to her face. They were tied. *Oh, Jesus. Oh Jesus.* Adrenaline coursed through her and she struggled against him.

Her legs gave way again.

'*Shh,*' he said, steadying her. 'It'll be fine. Just a few steps and then we're there.'

She pulled away from him, raised her arms, twisted in his grip, and jabbed backwards, hard with one elbow. He wrapped his arms around her, trapping her against him and put his mouth to her ear.

'It's a thirty-foot drop to the bottom. Think you'd survive the fall?'

He shoved her and her foot slipped off the step. She sensed an abyss, smelled moss and stagnant water. He held her, but she knew he might let go at any second, and she whimpered.

'That's more like it,' he said.

CHAPTER 16

It was seven p.m., and Rowan had already spent four hours on Saturday and six hours of her Sunday off-duty staring at a TV screen in the St Anne Street Station CID office. Grainy CCTV images from the Albert Dock car park, slightly better quality from the cameras covering the walkways around the central dock. It was tedious and frustrating work, but a hell of a lot better than listening to the angry silence at home.

In a repeat of Saturday's performance, Neil had eaten breakfast without a word and stamped up to his room. Seconds later, the house was booming with obnoxious bass. When she told him to turn the damn stereo off, he wordlessly, pointedly, clamped headphones to his ears and closed his eyes. For all she knew, he was still shattering his eardrums with Pendulum or Pearl Jam cranked up to a volume that could cause a small earthquake.

Beside her, within reach, were Penny Kominski's statement and an e-fit of her attacker. She would be home by now, at her parents' house in north London, no doubt being fussed over by her mother, her two brothers angry and protective. Penny's world could not be more different from Rowan's,

93

yet there was a connection between them: the Furman. He'd taken a risk in Penny's attempted abduction — there were people around. *But no police,* she told herself. *Penny was available, and gullible, and so much easier than taking a chance with the working girls, now that he knew he ran the risk of running into a cop.*

Rowan looked again at the e-fit. Penny had worked on it for over an hour with the technician the previous day. But despite their best efforts the face seemed oddly generic.

She played and replayed the CCTV recordings from around the dock until she was cross-eyed and by the end of it, she had isolated only four images of Penny Kominski with her abductor. One was at the restaurant. He was in the act of putting his cap on as he came out of the doors onto the dockside, his face hidden by his arm and the crown of the cap. That would be the instant at which he was transformed in Penny Kominski's mind from waiter to security guard. The second image was at the end of the enclosed square of the dock; she'd found two more from the car park cameras. Every time, he'd kept his head down, so that all she got was the peak of his cap and a tantalising glimpse of chin. He seemed to know where the cameras were.

She sat back and palmed her eye sockets. There had to be something better. Despair almost took hold, but then she thought, *since he knew where the cameras were, he had to have done a recce.* Maybe if she went back far enough, she'd find an image of him caught unawares.

She sighed, picking up a drive that was still sealed in an evidence bag, slit the plastic with her penknife and slotted the USB connector into a free port on her computer.

Light filtered in from the corridor, an odd lamp spotlit an empty desk, and a fluorescent strip light buzzed like a dying insect in the far corner, but otherwise, the room was in darkness. She worked through the CCTV images, exchanging greetings with the lucky few on overtime and the not-so-lucky on night shift who drifted in and out. With the exception of these brief interruptions, she was alone. The only sounds were the busy whirr of the computer hard drive, the fizz and pop of the faulty strip light, and the sound of her own soft sighs and muttered curses as she cranked the images backwards and forwards, willing into existence that one good, clear shot of his face.

A loud *crack!* She jumped, her hand convulsing on the mouse. Pulse racing, she peered into the dimly lit corners of the room, but the pools of light from the desk lamps only intensified the darkness — seemed almost to draw it in. The sound had come from her left. *The window?* She boosted herself out of her seat. Simultaneously, a shadow fell across the doorway. She turned back. A hooded figure stood silhouetted in the doorframe. Her heart rocketed to full fight or flight.

She braced, ready to charge, ready to take the bastard down.

The figure shifted from one foot to the other, uncertain of his welcome. 'All right, Cass?'

'*Shit*, Neil, what the hell are you doing here?'

His eyes widened. 'I brought food.' He lifted his right arm to show her two paper sacks bearing the name of her favourite Chinese restaurant. He seemed unsure of her, as though at that moment, he didn't quite recognize her.

She realised that she'd gone into street mode, aggressive, uncompromising, turning all that spare adrenaline on her brother. 'Sorry,' she said, unclenching her fists and relaxing her pose. 'How did you get in?'

He shrugged, still uncertain. 'I bribed Charlie.'

'Charlie Inghams is on front counter?'

'He sent a message,' Neil said. 'Get yourself off home or he'll have to start charging you rent.'

Rowan smiled, despite herself. Typical Charlie — she hadn't even realised he was back working in St Anne Street. The public face of the station was in a scruffy office block, fifty yards away from the reception building, and Rowan rarely used the front entrance — yet here he was, keeping an eye on her as he had done for the first three years of her career as a beat officer. Charlie's patch in those days had been Kensington — a narrow strip of Victorian two-up, two-down properties a couple of miles east of the city centre. Wedged between two busy radial roads, with the Royal Liverpool Hospital at its sharp end, 'Kenny', was one of the most deprived areas in the UK, with a high incidence of street crime.

Back then, a third of the housing stock was condemned and earmarked for demolition. Charlie Inghams had taught her to look for danger signs, how to be vigilant without becoming paranoid, to treat the decent people of the area with respect and the scalls with an iron fist. Charlie was one of a very few who knew about her family circumstances, and he had done way more than the rule book required to help her, switching shifts when she couldn't arrange childcare, and quietly covering for her when she'd had to take time off. He had almost certainly protected her job on a score of occasions — and if Charlie was telling her she should go home, it was because he knew that despite appearances Neil needed her there.

'You're on curfew,' she said.

Neil's face began to close, the barriers started to go up, and she softened to a smile, adding, 'On the other hand, that smells like Cantonese heaven.' Her stomach growled in anticipation; she'd eaten nothing but a digestive biscuit since breakfast.

'Well,' he said, 'I wouldn't want to break curfew.' Neil headed for the door, but she dodged in front of him, barring the way. 'Don't push it, squirt.'

He drew himself to his full height, as an eloquent demonstration that her old put-down simply didn't work anymore. He'd grown six inches in the past year and could meet her eyeball to eyeball in any argument.

'Hand it over,' she said. 'But if you bribed Charlie with the crispy duck, you're out on your ear.'

Ten minutes later, watching him guzzle his chicken and cashews, she thought it hadn't been easy for Neil, either, and she knew she was a poor substitute for their parents.

'Have I got oyster sauce dripping down my chin or what?' he demanded.

She angled her head to peer at his left earlobe. 'Just checking for signs of bleeding,' she said.

He touched his ear, momentarily concerned, then clicked it was a wind-up. 'You can't listen to Prodigy with your finger on the mute button,' he said.

'I get it,' Rowan said, mock-serious. 'Pump up the volume so that you can't actually hear the music. Brilliant — you'll be deaf before you reach forty.'

'Yeah, but at least I wouldn't be able to hear you nagging.'

She jabbed his hand with her chopsticks as he reached for the last spring roll and swiped it from under his nose. 'What's put you in such a good mood, anyway?'

'Why shouldn't I be in a good mood?'

She wasn't about to remind him, but she couldn't help it if she looked surprised.

He shrugged, took the last carton of fried rice and wandered to the window, out of chopstick range. Rowan felt a moment's anxiety, remembering the loud *crack* she'd heard just as he'd arrived. *A stone? A pistol shot?* In Liverpool, it wasn't unheard of for police stations to come under attack. They were on the first floor, but the way the land lay, it would put Neil at eye level with anyone on the roadway.

Take it easy, Cassie. It was probably a bird, confused by the street lights. Or a random stone thrown up by a passing lorry. Still, she itched to tell him to get away from the damned window and the darkness beyond it.

'Alex phoned,' Neil said, with studied casualness.

Alex! Rowan felt a mixture of excitement that her elder brother had called, disappointment that she'd missed it, and underlying both, a confused and guilty resentment that had been years in the making.

Neil drifted away from the window, riffling paperwork on desks and staring at Post-it notes tacked to computer monitors as he wandered towards the back of the room.

'He's coming next Friday,' Neil said, going back to his desultory inspection of the office. She knew he'd noticed her silence, but still couldn't find the right words to say. 'He's got to get back to New York on Sunday, though.'

'Two whole days. Terrific.' She cursed herself for finding her voice with a snipe at Alex.

Normally, Neil would have challenged the sarcasm in her tone, but he was staring, transfixed, at the whiteboard. 'Is this about the Furman?'

'Hey,' Rowan said, starting over to him. 'That's confidential police business.' The board carried details of all of the Furman's attacks: dates, times, names — and even forensic photographs of the victims.

'Is that Tasha?' She heard a slight wobble in his voice.

Oh, hell. He hadn't seen Tasha at her worst.

'Neil — come away from there.' She put her hand on his shoulder, but he didn't turn.

'Cass, why are you up on the board?'

'What are you on about? I'm not—' She followed his gaze and saw a six-by-four print of her: arms and face bruised, hair matted with dirt, her cheek oozing blood where the Furman's shoe had clipped her. 'Bloody *Wicks*.' She tore down the picture.

He turned to her, his eyes wide with shock. 'Is that how you got hurt?'

'Neil—'

'Is it?'

'It doesn't matter.'

He continued to stare her. 'Of course it *matters*, Cassie.'

'Neil.'

'*What?*'

'It's my job.'

A storm of emotions crossed his features. She saw the nine-year-old, lost and afraid as he was told that his mother and father were never coming home; the teen, fearful that he would be left alone again. And it made her heart ache to see, too, the young man Neil would become — wanting to punish the scum who had hurt his big sister.

She shrugged, said again, softly, 'It's my job, Neil.'

They looked at each other, and somehow, they reconnected.

Their parents had died in a car accident six years ago. Alex already had a career and a life away from home. Social services were concerned that the demands of Cassie's job would not provide Neil with the safe and stable environment he needed to grow. They had offered foster care, or the option of placing Neil with family.

'*We* are his family,' she told them.

'Oh,' they'd said. 'You and . . . ?'

'Alex — our brother,' she'd said. 'He's more than happy to share childcare responsibilities.'

Alex couldn't very well refuse and, having satisfied themselves that Cassie would have the support she needed, they had placed Neil in her care.

To his credit, Alex had covered her night shifts for a year, either staying overnight in the family home, or taking Neil back to his flat. Then Alex got a job offer in New York. Four weeks later, he was gone.

Rowan was twenty by then, working the Kensington beat on shift rotations that didn't make any exemptions for single parents — or a woman barely out of her teens looking after an eleven-year-old.

Terrified that Neil would be hauled off to their buttoned-up relatives in Scotland, Rowan had taken on the role of mother and father and big sister and big brother. The Graysons, their next-door neighbours, had stepped in as soon as they realised she needed help, and she'd enrolled Neil in every after-school activity available. But she had also lied and covered up, occasionally coercing Alex into attending parents' evenings with her to perpetuate the illusion that they had maintained family ties and shared responsibilities even across the Atlantic.

She had got Neil through night terrors and pre-teen tantrums, truanting and acting out. Stella Grayson had a child Neil's age, and she had provided a bed for him when Cassie was on night shift; Charlie Inghams had covered for her in his unobtrusive way, and somehow they had managed. There were days when she and Neil hated the sight of each other, days when their loss hurt so badly they didn't know how to comfort each other. But despite the loneliness and the arguments and the lies and the pain, they had always wanted to stay together.

Now, confronted by a photograph of his bossy, boring, killjoy big sister bruised and bleeding on a police notice-board, she saw in Neil's eyes for the first time an understanding that she had a life outside of home and family, separate from him — and a recognition that she was entitled to that independence.

''Kay.' He gave his trademark shrug, and a sly smirk touched the corner of his mouth. 'But you owe me — I'm supposed to have "quality family time".' He raked finger-quotes in the air. 'It's essential to my "emotional and social development".'

She gave his arm a friendly punch. 'I wish you'd hang on my words like you hang on every word your social worker says.'

The social worker was one of the more onerous conditions placed on them in return for allowing Neil to remain in the family home, and Rowan dreaded the monthly visits and 'core group' meetings that were imposed as part of his 'child in need plan'. But Neil had swiftly learned the right things to say and the subjects to avoid — while Rowan looked on with both begrudging admiration and alarm at the charming little manipulator her little brother had become.

By the time they reached the car park, Neil was trying to convince her that his emotional and social development would be enhanced by spending Sunday karting. She let him run on, debating the relative merits of the Ormskirk against the Aintree course, while she dug in her coat pocket for her car keys. The police car park was sunk below the level of the road, and pedestrians could look into the first-floor windows, and down onto the cars below. The security lights and street-lamps cast competing blocks of light and shadow. As she unlocked the car, she found herself trying to penetrate the glare from the streetlamp above.

'You see something?' Neil asked.

'I don't know.' She shielded her eyes, not sure what had caught her attention. Then she saw it: something flapping from the railing on street level. A hooded figure was standing next to it at the rail.

'Hey!' she yelled.

The object flapped again, then fell. Two arms spread wide, seemed to pinwheel through space. *Oh Jesus!* She shouted to Neil as she ducked. The object landed with a dull thud onto the roof of her car. Too light for a body. Rowan straightened, yelled again. The hooded figure stood for a moment, gripping the rail with both hands, then curled his fingers in a wave and disappeared from sight.

'Get in the car,' Rowan said, dragging the jacket from the roof and sliding behind the wheel. She fired the engine, shot toward the exit, screamed around the corner and came head-on with a surveillance vehicle. She hit the brakes, blinded by the headlamps, jumped out of the car, running. Skidded on loose gravel and lost her footing, regained it, ran along the footpath to the gateway that gave onto the single-storey building that housed the General Enquiries desk. It was locked. She rattled the padlock in frustration. 'Bloody hell!'

The van driver panted up behind her. 'Is that Cassie Rowan? What've you got, Cass?'

'*Nothing.*' She landed a vicious kick at the gate. 'Not a bloody thing.'

She saw Neil's anxious face over the driver's shoulder. His eyes were huge and his face so pale it seemed almost to shimmer in the stark white of the security floodlights. He held the jacket in his hands.

'Cass,' he said, holding it out for her to take, as though he was afraid he would injure it. 'I think it's Tasha's.'

CHAPTER 17

Monday, 23 November, early morning

'Cassie.'

'Ian.' Rowan hung up the phone and looked expectantly at the CSI. She had spent the last hour talking to Tasha's gallery staff. Chan had the jacket with him; Rowan could see the brown leather through the cellophane window of the evidence bag.

'Don't get your hopes up,' he said. 'It's been wiped over with an alcohol-based cleaner.'

'No fingerprints?'

'No fingerprints, no hairs, no fibres.' He shrugged. 'Look, it was probably just some drunk, trying to unnerve you.'

'The handrail on the street was clean, as well. It wasn't a *drunk*, Ian—'

'Oo-kay . . .' he said, making a visible effort to be patient. 'So it was some *scall* trying to unnerve you. Same difference. It was a wind-up, Cass.'

'He chucked a seven hundred-quid jacket at me.'

His limited reserves of patience exhausted, Chan said, 'Since when did you know the value of Milanese leather goods?'

'It's *Tasha's*, Ian. I was with her when she bought it. Can't you — I dunno — check the lining, do some techno-stuff on it? DNA? Trace? I thought you guys could get everything but a girl's vital statistics from a single cell, these days.'

'For God's *sake*, Cass.' He glanced around the room and she realised she'd raised her voice.

She closed her eyes for a second, and opened them again fast, when the room seemed to gyrate. 'Sorry.'

'In case you've forgotten,' Chan hissed, 'it's not a crime to drop a jacket. And without a case number on a bona fide crime, I shouldn't have run even the *basic* tests.'

'I said I'm sorry.' Rowan pressed her palm to her forehead. It was feverishly hot. 'Something's wrong, Ian — I know it. I've tried her mobile, left messages on her voicemail, spoken to the girls she used to work with. I've been to her flat I don't know how many times . . .' She raised her shoulders and let them fall. 'Nobody's seen her.'

'Hospitals?' He said it with a wince, as though afraid she might kick off again.

She nodded miserably. Since Sunday night she had tried every hospital in the city and beyond, given her contact details to A&E departments, and pestered Tasha's landline and mobile phones every two hours with new messages to call her.

'Look,' Chan said. 'She might've taken herself off for a few days. She's done that before, hasn't she?'

'Yes,' Rowan admitted reluctantly. 'But not since the Furman attacked her — and it still doesn't explain her jacket.'

'*If* it's hers.' He raised a finger, silencing her objections. 'Cass, she's probably sipping champagne in a spa as we speak: bubbles in the Jacuzzi, bubbles in her glass. Whoever did this, they were trying to wind you up. Which is not nice, but it's not a crime, either.'

He placed the brown evidence bag on her desk like a man relinquishing responsibility.

'And what am I supposed to do with that?' she demanded.

'Wear it,' he said. 'Give it away. I don't *care*, as long as it's off my hands.'

CHAPTER 18

DC Roy Wicks stood just outside a private room at the Royal Liverpool Hospital, copping an eyeful while the nurses helped his witness into a surgical gown. The dumpy one with the mousy hair fussed over her patient, offering her a glass of water, adjusting the pillows.

The patient gave a little gasp and the two nurses moved in close, helping her to sit more comfortably. She winced, pale and pretty, and for one moment he forgot her plainly silly story and felt sorry for her. What kind of man let a girl like this put it out for a few quid a jump?

The dumpy nurse came out and he made a point of frowning at his phone as if he'd been checking for important updates.

'She's still in shock,' she said. 'Be gentle.'

Wicks's gaze strayed to the woman in the bed. He couldn't help thinking how those gowns were split all the way up the back.

Dumpy shot him a look like she'd read his thoughts, and he felt himself colouring.

He stepped into the room and gave the victim the once-over: slim neck, a bit messed up with the bruising — apparently, her assailant had choked her. Face a bit mottled, which was understandable. Good jawline, shapely arms. No signs of needle tracks, no ulceration, and none of the tell-tale skin pigmentation that indicated collapsed veins. This one looked after herself.

The doctor had let her shower after they'd taken samples and the CSU photographer had got his photos. Wicks gave his head a shake to dislodge that image from his mind.

The second nurse left after pressing a buzzer into the girl's hand, and at the same instant, Finch appeared, looking like a wet lettuce. He carried three paper cups in a Costa tray.

'Well, come 'ead,' Wicks said. 'We're dying of thirst here.'

Finch crossed to the opposite side of the bed and handed one of the cups to the girl in the bed. *Chivalrous prick*.

'I've got sugar if you want it.' His face was blotched with colour.

The woman gave him a wan smile. 'No thanks.'

Wicks sighed and Finch took the hint, handing him his coffee and a few sugar straws before taking a sip from the third cup and looking around for somewhere to ditch the tray.

Wicks rolled his eyes and turned his attention to the girl. 'Comfy now, love?'

Her lips pressed into a thin line. 'Do I look comfortable?'

Posh accent, superior manner. *Uppity cow*. He sucked his teeth and reached into his jacket for his notebook and pen. 'Detective Constable Wicks,' he said, falling back on brisk formality. 'Sir Galahad, here, is Detective Constable Fincham.'

He waited. No answer. *Jeez, this is like pulling teeth*. 'What's your name, love?' he asked.

'You have my name.'

Wicks hadn't bothered to check the task sheet before he left the station. She did look familiar, though.

Fincham shuffled from one foot to the other. 'Wicksie, this is—'

Wicks silenced him with a look. 'For the record, please, Miss.'

She eyed him with dislike. 'Natasha McCorkindale.'

He wrote the name down, a frown gathering between his brows. 'Natasha . . .' He took in the blonde hair, the cool blue eyes. 'Bloody hell — *Tasha*? Cassie Rowan's mate?' He should have made the connection but to be fair, she wasn't looking her best. He sat down in the chair next to the bed. 'I thought you were off the game.'

'Have you come to take a statement or to pry into my private life?' she demanded, two spots of angry colour appearing on her cheekbones.

Stung, he said, 'Here's a tip: you want to keep your sex life private, don't sell it on the street.'

She fair quivered with indignation. 'I was *raped*.'

'Look, Tasha . . .' Wicks set his notebook down on the bedcovers. 'I know you've been hurt. I know you're pissed off and humiliated and wanting to get back at someone, but this story you told the paramedics . . .' He glanced at Finch. 'Well, let's just say Bashful, here, might fall for it, but not an old dog like me.'

She bristled and he held up his hands.

'Don't get me wrong — we take assaults like this serious.'

Finch did another little shuffle, cleared his throat. Wicks blanked him.

'I mean, lightning doesn't strike twice, does it?' He took a swig of coffee. He wanted to help her — he really did. 'Tell you what — if you want to change your statement, give us a name — we'll go and have a quiet word.'

She stared at him. 'With whom?'

She might get away with using that tone down the polo club, but she was on his turf, now.

He smiled. 'Your pimp — who else?'

Her face turned almost as white as the pillows that propped her up. 'I. Don't. Have. A pimp.'

Now she was *really* pigging him off. 'So how come your face isn't marked?'

'I have no idea what you're talking about,' she said.

He sighed. 'Sure you do. Pimps know the bruised peaches get left in the box.' His hand snaked forward to lift her hair, exposing the faint scar on her right temple. She gasped and twisted away from him.

'The Furman did that to you, didn't he? He wouldn't have turned a hair if he'd had your eye out — see, punters who turn violent aren't too bothered about making a mess of a girl's face. Which means this wasn't a punter. It was someone with an interest in the goods.' He spread his hands. 'Like a pimp, for instance.'

'I'd like to give my statement to a female officer.' Her voiced trembled, and she wasn't so lady of the manor now.

'What, gone all shy, have you?'

'I *said*—' She broke off, close to tears.

Finch stepped forward, but Wicks warned him off with a look.

The lad really was clueless.

'All right,' he said. 'We'll send one along when there's one available. But we're in the middle of a serious investigation — and you crying wolf just wastes precious police time.'

★ ★ ★

Rowan was glaring at Ian Chan, the leather jacket still on the desk, when Finch came through the doorway, looking anxious.

'Me and Wicksie just got back from the hospital,' Finch said. 'Tasha was admitted two hours ago. Sexual assault.'

'Is she—?'

'She's fine — or she will be. She was given a spanking by her pimp.'

The disrespect in those words coming out of Finch's mouth was like hearing a cherubic choir boy swearing like a builder's mate. Rowan exchanged a look with Ian Chan, and Finch blushed.

He avoided her eye. 'Sorry, Cass.'

'Tasha *told* you she was hooking?'

Another blush flashed across Finch's cheeks. 'Not in so many words — but she never denied it, neither.'

107

'Let me get this straight — you barged into a hospital room and accused a *rape* victim of prostituting herself?'

She saw from the alarm on his face that she was right.

'I brought her coffee,' he mumbled, and she laughed.

'Bravo! Did you throw it in her face?'

'You weren't there, Cass. I know what I heard,' he said stubbornly. 'Tasha's back on the game.'

She eyeballed him as she pressed Tasha's speed dial on her mobile phone for the hundredth time since the weekend.

'Tasha, it's Cassie,' she said. 'I just heard. Call me when you get this.'

Ending the call, she glared at Finch. 'I'd expect a pillock like Wicks to make lazy assumptions. I thought better of you, Finch. If Tasha was on the streets, I'd know it.'

'Yeah, well, there's other ways of hooking than on the streets.'

Rowan felt a flicker of uncertainty, remembering the night of Neil's party, when she'd asked Tasha to take care of him until she'd finished her shift. Tasha had been dressed for action. She shut the notion out of her mind.

'What happened to her, Finch?'

'Wicksie says—'

She cut across him. 'I've heard what Wicks says — his words keep coming out of your mouth.'

His colour darkened and Rowan knew she had hit home. Finch, in his desperation to be liked, stood on the sidelines, watching and listening, trying to fit in, getting it hopelessly wrong.

'What does Tasha say?'

His gaze darted to every corner of the room, but he couldn't look her in the eye.

'Did you even *take* a statement?'

He shrugged. 'She was uncooperative.'

Rowan shook her head. 'God, you're pitiful.'

She glanced down at the bagged jacket. It had just become evidence from a crime scene. Chan picked it up without saying a word.

She nodded her thanks, then unhooked her own coat from the back of her chair and headed for the door.

'Where are you going?' Chan asked.

'The hospital. Finch, d'you think you could give Ian an incident number, so he can start processing that jacket?'

'There *was* no jacket,' Finch said, unthinking. 'She was found naked.'

Rowan stared at him for a moment. 'She was—?' Anger and sorrow for her friend jostled her, and she felt a pressure building behind her eyes. If she stayed, she would regret what she said, so she looked at Ian Chan, focusing carefully on his face and avoiding even a glance in Finch's direction. 'Ian—'

'Go,' he said. 'I'll sort it.'

CHAPTER 19

Monday afternoon

Alan Palmer watched as Dylan Corbie performed his usual checks, moving slowly around the room, as if in pain. He wore a different jacket and hooded top — they looked newer, less comfortably worn-in. The right side of his face was swollen, the skin bruised and scratched from browbone to jaw.

Fading, Palmer thought. It must have happened a few days ago — over the weekend, perhaps — or just before?

Apparently satisfied that all was as he'd left it, Dylan slipped his phone from his pocket and performed his ritual of checks on wireless networks with access to the internet. There were ten, apparently — three unsecured.

He switched off his phone and sat opposite instead of taking his usual seat adjacent to Palmer. Then he took out his notebook and set it down on the arm of his chair, with a pen resting across the cover.

'Why do you do that?' Palmer asked.

'The phone? To see who's listening.'

'This room isn't bugged, Dylan.'

Dylan made bold eye contact. 'Virtual listening doesn't require a bug in the conventional sense.'

'I don't follow.'

He glanced over his shoulder, towards the desk, and Palmer saw him wince. He looked like he'd taken a serious beating.

Dylan jerked his chin, indicating the MacBook on Palmer's desk. 'Is that your personal laptop?'

'It is.'

'Is it firewalled?'

'Yes.'

'Are the firewall and operating systems set to automatic updates?'

Palmer was less certain of this, and Dylan must have read it in his face. He puffed air between his lips — a gesture of contempt. 'Your laptop has a camera and a microphone. Both can be turned on remotely.'

'Okay. But why would anyone want to eavesdrop on our sessions?' Palmer was sure that there was a rational basis behind Dylan's paranoia. If he could find that out, they could make real progress.

Dylan ignored the question.

'Do you use Wi-Fi hot zones — free internet access in your favourite coffee bar?'

'Occasionally.'

'You might as well go out for the day and leave your doors and windows open. A hacker can slip through, create a back door, and leave it wide open. You might feel the draught; you might even notice he'd moved stuff around — changed things. But you'd never see him.'

Changed things. An iteration of Dylan's obsession with checking the consultation room, his agitation if he found anything out of place.

Palmer reflected on Dylan's new communicativeness. Something had altered in him — his injuries, far from emphasising his vulnerability, seemed to make him harder.

'Are you going to ask?' Dylan demanded.

'Ask what?'

'Why I wasn't here last session.'

He had missed his Friday appointment. 'Do you know why?'

Dylan glanced up, his eyes flashing green. 'You're making fun of me.'

'No,' Palmer said. 'But I am surprised that you haven't said how you were injured.'

'You wouldn't make fun if you knew.'

Palmer heard the veiled threat in this last remark; he was in no doubt this was a power play and a second denial would hand power to his patient. So he said nothing, and waited instead for Dylan to elaborate.

'As a matter of fact, I *was* here.'

'You missed your session, Dylan,' Palmer said.

'I was here the whole time.' He sounded more triumphant than belligerent.

'Yet you missed your session. Why was that?'

'I wanted to see what you'd do.'

'I waited for you,' Palmer said. It's what therapists did when their clients were late — or even failed to show up.

'Yup,' Dylan nodded. 'The whole time.' Again, that note of triumph.

'It's *your* time, Dylan.'

'Yours, too.'

There it is again, Palmer thought. *Power, and control.*

'I was with you all the way from Strand Street.'

Palmer felt a prickle of apprehension. *Did he follow me home? If Elspeth were to find out— Stop it. Focus on what he's telling you — on the emotions behind the words.*

'You've been following me?'

Dylan had lowered his eyes. *Was that a hint of a smirk?* 'Sometimes.'

'But not *only* me?'

Dylan lifted one bony shoulder. *Maybe.*

'Why?'

The question seemed to take Dylan by surprise. His eyes kindled. 'Because I like it.'

'What do you like about it?'

The light in Dylan's eyes dimmed and his gaze shifted to the right of Palmer's shoulder. 'I don't know.'

He kept his voice low, almost toneless, but for a fraction of a second Palmer felt a thrill of excitement. *Following someone, them not knowing, gives him power over another human being.*

'Well, how does it make you feel?'

'Better.'

'Better than what, Dylan?'

'I don't know,' he repeated stubbornly. 'I forget.'

'We've talked before about the importance of feelings,' Palmer said. 'By thinking about how we feel, we begin to understand why we act or *re*act in a certain way.'

Dylan shrugged dismissively. He was withdrawing, his shoulders hunched, a determined frown on his face.

Go back to where he's more comfortable — go back to the facts. 'When did you start following people?' *Women?* The word seemed to whisper in the silence that followed.

'I forget.'

'Is that why you keep notebooks, to help you remember?'

Dylan looked up slowly, coolly assessing Palmer, and his eyes shifted from bright emerald to the deep unfathomable green of moss seen through a shivering cascade.

'Didn't Dr Atherton tell you?' he asked. 'I have eidetic recall.'

It sounded like a warning: 'Don't underestimate me, don't presume you know anything about me. Do *not* push me.'

Dylan moved stiffly towards the door, and Palmer said, 'Are you leaving so soon?'

Dylan glanced back him. 'Like you said, it's my time.'

'To use — or waste,' Palmer said.

Dylan gave a short, dismissive grunt and kept walking.

Watching him limp out onto the street below, Palmer wondered again how Dylan had been injured, recalling the tone of warning when he'd said, *You wouldn't make fun if you knew.* Thinking about the angry swagger that Dylan had apparently acquired along with his bruises, Palmer had the uneasy feeling that his client's assailant had probably come off worse.

CHAPTER 20

Tuesday, 24 November, early morning

Rowan groaned. Her limbs were stiff, and her mind unrested after a night of sweat-soaked dreams. She had fallen asleep worrying about Tasha. She'd already signed herself out when Rowan got to the hospital on Monday morning. Rowan's warrant card had got her past security at Tasha's apartment building, but the flat was shut up tight and the security guard on duty said he hadn't seen her come in. He had checked the residents' car park, too; there was no sign of Tasha's Mini Cooper S.

During the night, Rowan had snapped awake a dozen times, hearing the crack of stone on glass. Every draught in the old house became a furtive sigh, every shadow a crouching threat. Twice, she was jolted from sleep seeing a body fall, twisting, arms reaching as if to snag the air and save itself.

She rolled over and groaned again: her alarm clock read six thirty — time to get up. She kicked the bedclothes aside, dreading the demands of the day ahead on so little sleep, yet grateful to be able to leave the tormenting nightmares behind.

She padded to the kitchen and filled the kettle for tea. Last night's dishes were waiting to be washed, and she ran a bowl of water, going over the facts, and asking herself the same questions she had been asking over and over since Monday morning. Maybe Tasha had gone home — wherever home was — to find solace. Rowan realised with a pang of guilt just how little she really knew about her friend. The hospital had confirmed that Tasha had been found naked, bound and blindfolded on wasteland in Kensington. The rapist had taken her personal possessions, including her mobile phone — which explained why she hadn't replied to Rowan's messages. He had also taken her clothing. *Except her jacket*, Rowan thought. *He made a special effort with Tasha's jacket*. Why would he risk coming to a busy police station to do that? The answer was plain: to deliver a message. Which meant it had to be the Furman. But what kind of message? Tasha was a former victim — she wasn't stupid or desperate — she wouldn't go willingly with a man she knew had attacked her on a previous occasion. But Tasha had little memory of the first attack. Could the Furman know that? Rowan racked her brains, trying to remember if Tasha's amnesia had been reported in the press, and made a mental note to look out the reports when she got to work. The Furman had always been cocky — was he showing them that he could get to the girls even when they were on their guard? Did he know that she and Tasha were friends? Could this be revenge for the injuries Rowan had inflicted on him — or even a not-so-subtle threat to Rowan herself? Had he been watching her as she worked in the CID office on Saturday? She shivered, then gave herself a shake.

'Spooking yourself, Cassie,' she muttered.

Relations with Neil had slipped back a bit since the weekend. She just hadn't had enough time or energy to talk to him. He was worried about Tasha — she could see that — but he wanted to know what she was doing to find her, demanding that she put out a missing person's report. He couldn't accept that when an adult decides to go away, you had to allow them the privacy to do just that.

Only the promise of their brother's visit at the end of the week was keeping him from a full retreat into sullen silence again. Alex had phoned the night before, apologising for the late hour. 'You'd think I could get the time zones straight by now, wouldn't you?' he said.

Recalling his words, Rowan thought, *Yes, you would.* Alex was a businessman; he made frequent calls from the US to associates in the UK — she couldn't imagine him ringing them at eleven thirty at night just because he couldn't get the time zones straight. She scooped the phone out of the cradle mounted on the kitchen wall and dialled 1471. The area code of the last incoming call was 0207. Central London.

You bloody liar, Alex. How long had he been in the UK — avoiding coming home. Avoiding them?

She threw a teabag into a breakfast cup and poured boiling water onto it, clicked the radio on as a distraction, and returned to the sink to dry the dishes while it brewed. A grey light seeped through the wooden slats of the window blind. One slat had caught in her haste to shut out the dark the previous night. She had been staring at her reflection in the glass, when she felt a terror of what might be watching, unseen, on the other side.

In the six years since her parents' death, Rowan had thought often of her father's dying words to her. He had taken her hand and looked deep into her eyes, as if these were the most important three words he would ever say to her. He had said, 'Don't be afraid.'

He might have said: 'Think of me', or 'I love you', but he wasn't looking to reassure or comfort her — this was a command. To throw her shoulders back, stare the world in the face and fight the fear that would inevitably come.

'Way to go, Cassie,' she muttered, leaning across the sink to raise the blind. The window cleaners had been just before the weekend, and the glass gleamed in the gruel-thin light. But the pristine surface was marred by two hook-shaped smudges.

Something about the symmetry of the marks unsettled her. She unlocked the back door and stepped outside. Two crescent shapes, each about seven or eight inches long, bracketed the centre portion of the windowpane.

A bird, perhaps, had flown into the newly polished surface, mistaking the reflection for space and air. But the marks showed no imprint of feathers, and birds' wings usually splayed up and outward when they hit glass, while these curved downwards. Rowan was tall, but she needed a few more inches to see the marks properly. She cast about for something useful, settled on the wheelie bin, parked next to the back door. She laid it on its side and tested her weight on it with one foot. It held.

She climbed up, balancing precariously, brought her face closer to the marks and saw tiny lines and ridges, like a simian paw. Like a—

She jerked away, almost lost her balance, teetered forward again and clawed at the sill to steady herself. A sick horror rushed over her.

Someone had been at the window, had cupped their hands to the glass to see past the reflections into her kitchen.

CHAPTER 21

Rowan covered a yawn and tried to focus on what DCI Warman was saying.

'Emma Hammond's forensic reports are in,' Warman went on. 'Nothing useable.'

A collective groan from the rest of the team.

'We're closer now than we've ever been,' Warman insisted. 'He made a mistake, and a potential victim got away. The analysis of samples taken from Miss Kominski's fingernails and clothing didn't yield any DNA, but . . .' She raised her voice over a fresh chorus of dismayed complaints: '*But* . . . they *did* find fibres — which might give us something in the longer term — and we know now that he drives a Lexus hybrid. Who's looking into that?'

A hand went up. 'Lexus sold just over two thousand Lexus IS models in 2019,' he said. 'But the hybrid model was launched in 2013 — there's a lot of them in circulation.'

'Focus on new and recent sales,' Warman said. 'The last two or three years — we're looking for a man in his mid-twenties or early thirties. Cassie — anything from Miss Kominski's e-fit?'

Rowan shook her head. No one was surprised; composites only gave a twenty per cent hit rate at best.

'Finch — how're you getting on with the shoe?' After returning from the hospital, Finch had spent the day on a credit card search, trying to trace the shoe the Furman had left behind at the freight yard.

Wicks clasped his hands to his man-bosom. 'Oh, Prince Charming, have you found your Cinderella?'

Warman silenced him with a look. 'In your own time, Finch,' she said. Finch began to stand, decided that he should remain seated and almost knocked his chair from under him. He cleared his throat.

'The brand is available at John Lewis, House of Fraser, Debenhams and Clarks branches across Merseyside, as well as in a couple of discount outlets at Cheshire Oaks on the Wirral. I'm working with the stores to check through credit card purchases over the past six months.'

'And?' Warman said.

'I've drawn a blank so far, boss,' he admitted, deflated.

A muscle twitched in Warman's jaw. 'So . . . ideas, anyone?'

Rowan spoke up. 'I think we should be investigating Tasha McCorkindale's abduction alongside the rest,' she said.

Warman shot her an irritated glance and Wilks sighed, but Warman said. 'All right, let's hear it.'

Rowan went through the events of the weekend: Tasha's abduction, the stone thrown at the window of the CID office, Tasha's jacket tossed over the rail as she walked to her car. The way Tasha had been dumped, naked and bound on waste ground. She left out her discovery of handprints on her kitchen window.

'There are similarities . . .' Warman said, sounding doubtful.

'The MO is identical.'

'I think that's a bit of a stretch,' Warman said. 'If you're right, he'd have to have tried to snatch Penny Kominski, and when she got away, gone looking for his next likely victim on the same night — within hours.'

'Why not?' Rowan said. 'He's been working on a shorter cycle recently, anyway. Maybe he's frustrated Penny got away, goes looking for someone else.'

'And just happens to chance on Tasha Mac,' Wicks said. 'That's a hell of a coincidence, Cassie.'

There was a murmur of agreement.

'Anyway, we don't know the exact circumstances of Tasha's abduction,' Warman added.

'She told the paramedics that the man who abducted her approached her in the Malmaison hotel bar. She said he drove a Lexus.'

'Agreed. But since Tasha has vanished, and didn't give a full statement, we can't corroborate her story.'

'The medical report—' Rowan said.

'The medical report says she was injured,' Wicks said. 'It doesn't say how.'

'The medical report says she was *raped*,' Rowan interrupted.

'All right, *all right*,' Warman said, raising her voice over them both. 'Who interviewed her?' she asked.

Finch cleared his throat again, but Wicks got there first: 'Me and Finch. There's no doubt she'd been roughed up pretty bad. Refused to give a statement though, boss.'

Finch flushed and shot Wicks an uneasy look.

'And how does the hotel bar story check out?' Warman asked.

'The barman remembers Tasha,' Hoff said. 'Saw her with a guy.'

'Description?'

'Said he was "ordinary".'

That was the thing with Tasha: when she walked into a room, other people seemed to fade like sepia tints in a photograph.

'They left together after a drink,' Hoff added. 'Barman said she seemed fine.'

'She admitted she was back on the game,' Wicks said.

'Well, actually—'

'As good as,' Wicks cut across Finch, giving him a hard stare. 'If it *was* the Furman, she'd've recognized him, wouldn't she? And anyway, he'd have to have had a brass neck to approach her a second time — and in a busy hotel bar.' He shook his head. 'It just doesn't add up, boss.'

'He laid in wait outside the station and chucked Tasha's jacket at me,' Rowan said. 'Who else would do that, but the Furman?'

'*If* it's her jacket,' Warman said. 'But since Miss McCorkindale has taken herself off somewhere, we can't test your theory, can we?' Warman said, tartly. 'And why on earth would he target *you*?'

'Because I chased him down, cornered him in the freight yard — almost caught him.' She could have bitten her tongue off. *Almost caught him? Jeez, Cassie — what do you want, a gold star?*

Warman let her silence speak for her, and when sufficient time had passed for Rowan to feel sweat break out on her brow, she said: 'All we have in Tasha's abduction is hearsay from the paramedics and a jacket that may or may not have belonged to her.'

'And the rope,' Chan said, and Rowan could have kissed him. 'We've got that.'

Warman paused, and after a few seconds she said, 'All right — check it for trace, see if it's a match to the other abductions. In the meantime, we follow the evidence that we have. And we do *not* speculate ahead of the facts.'

She switched her attention to Finch, and Rowan didn't know whether to be angry at being summarily dismissed, or grateful to have the team's attention drawn away from her.

'Focus on inquiries with the shoe shops,' Warman told Finch. 'Roy — you can help with that.'

Wicks groaned.

Then Warman said the words that Rowan dreaded: 'Hoff, Cassie — go home and get some rest — as of tonight, you're back on Operation Kerbwatch.'

CHAPTER 22

Jodie Pickersgill strode out of the Arnott Hotel in the city centre, a wealth of designer carrier bags swinging at her sides. Late November — soon the party season would begin, and she was already on the way to making a real impression; she was twenty-three, single, *very* pretty, and her man adored her in the way that mattered most.

She bit her lip to stop a laugh of sheer giddy delight. Life — and love — seemed eager to spill a cornucopia of possibilities into Jodie's manicured hands. The traffic signal changed and she trotted across the road, quick on her feet, light on her four-inch Manolo Blahnik heels.

In Williamson Square she tottered past workmen repairing the parallel rows of fountains, shook her curls at them, smiling when they whistled after her. *Oh,* she thought. *Today is just so . . .* She didn't have the words for it — even the rain had held off, though it was cold enough that her lovely man had snuggled her under his arm like a great handsome eagle. She loved the smell of him, his musky animal scent, the sharp tang of his aftershave, the soft blunt fingers of his big hands.

She shivered; the wind now came in blasts from the river, and the cloud seemed to crouch lower over the buildings. If she hurried she would make it to her car in time, her hair would keep its bounce and shine and her MaxMara trench coat — one of her new purchases — would make it home unspotted by rain. She pictured herself in her tiny flat, surrounded by her glossy bags with their soft cord handles and low-key, high-class logos. Imagined herself pouring a cold Chardonnay and gazing at them for a long time before she slid her hands inside to disturb the whispering layers of tissue paper.

A gust blew up a swirl of dust from the street and a dumpy woman in a badly-fitting parka cursed. Why did everybody look so glum? It seemed unreasonable of them to go about scowling when she was so happy.

Suddenly Jodie *had* to talk to someone who would understand. She sighed with anticipatory contentment, dipped into her handbag — the *sweetest* little Radley — and took out a new, ultra-sleek, fashionably, *passionately* pink mobile phone. 'Guess what I'm phoning you on?'

She heard a satisfying gasp from her friend. 'Jodie?' Stacey had shared a house with her at uni, swapped gossip and clothes and even boyfriends ever since.

'Omigod, he never bought you the iPhone?'

'Here, in the palm of my ickle hand. The one with the triple lens! And it's got the new night mode — can't *wait* to give that a try,' she added saucily. 'It's *impossibly* sexy. Honestly, Stacey — this gorgeous little gadget does practically everything except give you a bikini wax.'

Stacey squealed. 'Fingerprint activation?' she asked.

Jodie giggled. 'Just like me.'

Stacey gave a scream of outraged delight.

She *knew* Stacey would understand. 'Where are you?' she asked.

'At work.'

Jodie felt an unworthy twist of spiteful pleasure remembering that her friend had another hour to go. She quickened her pace, feeling a spot of jealous rain on her cheek, scowled at the darkening clouds. 'Give me a minute, I'll call you back. Have to make a diversion.'

She smiled, hearing Stacey's squawk of complaint as she broke the connection. If she scooted right, she could cut through the John Lewis store, take the skyway to the car park. Call it a reconnaissance trip. She stepped through the entrance into the golden light of John Lewis and was enfolded in its warmth.

Minutes later, AirPods in place, she called Stacey.

'So, it's convenient to talk again, is it?' Stacey said, sounding miffed.

'Oh, Stacey,' Jodie said. 'Don't be mad. I think I've just had the *best* day of my life. How can I make it up to you?'

'Well . . .' Stacey said, maintaining the pretence of hurt pride for a few seconds longer, but finally succumbing to curiosity, as she always did. 'You can start by telling me *everything*. Don't leave *anything* out.'

'Oo-kaay,' Jodie took the escalator, talking loudly and unselfconsciously. 'Morning was shopping: Chanel handbag, MaxMara coat — which I happen to be wearing right now.' She checked her look in a full-length mirror as she made her way through the store towards the skyway to the car park, viewing counters and racks with evenly suspended attention, knowing that she would recall anything of real import.

'Colour, fabric — *tell* me.'

'It's a trench coat — what do they make those from? It's black—'

'Bo-*ring*.'

'Ah, but the genius is in what I'm wearing under it: Chinti & Parker, figure-hugging jersey to the knee, three-quarter-length sleeves, linear op-art in fuchsia and black. The contrast is *divine*.'

Stacey sighed.

'I'm also wearing Manolo Blahniks to die for—'

Stacey's sigh changed to a moan of ecstasy. 'And do they fit like a silk slipper?'

Jodie snorted. 'They're *killing* me — but I found a four-inch pair in patent leather with fuchsia edging to match.' She had to stop and catch her breath. 'Stacey, I would have my little toes *amputated* to fit into these honeys.'

Stacey laughed. 'You are so twisted.'

'So many inter*ruptions*,' Jodie exclaimed. 'I thought you wanted to hear this.' She was joking and knew Stacey would know it. 'So-ooo,' she went on, 'We stopped for lunch, Si invited me to his room to try on a few of my goodies. When I say *room*, I should say it's one of their larger suites. I modelled for him, he poured us both a snifter of brandy, and then we had good sex — not spectacularly good, but comfy, you know — the kind of sex that makes you want to purr like a cat.'

'*Jodie.*' Stacey sounded scandalized. 'You are so bad!'

Gratified, Jodie embellished: 'Champagne, a little snifter of a more stimulating kind—'

'Oh, Jodie, you *didn't* do coke!' There was no playfulness in Stacey's tone this time. She was in dreary earnest. After a disastrous weekend during their second year, one which featured Es and skunk — and sex with a gang of boys whose faces they could barely remember afterwards — they had sworn off drugs.

'Don't be a buzz-kill,' Jodie said, rolling her eyes at a man who passed in the opposite direction. *Nice looking, well dressed,* she noted automatically. He smiled — an easy, complicit smile, like he knew what she'd been up to all afternoon and approved. She lowered her voice. '*Everyone* uses it. Makes you horny as hell.' She thought how he had sliced and scraped and patted and teased the white powder into neat lines, calling it 'Charlie' with a proprietorial familiarity, as though it was a favourite nephew. And his largesse had extended to her in a way that made her blood sing in her ears to think of it.

She gave a throaty chuckle.

Stacey, beside herself with curiosity, said, '*What?*'

Jodie glanced around. People were funnelling towards the exit for the skyway and she might be overheard, but what the hell. 'Listen up,' she said. 'He was so jazzed he took me on a post-coital shopping spree to Boodles.' She lifted her right hand to better catch the light on the sapphire-and-diamond ring he'd bought her.

'He took you *jewellery* shopping? Jodie, you're practically *engaged*.'

'It's not like that,' Jodie said, affecting unconcern, but wrapping her secret hopes up warm and slipping them next to her avaricious heart. 'He stands to make 800k in bonuses this year. In BONUSES!' She swallowed a laugh at the outrageousness of that kind of money. 'He said this is his way of celebrating.'

Cocooned in the warmth and dry of the aerial walkway, she congratulated herself on her foresight: rain lashed in blustery bursts against the glass walls and roof. 'Do you want to come over? Try on some designer chic?'

'Try on? I don't intend to leave empty-handed,' Stacey said. 'And I expect you to get the food in.'

Jodie had bought — or rather she had *chosen*, since she hadn't been allowed to pay for anything — a fabulous glitter shrug which would be just perfect with Stacey's new party dress. It was to be a surprise, a compensation for listening and not being jealous and for magnifying the glory of this heart-stoppingly wonderful day.

'Everything's been tagged and audited,' Jodie warned her, heading down the ramp to the next level, where her Fiat 500 was parked. She would have to stop soon, look for her car keys. 'And a body search is *not* out of the question.'

Stacey said something obscene, but Jodie barely heard her. There was that guy again. He was standing in the middle of the ranks of vehicles with a button fob in his hand and peering at the ranks of parked cars with a baffled look on his face. He didn't seem to notice her at first. He held his hand up and pointed the fob, pressing it again and again as he turned full circle. When he saw her, he smiled. He had such a *nice* smile.

'Damnedest thing,' he said, his face quirking into a rueful grin. 'I seem to have lost my car.'

CHAPTER 23

Alan Palmer shrugged into his overcoat. He had two sessions at the NHS clinic, one of which was with Dylan Corbie; it would take him fifteen minutes at a fast walk from his private practice. Turning to the window behind his desk, Palmer angled the blinds to get a view of the street; he had to admit he had been rattled by the revelation that Dylan had been stalking him. He would need to discuss that with Karl.

A rap at the door broke through his ruminations. Lara.

'I know you're on your way out, and I thought you'd want this before tomorrow, Mr Palmer,' she said, handing him an envelope. 'It looks important.'

It was thickly wadded, A4, marked special delivery. He thanked Lara and she left, with one last curious look at the package. He would have to drive if he didn't leave immediately. But, like Lara, he was curious. *To hell with it, I'll drive*, he thought, tearing open the envelope.

The header made his heart jump in his chest.

A solicitor's letter. His heart dropped and he felt a simultaneous wave of nausea. Hands rattling the paper, he skimmed the text: it stated in stark, cold legalese that Elspeth had filed for divorce.

No.

He skipped to the end. 'I enclose copies of the relevant documents, which you should sign and return to this office without delay.'

Jesus, why? Last Saturday they had spent the day together, all three of them — like a proper family again. They had even gone to their favourite Italian restaurant. But thinking about it now, he recalled that Elspeth had returned to the subject of employing a nanny to take care of Lucy.

'I've had a good response from the agency,' she'd said, over her glass of wine.

'I told you, we need to discuss this,' Palmer had said. 'She'll be going to school soon. I don't see the point of—'

'The *point* is it will make life easier for me.' Elspeth tucked a hank of hair behind her ear in a gesture that signalled her impatience.

'And push me further away.'

'I came with you today,' she said.

'And how precisely does that give me more time with Lucy?'

Lucy crunched on a breadstick, her gaze flitting from one to the other.

Elspeth had glared at him, twin flames flickering in her irises, hardening them. 'I *thought*—' She broke off, seeing the waiter approach with their meals.

When the waiter was safely out of earshot, Elspeth began again: '—that you might have *wanted* me to be here.'

'I do.' He wanted to say, *I love you. Come back to me — I wish we'd never got into this mess.* But they had, and now, staring at the letter in his hands, he realised that it didn't matter what he said or did — Elspeth could not, could *never* — forgive him.

The divorce petition cited 'unreasonable behaviour' as grounds. He turned back to the letter. Elspeth had filed the petition over a week ago. Sweating, he tore through the rest of the sheets: a request for declaration of earnings and assets, a contact order. *Contact order?* It felt like a punch to his heart.

He fumbled in his shoulder bag for his mobile phone and turned it on. Elspeth's number was switched to answerphone.

'What is this, Elspeth?' he said, his voice harsh with emotion. '*Christ*, you'd filed the papers before the trip to the park, before our day out on Saturday — what were they, our little family away-days — some kind of fucking *test*?' He crumpled the papers and threw them from him.

The nausea overtook him and he stumbled to the loo adjacent to his consulting room, splashed his face with cold water and stared at his harrowed reflection.

A few minutes later, he dropped his phone into his overcoat and retrieved the crumpled sheets of paper, staring in disbelief at the envelope that had taken a sledgehammer to any fantasy that they might have a reconciliation.

Driving out of the basement car park, the injustice, the hurt, the possibility of losing Lucy surged in him like hot sulphur. Not that she would vanish overnight — Elspeth was more subtle than that. She had set about disentangling herself from him with clinical precision, and he had no doubts that her fastidious conscience would find it easier to justify an erosion of his place in the family, rather than an excision.

Clouds had hung low over the city all day, sending bank after bank of sluicing rain, and creating a grey half-light that made it feel like dusk before they'd ever had a proper dawn. He merged with the traffic on Strand Street, bumper-to-bumper with lunchtime traffic. He would have to cut east as soon as possible, or he would be late for his appointment with Dylan.

His phone trilled and he reached into his pocket. It caught on the lining and, cursing, still trying to manoeuvre through the traffic, he dragged it free, hearing the stitching tear. The caller display read 'Elspeth'. He hit the answer key and switched to hands-free, glancing in his mirror, guiltily on the lookout for police.

'You think my behaviour is *unreasonable*, Elspeth? You think I can't be trusted with our daughter?'

'Alan, I'm not trying to take Lucy away from you.' Elspeth sounded calm.

'Like hell you're not. There's notice of a *contact order* in that bundle of shit. So, either your solicitor is super-efficient, or you instructed him well before today.'

She was silent. At least she wasn't going to insult him by denying it.

A gap opened ahead and he accelerated, but the brake lights of the car in front flared suddenly and he jolted to a halt, inches from its bumper. The driver glared at Palmer in his rear-view.

Palmer looked for somewhere to pull over. 'What the hell do you want, Elspeth?'

'I want Lucy to be happy.'

'And I don't?'

'I didn't say that.'

He felt another blast of fury and clamped down on it. 'But you think she'd be happiest with you, is that it?'

'Safest, anyway.'

That was a low punch.

The lights changed and he nudged through, quickly scraped left, steered into a bus lay-by, and turned off the engine.

'I'm coming over,' he said.

'No, Alan.'

'I'll be finished by six,' he insisted. 'We need to sort this out.'

'That's what solicitors are for.'

'Solicitors are for creating rancour while they rake in the money.'

'I feel the need of an intermediary.' That sounded rehearsed.

'You want to punish me,' he said. 'Fine — I get it — really, I do. But does Lucy have to suffer too?'

He heard her catch her breath and after a short angry silence she said with icy control, 'Don't bother coming to the house. We won't be here.'

'Elspeth, don't hang u—' The line went dead. 'Fuck!' Palmer slammed the steering wheel with both hands, breathing hard through his nose.

A siren whooped beside him and he jumped like a startled cat.

Police. The officer pointed to the road markings in front of Palmer's car that read 'buses only', and Palmer mouthed an apology. Flustered, he over-cranked the ignition on the first attempt and got a scream of protest from the ignition coil. The cop widened his eyes and jerked his thumb. His meaning was unmistakable: *Beat it.*

CHAPTER 24

Rowan had arranged to meet with Ian Chan in a bar half a mile from St Anne Street Police Station at lunchtime. He breezed in, checking out the talent as he walked to her table, slipped his shoulder bag off and placed it on the chair next to him, then sat opposite, casting a critical eye over her.

'Well, don't you look like hell? I mean, how long is it since you got a good eight hours?'

It was five long days and nights, but an honest answer would just give Chan more ammunition, so she said, 'Probably more recently than you.'

He smiled. 'Ah, but sex floods the brain with endorphins and endorphins induce sleep. And the sleep of the *just after* is far more restful than the sleep of the *just*.'

She snorted. 'What would you know about the sleep of the just?'

He studied her a while longer, and his mood softened, his eyes darkening with concern. 'Still no word?'

'No word.' Rowan swallowed, cursing the swell of emotion triggered by his simple inquiry.

It was the busiest hour, the clientele was transient, and this was not a cop drinking spot, so the handover should be safe from the canteen gossips.

Chan reached into his shoulder bag and slid a buff folder across the table.

'Thanks, Ian,' she said.

'Don't thank me, Cassie — I shouldn't even be showing you this — you two being so close.'

Rowan was suddenly reluctant to pick up the folder.

He kept his eyes on her. 'If you want, I can take it back.'

'No.' It was a lie — she wanted him to take it, hide it, shred it — burn the damn thing till nothing but ash remained. But that would not undo all that had been done to Tasha. She laid a palm on the folder, as if to quell the anguish that lay within.

'I've tried everything else. Tasha doesn't want to be found, right now, so I can't get a description from her. DCI Warman isn't convinced she was even abducted by the Furman. If I can find points of similarity between Emma Hammond and Tasha, maybe she'll take her more seriously.'

'Any luck with the car?' Chan asked.

'She told the paramedics it was a Lexus.'

'Same make as Emma's would-be abductor. What about colour? Model? Number plate?'

'Emma says it was a dark Lexus IS, and unless it was a custom job — which is unlikely — that would mean velvet black, graphite, or azure blue. Tasha said dark azure blue — and she's an artist — so I'd trust her judgement on the shade. But since the two numpties who interviewed her didn't manage to get a statement, we don't know the model, and it's unlikely she would have got the number plate, anyway,' she admitted.

'Sweetheart, you've got your work cut out,' Chan said.

CHAPTER 25

Rowan sat at her desk, building up the courage to open the plain buff folder Ian Chan had given her. It contained the medical examiner's report on Tasha's assault, and was just on the periphery of her view, close to her left hand. Open in front of her, the case files for Penny Kominski and Jade Nulty — another sex worker who had been robbed and raped by the Furman — as well as three more statements from girls and women who had phoned the newspaper after reading the article about Emma's abduction. He had posed as a security guard, a plain-clothes police officer, a man in a plaster cast, needing help to load his car — always charming, always persuasive. In amongst the statements she had found a copy of Roy Wicks's report on his interview with Tasha.

The office was quiet — most of the day crew would be out on calls. A couple of guys came in with a mug of coffee in one hand and a bundle of blank forms in the other; she knew them from a brief spell working undercover on a drugs inquiry the previous year. End of the day for them, or the beginning? Hard to say — the drugs guys didn't talk much about their work. They gave her a nod and sat at the far end of the room. Minutes passed and they were deep into the tedium of form-filling — expenses, hours worked — the unglamorous side of the job. A phone rang on a desk near the office door, but rapidly switched to answerphone and then the only sounds were the distant hum of traffic on St Anne Street and the occasional sigh from the two men. Finally, exasperated with herself, Rowan snatched up Wicks's report.

It was less than a page long. Tasha was referred to as 'the complainant' except for one line at the beginning, identifying her. 'The complainant', according to Wicks was 'uncooperative'.

'She admitted that she had been soliciting for sex. When I asked her to describe what had happened, the complainant told me to "F*** off."' Three of the four letters blanked out — as if the Anglo-Saxon utterance had shocked him pink. *Bloody hypocrite.*

'She refused to describe her attacker and when I suggested that the man was her pimp, she swore at me a second time. She would not confirm that the sexual assault had been committed by him.'

Tasha had not signed the statement.

She read the report again but found nothing of use. It had fabrication written all over it: no follow-up, no request that Tasha should come in to work on an e-fit. Rowan's eye strayed once more to the buff folder on the edge of her vision: the forensic medical examiner's report. She sighed, giving in to the inevitable, and slid the folder to the centre of her desk.

The FME had been thorough, she'd give him that. Time and again, Rowan had to stop: the unblinking details of fifty separate injuries, internal and external, were too much to stomach in one reading. And Ian, with his usual technical skill, had captured on camera the bruises and burns, the red pinpricks of petechial haemorrhages in the whites of Tasha's eyes and on her face — her tormentor had repeatedly strangled and revived her during the rapes.

'Cassie?'

Rowan jumped, instinctively covering the pictures with both hands.

'You okay?'

135

Finch, a worried look on his schoolboy face.

Rowan scrabbled for the rest of the photographs and jammed them into the folder. Tucked the flap inside — slammed the vile thing into the desk drawer. It felt like she'd dragged her friend into the centre of the CID room and stripped her naked for the curious to point at and comment.

'What do you want, Finch?' She wiped tears from her eyes. *Shit*.

'I — nothing. The boss said she wants a report on the Lexus.'

'Why wouldn't she talk to you, Finch?'

'Who, the boss?' he said, bewildered.

'Tasha McCorkindale.' Rowan lifted the one-page slip that constituted the full police report on the rape and torture of her friend. 'What did you say to her?'

'Nothing, honest. She shut us down, that's all.'

'There isn't even a mention of an e-fit.'

'We didn't get that far.' A storm of emotions troubled the smooth surface of Finch's face. 'You know Wicksie . . .'

Rowan had thought so — she'd had Wicks pegged for a buffoon — a crass and unthinking, but harmless idiot. But in the past few days, she'd begun to rethink.

Finch shuffled his feet, avoiding her gaze.

Rowan glanced at the clock above the door frame, saw Wicks arrive, scratching his stomach just above the waistband and yawning cavernously.

She came around the desk so fast that Finch took a step back. 'Why didn't she give you a statement, Roy? Why didn't you ask for a description of the man who took her?'

Wicks shot a hard look at Finch then, recovering, forced a smile. 'Change the record, will you? I've got as much sympathy as the next Joe, but the work she does, what do you expect?'

Anger bubbled up in Rowan, hot and uncontained. She slammed the report on his desk. 'This isn't a statement, it's your wet dream.'

Wicks snapped from patronizing to aggressive in a heartbeat. 'What the *fuck's* that supposed to mean?'

Finch stepped between them, a look of wide-eyed panic on his face. '*Cassie.*'

The room went dead quiet. She felt the attention of the two drugs guys steady at her back, watching to see what would happen. 'What about you, Finch? Do you really think "the complainant" was raped and tortured for two days by her *pimp*?'

Finch glanced nervously at Wicks.

'Don't look at him,' Rowan said. 'Why didn't you get a description? *Look* at me, Finch.'

Finch's gaze snapped back to her, but it wouldn't hold and slipped away again. 'I wasn't the lead investigator,' he mumbled.

She eyed him up and down. 'Yeah, well, tell that to the next victim who turns up, brutalized and humiliated, her life a wreck — explain to her that you couldn't do your *job*, because you weren't the lead investigator.'

'Cassie!'

Rowan turned to face DCI Warman.

'My office,' Warman said. 'Now.'

* * *

The investigation was taking its toll on DCI Warman. Her skin, always sallow, had taken on a greyish tinge, her eyes were rimmed red and the fine mesh of lines and wrinkles under them were bluish with lack of sleep. Rowan knew how she felt but couldn't muster much in the way of sisterly feeling.

Warman took in Rowan's leather jacket, her jeans and boots. 'You've been here for hours — and you've a full shift on Kerbwatch tonight.'

Rowan lifted her chin. 'I'm not claiming for it.' She knew she sounded defensive — she *always* sounded defensive around Pat Warman.

'I'm glad to hear it.' Warman managed an ironic smile. 'But what does it achieve?'

'I'm just trying to get the job done, Ma'am.'

'We *all* are, Cassie.'

Rowan scoffed.

Warman picked up a sheet of paper from the pile on her left and transferred it to the tray on her right. 'I'm not saying it wasn't traumatic. You care about Tasha, and that's commendable.'

Rowan began to speak and Warman raised a hand to stay her. 'But you're taking this far too personally, Cassie. You're alienating the rest of the team — and it's got to stop.'

Later, she would realise that Warman was offering tactful advice, but right at that moment, all Rowan heard was an accusation.

The DCI clasped her hands in front of her. 'You're in danger of turning this investigation into your own personal vendetta.'

Later, Rowan would reflect that if Warman had been capable of softening the grating timbre of her voice, if Rowan herself had been less tired and felt less beleaguered, she might have heard the note of conciliation in her boss's tone. But right now, she was exhausted and frustrated and more than a little scared, remembering the handprints bracketing her kitchen window.

'The stone lobbed at the office window, Tasha's jacket — it *is* personal.' Rowan kept her voice low, but heat came off her words like the dark smoulder of a magma flow.

'Very well,' Warman said. 'You need to get ready for your Kerbwatch shift. I suggest you take the opportunity as you bond with the nightlife to reflect on your priorities, and where your loyalties should lie.'

Burning with impotent rage, Rowan reached for the door handle and stormed out, practically bouncing off Finch. He put out a hand to steady her.

'Cassie,' he said.

She shook her head. 'Not a good time, Finch.'

He caught her arm, held it tight. 'You need to hear this.'

'Well?' Warman said, peering past Rowan.

Finch's gaze flickered uncertainly to the DCI, then back to Rowan. 'Probable abduction, boss,' he said. 'Paradise Street car park. The victim is a Miss Jodie Pickersgill — her mate heard the whole thing.'

CHAPTER 26

'Let's get on with it.'

This in itself was a unique opening gambit. There was an urgency in Dylan's Corbie's tone, in the swift, careless way he hung up his coat, his perfunctory examination of the room for alterations, and the abandonment of his usual rigid routine.

'Where would you like to start?' Palmer asked.

Dylan sat opposite, as he had done on Monday. Two more days of healing had painted the boy's face in a mosaic of yellow and tan, the concavity of his right eye a dark peaty brown. His uninjured eye was the deep fathomless green.

He leaned forward, clasped his bony hands between his knees, and stared at a point on the industrial weave carpet as though an image replayed there. 'I've been thinking about why I do the things I do. Writing things down. Following people.' He glanced at Palmer. 'Following you.'

For a minute or two he was silent, and Palmer was aware of an inner struggle in the young man.

'It's my fault,' Dylan said. 'He died because of me.'

'Are you talking about your father?' Dylan never used the word 'suicide' — twelve years on, the manner of his father's death was still literally unspeakable.

Dylan gave a stiff nod. 'I told him about his imaginary rival — that's what Mummy called him.' His voice, always light and boyish, took on a childlike quality. 'Daddy came home from work and asked if I'd had a good day — I think it must have been a holiday because I said I was bored. I told him Mummy only wanted to play with her friend and not with me. She said most little boys invent imaginary friends, but I'd invented an imaginary rival for Mummy's affection.'

'How did you father respond?'

'He was angry, of course. She was s'posed to look after me.'

'Is that the only reason your father was angry?'

'No.' Dylan tilted his head, as though listening to a recording of the conversation replaying at a low volume nearby. 'Dad said, "Kids don't have that sort of fantasy."' He looked at Palmer. 'I didn't know what he meant then.'

'But you do now?'

'I think he believed me,' Dylan said simply. 'I was sure he did, at first. And I knew I was right. But she gave me sweets and cakes and I got fat and stupid and started to forget.'

Skinnerian rewards — positive reinforcement of the bedtime stories that reinvented his day? It fit with the medical history Karl Atherton had provided of Dylan's childhood obesity.

'What did you forget?' Palmer asked.

Dylan frowned. 'Perhaps not "forget" exactly.' He stared into Palmer's face for a few seconds, then shook his head as if trying to dislodge a double image. 'I got confused.' His cat-like green eyes were steady and unreadable.

Palmer was thinking of his conversation with Karl — was it really only a week before? 'Why would a person who has almost perfect recall need to make a written record of the tiniest details of his day?' Karl had said.

'Because he doesn't trust what he sees,' Palmer had replied.

Could it be . . . ? Could Dylan's mother have drugged a seven-year-old boy — her own child?

'And after your father died?' Palmer asked. The obesity had lasted well into his teens then, suddenly, Dylan had become anorexic.

Dylan stared at him blankly. 'I don't understand.'

'Did you still see your mother's imaginary friend?'

'I don't know.' Dylan's gaze darted left and right, but he couldn't meet Palmer's eye.

'Why did you stop eating, Dylan?'

'Because I couldn't *think* — I told you — it made me *stupid*.'

'When did you start keeping your diaries?' Palmer lowered his head, trying to catch his patient's eye, but Dylan refused to look at him. 'Dylan?'

Dylan shot him a sly glance. 'You *know* when. It was when I stopped eating.'

'But you said it was the sweets and cakes your mother gave you that made you "stupid"; why would you stop eating altogether?'

A flash of anger at the challenge to his logic, then Dylan shrugged and looked away. 'Her friend stopped coming when I stopped eating.'

'That isn't really an answer,' Palmer said. No response. 'I notice that you didn't describe the friend as "imaginary".'

Dylan's nostrils flared, but he wouldn't meet Palmer's gaze. 'I made him stop,' he muttered, his teeth clenched.

'Why do you think your father believed you about your mother's friend?'

'I wasn't a liar.' This was said with the fury of a child who is unjustly disbelieved.

'No,' Palmer said, quietly. 'I don't believe you were.'

Dylan seemed startled by the affirmation. He looked into Palmer's face, his eyes wide with shock, and Palmer thought he saw a dawning realisation in his patient that his unhappiness, his instability, his descent into psychosis was his mother's doing.

Dylan broke away from Palmer's quiet regard as if tearing himself from a vile horror, and searched his pockets, muttering to himself.

'I have to go,' he said, producing his notebook and pen. 'There's things I need to do.'

'You've only been here ten minutes.' Palmer kept his voice calm, despite the urgency of the situation: Dylan had made a momentous discovery, but a horribly disturbing one. If Palmer could persuade him to consider the implications in the safety of the therapeutic setting, they might make progress — but facing his mother's betrayal of trust on his own might send Dylan on a downward spiral.

'There's still forty minutes of your session to run,' Palmer added.

'No. No.' Dylan began writing in his notebook in his jerky, crabbed style.

'We could talk about what you just told me,' Palmer suggested, in the same soothing tones. 'I believe we're close to a breakthrough, Dylan. I know it's hard for you to—'

'Enough!' Dylan stood. Rage shook his spare frame and seemed almost to *pulse* in the weird light of his eyes. He stuffed his notebook and pen in his pocket. 'I'm going. I have somewhere I need to be.'

He looked around him anxiously as if suddenly finding himself in strange surroundings. 'I almost forgot.' His mood flipped again and suddenly he was yelling in Palmer's face. 'You almost made me forget!' Then he was gone, leaving Palmer shaken, struggling to process the storm of emotional transference he'd just experienced. The venom in that one word, 'Enough!' had felt like a physical threat.

CHAPTER 27

Wednesday evening

Alan Palmer drove from the NHS clinic to his private office still fretting about Dylan's session. Heading down the steep incline of Duke Street in the teeth of a stiff wind, he replayed the short session in his head. If he was right — and Palmer was confident he *had* read the situation right — Dylan had made the sudden and deeply wounding discovery that his mother had coerced and planted false memories in his mind, obliterating the truth and making him doubt his own sanity. Palmer believed it likely that she had even poisoned her son with drugs. Such a devastating betrayal could be catastrophic to Dylan's psyche, and he would need a safe environment to examine the violent emotions it had triggered. Liverpool One was still busy with late-night Christmas shoppers, but the decorations seemed dull and cheerless. He made a quick left before Chavasse Park to avoid the crowds, then right onto the waterfront. For now, Dylan was projecting all his bitterness and anger onto Palmer, and that might make him impossible to reach, but Karl might be better placed to broach the subject; as Dylan's psychiatrist, the therapeutic dynamic was very different. Palmer made a mental note to call his friend immediately when he got home.

Jake Osbourne was waiting for him when he arrived. He was leaning with one elbow on the receptionist's counter and she inclined her head towards him as if in intimate conversation.

As Palmer crossed the marble tiles to her gleaming marble island, Osbourne noticed him and turned slowly, a look of amusement on his face which said, *See the effect I have on them?*

The receptionist, Lara — named, she had told him, for the feisty heroine of the *Tomb Raider* games — blushed and tucked a lock of hair behind her ear like a tidy schoolgirl. She seemed to realise the gaucheness of the action and with a quick, self-conscious movement, fluffed her hair with her fingers and gave a defiant toss of her head.

'Doctor Palmer,' she said. 'Mr Osbourne is here to see you.'

'Thank you, Lara — and *Mister* Palmer is fine.' Lara had never quite grasped how anyone could be a psychoanalyst and not have a medical degree.

Osbourne eyed him sardonically, putting his back to Lara and leaning with both elbows on the raised section of the receptionist's island. 'Raining is it, Doc?'

Palmer had been caught in a sudden downpour on the last few hundred yards of his walk across town; his hair was plastered to his scalp and his overcoat dripped onto the polished floor. Osbourne, on the other hand, was dry and immaculate in a charcoal-grey suit and lemon-yellow tie, his hair   trimmed short and waxed into soft peaks calculated to look casual rather than contrived — was salon-perfect. No doubt he had blagged his way into the residents' parking in the basement.

Osbourne seemed untroubled by Palmer's lack of response. He clapped his hands and smiled. 'I'm ahead of schedule,' he said. 'Shall we make an early start?'

The second week of therapy and his patient was already testing the boundaries, asking for concessions, trying to exempt himself from the rules. Palmer had seen it too many times in his ten years as a psychoanalyst to be so easily coerced.

'I'll see you at the regular appointment time, Jake,' he said.

'Come on, Doc—' Osbourne pushed off from the counter. 'You could be home by eight thirty — what d'you say?'

'You can wait upstairs,' Palmer said, with an involuntary glance in Lara's direction. She seemed surprised by the hard edge to his tone. 'Or you can go and have coffee. I'll see you in' — he checked his watch — 'twenty-five minutes.'

Despite the inconvenience of Osbourne's early arrival, the little cameo Palmer had seen with the receptionist was instructive. Osbourne was neither handsome nor ugly — his mouth perhaps a little wide and slightly thick in the lower lip — but beyond this, he was unremarkable. His skin was smooth and always close-shaved, his hair a nondescript brown; he wore good-quality suits, and black, well-polished shoes. Yet, despite his ordinariness, Lara was clearly sexually attracted to him, and in Lara's presence, Osbourne was a different man. The usual aggression of the consultation room was absent in his flirtation with the young receptionist — with Lara, he was confident and charming, his aggression smoothed to an acceptable assertiveness. Palmer saw how Osbourne might use this in his business transactions — or to persuade women into his bed.

CHAPTER 28

Wednesday night

A splinted arm, a broken leg — they bring out the nurturing instinct in women. One hint of vulnerability and they're all over you, wanting to help. Makes them feel superior. And safe . . . But a crutch is as good as a baseball bat for crushing a skull. A plaster cast is a concealed weapon carried in full view.

* * *

Ian Chan sauntered into the office, the camera around his neck giving him the look of a paparazzo chancer. He went straight to Rowan's desk and hopped up. 'What happened to you?' he said. 'I'd've thought you'd be there like a shot.'

Rowan abandoned typing up her report and shoved her chair a little way back from the desk to face him. 'Warhorse.'

He raised his eyebrows. 'Been mouthing off again, have you?' He cocked his head, waiting for her to confess.

Rowan sighed. 'She told me I'd lost my professional objectivity. I didn't take it very well.' Rowan sighed and ran a hand over her face. 'In fact, I behaved like a teenager in a strop.'

Chan rolled his eyes. 'What *are* you like?'

'I know, you don't have to say it. I'm a bloody disaster.'

Chan shook his head. 'When will you learn that you don't have to fight everyone to get what you want? Bosses are insecure at heart. You'd get a lot further with a bit of tact and the intelligent application of flattery.'

'Ian, I'm really not in the mood for one of your *Work is Politics* lectures.'

But Chan wasn't listening. 'There's something you need to understand about Pat Warman, Cass. She joined the force when women were expected to do the filing, make the tea and keep their mouths shut. She's obeyed the rules, read the manuals, attended the courses, worked to protocols, and where'd it get her?'

'She made Detective Chief Inspector,' Rowan said.

'But she wanted *so much more*,' Chan said. 'Probably even deserved it. And what did it cost her? Can't you see it in her eyes — all that thwarted ambition? She looks at you, and she sees herself before she got old and bitter. For all her ambition, at fifty-then-some she'll never make Detective Superintendent.' He shrugged. 'Time just ran out for the old warhorse. And here *you* are, twenty-six, bright, couldn't give a shit what people think — and you'll go as far as you want to. *That's* what pisses her off. That, and your spectacular lack of tact.'

'Ian . . .'

'If you listened to her once in a while, you might see that she's trying to help.'

'She put me back on *Kerbwatch*!'

'Well, she couldn't exactly put *Hoff* in a pelmet skirt and feather boa, now could she?'

Rowan had to admit he had a point.

Chan took a breath and stared at the tip of one Ted Baker Chelsea-booted foot before exhaling in one loud *woosh*. 'Ooo-kaay . . . I'm glad we got that straightened out. So, getting back to my original question — where *were* you when the rest of Merseyside Police were swarming over Liverpool One?'

'Warman sent me to interview the girlfriend — Stacey Kirkwood.'

'Anything useful?'

Rowan grimaced. 'Not much.'

Three sharp raps from the front of the room. The DCI had somehow got past them, and Rowan wondered how much she'd heard. They exchanged a guilty look and Chan mouthed, 'Cloak of Invisibility.'

People were hungry for news, and Warman didn't have to wait long for silence.

Chan grabbed a chair from the desk next to Rowan's and sat facing the DCI. Another thirty detectives, Scientific Support and clerical staff settled on chairs and desks.

Warman said, 'Eddie Hayes is CSM on this one — Eddie.' The crime scene manager had the responsibility of maintaining the integrity of the scene, as well as coordinating the collection of forensic evidence. Hayes stepped forward.

Like the rest of the men in the room, he was dressed in a business suit and tie. He was around forty, tending to thicken around the middle, with the same calm, unreadable stare Rowan had seen in every good cop she'd ever met. But Hayes had never been a cop — he was a scientist, first and last. Even so, he commanded their attention like a man who was accustomed to being listened to.

'Jodie Pickersgill was last seen on level three of Paradise Street car park,' he said. 'Her car was found on level two. I'll have floor plans and photographs ready for the morning briefing. For now, I can tell you that level two has six CCTVs. Every one of them had been put out of action — and as each level has its own circuitry, someone shorted out that specific circuit on the motherboard.'

'Wait a minute — nobody reported this?' Wicks said.

The crime scene manager didn't miss a beat. 'The cameras are checked every three hours, and the fault was reported at seventeen hundred hours — during a routine security check,' he said. 'They couldn't find anything visibly wrong with the cameras, so they assumed a technical problem and the supervisor called out their area electrician. He was due to arrive at nineteen hundred hours. Unfortunately, Jodie went missing at seventeen thirty.' His delivery was carefully enunciated, and he adjusted his pace to ensure that people could note the times.

'Suggests someone tech-savvy,' Rowan said.

Hayes lifted one shoulder. 'Actually, it wouldn't take much technical knowledge to knock out the circuitry. It's far more impressive that they got through two sets of high-security locks to access the cabinet that houses the motherboard.'

He waited a moment to see if there were any other questions, then continued at the same unhurried pace. 'Examination of CCTV recordings at the entrance of the car park show Jodie arriving at 09.05 — they have a piece of software that can scan twenty-four hours of digital footage, and isolate a single number plate in less than an hour.' His eyes gleamed, and Ian Chan leaned closer to Rowan.

'Eddie loves Big Boy tech-toys,' he whispered.

'We've done a preliminary check of the recordings covering access points, but nothing out of the ordinary showed up. Jodie entered the lift and crossed the skyway into John Lewis by 9.10. She returned to the car park at seventeen twenty-seven. And vanished.'

'What about the stairwells?' Finch asked. 'Could she have left that way?'

Hayes shook his head. 'There's nothing on the cameras.'

Warman spoke up. 'I've requested street-cam access from the council, but it'll be a couple of days before we get it.'

'What happened to her phone?' Rowan asked.

'We found her earphones on level two, along with a number of shopping bags. The phone itself was dumped on level one.'

'Any signs of a struggle?' Rowan asked. 'Jodie's friend said she heard a scream just before the line went dead.'

'We found a small amount of fresh blood on level two,' Hayes said.

'I've asked for premium service on the DNA profile,' Warman said. 'Jodie's parents have already provided samples for comparison.'

'Stacey — the girlfriend — said Jodie was in conversation with someone,' Rowan said. 'She couldn't hear the other side of it, but she thought it was a man.' She flicked through her notes. 'Jodie said, "I do that all the time."' The other person spoke, then she said, "What's the make?" — again, Stacey didn't catch the reply. *Then* Jodie said, "Nice — my boyfriend's got one."' She waited a moment for the significance of it to sink in. 'So, I'm thinking, we find Jodie's boyfriend, we've got the make of the abductor's car.'

There was a murmur of approval in the room.

Even Warman nodded. 'Do we have a name?' she asked.

'Stacey knows the boyfriend only as "Si" — he's new, and Jodie's been secretive,' Rowan said. 'Wouldn't even say where he's staying. Stacey suspects he's married.' She turned to Hayes. 'Were there any receipts in the bags?'

Hayes nodded, following her line of reasoning. 'Paid for by credit card — could be a way of tracing him.'

'Apparently, he bought her a sapphire-and-diamond ring from Boodles. If it was flashy enough, the staff might remember,' Rowan said. 'I'll get onto it first thing.' She ran through the list of purchases Stacey had spoken of: the shoes, the coat, lingerie, the sapphire, then stopped short — *the phone.* 'Isn't he listed on her mobile?'

'New phone,' Hayes said. 'The only contact listed was the girlfriend, Stacey,'

'What about the old one?' Rowan asked. 'Stacey said they'd bought an iPhone that morning — so what happened to the other one?'

'There was no sign of a second phone.'

Rowan felt a rising excitement. 'If Jodie has it on her we can get the service provider to ping her phone, get a location.'

Warman said, 'It's worth a look.'

'Boss, he'll ditch it as soon as he finds it — the sooner we act, the more chance we have of finding Jod—'

Warman raised her voice. 'I *said*, I'll look into it.'

Chan kicked her ankle hard enough to remind her to maintain a professional coolness, and Warman called on Roy Wicks.

He sat up from his slouch. 'Boss?'

'First thing tomorrow I want you to co-ordinate a blitz of the car park — talk to shoppers, hand out photos. Did you ask for a picture of Jodie from her friend, Cassie?'

'I'm having some run off now, ma'am,' Rowan said, realising too late that 'ma'am' probably sounded *too* coolly professional. 'They'll be with us by the end of the briefing.'

Warman looked at Wicks. 'Take copies with you, Roy — see if anyone recognizes her. Finch can help with that. Cassie, you'll be on the purchases — follow the paper trail.'

'Don't we have any other witnesses to interview?' Rowan asked.

'I'll talk to the media,' Warman said. 'Ask them to put out an appeal.'

'Pity *your mate* didn't stick around long enough to work up an e-fit, Cass,' Wicks said.

'Changed your mind, have you, Roy?' Rowan asked.

Warman said, 'Cassie.'

'I mean, you were so convinced Tasha had been beaten up by her pimp.'

'Constable Rowan.' Warman's voice had the scratch in it that said she was angry.

But Rowan was in too much of a rage herself to notice. 'If you'd taken thirty seconds to look at the medical report—'

'*Rowan.*' The room went unnaturally quiet, and Warman's jaw pulsed as if she would shatter a tooth. 'Everyone — a warning.' She looked into the faces of each of them in turn. 'The media is all over this — leaping to all kinds of conclusions. *However* — we have *no* proof of any link, so I *do not* want any rumour-mongering.' Her gaze lingered on Rowan a moment longer than on the others, and Rowan felt herself blush.

'Have I made myself clear?' She got a murmur of response. The odd chair shifted, but she continued to stare at Rowan. 'Constable Rowan?'

'Clear, ma'am.'

'Refer any questions to the press office — or me.' Warman gathered up her papers. 'It's late,' she said. 'There's not much we can do until the workers start to come into the city tomorrow. Go home, get some rest — I want you all back here at seven thirty a.m. for a briefing.'

CHAPTER 29

Rowan and Ian Chan fetched up at the Pump Room pub at the Albert Dock. Rowan stared morosely into a half of Stella, while Ian Chan sipped a white wine. 'You shouldn't take it so personally,' he said.

'She practically accused me of rumour-mongering.'

'She warned *all* of us, Cass. She was ready to congratulate you on the interview with Stacey — working out the Boodles connection — but you had to go charging ahead, telling her how to do her job. Pissing her off — again. She will ping the damn phone — of *course* she will — you haven't got the monopoly on common sense, sweetheart.'

Rowan took a sip of beer and thought about it. 'Okay, I overreacted, but she let Wicks mouth off about Tasha, when it's his fault we don't have a witness statement.'

'He's a pig,' Chan said. 'But he has a point: why would the Furman take a huge gamble on Tasha not recognizing him? It wasn't as if her amnesia was reported in the papers.'

It was true — Rowan had checked and checked again — there was no word of Tasha's memory loss in the news reports. *On the other hand, he took a huge gamble coming down to St Anne Street to lob Tasha's jacket at me; and again, when he dumped her in broad daylight.* 'Maybe that's what he does, Ian,' she said. 'He takes huge chances — probably gets off on it.'

'Well, until Tasha resurfaces, it's all academic isn't it?' Chan's gaze flickered away for a second.

She followed his line of sight and saw someone she vaguely recognized. 'Doesn't he work in the press office at HQ?' she asked.

'Oh, yes indeed.' Chan smiled and raised his glass to press guy. He smiled back.

'And I'm in the way.' Rowan downed the rest of her lager.

'For God's sake, Cassie,' he laughed. 'I'm not going to jump his bones right here.'

Rowan stood, unhooking her jacket from the back of the chair. 'Ian, you're practically purring.'

'Mm . . .' He flashed her a wicked smile. 'He can stroke me anytime.'

'Subtle, Ian. Very subtle. Anyway, I thought I might stop in at the Arnott on my way home.'

Ian's attention snapped back to her. 'The Arnott? It's a bit upmarket for you, isn't it?'

'Gee, thanks,'

Chan's eyes narrowed. 'You're up to something.'

Rowan set down her glass. 'Could be.'

'Tell,' he demanded.

'Jodie told her friend she'd had a little afternoon delight in the mysterious Si's hotel room.'

'Ye-es,' Chan said. 'I was awake for that part of the briefing. But she also said that Jodie didn't *name* the place.'

Rowan looked at him over the rim of her glass. 'I checked the inventory of Jodie's possessions before I left. She'd squirrelled a couple of sheets of headed stationery into one of her shopping bags — memento of her ever-so-brief stay in one of the classiest hotels in the city.'

'The girl's so sweet it almost breaks your heart,' Chan said. 'But Warhorse won't like it. You're supposed to go home, get some rest.' He was going through the motions, being her conscience — her voice of reason — because that was his self-appointed role in their relationship, but his mind was elsewhere.

'Warhorse doesn't like *anything* I do,' Rowan said. Press guy had been served and was heading their way, pint glass in hand. Rowan shrugged into her jacket and dropped Chan a wink. 'And we all have our different ways of taking our relaxation.'

* * *

The Arnott was a boutique hotel. Once part of the city council's building stock, it had been bought up by an enterprising designer and her architect husband in the big equity sell-off early in the new millennium. The entrance was an imposing lemon sandstone portico up a flight of shallow steps.

During the daytime, cars and lorries ground past in sludgy pulses, but at this time of night, traffic on the outer rim of the business quarter was light. Rowan parked on a meter and jogged across the road.

The reception area floor was tiled in apricot marble. Pale ash panels with black inlay were designed to give an impression of nouveau Deco.

The receptionist stood behind a counter topped by black granite in a long curving sweep like an arched eyebrow. The receptionist was in her early twenties, medium height, brunette and catwalk elegant, minus the sulky pout. Her name, according to her lapel badge, was Lisa. She smiled a professional welcome and asked how she could help.

Rowan returned the smile. Her casual dress would not be out of place at the Arnott — its laid-back style welcomed the bohemian as readily as it embraced Italian chic. *One of the grander suites, Jodie had said.*

'I believe you have an executive suite?'

'We have three, in fact.' The receptionist reached under the counter and brought out a brochure, began pointing out features as she spoke. 'Fabulous views over the city; each

156

decorated to a very high standard, with original artwork by local artists. The suites are equipped with large screen TVs, Sky, Netflix and Virgin cable, plus Bose sound systems — the largest has two reception rooms as well as—'

'Sounds wonderful,' Rowan said, feeling bad about interrupting her carefully rehearsed spiel. 'But I'm interested in one in particular.'

'If you know which, I can show you a list of prices.' Lisa remained pleasant — keen to please the customer, but not too eager.

'The suite occupied by "Si" or "Simon",' Rowan said, showing her ID card.

The smile wavered and the receptionist wrinkled her nose as though she'd smelled something bad. The Arnott's clientele included celebrities and footballers; it prided itself on its discretion.

A guest came through the automatic doors and the receptionist renewed her smile, though it seemed less genuine this time around. She pressed a buzzer and said, 'Someone will be with you in a moment, madam.'

She sidled along the curve of the desk to the trailing point of the brow and Rowan followed. 'I'm afraid we don't give out guests' details,' she said, lowering her voice. 'But if you have a name, I'd be happy to pass on a message.'

She tilted her body back to look below the counter again and Rowan said, 'Don't.'

Startled, the receptionist placed her hands on the granite counter like a barman caught reaching for a shotgun.

'Don't fetch out your little message pad, or I'll be insulted,' Rowan said. 'I'm here as part of an enquiry into the abduction of a young woman.' She saw nervy recognition in the receptionist's eyes — Jodie's abduction had been reported on every local news bulletin since six o' clock — the commercial stations had even begun to draw comparisons with Tasha's abduction and rape.

A door opened to Rowan's left, releasing the soft murmur of well-bred conversation and a waft of warmth and music. Rowan kept her focus on the receptionist, but in the periphery of her vision she could see a man approaching the desk. He wore a brushed bronze name-clip and had the polished look of a business graduate with an eye on promotion.

'Look, Lisa. I just want to talk to this Simon. We believe he and the victim spent the day together. There's no reason to think he's implicated in any way.'

'I heard about the abduction,' Lisa admitted. 'And it is awful.' Her eyes darted towards her male colleague. 'But I really can't give out guests' details.' She lowered her voice. 'I just *can't*.'

The hotel guest drifted past Rowan, trailing expensive perfume. A moment later she heard a muted *ping* and the polite swish of elevator doors.

Rowan pushed harder. 'Lisa, listen to me. This guy — this Simon — spent the best part of ten grand on his girlfriend today. Don't you think he'd want to know if something's happened to her?'

Rowan thought she saw a slight wavering of Lisa's resolve; she turned her back on the male receptionist and leaned closer, so she wouldn't alarm the guests. 'She was dragged off a busy car park at the peak of rush hour. This guy is reckless and vicious — we need to find Jodie. Fast.'

The victim's name seemed to flick a switch in Lisa's mind. She struggled with her conscience a second longer, then leaned forward confidentially, mirroring Rowan's body language.

Suddenly, the man was at her shoulder, a faint smile playing about his lips, as if someone had told him a joke and he'd anticipated the punch line. 'Forgive me,' he said. 'I couldn't help overhearing. As Lisa explained, we make it a policy not to give out guests' names.'

'And as *I* explained, a woman's life might be at risk.'

'As I understand it, the young lady didn't disappear from the Arnott?'

'No,' Rowan admitted.

'Then I don't see how our guest can help you.'

'That's not your call to make.' A glance at his name tag revealed that he was *Mister* Rossiter. *Ah, the subtle distinctions of hierarchy.* 'Let me talk to your guest, Mr Rossiter — he can make that decision for himself.'

'Sorry,' he said. 'Obvious question — do you have a warrant?'

'Why the hell would I need a warrant?'

He smiled, nodding, and delivered the punchline himself. 'To see the guest list.'

CHAPTER 30

Rowan sat fuming in her car for half an hour. A wind whipped up from the Mersey, buffeting and rocking it like a crowd of football hooligans out on the lash. Guests arrived in taxis, returning to the hotel after a night out, a few left. Rowan replayed the last few hours in her mind. Ian was right — if she played the game, flattered Warman a bit, she would probably get on much better — on a personal level and in her career.

A people-carrier pulled up near the entrance to the Arnott. Sleek black, darkened windows. Six got out, four women, two men, all in evening dress, the women shivering in their silk wraps.

Rowan recognized one of them as an American actress — or maybe a British actress who played Americans — either way, she was a recognizable face. The tall bearded man looked familiar, too. Producer? Director? He'd been interviewed on daytime TV recently, Rowan was sure of that — and she was equally certain that the hotel staff would know exactly who their celebrity visitors were — which made their arrival the most useful of things: a potential distraction. She snatched the ponytail ring from her hair and shook it loose, slipped off her leather jacket and sprinted across the road as the coterie headed up the steps. She huddled at the back of the group, waiting for the flutter of excitement as they reached the reception area.

To their credit, the staff made the minimum of fuss, Lisa simply smiled, and Rossiter welcomed the party with a nod and a polite, 'Good evening.' But they continued to watch as the group moved left towards the bar and Rowan, taking advantage of the momentary lapse, slid right, towards the bank of lifts.

One lift door stood open. Rowan stepped inside, punched the button for the top floor, checking her look in the mirrored walls of the carriage. The wind had ruffled her hair and she ran her fingers through it so that it fell more obediently into place. She had no plan, beyond maybe knocking on doors. But Rowan had spent months out on the streets, flattering men, using her body as both decoy and bait: if the occupants of the suites were male, she was confident she would be able to keep their minds on things other than hotel security. She wore no make-up, but the surge of adrenaline had given her some colour. She unfastened a button of her blouse and rearranged the fabric to reveal her cleavage. 'The glamour of police work,' she murmured, grimacing at her reflection as the lift pinged and the doors slid open.

The corridor was empty. There were two doors along the facing wall. The nearest, a wide polished plane of oak, was inlaid with mahogany in the shape of a stylised rose. A *Do Not Disturb* sign had been hung over the thin brass blade of the handle. It might be wise to leave that one till last — waking sleeping occupants was a sure way to get herself thrown out. The fire exit was tucked in the far corner — if she had to slip away quietly, that would be her best route. She tried the furthest suite. No reply. Knocked again, listening for signs of movement inside. Nothing.

Her heart tripping rapidly in her chest, Rowan moved to the adjacent suite, alert for the sound of the lift. The next door was decorated with a tulip motif; neither door had a name plate or number. She raised her hand to knock and heard the mechanical swish of the lift doors. *Damn*. She was ten metres from the fire exit.

Run, or brazen it out? Her instincts told her to flee, but she hesitated a moment too long, and someone stepped out of the lift. *They haven't seen you yet. Walk away — use the emergency exit — keep out of trouble.*

A searing picture flashed across her mind: Tasha in the forensic images, taser marks on her breasts — small angry burns a couple of centimetres apart, like snake bites. A mutinous resentment rose up in her — Jodie Pickersgill had already been missing for six hours and it would be another seven before the investigation continued in earnest. Terrible things could happen to a woman in that time; things that would haunt her for the rest of her life. If they knew the identity of the mysterious 'Si,' what kind of car he drove — at least they could start looking for the sexual sadist who had Jodie.

She rapped smartly at the door. 'Si — it's Cassie.'

From the corner of her eye she saw someone hesitating by the lift, turned, smile on full beam. For one horrible moment she thought Lisa had followed her from reception. But this was a girl, a pale waif in the uniform of housekeeping staff. Too young to be a student, too young — judging by the fearful look on her face — to be out in the world of work.

Rowan pushed her fingers through her hair. 'Hi,' she said, affecting a slightly breathy, girlish tone. 'Looking for Si — haven't seen him, have you?'

The waif glanced into the lift as though looking for reassurance, and Rowan's heart sank. If there was more than one of them, she'd never get away with it. The lift door began to close and the girl gave a little yelp, blocking it with her body. Rowan winced at the sound of the impact — the girl was skin and bone — and heard the doors glide open again. The girl leaned in and dragged a trolley out onto the carpet. She eyed Rowan with faint terror.

'I'm Cassie,' Rowan said, tossing her head. 'Simon's PA? Or I *was* until I *totally* cocked things up.'

The girl pushed the trolley towards her, keeping her head down, as if she hoped that this gabbling woman would simply vanish.

'I mean I've only been in the job for a week — but they expect you to know *everything*, like there's a rule book or something and you'd, like, have to be OCD or something to read it, but honestly I've *really* tried—' Rowan surprised herself with a tearful sob. 'And I thought he'd at *least* pick up his own bloody text messages. But no-ooo. *He* doesn't answer his mobile all day, and for some reason it's *my* fault he hasn't got back to the office.' She pushed her fingers into her hair, left them there long enough to make it stand up in mad tufts. 'And it *really is* important — customers in Japan, and they just take it for granted you'll be working twenty-four/seven, because — hey, this is the global work-place, right?'

Rowan raised her fist to rap again on the tulip door. The girl stopped at the Rose door with the *Do Not Disturb* sign and turned her frightened eyes on Rowan. 'Mr Carstairs?' she asked, her voice a thin, child's falsetto.

Rowan's smile broadened. *Simon Carstairs — thank you.* 'Simon,' she said. 'Yeah.'

'That's the Tulip Suite — Mr Carstairs is in the Rose Suite.'

The girl turned to the door with the *Do Not Disturb* sign hanging rakishly on the handle, pointed timidly. 'This is the Rose Suite.'

Rowan slapped her forehead. 'See — it's like I said — I mean, who wrote this bloody rule book — and where can I get a copy?'

The waif giggled, and Rowan faked a shaky laugh.

'He's not even in,' the girl said. 'He's asked us to tidy up a bit — says he's bringing clients back.'

Rowan gasped. 'Oh, thank God. If I could just leave him a note, he'd maybe think I left it earlier.' The chambermaid chewed her lip, uncertain, and Rowan groaned theatrically. 'I am *so* fired . . .'

Suddenly the girl seemed to make up her mind. 'We're not supposed to push the trolleys against the doors,' she said, 'In case it marks the wood.' She lifted a swipe card from a narrow chain attached to the belt of her uniform dress and slid it through the reader. The lock clicked and she put her shoulder to the door; it gave with a sigh. 'We have to fasten the doors open with the hooks,' she explained, reaching around the back and latching it in place. 'My supervisor says they're just asking for someone to sneak in and rob the place while your back's turned.' She smiled shyly, and Rowan's spirits lifted.

'Oh, my godfathers . . .' The girl stood in the doorway staring open-mouthed at the aftermath of Jodie and Simon's celebrations. Newspapers and wrapping tissue were strewn across the floor. Two brandy glasses, one still with traces of liquor, stood on the table and a damp towel and a bathrobe hung on the back of an armchair. A woman's jacket lay on the floor with one sleeve pulled inside out; next to it, an empty shoe box and beside that a pair of black stilettos, one fallen tipsily on its side. Shopping bags had been heaped on the second sofa — it seemed that Mr Carstairs had treated himself as well as Jodie on their spree — instruction manuals for a Sonos Move speaker and an iPhone cluttered the coffee table, the gadgets themselves discarded among the packaging like forgotten toys.

'He's coming back any minute,' the girl wailed, darting forward to pick up a newspaper and folding it distractedly. 'How'm I supposed to sort out this mess?'

'Call Housekeeping and tell them you'll need help,' Rowan said.

The girl's eyes widened. 'I can't — they already think I'm a waste of space . . .'

Rowan was eager to check out the room off to her left, but then she felt for this child sent to clear up Carstairs's orgy of consumption and sex. 'Tell your supervisor the place is a pigsty — if she wants it ready for when his lordship gets back, you'll need someone to give you a hand — just say it like you mean it.'

The chambermaid gazed at Rowan with a mixture of awe and mistrust — this was not the same anxious menial who had begged to be allowed to leave a note for her employer.

Rowan shrugged. 'Up to you. But if this place is still a tip when Carstairs gets back with his clients, you know who'll get the blame.' She moved swiftly across the room and smiled to herself when she heard the girl pick up the phone receiver and key in a number.

The door gave onto a bedroom. The bed was unmade, the duvet half on the floor. A champagne bottle lay on the pillow, and on the bedside table a half-full champagne flute, the fizz gone out of it. The room was ripe with the smell of sex.

At the top end of the room a door through to an en suite bathroom stood ajar. A chaise longue, draped with a dressing gown and another damp towel, stood before a glass coffee table. On it, a business card and a silver snuff box. Rowan snatched the card up. Simon Carstairs was a commercial lawyer with a London firm. The card gave his office address, phone number and mobile. Rowan fished in her jacket pocket for her phone and snapped a picture. As she replaced the card, a talcy dryness under her fingertips made her look more closely: a tell-tale dusting of white powder clung to the edge of it. Stacey had told her she thought Jodie had taken cocaine.

She glanced towards the door. Faintly, she could hear the girl's quick steps, the rustle of paper. Then a woman's voice, older: 'Bloody hell, you weren't kidding — the kip of the place! Look, girl, just straighten up a bit — chuck them bags behind the sofas, he's on his way up.'

Rowan's heart skipped a beat. Best clear out — wait outside the room, catch Carstairs as he returned. But the snuff box stared up at her from the table. *It's not like you could do him for cocaine possession*, she told herself. *You practically broke into the place. And you've got what you came for.* But cops, like cats, are curious, and she simply couldn't resist taking a look.

'Do I know you?'

Rowan wheeled to face the questioner, her hand closing over the snuff box in a reflex response. 'Simon Carstairs?' she said.

He stood in the bedroom doorway. A tall, dark-haired man in his late twenties — not spectacularly handsome, but glossy, in the way the very rich are. She would bet the suit he wore had a Saville Row label hand-sewn to the inside pocket. His shirt probably cost more than her entire outfit.

'You don't look like hotel management,' he said.

She heard two more voices in the corridor, both male — his guests, following on. Carstairs turned to greet them. 'Come in,' he said, 'the cleaning staff are just finishing up — isn't that right, ladies?'

The older woman spoke for both of them: 'Did you want us to straighten up the bedroom, sir?'

He had his back to her — Rowan could have replaced the snuff box, but something made her hold onto it.

'That won't be necessary.' He waved Rowan out of the room, but she wasn't ready to leave.

'I need a word in private, sir,' she said.

A frown crossed his smooth white forehead. 'Now is not convenient.' Impatient, he gestured again for her to leave and she noticed he wore a gold wedding ring.

Rowan stood her ground. 'It's urgent.'

His clients peered past him to get a look at the stroppy hotel employee.

'Pour yourselves a brandy, gentlemen,' he called over his shoulder. 'I'll be right with you.' He sounded congenial — he even smiled, but there was no humour in his eyes.

She heard the clink of crystal, a whispered exchange between the two housekeeping staff, then the rattle of their trolley leaving and a soft creak as the door swung closed behind them.

'Now,' he said softly. 'Either you leave, or I call hotel security.'

A pulse throbbed in Rowan's throat. *For God's sake, Cassie, he's a lawyer — if he calls security it won't end there.* She

166

would be in deep trouble — with her boss and with the law. *Yeah, and he wants rid of me, and he doesn't even know who I am — these clients must have clinched him his big bonus or something.* She decided to play her trump card.

'All I want is a quiet word on an urgent matter,' she said, opening her fist to reveal the silver snuff box.

Carstairs paled, made a move towards her, but Rowan stepped back, palming the box again. He went to the door and closed it firmly.

'Who the *fuck* are you?' he snarled.

'Jodie Pickersgill is missing,' Rowan said. 'Possibly abducted.'

The angry tightness around his eyes vanished and his face sagged. 'No,' he said. 'That's— I mean, just saw her a few hours ago.'

'She was talking to a friend on her mobile when it happened,' Rowan explained. 'Her phone — the new one — was found smashed in the car park at John Lewis. Has she made any contact with you?'

'Not since she left the hotel.'

'When was that?'

He groped for the bed, sat down heavily. 'I dunno, around five?' He stared up at her, his eyes glazed. 'Are you police? Shit—' He blinked, and his skin greyed to ash. 'Are you *press*?'

Rowan showed her warrant card and his mouth set into a hard line.

'I was with my clients all evening.'

'I haven't accused you of anything,' Rowan said.

'You threatened me with *that*.' He glanced at the hand that held the snuff box. 'Which, need I remind you, was found as the result of an illegal search?'

'I'm not here to arrest you, Mr Carstairs — I just want to talk.'

He took out his mobile and keyed in a number. After a few moments he ended the call and pocketed the phone. 'That was her old number,' he said. 'She's not answering.'

'We know. Jodie's friend heard her talking to a man—'

'I told you, I was with my clients.'

'And I told you, I'm not accusing you of anything — but your concern is touching.' Fresh colour rose into his face, but he said nothing, and Rowan went on, 'During her conversation with the mystery man, Jodie said her boyfriend — presumably you — had the same car.'

'A Lexus?' His tone implied it was inconceivable that criminal riff-raff would be allowed membership of his exclusive owners' club.

Adrenaline zinged through Rowan's bloodstream. *A Lexus IS — I knew it!* She grabbed Carstairs's hand and slapped the snuff box into his palm. 'Here,' she said, 'You've earned it.'

* * *

She squeezed through the lift doors as they opened at ground floor level, strode past a perplexed Lisa at reception, shrugged her jacket back on, and trotted down the steps to the street scrolling down her cell phone list for Ian Chan's number. She was banking on Ian knowing the crime scene manager's number. If she could persuade him to go back and check the digital recordings at the car park exit, they might get an ID, catch the bastard.

She glanced up to check for traffic and saw a man leaning through the passenger window of her car. 'Hey, you!' she yelled.

The figure at her car straightened, in no hurry. He wore a hooded jacket, so she couldn't see his face clearly, and as he brought his right hand to the roof of her car, she saw he had a fistful of her CDs.

'Police!' she roared. 'Stay where you are!'

He turned away.

Rowan darted forward. A horn blared and she threw herself back, caught her heel on the kerbstone and landed on her backside. A car had come from nowhere. It swerved, tyres squealing, straightened, fishtailed then shot off, its horn a nerve-jangling wall of sound.

Heart thumping, fingertips tingling with shock, Rowan pushed herself to her feet and took off after the hoodie.

He had twenty-five yards on her, but she was fit, and the adrenalin burst of a narrow escape helped her to cover the first ten yards in seconds. At the twenty-yard mark, her chest started to ache: the lucky kick the Furman had landed nearly ten days ago was still sore.

Is this him? Is this the Furman? Was this the man who had waited for her outside the police station at the weekend?

Ahead, the hoodie took a left. Taking the corner too wide, he almost overshot onto the road, but swung round a one-way sign, shedding a couple of discs. Rowan felt one crunch underfoot.

He dodged left and she followed without thinking. The roadway was too narrow to take more than one car in either direction. It was marked with double yellow lines on both sides. The hoodie had vanished. Rowan stopped, leaning forward with her hands on her knees. The cold air scoured her lungs and burned in her throat and, for a while, all she could hear was her own ragged breathing.

Then the slap of running feet echoed somewhere to her right, and she was off again. A narrow ginnel opened ten yards down and she skidded into it, ricocheting from one side to the other. She slowed again, seeing the low, squat form of a commercial wheeled bin almost blocking the tight space. A padlock on the lid oscillated fast, gleaming dully in the uncertain light, and beyond the dumpster, dimly, she saw a block of darker shadow — a doorway, perhaps. The harsh reek of food waste and urine caught the back of her throat and she coughed, the sound echoing back to her like the sound of pebbles in a well. She covered her mouth with her hand and waited.

The alley was still and silent. She cocked her head, holding her breath for a second. A faint rustle. Rowan slid her Casco baton from her belt and crept closer, senses on full alert. The buildings at this end of town had been constructed with the Victorians' eye for efficient use of land. No windows overlooked the alley, just a few steel-plated doors, all closed. There was barely room to edge past the dumpster.

She flicked the baton to full length, holding it low, ready to take a crack at knees, ankles, elbows. There were no street-lights here, and the dark was so intense all she could see was a faint glimmer from the dumpster and the red pulse of blood behind her eyes.

Give up, a voice in her head told her. *Go home.* For some reason, the voice had the exact tone and accent of Sergeant Inghams. Then she heard that low rustle again: the shuffle of feet? A furtive movement? Was he waiting in arm's reach, ready with a cosh, a knife — a taser?

Fuck it. She swung around the corner of the dumpster into the empty dark, yelling. Something brushed past her and she jumped like a cat, her heart clamouring in her throat.

She wheeled, swinging the baton wildly, remembered belatedly the key light on the fob in her pocket. Back to the wall, she fumbled for it. *What the hell were you thinking?* The dark seemed to close in, plucking at her. She stared into the suffo-cating blackness, widening her eyes, hoping to catch an extra gleam of light. The key caught on the lining of her jacket and tore it. She jabbed it like a weapon into the darkness, and the key fob burst into life, its tiny corona of light startlingly bright after the intense blackness.

She scanned right and left, her whole arm shaking. To her right, the alley ended in a ten-foot-high gate.

A third time, she heard the insinuating shuffle and scrape — this time to her left. Near the wheelie bin, block-ing her way back out to the street. She held her key light in her left hand, gripping the baton hard in her right, feeling it slick with sweat.

A gust of wind spun down the alley and something flew up at her face. She swept the baton in an arc, batting away a polystyrene food container. Before she could regain her balance, something launched itself out of the doorway, low and fast. It hit her hard in the shin and she felt small claws scrabble briefly at her trouser-legs. It landed heavily on her foot and she kicked it away with a scream.

'Jesus. Fuck!' A rat.

It hit the far wall, rolled and scuttled out of range of her key light and vanished. She was alone again.

CHAPTER 31

Thursday, 26 November, morning

Mornings were generally the quietest time in the Rowan household which, in her delicate state, suited Rowan just fine. She'd called Ian Chan at one a.m. It sounded like he wasn't alone — and he hadn't been pleased by the interruption. By the time she had spoken to the crime scene manager, reported the break-in to her car and taped plastic sheeting to the broken nearside window, it was two thirty a.m.

By rights, she should have crashed out as soon as her head hit the pillow, but she kept seeing the hooded figure at her car window, the man standing at the safety rail above the car park at St Anne Street. Was it the Furman?

For the next two hours she stared at the ceiling, listening to the hollow chuckle of rainwater in the gutters. When she closed her eyes, she saw flashes of Tasha in the forensic pictures, her neck bruised, layer upon layer, each one at a different stage of ripening. If she drifted off, she was jerked awake by imagined cries, and awake or asleep, she was haunted by Tasha's face, her eyes red and swollen, looking helpless and used. And beneath the churning misery of that memory was the knowledge that Jodie Pickersgill's torment had only just begun.

The shrill beep of the alarm clock at six a.m. had startled her from a sweaty dream in which Jodie/Tasha was in a car park, trying to hide from an unknown pursuer. She worried at car doors and boot locks until she found one open. She threw a panicked glance over her shoulder, then turned back. Tasha/Jodie's eyes widened in terror and suddenly, horribly, Rowan *was* Tasha/Jodie, and the man — the faceless pursuer — was inside the car. He reached up and dragged her inside.

Rowan had fumbled the alarm off-switch with a groan: a seven thirty briefing, followed by a twelve-hour shift, and all on two hours sleep.

She felt marginally better by the time she'd showered, dressed, and dabbed on a little make-up to hide the shadows under her eyes. She poured a bowl of cornflakes, slid two rounds of bread in the toaster and set the kettle to boil while she sat at the table, munching her cereal and listening dully to the seven o'clock news on Radio Merseyside.

They interviewed Stacey Kirkwood, the friend who had been speaking to Jodie when her abductor approached her. Rowan listened to Stacey's account, wondering if Warman had put the media onto her in an effort to strengthen the appeal for witnesses — there was nothing like a personal account to get the listeners to empathise.

The newsreader went on, 'Police say they're keeping an open mind about possible links to the attempted abduction of a businesswoman last Friday and the rape of a prostitute in the city over the weekend.'

Neil shuffled in a moment later. 'Shouldn't you be in bed?' he asked.

Rowan said, 'Shouldn't you?'

'I've missed your sparkling conversation at breakfast.'

'A listener called the Terry Hamblin chat show yesterday afternoon,' the newsreader said.

Neil poured boiling water onto the teabag and handed her the mug. 'I thought daylight turned your sort to dust,' he said.

'Early briefing — shh!'

They were playing the call back. 'He came up to me in the car park.' It was a bad line, the woman's voice slightly muffled, and extraneous noise suggested she was calling from an office phone.

'So, you're going in early?' Neil asked.

Rowan turned up the volume.

'He seemed like a nice feller.'

Neil dropped a teabag into another mug, added hot water and sloshed milk into his without letting it brew, then he swooped in to steal one of the rounds of toast. She rapped him on the knuckles, but he refused to relinquish his prize, retreating instead to the far side of the kitchen table.

'He was wearing a beanie hat,' the woman said — 'you know, one of them wool thingies.'

We've got a witness. Rowan snatched up the last piece of toast and headed for the door.

'Wait up,' Neil said, 'You can give me a lift.'

Rowan checked her watch. 'Neil, it's ten past seven. You're not usually out of *bed* till eight thirty.'

'Exaggeration.' Neil brushed the breadcrumbs from his hands.

She lowered her head and gave him the big sister look.

He rolled his eyes. 'Field trip. We're supposed to meet at Lime Street Station at eight.'

'And you didn't mention this because . . . ?'

'You've been kinda preoccupied.'

There was no arguing with that. 'Have you paid for this trip?'

'No, *you* did. Last month.'

Rowan had a dim recollection of filling in a permission slip and handing over some cash.

'You can drop me on Brownlow Hill,' he added, too casually.

'Ashamed to be seen with big sister?'

'Jeez — paranoid much? I just need to get a sandwich for lunch, all right?'

'You can get one in the M&S on the station concourse,' she said.

He rolled his eyes.

Following him out of the house, she grabbed Neil's Berghaus from the row of hooks by the front door and tossed it to him on the street.

'In case your field trip's in an actual field,' she said. 'And so you know? Just 'cos you're paranoid, doesn't mean they're not out to get you.'

Neil stopped at the kerb, taking in the damage to the passenger window. 'Nice look,' he said, pinging his nail off the sheet plastic she'd used as a temporary repair.

'Thanks for the sympathy,' Rowan said, relieved that he hadn't made the connection with the weird events of the previous Saturday. 'Replacing that window will cost me a packet.'

'Well I left a thumb drive in here — I hope they didn't nick it.' He slid into the passenger seat and checked the glove compartment.

Rowan quizzed him on his field trip while he searched — anything to keep him from thinking deeper and discovering the disturbing possibility that the Furman had paid her a return visit. They were heading to York, as it turned out. She kept up the pressure by asking what time he was expected home and whether he was up to date with his coursework.

As they passed the Royal Liverpool Hospital, Rowan's mobile rang.

'Can you get that?' she said, glancing at her shoulder bag in the passenger well.

'Someone called Finch,' Neil said.

'Put him on speakerphone.'

Finch's voice was tense with suppressed excitement. 'Cassie — you'd best get over to Kenny.'

Kensington — her old patch — Emma Hammond and Tasha had been dumped there.

'I'm just passing the Royal now,' she said. 'I can be there in under five minutes.'

'Warhorse checked with the service provider,' Finch explained. 'They've located Jodie's phone.'

Her heart skipped a beat. 'Where?'

She checked her mirror and performed a sweeping U-turn on Prescott Street, drove fast back up the hill and tore through the lights on amber, took a sharp right into Albany Road, braked hard, skidded into another right turn and Neil braced himself against the dashboard.

Hundreds of millions had been spent on the 'New Deal' regeneration project in Kensington until the money was stopped abruptly in 2010, but driving into its diseased heart, it was difficult to see where the money had been spent.

She killed the engine and flicked off the headlamps. It was still dark, the dawn still no more than a faint grey glimmer on the edges of her vision. The streetlights at this end of the terrace were out — in her days on the beat, drug dealers would shoot them out with air rifles.

'Got a torch in that boy scout kit?' she asked.

Neil opened a side pocket in his rucksack and handed over a slimline flashlight. 'Shouldn't you — you know — wait for backup?'

She threw him a side glance. 'And miss the chance of making the arrest?'

Neil opened his door at the same moment she popped her own door lever.

'Nuh-uh.' She held her hand out for the torch. 'You stay put.'

For once he didn't argue.

The house was boarded up, but the front door swung open to her touch. Inside, the building reeked of damp plaster and rotting wood. Sagging stairs led steeply into the darkness. It was bitterly cold. The previous night's rain had found its way in and a steady drip fell from the top of the house, landing every two seconds with a dull *thunk* onto the pulpy wood of the steps.

Rowan focused on the narrow hallway — her flashlight revealed one door on the left, one directly ahead. She knew these houses: front parlour and kitchen on the ground floor, two bedrooms upstairs. Many of them had been extended into the back yard to provide a bathroom and indoor toilet — luxuries the Victorian builders hadn't considered necessary for the working class.

Violent crime in Kensington was fifty per cent higher than the average for the rest of Liverpool, and despite her show of bravado for her brother's benefit, Rowan wasn't keen to add to the statistics. She listened, her senses hyper-acute in the oppressive dark. Heard nothing except the drip-drip of the roof leak.

She tried the room on her left, let the door swing wide. There were signs of a recent fire in the hearth, and the room was a little warmer than the hallway. Here, the smell of damp and rot was overlaid by a foetid, animal reek, and Rowan remembered with a shudder the rat in the alley, running heavy and warm over her feet.

Rowan pushed the door all the way back to the wall before stepping inside. Her heart thudding, she trained the torch beam on a tumble of blankets in the alcove on the far side of the fireplace. A couple of boxes had been opened flat and layered one on the other. The blankets, grey in the uncertain light, covered a hump of something. Rowan drew her Casco baton from her belt and called softly, 'Jodie?'

Her flashlight played on a mop of tousled hair. Blonde, dirty. Way too still.

She touched the shape under the blankets lightly with the tip of her toe. Nothing moved. *No. It can't end like this.*

'Jodie?' she said again.

Rowan leaned forward and pinched the blankets, tugging them gently back.

Afterwards, she blamed days of working double shifts with little sleep, the dream she'd had just before waking — adrenaline-fuelled clarity jostling with dreamlike surrealism.

The hair became golden in the torch light — Rowan felt it as a jolt of electrical charge — *Tasha?*

The figure stirred, grabbed a handful of blanket and yanked it back. 'Hey!'

She leapt a foot high and the light beam bounced off the walls, the ceiling, the floor. It was a man. He sat up, pulling the blankets around his shoulders and shielding his eyes with his free hand. 'Point that thing somewhere else, will you? And shut the friggin' door — you're letting the cold in.'

CHAPTER 32

Rowan dropped her brother at the railway station and made the journey down to the Dock Road in the rush hour, curs ing, swerving in and out of traffic, heading for Tasha's apart ment, her car tyres slashing through puddles flushed pink in the dawn light. She wasn't sure what she'd do when she got there — Tasha still wasn't answering her phone — she could be a thousand miles away. There was no sign of security at the gates to Tasha's dockside apartment, nobody she could flash a warrant card at to gain entry.

She buzzed Tasha's flat from the barrier, but she wasn't answering. Tried the landline. The answerphone kicked in. She threw her mobile onto the passenger seat in disgust, and looked over her shoulder, already reversing out onto the street.

Someone rapped hard on the bonnet of the car and she gave a violent start, swung back, hand on the gearstick, ready to jam it into first and run the bastard down.

He must have seen the glint in her eye, because he side-stepped, fast. 'You're Tasha's mate, aren't you?'

Rowan exhaled. The security guy.

'I thought you'd wanna know — she got back last night.'

* * *

Music was playing beyond the wide oak door of Tasha's apartment. Something raucous and raw. She knocked at the door and the music was cut off.

Rowan looked into the small security camera above the doorway and gave an encouraging smile. Abruptly the singer's voice growled from the speakers again.

'Tasha, answer the door — it's me, Cassie,' she shouted over the noise.

The singer's voice grated on like an angry saw, but Rowan sensed her friend's presence behind the door and pressed her palm against the gleaming wood.

'Open the door, Tasha,' she said, more softly this time. 'Please?' She felt the vibration of sound in her fingertips, but the door remained closed. Frustrated, she slammed the door with the heel of her hand.

'Listen to me: he's taken someone else. Her name is Jodie Pickersgill. We had a tip-off she might be in a squat in Kensington.'

The collision of dream and reality flooded her mind; she saw again the figure under the blankets as it morphed from Jodie to Tasha, and her body vibrated with the aftershock.

The song ended on a low sob.

'I saw this — body — lying under shit-stained blankets.' She spoke into the silence, her voice trembling with emotion. 'I thought it was you, Tasha. For one crazy, horrible moment the two of you switched places and I thought it was *you*.'

Nothing.

'Damn it, Tasha, open the DOOR,' she yelled.

As she was on the point of giving up, a shuffle, the sound of locks turning and a chain being rattled off its stays, and Tasha stood in the doorway.

'Was it her?' She was wearing loose combats and a baggy sweater as if to disguise her figure, and her hair looked greasy and unwashed. Rowan saw the horror of her ordeal in Tasha's pallor and in the slump of her shoulders.

'The girl in the house,' Tasha said. 'Was it Jodie?'

'No,' Rowan said, edging her foot into the gap between door and frame. 'No, it was nothing — a false alarm. We haven't found her yet.'

Tasha folded her arms across her chest, hugging herself, and for a half minute she seemed lost in thought. Just when Rowan was thinking she would have to say something, Tasha stirred and looked at her. She seemed surprised to see her still in the hallway.

'You'd better come in.'

Rowan stepped inside and her breath caught in her throat. Canvases and sketch pads, scrap paper pinned to the walls, charcoal, pencil, ink, acrylics, all of the same subject: a man. His sandy hair waxed into peaks. Straight, dark eyebrows and startling eyes. They glared out of every picture full of fury and hate. In some, only the eyes were clearly drawn, the pale blue-green of the irises flecked with fiery reds and oranges. It made her think of solar flares and volcanoes, of danger and sudden violence.

'Is this . . . ?' she whispered.

Tasha nodded jerkily, and Rowan stared at the pictures, trying to match them to her own fuzzy impression of the shrouded figure she had chased through the fog, the man she had studied though hours of CCTV recordings. There was something there — something that stirred the muddy waters of her memory, but she really hadn't got a good look at him. Could she swear that this was the man she brought down in the freight yard ten days ago? She didn't need to look any further than the frightened look on Tasha's face — it was the Furman.

It shouldn't have surprised her, but it did. He looked . . . ordinary. Except for those extraordinary eyes. In the acrylic paintings they were a minty blue-green that reminded her of Van Gogh self-portraits, Mediterranean seascapes. And madness.

Tasha picked up one of the pencil drawings. It rattled in her fingers and she clenched it into a ball in her fist. 'It's the only way I can stop the shaking,' she said, with a tremulous laugh.

'When did you *do* all this?' Rowan turned full circle: the walls, sofa, kitchen work surfaces and window ledges were buried under images of the man.

Tasha smiled weakly. 'I haven't been sleeping.'

Rowan reached out to touch her, but Tasha pulled away, as if human contact would rob her of the last remnants of self-control. 'Don't,' she whispered. 'Please, please, don't.'

For a while, the only sound was Tasha's breathing. She frowned, as if it required her full concentration — as if she was learning to breathe all over again. 'When he took me into that place,' she said, 'it was so *dark*. I couldn't see. I thought—' She broke off, and her fingers travelled up to trace the star-shaped scar on her right temple. 'I thought I was blind, Cassie.'

Rowan had visited Tasha in hospital after the attack last September. She was lying in bed; both eyes were bandaged. Tasha, who saw everything in colour — even mood had shades and tones and textures — lay still and pale in a white gown on white sheets in a plain white hospital room, and her terror of losing her sight seemed to suck air and colour out of the place.

'Why didn't you call me?' Rowan said. 'Why didn't you answer my calls? I could have helped, Tasha.'

Tasha frowned, tilting her head on one side, as if Rowan's voice came to her from a great distance, and slowly she came back to herself. 'No one can help me.'

Rowan wanted to tell her that she was wrong, that all she needed was time, that everything would come out right: she had lied easily to social services and Neil's school, to her bosses and colleagues and even to the creeps who tried to buy her body on Operation Kerbwatch, but the words stuck in her throat. She couldn't bring herself to tell her friend one soothing little lie.

Tasha shook her head. 'I keep hearing his voice — "*Is this how you like it?*"' Her voice took on a harsh, breathless rasp, and Rowan gave an involuntary shudder. Emma Hammond had said exactly the same thing.

'I thought if I got away, I could get him out of my head.' She covered her ears. 'But I can still hear his voice. I can smell him on my clothes, on my skin—' She fixed her gaze on Rowan, her eyes wide with fright. 'Cassie, it's like he's still watching me.'

Thinking about the palm print on her kitchen window, Tasha's jacket, the break-in to her car, Rowan felt an answering shimmer of fear.

Tasha opened her hand and stared at the tight ball of paper in her palm with faint horror. 'I didn't mean to lie to you, Cassie.' She groaned, letting the balled-up paper fall and suddenly gave a choked, wet laugh.

'How bloody stupid! Of *course* I meant to lie to you — I told you explicitly that I'd given up sex work.' She examined her paint-stained hands. 'I'm trying to tell you that I let myself down, and I lied to you, but I *swear* I didn't mean to hurt you.'

'Okay, you lied. So what?' Rowan forced back tears. 'D'you think I care? Did you think I'd judge you?'

The intensity of Tasha's gaze was disconcerting. 'Ask me that again tomorrow.'

Tomorrow? Rowan took in the acrylics and charcoal drawings and pencil sketches and had a flash of recognition, feeling it like a spasm in her gut. *Yes, it's the Furman all right.* And if his image had this effect on her, then for Tasha this place must be like waking from a bad dream into a nightmare.

Suddenly afraid for her friend, she said, 'Tasha — whatever he did to you, don't let him—'

Tasha read her perfectly, as she always did. 'I'm not planning anything dramatic, Cassie. Thing is—' She took a breath, seemed to struggle with what she had to say. 'The thing is,' she said, with a long sigh, 'the damage is already done.'

'I'm going to catch this fucker,' Rowan said, her voice hard. 'And when I catch him, I'll rip his frigging lungs out.'

Tasha smiled. 'You should do that. For yourself and Emma and Jodie. But I don't deserve your loyalty, Cassie. I've — I've done things I can't take back.'

'I told you,' Rowan said, holding her gaze, trying to fathom the sadness in it. 'I don't care.'

Tasha crossed to the window and looked at the view over the Liver Buildings and beyond, the Mersey River, winking steely blue in the pale winter light.

'Help me,' Rowan said.

A minute of silence passed.

'Help . . . ?' Tasha said at last, and it seemed at once a question and a plea. Tasha sketched something quickly on the window glass and Rowan knew it was another likeness of the man who raped her. Then she turned, clasping her arms tight across her breasts. 'What do you want me to do?'

CHAPTER 33

DCI Warman's door stood open. She was working at her computer, surrounded by neat stacks of paperwork, and she had the self-satisfied air of a woman who had completed half a day's work in half a morning.

'You missed the briefing.' Her gaze remained fixed on her computer screen while her fingers moved with eerie efficiency over the keyboard.

'I was following a lead,' Rowan said, holding up the buff card folder in her hand as if that would be sufficient proof that she hadn't been slacking.

'Like the "lead" that took you to the Arnott Hotel last night?'

Rowan's stomach did a flip. Had Simon Carstairs put in a complaint? She was well enough rehearsed in the tricks of interrogation to know that a vague question could often coerce the guilty into revealing far more of themselves than a direct one, so she said nothing.

'Do you know why we don't get on, Constable Rowan?' Warman said. 'You have no respect for protocols and proper process. You are not a team player.'

Rowan experienced a fleeting moment of guilt, before her defence mechanism switched in, turning to attack. She wanted to ask if six months pulling night shifts standing on street corners in the freezing cold dressed like a hooker counted as teamwork. But the folder she held in her hand would be of no earthly use without Warman's sanction, so she did what Ian Chan was always advising her to do, and kept her mouth shut.

'In your favour,' Warman added, 'you have enthusiasm.'

Rowan blinked. It was a surprise to hear that Warman thought she had anything going in her favour.

'But you need to learn when to rein it in,' Warman went on. 'And the occasional application of tact would not go amiss.'

'Ma'am,' Rowan said, more stunned than chastened.

Warman slid a file from the foot-high stack on her desk. 'Stills from Liver Street Car Park.'

'They found the Lexus?'

Warman tapped the cover with one bony finger. 'You had no authority to instruct Hayes to search the CCTV recordings.'

'All I did was tell him that Jodie's boyfriend drives a Lexus IS. He made the decision to search the recordings.'

Warman fixed her with her grey stare. 'Protocols and proper process, Cassie.'

Rowan nodded. She had to admit, she'd played fast and loose with both.

Satisfied, Warman said, 'We have a Lexus IS with a man driving.' She continued tapping the file. 'He arrived at fifteen thirty and left shortly after seventeen thirty.'

'He was trawling for *two hours*?' Rowan's mind raced. 'Maybe he went into John Lewis to keep out of the way of the car park security patrols. I could check — see if they got him on their CCTVs.'

'Finch is taking care of that,' Warman said, and Rowan heard Ian Chan's admonishment: *You haven't got the monopoly on common sense, sweetheart.*

Her attention was drawn again to the cover of the file, to the maddening tap of Warman's finger. 'And the car?'

Finally, Warman opened the file and rotated the picture for Rowan to see. The number plates were unreadable, and the driver wore a baseball cap pulled low over his eyes.

'As you see,' Warman said. She closed the file and placed it with forensic precision on top of the nearest stack. 'Now. What kept you from the morning briefing?'

Rowan squared her shoulders. 'I was on my way here when I got the shout that we had a location on Jodie's phone.'

'Finch reported on your behalf.' Her tone was so dry Rowan could practically hear autumn leaves rustling. 'Your detour does not, however, account for the ninety minutes it's taken you to finally get here.'

Rowan paused; she had to pitch this right.

'I got to thinking, if we had a decent e-fit of the abductor, we might get somewhere. Emma and Penny Kominski weren't much help . . .' Rowan took a breath. 'But there is one victim who wasn't even asked to provide a description.'

Warman threw up her hands. '*Really*, Cassie — not Tasha *again*?'

Rowan abandoned her carefully prepared speech about Tasha's intelligence, reliability and observational powers. 'She's good — an art student — she only works the street to put herself through her studies,' she blurted. *For God's sake, Cassie, just stick to the script.* She took a breath. 'That's where I've been this morning.'

Warman's nostrils flared. 'While it's good to know she's finally surfaced, I cannot see how this helps us to find Jodie.'

Rowan opened her folder.

'I've been working on an e-fit with her.' Ian Chan had done the tech side — a personal favour to Rowan. One of the scores of favours she owed him.

'If this doesn't convince you, boss, I promise I won't say another word on the subject,' she said, holding the sheet of paper up.

Warman raised her finger but seemed to check herself. Maybe it was because Rowan had called her 'boss', instead of 'ma'am', or maybe she thought it was worth a look on the promise of a let-up in Rowan's crusade. At first, she gave the sheet no more than a glance, then she leaned across the desk and plucked it from Rowan's hand. Her expression changed from irritable boredom to consternation, to genuine surprise. Then she laughed.

'This' — she held the sheet between thumb and forefinger — 'is Roy Wicks.' She was right. The fat face, the small eyes, the fleshy mouth. It was an unflattering but accurate portrait of Roy Wicks.

Rowan waited for her to slide the image onto her desk.

'Yes, ma'am. I asked Tasha to give the tech a description of the officer who came to the hospital to question her about the attack.'

The smile on Warman's face faded.

'Like I said, ma'am — she's good.'

'This' — Rowan set down a pencil sketch of Tasha's tormentor — 'is the Furman.'

CHAPTER 34

Warman went to the local TV news teams with Tasha's sketch of her abductor, and by midday, the emergency number was jammed. Overspill was diverted to the CID office and there were rumours that a separate incident room was about to be set up.

DCI Warman called an impromptu briefing as people filtered in for lunch at around one thirty. The phones continued to ring, some were picked up, and some weren't. Those who had bought food tucked in, keeping a weather eye on Pat Warman. For the present, she was in discussion with one of the clerical staff who had brought her a sheaf of papers.

Rowan finished her last call. Warman had sent her to show the sketch to Emma, then drafted her in to answer phones. Rowan couldn't blame her: she had performed the switcheroo with the two sketches with a flourish that smacked of spiteful glee. During the course of the morning, she had drunk enough sludgy coffee to silt up the Mersey estuary, but she still struggled to stay awake. The high-octane caffeine intake and lack of sleep created a jittery unreality, where noises jarred and waking dreams flashed across her retinas.

Warman finished her discussion and turned to face the room. A moment later she had silence. 'A hundred and twenty calls so far,' she said, placing the stack of papers on the table in front of her. 'A good fifty in response to the sketch that went out this morning.'

'Bloody hell,' Wicks complained. 'Every bint who's had some bloke look at her funny — how're we supposed to follow up on that lot?'

The DCI glared at him. 'What did you say, DC Wicks?'

Wicks gave her a look of wide-eyed innocence. 'I said even a *hint* some bloke's—'

'These are potential witnesses,' Warman cut in. 'They could provide valuable leads.'

Wicks ran his tongue over his teeth and folded his arms.

'Since we've had fifty calls from an appeal on lunchtime news, we can expect a lot more when the sketch makes the late edition of the *Echo*, and the *Mersey Daily* tomorrow,' Warman said. 'I'm getting more staff allocation on this but in the meantime, I do not want a foul-up because someone hasn't taken a complaint seriously — clear?'

She got a murmur of acquiescence from the room, and scowled at Wicks until he said, 'Yes, boss.'

'Cassie, what did Emma Hammond make of the sketch?'

Rowan had visited Emma at home. It had taken half an hour of coaxing to persuade her even to look at it.

'She couldn't be sure,' Rowan said. 'The fog, the hat and scarf — she didn't see much of him, so—'

'Okay, we rule her out,' Warman said.

'But Tasha's description of a deep echoing space, the smell of stagnant water, the steps down — they all match Emma's story.'

'Granted,' Warman said.

'What does Penny Kominski say?' Rowan asked.

'The Met are trying to track her down — she's taken a holiday. However—' Warman looked around the room to make sure she had their full attention. 'Calls to the hotline have thrown up a name: Jake Osbourne. Sales rep in security systems. So far, six female clients from Liverpool to North Wales have called in, identifying him from the sketch.'

Rowan had been drooping by this time, but now she sat up, her scalp tingling, and an excited murmur went around the gathering . . .

'*However*,' Warman went on, 'Mr Osbourne has no criminal record, he hasn't been out of the country, and since Emma is looking a bit shaky, we're relying on Tasha's word — and that could be risky. I do *not* want this to turn into a witch hunt. So, we will not approach Mr Osbourne until we have more. I need a tactful volunteer to interview Osbourne's clients.'

'I'll do it, boss.'

Roy Wicks? A few at the front of the room turned around to be sure they hadn't made a mistake. Even Warman raised her eyebrows.

'The Plods have got the canvas covered,' he said. 'I feel like a spare part wandering around with a clipboard. I'll have a chat with them.'

Warman thought about it for a second, then nodded. 'Tactful,' she repeated, raising a bony finger to emphasise the point.

Wicks was a picture of innocence.

'Mr Osbourne's boss also phoned in,' Warman said.

Glances were exchanged: if the man's boss phoned in, there had to be a good reason.

'Mr Osbourne hasn't shown up for work since Tuesday afternoon.'

Rowan shifted in her seat. *Send me,* she willed Warman.

Warman's gaze flitted to her, then away.

'Osbourne is seeing an analyst, apparently. I'll find out what I can when I talk to his boss — she's agreed to come in. Cassie,' she said, with the air of someone throwing a dog a bone. 'Talk to the analyst — sound him out — see what he has to say for himself.'

Tasks allocated, Warman set a time for the evening debrief and left them to it.

There was a breathless silence until they heard the fire doors along the corridor swing shut, then laughter broke out in the incident room and someone threw a sheet of balled-up paper at Wicks. It hit him squarely on the back of the head.

'Oy!' he yelled.

Someone shot a hand up. 'I'll do it, boss!'

Wicks smirked lazily. 'If you wanted it, all you had to do was speak up.'

Rowan shook her head. 'You really know you need a good night's sleep when you're beaten to the buzzer by Roy Wicks.'

As she walked past Finch's desk, he said, 'Good that she gave you the analyst to follow up, Cass,' he said.

'Finch,' she said, 'How the hell did you get into CID when you think so well of everyone?' Finch's smooth brow furrowed.

'She's sent me to chase a "no comment" — that's all you'll ever get from a bloody shrink.'

He shrugged, and she said, 'How're you getting on with the John Lewis CCTV images?'

'I got nothing,' he said.

'What?' Rowan exclaimed. 'We *know* Jodie walked through the store.'

He blushed, flustered. 'We got a few of *her*. When I said nothing, I meant nothing, you know, *useful*.'

She curbed an impulse to shake him by the scruff of the neck. 'So what *did* you get? The not-useful stuff, I mean.'

'A few of her smiling at a man who might be our man. But honest to God, Cassie, he must know the angle of every camera in the shop — we haven't got his face on any of them.'

Rowan gazed at him, feeling a fresh tingle of excitement running from her scalp to her fingertips.

'What?' he said.

'The guy who took Jodie disabled the cameras in the car park. He's security aware. Osbourne sells security systems. That can't be a coincidence, can it?'

Finch glanced over his shoulder, but Wicks was stuffing his face with fish and chips and took no interest in their

conversation. 'The boss said she doesn't want Osbourne contacted till she knows the details.'

'Who said anything about contacting him?' she said.
'I'm going to see his therapist.'

'I thought you said therapists were uncooperative.'

He looked so confused that she smiled. 'Even a "no
comment" can tell you something, Finch.'

CHAPTER 35

Thursday evening

You can hardly hear yourself think over the din of voices demanding answers — TV, radio, newspapers, Instagrammers, bloggers and Twitterers — wanting to know what kind of monster this is. Because surely only a 'monster' could do what's been done to these women? What utter bullshit. What they're really afraid of is the monster coiled inside their own hearts. They've leashed their rage, sublimating their lust into an officious anxiety for their wives and daughters. But the only real difference between them and me is I have the courage to act.

* * *

At six fifteen, Rowan approached the glass doors of Alan Palmer's office building for the second time. The infra-red sensors triggered the mechanism and the doors swept open with barely a sound. It was cold — the forecast was for frost — and Rowan felt it all the more for being exhausted.

Lara, the receptionist, was still on duty, but was packing up for the night by the look of it. She did a double take and tucked her hair behind one ear, then flicked it free again with an irritated frown.

'He hasn't been back, Constable Rowan,' she said, pre-empting her question. 'Did you try him at home?'

'Tried it, came up empty.' Apparently, she had just missed the therapist at lunchtime. Since then, between taking dozens of calls redirected from the hotline, she had trekked out to his home address and the NHS clinic, left messages on his office answerphone, and now she had come full circle. She pressed her fingers to her temples. 'You wouldn't have his mobile number, would you?'

Lara lifted one shoulder. 'Sorry.'

The weariness Rowan had been battling all day suddenly threatened to overwhelm her. She leaned heavily on the cold marble counter and closed her eyes for a second. An image of Tasha's abused body flashed behind her eyelids and the floor seemed to rock under her feet. She snapped her eyes open and took a few breaths.

'He'll be in first thing,' Lara said with a sympathetic look.

It rankled with Rowan that she would have to return to the day's final debrief with nothing to say, but she couldn't see any other option. She thanked Lara and turned away, bracing her back against the counter before moving off into the great marble expanse which seemed to tilt ever so slightly at the edges of her vision, like the horizon seen from the prow of a ship. Steadying herself, she noticed for the first time a camera, pointing from the doors towards the reception island. A three-sixty-degree scan of the foyer located two more, one of which was trained on the doors themselves.

If I could get footage of Jake Osbourne — compare it with the CCTV recordings of the Albert Dock, maybe get a gait analysis done—

But no. Osbourne hadn't even been ruled in as a suspect — Warman would have a fit. Despite the arguments against it, Rowan said, 'I don't suppose . . .'

'What?' The eagerness to help in Lara's voice encouraged her.

'You wouldn't know Doctor Palmer's patients by sight, would you?'

Lara tossed a skein of glossy hair over her shoulder. 'I know *all* the regular visitors to Quorum House,' she said. 'I've got a very good memory for faces.'

'He'd be about five-ten, sandy hair, late twenties or early thirties—' Rowan tried to visualise Tasha's sketches, cursing herself for not having brought a copy with her. In every one of them, it was the eyes you saw first, the eyes that held you.

Lara was staring at her and Rowan realised she must have flipped out for a second. 'Blue eyes,' she finished. 'Very intense.'

'Oh, that'll be Mr Osbourne.' No hesitation.

Rowan felt a prickle of excitement raise the hairs on the back of her neck. 'Wow, you *have* got a good memory for faces,' she said. Shameless flattery was a sure-fire way to gain a witness's confidence. 'Mr Osbourne. You're sure?'

'It's the eyes.' Lara leaned forward, folding her manicured hands in front of her on the counter, her bracelet clacking against the marble. 'He's normally here three or four days a week.'

The doors swished open, and a draught of icy air caught the back of Rowan's neck.

Lara straightened up. 'Here he is now.'

Rowan swung to face the doors, her heart beating fast.

'Mr Palmer — not Mr Osbourne,' the receptionist added, apologetic.

Rowan exhaled softly, forcing the tension from her shoulders, wondering what she would have done if it *had* been Osbourne.

'Mr Palmer—' Lara called. Then, to Rowan, whispering, 'He doesn't like being called "doctor".'

He didn't even break stride. 'Sorry, Lara, I'm in a hurry.' He kept a diagonal course for the lifts.

Rowan stepped forward. 'Police, Mr Palmer.'

He turned to look at her. Palmer was tallish, mid-thirties, brown hair, broad in the chest, athletic. She had expected someone older, someone more comfortable in his own skin

— Alan Palmer looked out of sorts with himself and the world. He was well dressed — a long black overcoat, good leather shoes, and a leather shoulder bag worn cross-wise. He looked like he'd walked a distance: cold air and good health radiated from him almost as strongly as the dull rage that showed in the bunched muscles of his neck and the set of his jaw.

Rowan took out her warrant card and held it up for him. He stayed put, his dark eyes appraising, faintly hostile.

'Detective Constable Rowan,' she said, holding her ground.

'What can I do for you, Constable Rowan?'

'Perhaps we should talk in your office, sir.'

* * *

It seemed he took her literally — didn't speak a word to her in the lift or on the short walk down the corridor — didn't so much as look at her.

In his consulting room, he went directly to a bank of three filing cabinets and unlocked the middle one. 'Are you going to tell me the reason for your visit or are the police using free association as an interrogation tool, these days?'

Rowan's irritation with the man was fast being displaced by a definite and solid dislike.

Rowan didn't get to see her father much in her child-hood: he worked split shifts in his black cab — early mornings and late nights, sleeping during the day — to keep his three children. He'd passed little advice on to her, trusting Cassie's moral and social instruction to her mother. In her first month as a uniformed officer, Cassie Rowan was hurt in a stabbing that nearly put an end to her career. She was back on the job after six weeks. But she got so jittery as the time got close for her to set off for work, she would throw up. This went on for a month. Her mother fussed, told her to find a safer way to earn a living; her brothers looked unhappily at one another and said nothing.

Then one night her father offered her a lift into work. He pulled up fifty yards from the police station and left the engine running, the 'for hire' light turned off. The throaty rattle of the diesel engine made her feel safe in a way she couldn't explain.

'I've been driving a cab in this city for nigh on twenty years,' he'd said, turning to her without preliminary. 'I've been chauffeur to drunks, medical emergencies, pimps, prostitutes, and lads whose idea of Saturday night action is to kick someone's head in. I've been threatened so many times I've lost count.'

She'd stared at her father, shocked. In those days, when she was barely out of her teens and more naïve than she cared to admit, it was almost unthinkable that anyone would dare give her dad a hard time.

'The most important thing I learned in all those years is this,' he said. 'If you go out expecting trouble, you're sure to find it.'

He had meant those dangerous situations she faced every day on the beat, but it applied just as much to occasions like this, when a small measure of forbearance and tact could make the difference between co-operation and running smack into a brick wall of sullen obstinacy.

'You have a patient by the name of Jake Osbourne, sir,' she said, maintaining a neutral tone.

Palmer was riffling through his files. He finally extracted a bundle and snapped the drawer shut. 'Do I?'

'According to our sources.'

He didn't answer directly, but he did look at her. '"Sources"? What "sources"?'

'I'm not at liberty to say, sir. What can you tell me about Mr Osbourne?'

Palmer placed the folders he had just extracted face down on the filing cabinet. His gaze never left hers.

'He's my patient. Beyond that' — he paused, emphasising the repetition of her own professional get-out — 'I'm not at liberty to say.'

Expect trouble, you'll find it, expect co-operation, maybe you get that, too. She tried again: 'A young woman is missing, Mr Palmer. Your client is—' She couldn't say, *Your client is our prime suspect* — that would be way off the mark. *Your client looks like someone we want to interview?* Lame. *Mr Osbourne's name has come up.* Lamer.

'We'd like to interview him.'

'In what context?' Palmer waved a hand, dismissing any reply before she'd even got started. 'Never mind — you're not at liberty — but I'm not sure what you want from me.'

She frowned, her thought processes limping behind his by a couple of sentences. *You're too tired for this, Cassie.*

He leaned with his elbow on the filing cabinet, as if her dullness made him weary. 'I assume the police can find an address and phone number without having to consult someone like me. So precisely what *do* you want, Constable? Insights?'

Tired or not, Rowan still recognized contempt when she saw it. 'There's a rapist on the loose in the city,' she said, her voice tight with anger. 'I thought maybe — being in a *caring* profession — you might want to help us out.'

He leaned off the cabinet. 'You're telling me that you think my client is a rapist?'

'No.' *For God's sake, Cassie.* 'I'm just asking for your impressions of the man.'

'You must know that what passes between a therapist and his patients is confidential.'

Pompous prick. 'Sanctity of the confessional, Doctor?'

Palmer's face darkened. 'I'm not a religious man. But there is a kind of sanctity in the trust people place in me. If I didn't respect that trust, I couldn't do my job.'

You're sleep-deprived, caffeine-jagged, she told herself: *Go home, sleep it off, come back in the morning.*

She'd made up her mind to do just that, so it came as a surprise to hear herself say: 'Don't you watch the news? Don't you *know* what's going on in this city? Your client has been named by six different women from a sketch of an abductor and rapist.'

199

Too much — she'd said too much.

In his line of work, Palmer must be used to hiding his emotions, but Rowan saw doubt cloud his expression. '*Six* victims have identified Jake Osbourne as a rapist?'

Is that what you're saying Cassie? Because the women who identified Osbourne were clients, not victims. She closed her eyes for a second, trying to clear the fog in her brain. 'No. They weren't victims — it's just — these women thought they maybe recognized the man in the sketch.'

He seemed genuinely confused. 'Constable, you're not making any sense.'

She looked away, trying to compose her thoughts. It had already been dark for nearly two hours and the larger of the two windows in the consulting room was a blank screen on which their shapes reflected faintly, like ghosts loosely tethered to their earthly forms. Rowan swayed for a moment, disorientated, thought of apologising, of taking one last shot at explaining, but her exhaustion, her resentment at her wasted journeys somehow became Palmer's fault. Her stomach burned with acid and her head ached, and somewhere deep in her chest, she felt a deeper, unsatisfied rage.

To hell with it. And to hell with you, Palmer.

She took a card from her jacket pocket and placed it on top of a bundle of files on the cabinet. 'In case, by some miracle, you grow a conscience and decide you want to help.'

CHAPTER 36

Rowan slept like the dead from ten p.m. to six a.m., but if anything, she felt worse on eight hours sleep than she had on the two she'd scraped by on the previous night.

Neil's chipper good humour only made it worse. He bounced into the kitchen at six thirty in an obscenely good mood, shook four Weetabix from the pack while the kettle boiled, and was slurping though his third milk-soaked biscuit when Rowan finally snapped.

'You're the only person I know who can make noise eating soggy Weetabix.'

Neil cocked an eyebrow at her. 'You should hear what I can do with toast and peanut butter.'

The mention of peanut butter made her stomach roil in protest and Rowan stood quickly, tipping the last of her cereal into the bin.

'Must be a hell of a hangover,' Neil said, between mouthfuls.

'I wish it was — at least I'd know I had a good time last night.'

He shoved his bowl aside and pushed his chair back with a squeal that sent a bolt of pain from the base of Rowan's backbone to the top of her skull.

'What the hell are you doing up so early?'

For a split second, he looked hurt, then he reverted to teenaged contempt. 'I suppose you've forgotten Alex is coming.'

Damn, damn, damn. She had. Forgotten it was Friday, forgotten Alex was coming, forgotten the damn wedding, and the damn dress she was supposed to buy to attend the damn wedding.

'He's due into Manchester at four o'clock.'

Rowan clenched her jaw. Neil didn't need to know that their brother's last call had come from London, that he had been in the country since Tuesday: four whole days of avoiding coming home.

'So,' Neil said, 'are you going to meet him?'

'Did he ask me to?'

'No, but—'

'He'll hire a car.'

'Brilliant,' Neil said. '*He* comes all the way from New York, and *you* can't be bothered to drive thirty-five miles.'

'I'm working, Neil.'

'You're always bloody working,' he muttered, slathering his toast with peanut butter in what, to her offended senses, seemed like an act of spite.

'Anyway, why would he want a lift in my old banger?'

'Because you're his sister,' he yelled. 'You're supposed to give a shit!'

'Like Alex does?'

'What the hell does that mean?'

If she'd stayed she would have told Neil exactly how much big brother Alex cared: that he'd lied to them both, avoided them — no doubt having a fine time in London. But that would hurt her kid brother in ways that might never heal, so she took the coward's way out and fled to the car.

The promised frost lay thick on the ground and glittered like fish scales on the windows of her car. Even the plastic sheeting on the broken side-window was clouded with crystals. It was still early, and fully dark, but the street thrummed to the sound of engines warming up. Against this, an insistent scratch-scratch-scratch, like fingernails on sandpaper. Rowan sighed and opened the driver's door: *Get the rear screen heater on, then tackle the windscreen.* She slid behind the wheel.

As she dumped her handbag in the passenger well, she saw something on the passenger seat. A thumb drive. Neil's missing thumb drive.

Rowan felt her hackles rise. She gripped the steering wheel, her heart rattling her rib cage, and forced herself to look in the mirror, expecting to see the man in Tasha's sketch staring back at her. Waiting for his arm to snake around the back of the seat, for his taser to spark blue light in the dark. She saw only her own frightened face staring back at her in the rear-view, her breath making smoke signals of distress.

She let out a slow, calming breath and turned to check behind the seat. Nobody hiding, nobody waiting to pounce.

Then he was at the door, flipping the door handle, his face distorted by the plastic sheeting on the damaged passenger window.

She froze, her heart clamouring in her throat.

'Come on, Cassie — open up!'

Neil. It was Neil.

'For God's sake, Neil!' She leaned across the seat to lift the lock pin.

He opened the door, bending at the waist to talk to her, his hands gripping his knees.

'Alex just rang.' He was smiling, excited, transformed from a surly youth into a happy boy again.

So that's why he was up early: he was expecting a call. Alex was going to some lengths to give the lie credibility — *no doubt he'd told Neil he was just about to board his flight. Bastard.* With the adrenalin still rushing through her veins, Rowan's fear and anger got tangled up. 'What the hell does he want at this hour?'

The puzzled hurt on her brother's face made her feel horrible.

'Sorry.' She closed her eyes, tried to catch up with Neil's latest mood change, to sound pleased. 'I had a crappy night. What did he say?'

'He says if you give me thirty, I can get some food in — he'll pay you back later.' His voice was flat — she'd managed to suck the fun out of it for him. *Nice one, Cassie. He sees Alex, what — three, four times a year?*

But she couldn't help thinking, as she dug in her purse for the cash, that this was typical of Alex's contribution to his brother's upbringing: chicken in a bucket and a promise to pay back later.

As he leaned inside to take the money, Neil saw the thumb drive. 'Woah, you found it!'

She slapped his hand away. 'Don't touch it.'

He looked at her like she was mad. 'Well, I'm not leaving it in this old skip — it's got my thrash metal compilation on it.'

'Neil—'

'*What?*'

'It wasn't there last night.'

'So?'

'So now, it is.'

'Call the Vatican — it's a miracle.'

She pressed the money into his hand and shoved him back. 'Not a miracle, Neil — a message.'

CHAPTER 37

When Alan Palmer needed to think, he walked. It was 6.45 a.m., the dawn was still an hour away and frost glistened on the walls and hedges of the narrow front gardens, pinkish in the glow of the streetlights. In the side streets it lay so thick that it ridged like trammelled snow under car tyres. He went carefully at first, avoiding patches of slick ice, keeping to the pristine white stretches, the frost crystals whispering under the soles of his shoes.

At Parliament Street he took the wide curve of road left, the Anglican cathedral a solid presence at his back; ahead the steep hill down to Queens Dock. A quick dogleg right and he was on the final stretch, the whiff of seaweed from the bay, the tugboat reek of diesel in his nostrils, the river air bitingly cold. From this vantage point the wide sweep of road displayed a postcard vista of the Liverpool skyline, and the clock towers of the Liver Buildings a mile distant, synchronised at seven fifteen, seemed to gleam phosphorescent in the feeble winter pre-dawn.

The previous evening, he had gone directly from his encounter with Rowan to dinner with Karl Atherton. The intention had been that they would agree strategy on Dylan Corbie; he had a regular Friday session, and this would be the first time they had met since his explosive exit on Wednesday. But he had hardly touched on Dylan's revelations about his mother.

Instead, over dinner, he had railed against Constable Rowan, infuriated by her patronizing tone, her pompousness: 'Not at liberty to say', her sarcastic comparison of analysis as confessional, psychoanalyst as priest.

Karl ate his meal thoughtfully, taking an occasional sip of wine, with little more than a glance or a nod to encourage Palmer to continue. But he listened with quiet attention, and slowly, by degrees, Palmer was able to listen to himself. Embarrassed, he came to the realisation that his anger — all his indignant bluster — was not against Constable Rowan at all. At last, he fell silent.

Atherton peered at him from under his eyebrows, a question on his face.

'Bad day,' Palmer said, feeling foolish.

'Hmm . . .'

Palmer looked into his friend's eyes. They might not be as sharp as when they had first met over twenty years before, but they still saw a lot. He sighed. 'Elspeth has filed for divorce.'

Atherton had been an analyst for too long to show surprise. He waited in sympathetic silence for Palmer to say what he had been building up to all night.

'She's already put in the papers.' He swallowed, tasting bitterness at the back of his throat. 'She wants sole custody.'

'And you're angry,' Atherton said, when he lapsed into silence.

'I'm angry and hurt and helpless and terrified. In all that's happened in the last six months, only Lucy kept me sane.' He rubbed a hand over his face, 'I know I've lost Elspeth — I can accept that. But I don't know what I'll do if I lose Lucy.'

Karl left him with his thoughts for a good while before asking, 'And where does Constable Rowan fit in?'

As usual, Karl had got to the heart of the matter. After a sleepless night, in terror of losing his daughter, he could admit that he had been ready to tear into anyone who crossed his path. When she'd asked about Osbourne, he might have explained his position gently and with professional courtesy. Instead, he had met Constable Rowan with head down and teeth bared; he had been overbearing, boorish, bullying and dismissive.

* * *

During the sleepless hours, Palmer had thought a lot about Jake Osbourne. It was just ten days since he'd taken the man on as a patient; in analytical terms, they had barely got past the equivalent of an introductory handshake. But Palmer had formed a sense of a deeply ambivalent and conflicted individual, often agitated, speaking fast and loud, as if he was afraid of being interrupted, but equally prone to slide into deep, troubled silences.

In the consultation room, Osbourne was often restless, moving from one piece of furniture to the next, straightening a picture, staring out onto the Mersey for a few seconds, before resuming his pacing.

He talked about himself only in terms of sales records, bonuses and strategies for persuading clients to buy.

'The salesman's art,' he had said, 'is the art of seduction. While you're giving the punter the blether — remarking on the decor, the layout, going into raptures about their crappy choice of art — you're sussing out the place, finding the weak spots, the keys left lying, the handbag perched on the kitchen table, the patio doors left on the snick — and then there's the cat-flap. God, I do love a cat-flap.'

He would turn away any attempt to talk about family or feelings, but Palmer sensed an anger and hurt, and aching loneliness behind the barrage of performance stats and category prizes and bonuses earned. His boastfulness sometimes had the tone of a small boy overwhelmed by feelings of inferiority yet struggling to find a way to assert his independence and sense of worth.

Palmer hadn't told Constable Rowan that Osbourne had an appointment with him this morning, but he reasoned that she must have Jake's work and home addresses, his phone number and car registration — it wasn't his place to do her job for her. He paused. *Am I being unfair to her again?* He had been rude and aggressive, but she had given a garbled account of why she wanted to speak to Osbourne, and he knew as well as the next man how unreliable e-fits were. The women — none of whom had been victims of the rapist — had identified a man who looked like a lot of other men in their late twenties. Osbourne had that kind of face.

He couldn't betray his client's privacy or jeopardise the psychotherapeutic relationship — the consequences could be devastating. Palmer increased his pace as he approached the glistening water of Albert Dock, unwilling to follow a train of thought that would lead back to the beginning of the year, and a mistake he hoped never to repeat.

That which we refuse to think about, we are doomed to repeat. The voice in his head was an approximation of Karl Atherton's measured tones.

Amy Sefton, Osbourne's previous analyst, had provided no history, and no analytic insights, pleading ill-health for the lack of case notes. Osbourne had been advised, she said, to seek help by his GP, 'To come to terms with the natural conflicts arising from significant psychic challenges since one of his mentees had been promoted to a senior position in the firm.'

Ambivalence and conflict, boastfulness and a struggle against feelings of inferiority: Osbourne was in trouble. He made a mental note to contact Ms Sefton.

The faint trill of his mobile was a welcome intrusion. He retrieved it from his overcoat pocket and pressed it to his ear. 'Alan Palmer.'

'Daddy?'

A liquid shiver of joy ran through Palmer. 'Hel-*lo*, darling! You're up early.'

'I'm too excited to sleep!'

Palmer had arranged to take Lucy to Blue Planet for her Friday afternoon treat. He remembered last Christmas, when she had bounced into their room at two in the morning, demanding to know what had happened to Santa. She snuggled next to him for an hour before she finally drifted into a deep sleep and he had carried her gently back to her own bed. The heat of her, the vanilla and cinnamon scent of her had kindled a fierce protectiveness in him, a searing happiness he had never experienced before or since. At that moment he thought he was blessed.

Now, listening to his daughter along a telephone line, separated by a thousand miles of alteration and distrust, a band of tightness constricted his throat.

But Lucy filled the silence with lists of all the creatures they were likely to see, and plans for a picnic, and what she was going to wear. 'I want to ride the sharks, Daddy,' she said.

'I'm not sure they allow people to ride them, Lucy,' he said, 'But maybe they'll let you stroke the little ones.'

'Mummy says you can walk *right under* them.'

'*Wow.*' Palmer smiled down the phone at her, suddenly tingling with the projected excitement of a four-year-old. 'We'd better make sure we get there nice and early, so we don't miss anything. I'll see you at one o'clock — make sure you're all ready to go.'

Lucy giggled, lowered her voice to a whisper. 'I already got my wellies on.'

'I don't think it's going to be wet today, Lucy-Lou.'

'Daaa-*dee* . . .' He imagined her rolling her eyes and clapping a hand to her forehead, pudgy fingers splayed. 'It's a *na-aquarium* — 'course it'll be wet.'

Palmer's smile broadened. 'They keep the water in the tanks, sweetie. But you do what you think is best.'

''Kay, Daddy. Bye!'

Too late, he said, 'Wait, Lucy — put Mummy on.' But she'd already hung up.

He pressed the speed dial for Elspeth's number and got an engaged tone. He hung up and the phone rang in his hand.

'Is this how it's going to be?' Elspeth said. 'Refusing even to speak to me?'

'That's funny,' Palmer said. 'Wasn't it *you* that cut *me* off, last night?'

'Don't be petty, Alan.'

He sucked back another sniping reply. 'We need to talk.'

'You should give yourself time to think things through, first,' she said.

'You know me, Elspeth — always thinking.' He instantly regretted his sarcastic tone.

'Have you even read the forms, yet?'

He had carried them around in his shoulder bag since they had arrived, nursing them like a grievance. 'I'll be there at one,' he said, feeling a thud of anger, complicated by regret and longing, but all he heard was the tension in his voice. 'Make sure she's ready.'

He thought again about Jake Osbourne's anger, and understood the helpless fear that fuelled it. He could keep going at full speed, but eventually he was sure to hit a patch of black ice and if he lost his grip, the consequences could be devastating. Palmer glanced down at the blackened flag-stones under his feet, suddenly unsure of himself, imagining a slight loss of traction. The ooze of frost-melt was viscous, and the taste of salt on his tongue had a coppery tang, like fresh blood.

CHAPTER 38

Rowan snagged a coffee from the machine in the station's basement and stumbled into the CID Room at 7.45 a.m. Ian Chan had promised to dust the thumb drive for fingerprints, but she didn't hold out much hope.

'You should go to Warman, Cass,' he'd said. 'The jacket was a message. *This* is a message.'

'Funny,' she replied. 'That's just what I told Neil.'

He raised his eyebrows. 'Well, I wouldn't want to make a habit of agreeing with you, but when you're right, you're right.'

'Okay — just for the sake of argument, let's say I go to her — what would I tell her? My car was broken into — oh, and a thumb drive I thought was stolen turned up.'

'Your car's been broken into *twice*,' he corrected. 'And he left hand marks on your kitchen window — which, by the way, I might have been able to lift, if you'd told me when it happened instead of three days later. Someone's *stalking* you, Cassie. I mean, how am I going to feel if you vanish without trace?'

She tried not to smile. 'It's always got to be about you, hasn't it?'

'Oh, yes,' he said, and she realised he was in deadly earnest. 'It's all a huge joke. Well, if you don't care about me,' he said in all seriousness, 'you might consider Neil.'

'*Okay*,' she sighed. 'I'll talk to Warman later.'

As she approached her desk, she saw that someone had taped an oblong of newsprint to her computer monitor. She looked around; people stood in small groups or sat at their own desks, looking tired and winter-pale. To her right, Wicks rattled a newspaper and she stared at his lumpy profile for a few moments, but he seemed unaware of her, his lips moving silently as he read.

She set down her coffee cup and peeled the oblong of pulpy paper from her monitor. Her heart jumped. It was a newsprint photograph — her and Palmer, Osbourne's analyst, in the foyer of his office building.

She glared angrily around the room. Wicks rattled his paper again, swivelling his chair to face her. He peered at her through a neat oblong cut from the front page, the size and shape of the picture she held.

'You bumped your pal's sketch off the front page,' he said, holding up the newspaper so she could read the headline.

PSYCHED!

'The boss is not a happy bunny.'

Rowan's stomach tightened. 'You buffoon, Wicks.' She swiped the paper out of his hand and dumped it in the bin as she walked out of the office. Better to face Pat Warman now than wait to be sent for.

* * *

The tabloid lay on Warman's desk like an accusation.

'Can you explain this?' she asked, her eyes hooded, her jaw so tight it seemed she held her fury clamped between her back teeth.

'I just found out myself,' Rowan said.

'I asked for an explanation, not a chronology.' Her voice, never attractive, was gratingly harsh.

Rowan retreated into stiff formality. 'No, ma'am, I can't explain it.'

'You're pictured in the local press with a key witness. Osbourne — who has no criminal history — is named when I distinctly said I wanted this kept low-key.' Warman prodded the photograph with one bony finger to emphasise the point. 'You must have seen *someone* — this wasn't done from fifty yards away with a long lens.'

'It was after six o'clock,' Rowan said. 'The place was empty.'

'Evidently not.'

'There was just me, the receptionist and Mr Palmer,' Rowan said, trying not to sound truculent.

'And the photographer.'

Rowan stared at the picture, feeling a sheen of sweat on her brow. *How the hell could this have happened?* She shifted her weight from one hip to the other and angled her body to get a better look at it, tilting her head. Something looked off.

She picked up the newspaper, and Warman took a sharp breath, as though Rowan had hooked the strap of her handbag from her shoulder and tipped the contents out onto the desk.

'The angle's wrong,' Rowan said.

'What angle?'

'The picture — it had to be taken from above.'

'So they took it from the stairs, or a gallery.'

Rowan shook her head. 'There's no stairs, no gallery — no mezzanine — no way anyone could sneak a few shots from that angle.'

'Then how *exactly* to you suppose—?'

'Security cameras.'

'What?'

'CCTV,' Rowan said. 'I counted three — and I wasn't looking that hard. If it's digital — and most of them are these days — it'd only take a few seconds to find a decent still from the hard drive.' She realised she was gabbling and stopped, handing back the paper so that Warman could take a look for herself.

The Chief Inspector stared at the picture, her expression unreadable. 'And who do you suppose tipped off the press? How would they know you'd even *be* there?'

Yes, Cassie — how would they? Realisation hit her and she closed her eyes briefly. 'Lara . . .'

'Lara?'

'Receptionist at the psychoanalyst's office building.'

'I see.' Warman let the silence become uncomfortable before she asked: 'And was Mr Palmer helpful?'

Rowan shook her head and Warman paused, tapping the desk hard with one fingernail.

'Since you've identified the receptionist as the source of this leak — and you, Cassie, are the only member of my team who has spoken to her — I can only assume that *you* gave Lara Mr Osbourne's name.'

'No, ma'am. She *assumed* I'd come about him.'

'Just like that?' Warman said. 'You ask to speak to Mr Palmer, who must have dozens of patients, and yet she *assumes* you want to talk to Jake Osbourne?'

Rowan took a breath. 'I . . . might have given her a rough description.'

Warman closed her eyes and pinched the narrow bridge of her nose.

'I'm sorry, boss,' Rowan said, and meant it.

'Is there anything else I should know?' Warman asked tartly.

Now would not be a good time to mention Neil's thumb drive. Or to tell her boss that she thought she was being followed. Rowan would have liked the luxury of feeling she'd been hard done by, but she couldn't get past the fact that Warman was right: in talking to the receptionist, and putting Osbourne's name out into the public sphere, she had warned a credible suspect they were onto him. This was all down to her. She had screwed up.

CHAPTER 39

Palmer felt an almost overwhelming compulsion to cut through Osbourne's complaints, to silence the harsh unmodulated grind of his patient's voice, his grievances against his boss, the incompetence of his co-workers.

He had checked his watch at five minutes past eight — halfway through the fifty-minute consultation. *I could be working through my notes of Dylan's session, I could be at home. I could be sorting out — trying to sort out — the mess my marriage is in. Instead of which, I'm hanging around — for what — to indulge Jake Osbourne's whining?*

He stopped short. *Whining?* Osbourne was aggressive, demanding, angry — but *whining?* Surely not. And yet examining his feelings, his overriding emotion for the past twenty-five minutes had been irritation.

He tried an interpretation.

'You perhaps feel that your needs are too easily dismissed.'

Osbourne glared at him. 'You fucking *fraud.*' He stood and leaned over Palmer, all of his usual hostility and threat returned, trapped in his curled fists. 'You think I don't know what you're driving at? You think your ABC of puerile analysis impresses me? You judge everyone else by your own empty life.' Osbourne paused. 'Well, you can keep your abandonment issues to yourself — *Doc.*'

Empty. Abandonment. Elspeth and Lucy had tumbled into Palmer's mind — and with them the acrimonious phone call from Elspeth, earlier, and his own futile trip to Elspeth's house on Wednesday night. He recalled, too, his sleepless pacing, the anger and hurt he'd felt, and the divorce petition he was even now lugging around with him.

He felt a tug of guilt: he had entangled his patient's unhappiness with his own.

Empty. Abandonment. Osbourne usually described his turmoil as bodily symptoms. Rage became a pressure in his skull, loneliness an animal need to rut. But today, he hadn't talked about *bodily* discomfort — he had talked about 'emptiness' and 'abandonment' — actual emotions. This was a howl of anguish from Osbourne's damaged psyche.

'You talk about emptiness and abandonment,' Palmer said. 'It might be helpful to talk about these two things and what they mean to you.'

Osbourne backed away as if Palmer had leapt from his chair wielding a knife. He caught his calf on the edge of the couch and flung out one hand to save himself.

'Fuck you,' he said, as though he had placed the furniture to trip him. Still backing away he said, 'You want me to *trust* you with my private thoughts? You fucking *betrayer*. You *sell-out*. It's a really sick mind that demands trust and peddles this, this — bullshit.' Unable to articulate further, he waved his hand to encompass the room. He looked like a man trying to ward off some invisible threat.

He kept moving until he reached the wide glass window overlooking the river. Until now, Osbourne's anger had always been a cover for his insecurity, a manifestation of his sense of injustice. But at that moment, his hands splayed against the sheet glass as though he was teetering on a narrow ledge, there was also a desperate fear.

* * *

216

Palmer's second appointment of the morning didn't show up, which was unusual: he was an obsessively punctual man. At ten a.m., the next patient was a no-show and Palmer's vague sense of unease became a palpable anxiety. He called his ten o' clock appointment.

'David?'

'What?' David Ennis's voice was flat, and he sounded depressed.

'It's Alan Palmer.'

'I know who it is.'

Palmer heard noises in the background, a man's voice, raised in the jolly, patronizing tone people adopt when they address the deaf or the sick or the old; Ennis must be at work.

'I'm wondering why you haven't come to your ten o'clock appointment.'

'Is this some kind of joke?' A touch of heat in Ennis's tone, now.

'I'm sorry, David, I don't understand.'

'You and me, both. *You* cancelled my session, and now you have the nerve to—'

Palmer felt a small flutter of apprehension. 'David, I didn't cancel your appointment.'

A bark of angry laughter. 'I'm neurotic, Alan, I'm not crazy — I know your voice.'

Palmer's mouth dried. *Oh, God.* 'David,' Palmer said, catching hold of himself, trying to keep his voice level and calm for Ennis's sake. 'Whoever you spoke to, it wasn't me.'

A shocked silence. In the background, someone's name was called.

'If not you — then who?' David Ennis was a health professional, a senior consultant in cardiology; he knew the implications of a breach of security.

'I don't know,' Palmer said.

'How much do they have?' Ennis demanded. 'Contact details? Notes? Audio recordings? Good God, Alan!'

'I'll call you back,' Palmer said. 'Give me an hour.'

Dylan Corbie wasn't answering. Unlike any other student Palmer had ever met, Dylan switched his phone off during lectures; Palmer left a message asking him to call, giving his office number.

He worked through the rest of his client list, experiencing over and over their dawning horror as they realised how much of their lives — their most intimate thoughts and feelings — might be exposed. He tried to reassure them, set up new appointments with those who were willing, and agreed a code word, should he need to reach them. By the end of an hour his shirt was soaked with sweat and he was exhausted.

He checked the clock. *Hell* — eleven-fifteen — he was due to meet Dylan at the Rodney Street clinic at eleven thirty. He could just make it if he took a taxi.

* * *

He left the building at a run, still fighting with one sleeve of his coat. A cab turned in from the main road on the right and, struggling to disentangle himself, he raised his arm to hail it. It swept past and he cursed, turning again towards the waterfront, and a movement in the shadows of the building opposite caught his eye. He trotted on, and a moment later he had reached the corner, flagged a cab almost immediately. It was only after he climbed in that his mind made the connection.

The figure in the shadows. It was Dylan.

'Where to, Chief?' The cab driver was staring at him in the rear-view mirror.

'I've changed my mind,' Palmer said. 'Sorry.'

'Not as sorry as me, mate.' He tapped the face of the meter. 'We're already on the clock.'

Palmer shoved a fiver through the grille. 'That should cover it.' He dived out of the taxi, heading back to the side street. Turning the corner, he cannoned into someone coming the other way — Dylan Corbie.

Dylan bounced off him and almost fell. Palmer caught him by the elbow. 'What the hell are you doing?' He didn't try to mask his outrage.

Dylan jerked his arm free. 'Following you. I *told* you that.'

Palmer looked into Dylan Corbie's face. It was a mask of calm, yet he was angry, raging like a warehouse fire; he just didn't know it.

Whenever they had touched upon his arrest at the boys' school in their sessions, Dylan always denied feeling any animosity towards the children. He had insisted that wanting to kill them was 'just a compulsion'. 'Like when you're at the top of a tall building, and you want to throw yourself off.'

'Why are you here, Dylan?'

'Why are *you* late?'

'You know you're not supposed to come here.'

'Well, people break rules all the time, don't they?' Dylan clenched his fists at his sides.

Palmer didn't know if he was asking a question or making an accusation. 'Some of my clients received phone calls this morning. I've been calling them to—' *To what? Reassure them?* That admission would only heighten Dylan's anxiety. He started again: 'I tried to call you.'

'An emergency, was it?'

'Yes,' Palmer said. Their agreement was that Palmer would only contact him by phone in extreme circumstances.

'Yeah, well, I got your voicemail — confirming my appointment.' Dylan glared at him, his jaw flexing, his eyes flashing dragonfly green. 'But I *always* see you at eleven thirty on Fridays. How's *that* an emergency?'

Palmer vacillated. If Dylan hadn't received the same call as the rest, he would doubt his own memory, but if he had — and Palmer told him that the caller was an imposter — it would only feed into Dylan's paranoia. Catch 22.

Dylan shook his head, a cynical sneer on his face. 'Good liars don't hesitate.' Then he turned and started walking.

This was their first session since Dylan's realisation that his mother had planted false memories in his mind, denying the truth that she was having an affair and making him complicit in the events that drove his father to suicide. *I can't let him leave!*

Impulsively, Palmer said, 'Dylan, wait. Come inside.'

Dylan faltered but didn't turn.

Palmer kept going, heading towards the lifts to his private office in the hope that Dylan's obsession with knowing — his voyeuristic desire to *see inside* — would be enough. By the time he reached the doors, Dylan was at his shoulder.

A few minutes later, he was touring the office as if making a careful inventory of the room, its size, the layout, the files Palmer had left in stacks on his desk.

'Busy morning?' Dylan asked, after a five-minute silence.

'What do you mean?'

'All those calls. And . . .' He gestured to the files on Palmer's desk.

Was there a hint of amusement in his tone?

'Why don't you sit down, Dylan?'

Dylan looked from the leather consulting couch to Palmer as though he suspected it might be some kind of trick — that if he sat on it, or worse, lay on it — he might make himself ridiculous. Then he shrugged, set his backpack on the floor and perched on the edge of the seat with his feet tucked under, his knees angled sharply, the denim of his jeans hanging loose at his thighs.

After another silence, Palmer asked again, 'So, why are you here?'

'I have an appointment.'

'Your appointment is at the Rodney Street clinic — I was on my way to see you.'

Dylan watched him carefully, his green eyes clear and bright; the bruises on his face were fading. Abruptly, he swung his rucksack onto the couch and pulled out a rolled copy of the *Mersey Daily*. 'I wanted to ask you about this.'

He tossed it onto the floor and the paper unfurled, moving and stirring like a living entity. Palmer picked it up, flattening it out to read it. His stomach dropped. A photograph of him looking far too cosy with Constable Rowan.

The headline read: **PSYCHED!**

'You think I knew about this?' Palmer said, unable to hide his shock. 'Dylan, a detective came to my office. She asked some questions. But you know my rules of confidentiality.'

'You said you wouldn't tell anyone what we talked about — unless I "became a danger to myself or others".' He had it verbatim.

'I also said that I would tell you before I went to anyone else.'

'What about Dr Atherton? You talk to him.' He wouldn't look at Palmer.

Had Karl spoken to Dylan about their Wednesday session already?

'Yes. We agreed that at the start of your therapy.'

Dylan fiddled with the straps of his rucksack, his face white, his lips pressed into a thin line.

'Do you think I told the police that you follow people?'

Dylan glanced up, and the green of his eyes sparked with hate. 'Did you?'

'Of course not.'

'Maybe I should follow *her* — see what *she* gets up to.'

'The detective?' Palmer said. 'Why would you do that?'

'I told you — I like it.' The gleam in his eyes took on a hungry look.

'People don't like to be spied on,' Palmer said quietly. 'And there's another name for what you do.'

'Stalking.' Dylan's fingers strayed toward the bruising around his eye.

'Is that how you were injured?' he asked, thinking that a few news stories online referred to the abductor as 'the Mall Stalker'.

Dylan maintained uncharacteristically bold eye contact.

'Did someone catch you following them, Dylan?'

The boy's mouth twisted into an ugly sneer. 'What do *you* think?' He shouldered his bag and stalked out.

Palmer dropped into his chair, exhausted. The newspaper still lay on his desk, and his eye snagged on Osbourne's name in the second paragraph. The unattributed source said that the police thought he 'may have vital information' relating to the case — that catch-all phrase which could mean extreme guilt or perfect innocence. He was beginning to understand Osbourne's fury.

CHAPTER 40

Names don't matter. All that matters is this one is a doozie — a one hundred per cent genuine honey. The city's been hopping with this type since the Paradise Street development opened — and boy, did they get the name right — it really is a little slice of heaven with these exotic birds of paradise flitting from shop to shop. Fair-skinned or dusky, blonde, auburn or brunette, blue-eyed, or green or tawny-brown — they're all here. Tall, short, thin and curvy. Curvy's best. Just make your selection and take your booby-Barbie home with you today! Smiley girls — happy girls — girls who will do just about anything, given the right incentive.

Her hair is a perfect yellow-gold. Her head lolls forward, her chin against her chest. Her arms are tied behind her, stretched tight around the brick pillar. Her breasts strain against the thin jersey fabric of her dress; it clings to her, the pattern accentuating the curves; bright colours, birds of paradise colours. The cold makes her nipples erect. And oh, jeez, that mouth . . .

I have the knife in one hand and the taser in the other. A hundred candles flicker and dance. It's exactly — precisely — how I imagined it. Emma was good, but the ambience wasn't quite right; Tasha was better, but there was still the problem of the blindfold. This is perfect: no blindfold, no obstacles to the full 3D, scent-o-matic, film experience.

Pools reflect the points of light, fracturing and multiplying in ripples caused by vibrations pulsing through the sandstone bedrock from

223

the underground railway five hundred metres away. Subtle and soft, the candlelight weaves threads of bronze and copper among the gold strands of her hair, adding depth and texture, giving the illusion of warmth to her pale arms, the fair skin of her face and neck.

She came designer gift-wrapped, her clothes so new they smelled of fabric and not of her, but she's had three days to wear them in, and now they carry the musk of sweat and sex and the bitter, arousing tang of fear.

I wait for her to wake, listening to the kiss of droplets onto the puddled floor. Sounds echo here, the hiss and sputter of a candle flame is magnified to a frantic whisper, a sob becomes a sigh of ecstasy.

She stirs and moans. The excitement is almost unbearable. Every nerve in my skin quivers, my scalp tingles with desire for her. I bend and lift a strand of hair from her face with the knife blade; she opens her eyes and jerks back, cracking her head against the brick pillar.

Names don't matter, but this one happens to be called Jodie.

* * *

'Hey, Jodie . . .' he says, as though she has wakened from a Sunday afternoon nap. 'Did you think I'd forgotten you?'

Jodie groans. Drifting in and out of consciousness, she has alternated between terror that he won't return and dread that he will.

'I've thought up a new game,' he says. 'Ready to play?'

He pounces on her, slices through the ropes that bind her arms, and she falls forward. The release of strain on the tendons and ligaments of her arms is agonizing and she screams. The muscles cramp and tear as he undresses her. Her screams seem to arouse him. He whispers, his mouth close to her ear: 'Sexiest thing on this earth is undressing a beautiful woman.'

He has told her that the taser burn on her neck — the one he used to incapacitate her in the car park — looks like a love bite. That mark must be overlaid with many bruises now — dark prints from his spoon-shaped thumbs. He likes to choke her.

She wants to live — despite all he has done to her, despite all he has made her do. She wants to go home — to Mum and Dad — not to the flat. She wants to be with her family, to be held safe in loving arms, to be comforted. She was on the phone to Stacey when it happened — she must have heard; the police would be looking for her. When they find her, they will want a description of the man who took her. So she tries to remember: his face, the colour of his eyes. But it's hard to see beyond the cruel glitter in them as he stares deep into her own, impossible to think with his fingers around her neck.

His thumbs press on her windpipe as he thrusts into her. 'Is this how you like it? Huh? Is this what you want?' he whispers, his breath warm on her skin. He bears down and eases off, crushing and releasing, so that she experiences over and over the terror of choking, suffocating, fighting for breath, the pain-filled dark creeping in like storm clouds sparking with electricity from the edges of her vision. A brief, desperate struggle for air, then the sudden rush of it, cold and soothing into her throat. The despair, seeing his face. And then the horror begins again.

At first she tried to fight him, but he was too strong, and the taser shocks have left her sick and dizzy. Her legs won't work properly — she has lost count of the number of times he has shocked her. She thought the electrically induced convulsions were agonizing, but now her muscles spasm without warning, sending shards of pain like hot metal through her buttocks and back and chest. It's hard to remember how long she has been in here; hard to remember anything except the fear and the pain and this man's weight on her, his lips hot on her flesh, hungry for her, his stinking breath in her mouth and nose.

He says names don't matter, but he calls her by name as he rapes her, saying it as he thrusts into her, filling her head with the sound of his voice, repeating her name over and over as he instructs her, cajoles her, torments her, so that she hates the sound of her own name almost as much as she hates the feel of him inside her, the wet slap of his flesh on hers, the reek of his breath, his hands on her, that taunting repeated question, '*Is this how you like it?*'

He makes her change position, arranging her arms and legs as if she were a mannequin. More friction and burning pain, and the threat of the taser if she doesn't cooperate, whispering those vile words in her ear.

At last, grunting at the climax, he pushes her away. Her arms have no feeling and she flops helplessly, powerless even to cover herself. She sees triumph on his face, and hate, and disgust and contempt. He has a small scar just above his right eye. This small detail — the possibility that he is not invulnerable — gives her the courage to at least try to—

Remember: twelve yellow brick arches; tall columns, twenty or thirty feet high. The softer, crumbling pink bricks that form the curve of the ceiling. The drip of water. *Remember*: the drone of traffic, a short distance away, the periodic rumble of a train. *Remember*: an occasional whiff of chlorine over the mossy smell of old water and hot candle wax.

She turns her head so that she doesn't have to look into his face — doesn't have to bear his hate, doesn't have to think of his voice in her head, his body inside hers. The candles a few feet away seem to offer a feeble warmth to her chilled body. On her right hand, the ring that Simon bought her catches the light and seems to pulse, like a star. Her hand is lying in a puddle, like something already dead. It seems not to belong to her any more — she can't feel it, and cannot lift it clear. She watches the reflected light of the flames caress the surface of the water.

The light seems to shiver. It ducks and rears again, steadying to a yellow glow and his shadow crosses her. He swoops down on her, lifts her, tearing the tendons of her upper arms afresh.

Jodie screams.

'Fuck you,' he says, as if she has insulted him.

He has taken her freedom, her dignity, her body, and still isn't satisfied. Perhaps she didn't look humiliated enough, or perhaps he knew she had gone somewhere he could not follow.

He slaps her. Then he tears the ring from her hand and forces it onto his own pinky finger. He crouches next to her and she sees that hungry glitter in his eyes again. And Jodie knows she will never leave this place.

CHAPTER 41

At twelve thirty, Alan Palmer was in his kitchen, making sandwiches in preparation for his trip with Lucy to Blue Planet. After Dylan's early departure, he'd rung the head of building security, and immediately after that, a locksmith, reasoning that since he didn't keep digital records of patients' contact details, whoever had cancelled his appointments must have accessed his physical files. Then he tried Jake Osbourne, fully understanding his anger during their session. But he wasn't answering his mobile or his landline. He had tried Amy Sefton, Osbourne's previous analyst, several times, but her machine was switched to answerphone.

He kept returning to the awful day in May, when his life changed forever. How many times had Karl Atherton asked if he was ready to take on a full caseload — counselled him to take more time? Palmer wiped his hands and went into the hallway to phone Amy Sefton again; her voicemail kicked in. He was leaving another message when the doorbell rang. Then the letterbox rattled.

'Dadd*eee*! Hurry up!'

He grinned. Lucy.

She flung herself at his legs, hugging him as soon as he opened the door, while Elspeth scowled over her daughter's head. Elspeth was dressed for work in a softly tailored skirt suit in charcoal grey. A turtleneck cashmere sweater in light olive set off her dark curls and she smelled subtly of some fresh, floral scent.

'I wasn't expecting you till one,' he said, unwrapping Lucy from his legs and swinging her into his arms.

'Look, Daddy.' Lucy squirmed in his grip so he could get a better look. She was wearing her favourite pink wellington boots.

He gave Lucy's left foot an affectionate squeeze and gazed at Elspeth. 'Will you come in?'

'I have to get to work,' she said. 'A bit of a crisis.'

Palmer felt a pang of guilt. He'd left a crisis of his own for his half-day with Lucy. But he wasn't about to give Elspeth another instance of his 'unreasonable behaviour' for her solicitor to stack up against him. He had contacted the head of security and shown him the photograph in the *Mersey Daily*. That had been enough for them to send a guard to keep watch over his office while he went out 'on urgent business'.

'If you want that talk, perhaps we could do it tonight,' Elspeth said, without looking at him.

'I have a late appointment.' He planned to sleep in his office overnight and keep watch on the place until he had supervised the fitting of new locks.

'Well, silly me, I thought this might take precedence,' she said with a tight smile. 'My mistake.'

He was too tired for an argument and he could feel Lucy's distress in the way her hand tightened around his neck. 'Ready for the sharks?' he asked, and Lucy cheered.

Elspeth looked ready to stamp her foot at his refusal to play her game, and Palmer suddenly wondered if her new and unaccountable anger was a defensive measure — a way to harden her resolve in going through with the divorce. Something in his expression must have betrayed him; she seemed to sense his flash of insight and turned on her heel with an exasperated snort.

Palmer closed the door softly after her, said, 'Come on Lucy-Lou. Let's finish packing the sandwiches and we can set off on our voyage of discovery.'

'Are we going on a boat?' Lucy said, her fingers, chilled from her parents' doorstep confrontation, crept inside his shirt collar, seeking warmth.

'We've got to drive two whole miles under the Mersey River before we get to the Wirral,' he said.

Her eyes widened in awe. 'Is that where Blue Planet is, Daddy?'

'That's right.'

Lucy stared solemnly at one booted foot. 'Good job I've got my wellies.'

* * *

After he had explained that there was no water *inside* the Mersey Tunnel, Lucy became convinced that it must be like the giant aquatunnel at Blue Planet. She was expecting to see fish and maybe even the odd dolphin on the drive   but any disappointment was forgotten when they came up onto the motorway flyover and Palmer pointed out the horses grazing on Bidston Moss. A minute or two later, he glanced in the rear-view mirror. Strapped into her booster seat like a tiny astronaut, she seemed to be playing a counting game — cars or lampposts, he couldn't tell which. He remembered her counting game at the Fairy Glen and felt a shimmer of worry ripple through him.

The next exit sign came up and Lucy patted the seat in front of her to gain his attention.

'Are we nearly there, Daddy?'

'Junction three, darling, seven more to go.' Junction three was Amy Sefton's turn-off.

Palmer scooted off the motorway, telling himself that it was practically on the way to Blue Planet. He was just going to swing by that way; he wouldn't necessarily call in — he would make up his mind when he got there. He didn't question too closely the fact that he had made a point of memorizing her address when he went through her referral report — it wasn't like he had *planned* the visit.

The sky had cleared to a crisp autumnal blue and Heswall looked affluent and pleased with itself in the late autumn sunshine.

Palmer drove past the shops and restaurants in the village centre, slowing after the library and village hall, on past the police station and rows of neat Victorian cottages with their front doors hard against the pavement. A little further, after another row of shops, the houses drew back from the road; their large front lawns, scattered with the vivid red leaves of cherry trees, demarcated the shift from the comfortably-off to the truly affluent.

Palmer slowed, looking for a house number. He had to double back before he found Amy Sefton's house, set well back off the road behind a tall beech hedge whose coppery autumn colour gleamed as if every leaf had been polished. The house itself was a nineteen-sixties flat-fronted oblong in honey-coloured brick. He pulled into the drive, the gravel popping and crackling under the car's wheels.

Lucy stared around her in consternation. 'Is this the Blue Planet?'

'Not yet, Lucy,' Palmer said. 'I won't be a minute.' He left her in the car while he rang the doorbell, heard quick footsteps on the gravel path at the side of the house.

'May I help you?'

He turned to face a small, trim woman in her late thirties or early forties. He smiled. 'Amy Sefton? I'm Alan Palmer.'

'Oh.' She took a step back, as if she wished she could turn and run, but she seemed to get a hold of herself. After another moment's hesitation, she slid off one green gardening glove and shook his hand, searching his face.

'I left messages on your answerphone,' he said.

'I would have replied,' she said coldly. 'If I'd been given the chance.'

'I know,' he said. 'It's . . . irregular — but I feel there is some urgency.'

231

She gave him that searching look again. 'You'd better come in,' she said.

He gestured toward the car. 'I have my daughter with me.'

Her eyebrows shot up and he caught a flash of disapproval, then she said, 'Bring her through to the garden — she can play while we talk.'

She disappeared around the corner of the house, leaving him to explain to Lucy.

'But we'll be *late*,' Lucy argued, struggling to stop him unclasping the seat buckle.

'It's all right, darling. We can go in anytime.'

'But we'll *miss* things,' she insisted, her face pink with the effort of fighting him.

'We got here early because you and Mummy came early, so we won't be late and I promise we'll see everything. Ms Sefton says you can play in the back garden.'

'Don't *want* to play in her smelly back garden.'

'Well, you can play or not play. That's up to you.'

Given a choice, Lucy was confused into silence, and although she refused to take his hand, Palmer was able to get her out of the car and around to the back of the house without too much fuss.

The garden was neat, the lawn swept. A large pile of leaves was smouldering in one corner, raked to a neat cone and trailing a thin grey plume from its top, like a spent volcano. Lucy gasped at the sight of a swing and a full-size slide, and Palmer saw her struggle with her excitement at having them all to herself and her fury at being delayed on their afternoon adventure.

Amy Sefton was waiting for him in the conservatory. Her fair hair was cut into a bob which she seemed to feel was too short, since she frequently combed her fingers through it giving it a sharp tug at the end of each pass as if trying to adjust the length.

She indicated a seat and sat as far away from him as the room would allow, facing out into the garden. Palmer began apologising for the intrusion, but she cut him short.

'Can we get on with this? I'm really rather busy.'

He nodded. 'Of course. I'm concerned about Jake Osbourne.'

She glanced at him quickly, then out into the garden. 'I don't know what you expect me to do.' Her voice was high and piping, with a sharp brittle quality.

'I thought you might be able to give me some background,' Palmer said.

'You have my report.'

He had a single page of sketchy and incomplete notes and he was having difficulty extracting anything useful from it. He smiled. 'Perhaps you could help me match the notes to the man.'

Her head jerked a little and her hand fluttered to her hair, separating the strands of her fringe.

Amy Sefton had asked him to take on Jake Osbourne for what she had described as 'personal reasons' — adding reluctantly, he thought, 'Ill-health'. He wondered if Amy's mental health was the problem.

She tugged again at her short fringe of hair and he saw a few strands pull out at the roots. 'Everything you need to know is in my report,' she said. 'If you would like clarification on any specific aspect, I'm willing to answer your questions.'

It seemed she wasn't going to volunteer information. But Palmer hardly knew Osbourne; how was he supposed to know the right questions to ask? He gazed through the window, feeling her hostility, and watched as Lucy stamped up and down on the lawn, pretending not to notice the slide, beaming hostility at him like a radioactive isotope.

He gave a mental shrug: a patient's childhood relationships with his parents were always a good a place to start.

'How does he get on with his parents?' he asked.

She sighed, opening her fingers to examine the loose strands of hair, letting them fall to the tiled floor. 'His parents are divorced. He sees his mother regularly. She lives in Threlkeld, in Cumbria. His father remarried. He's retired.'

It was an oddly evasive answer. 'Can you tell me anything about them?'

'He didn't really "share".' Despite the attempt at sarcasm, her voice caught on the last word.

He looked at her without speaking and she fiddled again with her hair.

'Ms Sefton, he left his session this morning early, and—'

'Consider yourself fortunate, Mr Palmer.' Amy Sefton's mouth twisted into a smile.

'Fortunate?'

Her mouth clamped shut, and she looked horrified at the slip. She stood abruptly, seemed startled by her own action, unsure what to do with her arms and legs.

'Ms Sefton, are you all right?'

Her fingers strayed to her hairline, then veered away, and finally she clasped her hands tightly in front of her. 'It's not unusual for patients to walk out of sessions: testing the boundaries, avoiding issues — I shouldn't need to tell you this.' He heard the barbed edge in her tone, the slight suggestion of contempt.

'I believe Jake desperately needs help — I think he believes I betrayed him. He used the words "betrayer", "abandonment".' He remembered feeling as Osbourne looked out of the sheet glass window of his office, high above the city, that he was a man teetering on a narrow ledge. 'I think he may be on the verge of a breakdown.'

She gave a bark of laughter.

'Did I say something funny?'

'Are you sure that's not a projection of your own anxieties, Mr Palmer?' She stared at him, her contempt open and frank now.

Of course, she would have checked him out before making a referral. *She's read the British Psychoanalytic Council's ruling. She knows my history.*

She broke eye contact. 'I think you've kept your daughter waiting long enough.'

Lucy had sidled over to the slide. She climbed the steps and slid down with no outward sign of enjoyment, the scowl on her face her mother in miniature.

Amy Sefton moved briskly to the conservatory door and opened it, letting in a blast of cold air. Her face was pale, but large red blotches bloomed on the skin of her neck.

'Daddy's just coming dear,' she called shrilly, her fingers dancing on the curve of the handle, a tight smile on her face.

As he stepped past her into the garden, she tugged at her short fringe one last time and he noticed with a shock that her eyebrows were pencilled on and her eyelids were completely naked, as though she had plucked out every brow hair, every eyelash, in an orgy of compulsive self-destruction.

CHAPTER 42

Friday evening

Neil had selected their favourite Chinese takeaway, rather than the McNugget option. It seemed that even he wasn't above trying to impress Big Brother. Sated, the two of them sprawled side by side in front of the TV, watching *The X Factor*, occasionally making a damning remark about the awfulness of the acts, or the sorry dress sense of a contestant.

Alex was in his thirties now, grown into his skin, comfortable with himself, if a little vain. Always their parents' favourite child, the golden boy was now a man, and the touch of precious metal seemed still to glow on his skin. Neil was darker — more like Cassie — but she saw the family resemblance in their gestures, their laughter, even in the way they slumped on the sofa, heads on their chests, hands folded across their stomachs.

This is how it's supposed to be, Rowan thought. She could almost imagine that Mum was in the kitchen, Dad out bimbling in his taxi on one of his complicated split shifts — except that Alex looked too big for the room, too glossy — out of place. He seemed almost to be tucking his elbows in to avoid greasing up his good jacket. Or maybe it had all got too small for him: her and Neil, the house, the city — the whole damn country.

Alex noticed her watching and asked, 'What're you wearing on Sunday, Cass?'

'Haven't decided,' she said.

'Cutting it fine, Sis.' Since he'd emigrated to America, Alex said things like 'Sis'.

'She hasn't *bought* anything, yet,' Neil chipped in, enjoying the fact that she was on the receiving end of a quizzing, for a change.

'I've got plenty of stuff in my wardrobe,' Rowan said, on the defensive.

'"Stuff?"' Alex repeated. 'Well, I hope there's a dress or two—'cos this *is* a Rowan wedding — conventions must be observed.'

'We're Rowans, too, and maybe I want to buck the conventions.'

'Tasha's always telling her she should wear dresses,' Neil said lazily, his eyes fixed on the TV.

'Who's Tasha?'

'She's—'

'—a friend,' Rowan said, firmly. There were some things that were off-limits, even to Alex.

Neil shot her a look that said, *What?* Then his eyes swivelled back to the TV screen. 'You could always borrow one of those outfits you wear on night shift.'

'Is this going where I think it's going?' Alex asked, amused.

'I'm investigating a series of rape-assaults,' Rowan said, feeling a slow creep of blood into her face.

'If you can call going out dressed like a hooker "investigation",' Neil said with a smirk.

'Hey! Show some respect.'

Neil hunched his shoulders and lapsed into shamefaced silence.

'C'mon, Cassie,' Alex said, always ready to mediate. 'He's just teasing.'

Rowan scowled at both of them. 'It's bad enough listening to that kind of crap from the men in work. I don't have to take it from my kid brother.'

Usually, that would have been enough to put Neil in a sulk for the rest of the night, but Alex's presence changed the dynamic. Cassie always felt that she was faking the matriarch role when Alex was around, that she sounded more like an ineffectual nagging mother than the big sister who had held the home and family together for six years. Neil, sensing her insecurity, played on it.

'She's just annoyed 'cos I haven't told you she got her face in the paper,' he said, staring straight at the TV, the corner of his mouth quirking into a smile.

'*Neil*!'

Alex raised his eyebrows, enjoying her embarrassment, and Neil reached behind the sofa cushion, produced a copy of the *Mersey Daily*. 'Front page — see?'

'And above the fold,' Alex said. 'Well, this gives me hope for your romantic life — who's the hunk?'

'It's all there in black and white,' Rowan said. 'Since you're so keen on him, why don't I see if I can hook you two up?'

'Ouch.' Alex didn't look in the least bit hurt. He scanned the text. 'Seriously, though, Cass — he must be worth a few bob. And he could help you work through your anger issues.'

Neil chuckled. 'Oh, you are looking for a pummelling, Alex,' he said, his eyes fixed on the TV screen.

Rowan levered herself out of her chair long enough to snatch the tabloid from Alex's fingers and dump it on the floor beside her chair. 'If you're such a matchmaker, why don't you go and find yourself a wife?'

'Oof,' Neil's eyes widened, and he actually dragged his gaze from the television. 'Below the belt, Cass.'

'She's just sore over the slight misunderstanding at the Chamber of Commerce bash, last year.' Alex was smiling, enjoying the verbal sparring. He always had — it was why he was so good in PR.

'What happened?' Neil asked.

'Nothing happened,' Cassie said, firmly, bugging her eyes at Alex.

But Alex was enjoying himself too much to stop. 'It's a bit X-rated,' he said, 'but since you've seen your big sis dressed like a hooker, I reckon you can hear it—'

Given the choice between letting Alex give his version of events and telling it her way, Cassie stepped in: 'Your "big brother" conned me into going with him to a boring business party.'

'I *invited* your sister to a highly prestigious Chamber of Commerce party—'

She glared at him. 'He introduced me to a *very* sleazy man, who tried to grope me. I put the sleazy man straight. The end.'

'It was an opportunity to hobnob with senior police and, more importantly, some very wealthy young men.'

'I can't begin to tell you how sexist and patronizing that is,' Rowan said, knowing it was a wind-up, but unable to rise completely above it. Something itched at the back of her brain, though.

'Some poor sod came on a bit strong. Nearly got his arm broken,' Alex said.

'*The sleaze* trapped me in a corner and made a grab at me. He's lucky I didn't snap his dick off at the root.'

Her brothers winced and Neil even crossed his legs.

Alex clucked in mock disapproval. 'Street work has certainly added colour to your language, Cassandra.'

Cassandra. The guy at the party had insisted on calling her Cassandra.

Rowan's heart jumped to her throat. *No — not possible.*

'What was his name?' Alex mused. 'John . . . ? Jack, maybe.'

Jesus, I saw him at the bar in the Baltic Fleet — standing right next to Roy Wicks. I was literally staring him in the face. 'No.' Scooping the paper off the floor, she turned to page two and found Tasha's sketch of her abductor.

'Not Jack,' she said, and her hands shook as she stared into the eyes of the Furman. 'Jake. His name is Jake Osbourne.'

CHAPTER 43

Saturday, 28 November, early morning

A body dumped in the River Mersey would normally be washed out into the Irish Sea within hours. But Jodie Pickersgill had gone into the water just as the tide was turning, so she skimmed along the silty river bottom for half a mile with the ebb, then stopped, floating on a slow surge of seawater, her body gently rising and falling, rising and falling, so that it seemed the river had breathed life back into her.

The flow gained momentum, creating whorls and eddies, and she rolled with the ease of an otter, her trailing hand scooping a red cumulus from the fine sediment. Seawater flowed steady, cold, turning the river brackish, increasing her buoyancy, pulling Jodie this way and that until, at a bend of the river, where sand and mud accumulated, she was nudged into the shallows and marooned on the muddy banks. Jodie Pickersgill had come to rest at the place local sailors called Dead Man's Elbow.

* * *

Rowan sat at her desk while the investigation team gathered around her. Jodie had been found at five a.m., and her case file had been upgraded from possible abduction to murder.

Wicks was talking to some of the newly arrived officers, swapping jokes, jingling the loose change in his pockets, and all Rowan could think was that he had stood at the bar of the Baltic Fleet, elbow to elbow with Osbourne. Still, that didn't mean they knew each other, did it? And yet, if it *was* pure chance, why had Wicks been so keen to interview Osbourne's clients — the women who had identified him from Tasha's sketch? Wicks never volunteered for anything that didn't benefit him directly.

She felt paralysed: if she went to DCI Warman, as Alex wanted her to, she would be accusing a fellow officer of withholding evidence — or worse. And it wouldn't look good for Rowan: The fact she'd had a set-to with Osbourne at the Chamber of Commerce party meant she had an agenda — that she'd already made up her mind he was a bad man.

She remembered the way Osbourne had looked her over in the pub. He knew her. Even if she hadn't recognized him, at first, she had responded to him on a primal level — the animal part of her brain had told her, *be wary, be afraid*. She was sure that Osbourne had targeted her after he abducted Tasha — the jacket and the stolen thumb drive were specifically aimed at her. *Dear God* — had he targeted Tasha because of her? She remembered his answer to her challenge in the pub: 'Do I know you?' she'd said, and he'd replied, 'Apparently not.' Men like that thought themselves unique, special, yet she had humiliated him and then forgotten him.

Poor Tasha . . .

'Cass? Cassie?'

Rowan blinked and looked up, finding Finch standing over her.

'Come on — you're going to be late.'

She looked about her in surprise: the room had emptied. 'Where is everyone?'

'Weren't you listening? There isn't enough room in here for the entire crew. We're using the office space on the second floor for the briefings.'

'I thought they were refitting that room.'

'They are,' he said. 'Like I said, it's just for briefings.' Flustered, he rummaged through his desk, picking up a notebook, a pen, a wodge of notes. 'It was announced five minutes ago — are you coming?' He was already backing for the door, his fair skin turning slightly pink in his anxiety to be on time.

'Yeah, sure.' Rowan lifted and replaced the files she'd been working on, and stared in dismay at the mess of handwritten notes she hadn't got around to typing up. 'I'll be there in half a minute.' But Finch had already gone.

Wicks's desk was, as usual, littered with rubbish: sweet wrappers, a coffee cup, the mangled copy of yesterday's *Mersey Daily*, and task sheets. She checked the room. Everyone was upstairs — the place was empty. She shifted position so that she could keep one eye on the door and sifted through the pink flimsies in his in-tray — half a dozen giving contact details for Osbourne's female clients. Some tasks were still not completed, others were completed but not filed. Not giving herself time to think, Rowan slipped her notebook from her pocket and jotted down the names and addresses.

* * *

She could hear the gabble of fifty-plus officers, clerical and forensic specialists as soon as she pushed open the fire door onto the second floor. The smell of paint and the vinegary taint of silicone filler grew stronger as she jogged down the corridor. Merseyside police set aside a few 'sterile' rooms with enough space and sufficient phone and power sockets to house CID and clerical staff on a shift rotation, as well as the computers and trained indexers that would run the HOLMES 2 database, in the case of a major incident. The sterile room at St Anne Street Police Station was undergoing an upgrade.

CID, Scientific Support, CSIs, clerks and indexers stood in huddles or lounged in chairs, acquainting, reacquainting, sizing each other up, sussing out the grafters from the bullshitters, the workers from the wasters. Wicks and Finch sat together. Rowan hesitated on the threshold, apprehensive, feeling like the new girl on the first day of school. *For crying out loud, Cassie . . .*

Ian Chan saw her at the door and waved, pointing vertically down, indicating a free chair. Rowan weaved through the crush of bodies, feeling eyes on her: men in the room outnumbered women by about four to one. Chairs had been dragged in from every available office, but the room was devoid of desks. A couple of stepladders leaned against one wall, and four or five filing cabinets hunched under dust sheets in the centre of the room — evidence of the decorators' hasty retreat. On the walls, a strip of raw new plaster ran like a scar at waist height, punctuated by double plug sockets and new phone jacks.

She slid in next to the CSI. 'Ian, you saved me a seat — are we in high school or what?'

'You certainly *looked* like it when you came through the door.'

'That obvious, huh?'

He patted her hand. 'Only to me.' He looked at her askance. 'So. Big day.'

'Meaning what, exactly?'

Chan raised his eyebrows. 'Meaning we've got something to work with now.'

'We've got a *body* to work with, now.'

He sighed. 'For some people the glass will always be half empty.' He nodded towards the door; DCI Warman had just entered. 'Who's the cutie in the Hugo Boss suit?' he asked.

'Detective Superintendent Beesley,' Rowan said. Peter Beesley was forty-five and looked ten years younger. He had the air of a man who was on the way up.

DCI Warman seated herself at the only table, alongside the superintendent.

She made a few adjustments to her laptop, then tapped twice on the table with her pen.

Detective Superintendent Beesley spoke first, introducing both of them. 'In case anyone is in any doubt, this is now a murder inquiry. I'll be Officer in Overall Command. DCI Warman has briefed me on the abduction-rapes, and I'll deal with crossover relating to that. DCI Warman will be running day-to-day aspects of the murder investigation.' Beesley nodded to Warman and she took over.

'The body was found at five a.m., today; it wasn't in the water long, so it's in good shape. The Home Office pathologist is conducting the PM now, but the prelim report indicates evidence of torture on the body — including burn marks, probably from a taser — which gives us a direct link to Emma and Tasha, as does bruising on her neck, which is consistent with repeated strangulation.'

Wow, Rowan thought. *They're taking Tasha seriously.*

Wicks asked, 'Do we need to bring Tasha in again, get a clearer picture of the details?'

Warman considered this. 'Good idea, Roy.'

'Ma'am,' Rowan said, alarmed.

Warman kept her gaze fixed on Wicks. 'Let's get some more detail on that report — see if she can approximate a geographical location.'

No — *No way* would she let Wicks loose on Tasha again.

'Ma'am.' Rowan raised her voice. '*Boss.*'

'*Yes*, Cassie?' she said heavily.

'I interviewed Tasha on Thursday. It's all in my report.'

'Perhaps you can give us a précis,' Beesley said. 'Bring us all up to speed.'

'The physical assaults — the use of the taser and the repeated strangulations — are in the medical record. He treated her like a sex toy.' Rowan tried to keep a professional objectivity, but she had to clear her throat before she continued. 'He kept her tied to a pillar with her hands behind her most of the time. He strangled and revived her during the rapes. Made her dress between the attacks.'

'A pillar,' Beesley repeated. 'An old church — a warehouse?'

Rowan shook her head. 'She said it felt like a swimming baths. A lot of glazed brick work. Yellowish.' Tasha had given a precise shade, but with the scrutiny of the room on her, Rowan couldn't remember it.

'It was wet — puddles of water everywhere — she was blindfolded, but she saw that much. He made her walk down two steep flights of steps.'

'Basement swimming baths . . .' Beesley frowned, but there was no hint of scepticism. He was just puzzled, as she had been, by the description. 'Does this mean anything to anyone?'

Bemused glances were exchanged.

'She has no idea of the location?'

Rowan shook her head, gaining confidence. 'She was blindfolded the whole time. She thinks she was driven in circles for a while before he dumped her.'

'Okay,' he said. 'Anything else?'

'He has a thing for candles — there were hundreds of them. She could feel the heat off them.'

'*Like a bad rock video*,' Tasha had said, wiping tears from her eyes and forcing a laugh that tore painful strips from Rowan's heart.

'Well,' Wicks said, with a fake enthusiasm that made Rowan's face burn, 'we could check church suppliers.'

'That's not a bad idea,' Beesley said in all seriousness. 'Such large quantities won't go unnoticed.'

Wicks shot him a look of bemused contempt, but Beesley carried on: 'The boyfriend — Simon Carstairs — is he definitely out of the frame?'

Warman jumped in. 'Half a dozen witnesses are willing to confirm that he was in a business meeting at the time of the abduction.'

'Any luck tracing the man in the sketch?' Beesley glanced down at his notes. 'We had a Jake Osbourne as a possible suspect?'

Wicks said, 'I tracked him to his mother's up in Cumbria today.'

Rowan stared at the back of his head. *Yeah, I bet you've been swapping texts like a couple of thirteen-year-olds.*

'She says he's been with her on and off the last few days; he headed out on business this morning.'

'What "business"?' Rowan demanded. 'Didn't his boss say he hadn't shown up for work all week?'

Wicks shrugged his shoulders like he didn't much care, but Warman said, 'Yes, she did.'

'Why's he in analysis?' Rowan asked. 'Did the boss know?'

'No,' Warman said.

'So how did she know he was even *seeing* an analyst?' Rowan asked.

'Pillow talk,' Warman said, raising an eyebrow. 'Osbourne and his boss were in a relationship some months back.'

'Well, they must've fallen out big time if she thinks he's the Furman.'

Warman shot her a narrow look. 'She *said* he looks like the man in Tasha's sketch. Let's not get ahead of ourselves, here.'

Rowan wasn't convinced, but a dig in the ribs from Ian Chan was enough to persuade her not to push it any further.

Warman turned to Wicks. 'You've been talking to his clients, Roy.'

Rowan leaned to the side to try and get a better look at Wicks's face.

'Yeah. They thought they recognized Osbourne from the sketch. No complaints, though.'

'*Nothing* untoward?'

He turned the corners of his mouth down. 'Nope.'

'All right,' Warman said, 'I want him traced, interviewed and eliminated.' She addressed the room: 'And we keep looking. The Furman left a new-looking shoe behind during the failed arrest ten days ago. Finch has been checking credit card transactions at local footwear stores.'

'No luck, boss,' Finch said. 'Nothing on the armed forces checks, either — at least, nothing that matches the Furman's MO.'

The DCI tapped in a command on her laptop, and a slide was projected onto the wall behind her: a post-mortem image of Jodie. 'The pathologist thought we might like this ahead of his report.'

She zoomed in on the image, magnifying two angry taser burns on Jodie's thigh. But that wasn't what she wanted to show them. She slid the scroll bar right and Jodie's hand came into view, fish-pale, the fingers slightly curled. There was something written on the palm of her hand.

'A phone number,' Warman said, clicking the mouse to magnify the image.

Bloody hell! Rowan sat ramrod straight. 'Ma'am — that's Palmer's number — the analyst.'

Wicks swivelled in his chair with the rest. 'Got it on your speed dial, have you, Cassie?' Nobody laughed.

'You're sure it's his?' Beesley asked, scowling in disapproval at Wicks.

'I called it enough times. It's Palmer's office number.'

'Follow that up, will you — DC Rowan, is it?' Beesley said.

'Sir.' Rowan felt a childish pleasure that he knew her name.

Tasks were allocated, a stern warning issued that trained indexers *only* were allowed access to the HOLMES database, and Beesley reiterated the need to check out the swimming baths lead. Rowan could tell by the glint in Warman's eye exactly who she had in mind for that task.

CHAPTER 44

Alan Palmer woke with a crick in his neck. He washed at
the sink in the facilities off his consulting room and ran his
electric shaver over his chin. A change of clothes would have
to wait until later. He was expecting the locksmith at midday,
and he wasn't going to budge until the locks were changed
and the keys were in his hand.

He brewed coffee in the kitchen and carried it through
to his office, the nutty aroma of Colombian roast triggering
a Pavlovian response that convinced him that he was wide
awake even before he took the first sip. Every surface was
piled high with buff folders and document wallets; whoever
had accessed his files had left no trace. Dylan had said that a
back-door hacker was invisible: 'You might feel the draught,
but you'd never see him,' he'd said. Palmer wondered now
whether that had been a warning, or a threat.

He sat with his coffee at his desk and checked his email
account. A new message had come in from Amy Sefton. No
salutation, no message beyond a terse, 'See attached.' He
downloaded and opened the file: sixty pages of single-spaced,

small-print typescript on Jake Osbourne. She must have been up all night. He sat down to read.

An hour later, his coffee untouched, he sighed and sat back. As he reached for his phone to try Osbourne's number again, it rang and he picked up.

'Alan?'

'Elspeth?'

'What the *hell* are you playing at?'

'I don't understand,' he said.

'Lucy tells me it's just as well she wore her wellies, yesterday, because the "Lady's Garden" was all squishy.'

The ground seemed to plummet from under his feet.

'I thought it must be a new attraction at the centre, but I checked, and there's no "Lady's Garden" at Blue Planet.'

'Elspeth, it's not what you think—'

'Really — you mean you *didn't* take her to a client's house?'

'No — Elspeth—'

'You irresponsible bastard!'

'Look,' he said. 'It wasn't—'

'How much do you think a little girl can take?' she interrupted again.

'Elspeth, she isn't—'

'I mean you're the therapist. How much — in your *professional opinion* — before she's irreparably harmed?'

'For God's sake will you listen!'

There was a shocked silence on the line.

'I'm sorry,' he said. 'I didn't mean to shout, but the woman we visited isn't a patient.'

'Who then? Who was this "funny" woman that your daughter didn't like?'

'She's a therapist. I needed to talk to her about—'

'Don't tell me,' she said. 'I don't want to know. You were supposed to be looking after her. You *weren't* supposed to be working.'

His temper flared again. 'And I suppose you didn't make a few calls yesterday morning while you were looking after her? You wouldn't *dream* of checking your emails while she was watching CBeebies, would you?'

'You took her to a stranger's house,' Elspeth said with cold control.

'A fellow *professional's*. Lucy played in the garden while we talked — and before you say anything, I was watching her the whole time. *Jesus* — why the hell should I have to explain myself?'

Her silence was answer enough.

Palmer felt the old guilt return, displacing the anger and settling like a familiar coat around his shoulders. 'Elspeth, I wouldn't have gone if it wasn't absolutely necessary.'

'"Necessary". Is that how you justify it to yourself? She's your daughter, Alan. You put her in harm's way.'

She wasn't talking about today, but a morning six months ago. The blame on her side and the guilt on his were as raw now as when it first happened. He struggled to find the words to comfort her, but none came, and after a few seconds, she hung up with a sharp click.

He set down his coffee mug and keyed in his wife's phone number.

After five rings, the answerphone clicked in. He tried Elspeth's mobile phone, but it was switched off.

As he replaced the receiver, his desk phone rang again. He made a grab for the receiver and knocked over the mug of coffee. Cursing, he lifted notes and folders out of the way, cradling the receiver between his ear and his shoulder.

'Elspeth?'

There was no reply. The coffee spread in a widening arc towards his mobile phone and he swore again, snatching it out of the way.

'You're angry. I understand that—'

Elspeth maintained a hostile silence.

To hell with her passive-aggressive crap. 'Okay,' he said. 'You've made your point. Now put Lucy on, will you?' Though he hadn't one single notion of what he would say to her. The silence continued a couple of seconds longer, then:

'You must have a death wish, pissing off two women at the same time.'

'Jake,' Palmer said, striving for neutrality of tone. 'I've been trying to get in touch with you.'

'Have you?'

'I tried your mobile and left several messages on your voicemail.'

'I *bet* you did.'

The copy of Friday's *Mersey Daily* still lay on Palmer's desk. The picture of him with Constable Rowan.

'I can see how it might look, me talking to a police officer. Perhaps you thought I'd broken confidentiality.'

'No "perhaps" about it,' Osbourne said. 'I trusted you. And don't patronize me with your psychoanalytic word-wank. We're not "in session" now.'

'Why don't you come up — talk about this?'

'On a *Saturday*? Goodness — wouldn't that infringe the "time boundary"? And what about the cost, Alan?'

Palmer was sure he wasn't talking about money, but that wasn't a discussion to have over the phone. 'I won't charge you.'

'A shrink talking value for money?' Osbourne laughed. 'That's a first. Still, I can see you'd be keen to hold onto clients — I mean, the *Mersey Daily* has a wide circulation. Are you shagging her — 'cos I gotta tell you, Alan — she's *way* too young for you.'

The line went dead.

'Wait!' Palmer actually reached out as if he could hold onto Osbourne. His heart pounding, he tried Osbourne's mobile, but it was still switched off. Reluctantly, he replaced the receiver.

How many times had Osbourne been let down? By Amy Sefton, who didn't understand that his aggression was a defence against the psychic injuries of his childhood; by the ill-thought-out way she had handed him off to Palmer; by the shoddy and incomplete notes she'd sent on to him. And by Palmer himself — he wasn't blameless by any means.

If he hadn't been so preoccupied with his own life crisis, he might have demanded a comprehensive report from Amy sooner. And now, it must seem that Palmer had named him to police — had violated his right as a patient to privacy. And the desperation in Osbourne's tone had been unmistakable.

The phone jangled him out of his reverie and he reached for it, then stopped, seeing his hand tremble. *You need to be calm. You need to keep it together.* He took a breath and lifted the receiver, speaking as he usually did when answered his office phone. 'Alan Palmer, how may I help?'

His voice sounded all right.

'That's your fucking tragedy, Alan — I doubt if you ever helped anyone.'

Osbourne again.

He really needs this conversation, Palmer thought. *Enough to agree to meet?*

'I promise you, I didn't break confidentiality,' he said, 'and I'd like the chance explain face to face.'

Osbourne snorted. 'I don't trust you. But I trust your office security even less.'

'We don't have to meet in my office,' Palmer said.

'We don't have to meet at all.'

'No. We don't.' The silence stretched for half a minute. If he could hold his nerve, keep quiet for long enough, he felt sure that Osbourne would agree to meet.

Palmer swung his chair to the window behind him and looked down onto the street. It had started raining; a steady, slanting, icy rain that looked set for the day.

'Tate Gallery café, Albert Dock,' Osbourne said at last. 'Fifteen minutes.'

CHAPTER 45

Palmer waited thirty-five minutes. By then, he had finished breakfast and was on his second coffee. He called his office building to ensure that security was checking his office regularly, and after he'd finished the call, there was still no sign of Osbourne. Ten minutes later, the waitress came to clear away his dishes and he ordered a bottle of water to quiet the buzz in his head caused by two double shots of caffeine and three hours of sleep.

She brought it and moved swiftly on to a group of three teenaged girls seated by the windows. Then the main doors swung open, admitting a gust of cold damp air, and Osbourne walked in. He stood still for a moment, blinking in the bright uncompromising light of the white-walled room like a potholer fresh from a cave.

He hadn't shaved, and with a guilty thud, Palmer wondered if the beard growth was an attempt to hide the slight thickness of his lower lip that the sketch in the newspaper had illustrated so well.

At that moment, he saw Palmer and grinned widely. 'Alan, you waited!'

He touched the waitress's arm as she passed. 'Coffee, breakfast — the Full Monty, sweetheart.' He nodded towards Palmer's table and said, 'I'm with him.'

'Sorry about the delay,' Osbourne said, with calculated insincerity. He swept off his mac, swirling it like a matador's cloak and drawing the attention of the trio of girls at the table near the window. He gave his head a shake to dislodge droplets of rainwater that had gathered decoratively on the soft peaks of his carefully styled hair and smiled over at the girls. They giggled and drew together in an excited huddle.

'Sexual danger,' Osbourne said. 'Acts like a pheromone at that age.' His eyes swivelled to Palmer.

Palmer accepted the provocation for the challenge that it was and said calmly enough, 'Why don't you take a seat, Jake?'

Osbourne scraped back a chair, sending an echo to the high white ceiling of the café. He draped his mac over the chair and slumped into the seat with his knees apart, hands resting on his thighs, fingers pointing inward to the crotch in classic alpha male pose, but his fingers tapped incessantly and he glanced about the room, his gaze rarely resting on anything for more than a second or two.

He looked like he hadn't slept; his eyes were red-rimmed, the whites shot with blood, and the oceanic blue of his irises had taken on a duller tone, like the muddy waters of a shallow lagoon after a storm.

'So,' Osbourne said. 'You've been trying to reach me. Feeling lonely, Alan?'

Palmer's gaze tracked from his patient's nervously tapping fingers, upwards to his face. 'You seem agitated, Jake.'

'Never better.' Osbourne smiled — all teeth and no warmth of feeling.

Palmer left a point of silence. 'Being lonely isn't always about being alone.'

Osbourne laughed. The harsh sound of it bouncing off the walls and ceiling, shivering the decorative streamers above them.

'"Loneliness is a state of mind."? Bull. *Shit*.'

Osbourne's breakfast arrived and Palmer watched for a time as he attacked his food like he held a grudge against it.

When he thought his patient seemed calmer, Palmer said, 'I didn't give your name to the press or the police. But they do want to speak to you. That's why they came to see me. I don't know who took the photograph in the newspaper.'

'And you expect me to believe that? I mean, did you look at page two in the *Mersey Daily*?'

An artist's sketch that was so like Jake Osbourne that he'd gasped. The caption: *Is this the face of a serial rapist?* 'I did,' Palmer said.

'And you know what I do for a living.'

'Of course.'

Osbourne spoke of little else.

'How d'you think that'll go down at work? With my clients? With *prospective* clients? Do you think they'll be happy to let a man who looks like a *serial rapist* into their house?'

'It must be wounding to see your name in the press like that. It should not have happened,' Palmer said.

'Damned right it shouldn't. But, you know, life isn't fair.'

He sounded bitter and raw — and who could blame him? But Palmer felt that the bitterness went a long way back in his history, and the words sounded like a scolding mother's snipe at a child.

'I spoke to Amy Sefton,' he said.

A flash of anger. It held for a second or two, and then Osbourne sat back in his chair. 'Oh.'

Palmer read the tension in the muscles of Osbourne's neck, and in the tightness around his mouth.

'What's the crazy bitch been saying?'

'She asked me to leave.' He didn't add that the notes she'd sent this morning had revealed a sad history of alternating neglect and smothering attention from a mother who suffered from bipolar disease.

Osbourne smiled and waved to a passing waiter. The café was filling steadily with bedraggled tourists and day-trippers, but he got the attention he wanted and pointed down to his coffee cup. The waiter turned and made for the bar.

'Didn't you find her a twitching bundle of obsessions? Did you notice the trichotillomania? —The woman looks like a plucked chicken!'

Palmer didn't comment, but he was interested that Osbourne must have looked up the disease.

Osbourne chuckled. 'Gotta say, Alan, if your lot go into this business to deal with your own shit, Amy's hardly a poster girl for "the talking cure", is she?'

'You seem angry with her,' Palmer said quietly.

'Wouldn't you be?'

'I'd rather hear your perspective.'

Osbourne gazed out of the steamy windows and refused to speak for several minutes. When the coffee came, he organised the waiter in clearing the plates and then eyed Palmer with amusement. 'Do I look angry?'

'We often hide our true feelings,' Palmer said. 'Anger with laughter, for instance, hurt with indifference.'

'Now, why would I be angry with Amy? She's such a mouse!'

'I think that Ms Sefton's refusal to continue your therapy and her decision to send you to me felt like a rejection. That was hurtful, and it made you feel angry.'

The flicker of amusement remained, and Osbourne sat up straight, clasping his hands in front of him. 'Really?'

'I told you she wouldn't speak to me — and that's true,' Palmer said. 'But she sent me a written report this morning. Ms Sefton said that your mother was bipolar, that during her manic phases she "entertained" men.'

Osbourne was visibly upset. 'I told her that in confidence — she shouldn't have said.'

Palmer felt for the frightened lonely child Osbourne must have been.

'It's her duty as a psychotherapist,' he said gently. 'I can't help you, unless I know these things. She said that as a nine-year-old boy, with your father gone, you found that hard to cope with. You felt betrayed and rejected.'

Osbourne's eyes were empty of emotion.

Palmer held Osbourne's flat stare. 'I believe that seeing your name in the paper — and my photo with the police officer — must have been terribly painful. It must have felt like another betrayal of trust.'

Slowly, by small increments, Palmer saw some of the tension leave Osbourne's shoulders and neck. Then, abruptly, he sat back in his chair and laughed, throwing his head back and barking at the ceiling. But despite the laughter, Palmer felt a rising panic, a pain, sharp and bright, a building, blinding light behind the eyes. This was Osbourne's true emotion. He was desperately afraid.

'Oh, you are *bad*, Alan,' Osbourne chided, talking over his thoughts. 'You want me to say Mummy Dearest needed a good seeing to, and I was the little man to do it. If only father would die and get out of the way.'

'But he didn't die,' Palmer said.

'True, but he did get *right* out of the way — moved abroad with a twenty-something business graduate.'

'How did you deal with that?'

'We comforted each other.'

Palmer didn't comment. He didn't need to: Osbourne saw the significance of the phrase as soon as he said it and Palmer saw fury building again in his patient's eyes.

'Fuck off, Alan.' He spoke barely above a whisper, and he glanced around, for the first time seeming aware that others might overhear — or perhaps he had always been aware — perhaps this was the first time that it actually mattered to Osbourne.

He leaned forward, gripping the edges of the table. 'Just you fuck *right* the hell off.' He breathed hard through his nose as if the rage and the effort of controlling it was physically demanding. 'You and your twisted insinuations — I'm not some Norman Bates character, jerking off inside his mother's stinking skin.'

His eyes widened in shock and Palmer was certain that at that instant Osbourne recognized that these were his true feelings for his mother. Osbourne broke eye contact and muttered again, 'Fuck off.'

For some minutes they were silent. Osbourne's coffee sat, untouched, visitors came and went, but the staff let them be.

The noise around them, the scrape of chairs and clatter of crockery, the high canteen clamour of voices served to increase their isolation from the ordinary: the other diners seemed to sense it, and the tables adjacent to them remained free.

After five minutes Osbourne said, 'I'm leaving.' He sounded exhausted, wrung out, and depressed.

'Jake,' Palmer said. 'I want to help you. I think I can.'

Osbourne took out his wallet and Palmer thought, *He really is going.*

'Come and see me again tomorrow, when you've had time to process this.'

Osbourne's eyebrows shot up. 'Yeah, sure,' he said. ''Cos this has been so much *fun*!'

He seemed in a moment to have recovered some of his good humour — another bad sign, this unpredictability of mood. There was a tipping point between flippancy and self-destructiveness, as Palmer knew too well.

Osbourne tossed a couple of notes onto the table. 'News flash, Doc: if I feel the need to talk, it won't be with you.'

He turned to leave and impulsively, Palmer stood and put a hand on his arm. Osbourne spun round, his eyes suddenly blazing with that weird blue light.

'You know what you are, Doc?' He shook free of Palmer. 'You're a receptacle for all the rage and hate and perversions of a score of twisted minds. We fuck with your head to make ourselves feel better. Then we pay you and go home to our wives and families.' He straightened his mac and summoned a smile. 'And you know what that makes you, don't you?'

CHAPTER 46

When Palmer got back to the office building, DC Rowan was just walking into the foyer. Lara didn't work weekends, so a security guard in uniform sat at the desk. DC Rowan's hair, glossy, brunette with hints of auburn, was tied in a loose ponytail at the nape of her neck, and she wore a down jacket and wool trousers over low-heeled ankle boots. She moved with a smooth easy grace. She reached the desk, and the guard was just beginning to shake his head when she saw him.

'Thanks, Brian,' Palmer said, then, 'Constable Rowan. What can I do for you?'

'Some follow-up questions,' she said, her face closed and unfriendly.

He led her to the bank of lifts, and as they stepped inside, he cleared his throat. 'I owe you an apology.'

They were standing side by side, but she turned her head to look at him.

'I was rude and aggressive when we last spoke. I'd had an argument with . . . someone, and I'm afraid I took it out on you.'

Her eyebrows twitched. 'Does that mean you'll help us to locate your patient?'

'I'm afraid I haven't changed my position on that. But I have told him that you want to speak to him.'

Her eyes hardened. 'You've seen him?'

He took a breath, but she stopped him with a sharp laugh.

'Don't tell me — you're not at liberty.'

He supposed he deserved that.

Inside his office, her gaze travelled over the chaos of folders stacked on his desk and in piles on the floor next to it.

'Catching up on the filing?' she asked.

He felt a spurt of defensive anger, but he kept it in check, remembering Karl Atherton's gentle chiding: his family problems were not Rowan's fault.

'I had a break-in.'

'Want to report it?'

'There's nothing missing.'

Her eyes tracked over his rumpled clothing, studying him as a scientist might study a bug.

'I take it you slept here, overnight?'

'Yes.' It seemed an odd question.

'So you won't have heard the news.'

Her eyes, like his, were brown, but at that moment they darkened almost to black with the knowledge she carried. 'The missing girl — Jodie Pickersgill — is dead. We found her body a few hours ago.' She gave him her professional face, her seen-it-all, believe-nothing, unshockable cop's face, but he felt the anger and outrage she was keeping in check.

'And you think Jake Osbourne is implicated? Is that why you're here?'

She watched him closely. 'Right now, I'm more interested in you.'

He frowned. 'Me?'

'Did you know Miss Pickersgill?'

'No — I . . .' The question had thrown him completely. 'Of course, I've seen her picture on the news, but I don't *know* her. How would I?'

'I was hoping you'd be able to answer that, sir.' She didn't even blink. It was as if she didn't want to miss some tiny gesture, something that would give him away. 'You see, your office number was written in waterproof ink on her hand.'

'What?' He couldn't make sense of what she was saying.

'Can you explain that, sir?'

'No,' he said, completely at a loss. 'I can't. I—'

'Can't — or not at liberty?' she asked, her head cocked on one side.

'If I thought I knew, I promise you, I'd tell you,' he said. But that wasn't entirely honest, because a thought had started to form at the edge of his consciousness, and he turned to his last encounter with Dylan. He *liked* following people, he'd said. And that word 'stalking' that had come so easily to his lips. Palmer looked into Rowan's eyes and remembered the hate sparking in Dylan's eyes when he'd said, 'Maybe I should follow *her*.'

He opened his mouth to tell her — he would have warned her at that moment, but her phone buzzed and she held up a finger — a gesture to wait.

She said her name, listened for a few seconds, said, 'When?' Then, 'I'm on my way.'

A moment later, she was gone.

CHAPTER 47

The phone message was from Finch: Jake Osbourne had just given himself up — walked into St Anne Street Station and asked to speak to the senior investigating officer.

Palmer's waterfront office was a nine-minute drive from St Anne Street Police Station, if you knew the rat runs around the city. Rowan made it in eight and took the fire escape stairs to the Major Incident Room two at a time. Finch was heading out as she arrived at the door.

'Can't stop,' he said. 'I'm interviewing him.'

'Who's taking the lead?'

'Wicks.'

Bloody hell . . .

Finch carried on, barely slowing his stride.

'Has he been arrested, or what?' she called after him.

He paused at the fire escape door. 'He's being interviewed under caution.'

'*What?*' They couldn't take a DNA sample until a suspect either volunteered it or was formally arrested.

'According to his brief he's here voluntarily "to clear up this mess".'

'He's guilty as sin.'

Finch shrugged. 'Well, you've obviously made your mind up.' He pushed through the door and was gone.

When Rowan turned back to the MIR, the DCI was watching her. Warman's grey eyes were like two hard pebbles. 'Constable Rowan, could you wait in my office, please?' Her words might be honey, but there was no mistaking that angry rasp in her voice. She was in for a bollocking.

Warman's office was tidy. The paperwork had built up over the past week, but she kept the stacks neatly squared off in three equally spaced piles. Rowan's report, containing Tasha's full statement, was front and dead centre.

The Chief Inspector arrived a few minutes later, carrying a clear plastic evidence bag. Her eyes skimmed the room as if checking that Rowan hadn't touched anything. She dropped the bag in her in-tray and went around the desk, but she remained standing.

'Did you interview Mr Palmer?'

'Yes, ma'am,' Rowan said.

'And did he have any explanation as to why Jodie would have his phone number written on the palm of her hand?'

'No, ma'am. He seemed genuinely foxed.'

'Foxed — as though it were an interesting conundrum?'

'No — he was shocked, too — I just meant—'

'That he had no satisfactory explanation?'

'Yes, ma'am.' Why was it Warman always got her tied in knots?

Warman plucked a folder from one of the stacks on her desk. 'Now, I want you to think very carefully before you answer this question.'

Rowan heard the warning in her voice and tried to clear her head.

'Can you swear that Osbourne is the man you chased to the freight yard that night?'

Something's coming. Be very careful how you answer, Cassie. She knew Osbourne from the pub, that night at the Baltic Fleet. She knew him from the Chamber of Commerce party her

263

brother tricked her into attending. She knew he was a creep and a bully. She knew he'd been following her. She knew he was baiting her when he threw Tasha's jacket down to her on the car park.

Except you can't know — not really. Because you didn't see him — not properly — not in the street above the car park, or at the freight yard, or when he broke into your car.

'Cassie?'

'It was foggy,' Rowan muttered. 'He wore a hoodie and scarf.'

'So, you can't swear.'

Rowan took a breath, ready to argue. *Stop it, Cassie. No amount of justification can make up for lack of proof.*

'No, ma'am,' she said quietly. 'I can't swear.'

'All right.' Warman opened the folder and brought out a CCTV still, turned it so that Rowan could see the time and date. 'This is Victoria Square, St Helens. Do you recognize the man in the picture?'

'It's Jake Osbourne.' Rowan felt a sinking hopelessness.

'Yes,' Warman said. 'It is. Mr Osbourne had just finished selling a security system to councillors at the Town Hall in St Helens, fifteen miles away, at the exact moment that you, Cassie, were trying to arrest the Furman.'

The room seemed to spin and the ground shifted beneath her feet. She'd been so certain!

'This is the consequence when you lose your professional objectivity,' Warman said, her face unnaturally flushed.

Rowan bristled, but before she could utter a word, Warman slid a newspaper from under the files on her desk: the Saturday edition of the *Mersey Daily*. She placed it, folded to show the headline, onto the desk in front of her.

'ARTIST'S NEW ORDEAL'.

Rowan glanced in question at her boss.

'The "artist" is Natasha McCorkindale,' Warman said. 'She sold her story to the *Mersey Daily*. You will notice the "exclusive" tag.'

Rowan skimmed the first few paragraphs, her stomach roiling.

'Tasha isn't named,' she said.

Warman picked up the paper and showed Rowan the photograph below the fold. It was in silhouette, but it was Tasha — no question. She remembered the mad chaos of paintings and pastels and charcoals in Tasha's flat — all of her attacker — his eyes full of hate. She remembered Tasha saying she didn't deserve loyalty. *'I've done things I can't take back,'* she'd said.

The article told Tasha's story from the previous summer when she'd first brought the serial rapist to the attention of Merseyside Police, through the failed abduction in September, to her abduction and rape only days ago. The journalist didn't name Osbourne, but they did feature several of Tasha's paintings and sketches of him.

Rowan stared at the paper. 'I can't understand why she would—'

'For the *money*, Cassie,' Warman exclaimed. 'For Tasha, it's *always* been about the money. Whether Osbourne has a case to answer or not, her evidence is tainted by this — you *must* see that,' Warman said, sounding more disappointed than angry.

She retrieved the evidence bag up from her in-tray. 'These are receipts, invoices, time-stamped car park tickets. Mr Osbourne brought them with him this morning. He says they will prove his innocence. I want every one of them itemised, in detail, and then I want *you* to check them.'

CHAPTER 48

Chief Superintendent Beesley called a late-morning meeting; he asked Rowan for an update on the swimming baths. She had found five disused facilities in the city; two were in the process of demolition. Of the rest, one was under a preservation order, with planning permission pending on a proposal to convert it to a private health spa, the other two were featured on the Liverpool Victorian Appreciation Society website, members of which were trying to raise money to have them restored.

'I've made an appointment with the Society's secretary,' she finished. 'He said he'd show me around.'

Beesley nodded, approving.

'How does Osbourne check out?' Warman asked.

It was a bitter task, but Rowan relayed the news as dispassionately as she could. 'I cross-checked times and dates on the invoices, till receipts and credit card slips Osbourne brought with him. The time stamps put him in the clear for Tasha — seems he's spent a lot of time up in the Lake District over the last few days. But none of the receipts go as far back as the date of Emma Hammond's abduction.'

Wicks spoke up. 'He was out on calls when Emma was taken, but since she can't even give a reasonable description of her attacker, the lack of an alibi doesn't exactly put Osbourne back in the frame.'

Warman added: 'And Penny Kominski didn't recognize Osbourne from Tasha's sketch.'

A few people made notes, others continued eating, amid a general murmur of disappointment.

'He's been visiting his mother in Threlkeld in the northern Lakes quite a bit, recently,' Wicks went on. 'He was there Wednesday to Friday — she took sick.'

'You've checked his story?' Beesley asked.

'Yes, guv.'

'We've only got his mother's word he was there the whole time,' Rowan said, thinking Palmer hadn't been straight with her about when he'd seen Osbourne.

'He didn't stay with his mother,' Wicks said. 'He checked into a Travel Inn near Penrith on Wednesday.'

'Can the hotel confirm time of arrival?' Warman asked.

'Eleven a.m.,' Wicks said. 'And staff say he didn't leave his room until the following morning. Which puts him well out of the way at the time of Jodie's abduction.'

'And he stayed in his room the entire time?'

'Doing paperwork, apparently.'

'How can they be sure he was there?' Warman asked.

'Security cameras on the entrance and car park. Mr Osbourne's a regular — he parks where he knows it'll get max surveillance. Security swears it didn't move.'

Warman nodded. 'We'll need to see the CCTV footage.'

'They're copying the recordings to a thumb drive for us,' Wicks said. 'Cumbria Police said they'll get it to us this afternoon.'

'Good work,' Warman said.

'What does he drive?' Rowan asked. She knew she'd made a mistake as soon as the question was out of her mouth: with Tasha's testimony discredited, the make of car was irrelevant.

Wicks rolled his eyes. 'Back on the prostitute angle again, are you, Cassie?'

She set her jaw and decided to brazen it out. 'Just trying to get the facts straight, Roy.'

Wicks did a slow scan of the room, inviting the others to share in his weary indulgence of her. 'He drives a Lexus. Like thousands of other business types. But Tasha would know that.' He paused for dramatic effect. 'Because Osbourne is one of Tasha's regulars.'

'That's crazy.' Rowan said. 'She stopped sex work after she was attacked.'

'Soon as the scar on her face healed, she went back on the game,' Wicks said.

Rowan shook her head in disbelief. 'She would have told me.' But was that true? Tasha hadn't told her that she'd sold her story to the *Mersey Daily*.

'She's been telling you porky pies,' Wicks said. 'Mr Osbourne's one of her punters.' He paused, flicking through his notes. 'He had a fall-out with Tasha a couple of weeks ago, over' — he coughed politely — '"unsatisfactory service". Didn't pay her the full amount.'

'So the sketch was payback,' Warman said.

Rowan felt the muscles of her face go slack. 'It's not possible.'

''Course it is. She made a pot of cash selling her pictures when she got her face in the papers after the Furman attack. She goes back on the game 'cos she's a greedy cow, gets a bit of a spanking off a punter — thinks she'll milk it for a few more bob.'

Rowan bristled. 'She was tasered, raped and choked half to death—'

'Cassie,' Warman's voice cut her off before she'd really got going. 'We've been through this. This is not a profitable line of inquiry. The matter is closed.' She looked away from Rowan, dismissing her. 'Now, we've had a set-back, but looking at it another way, we've eliminated a suspect. We still have the shoe, there are witnesses to interview, and the PM results on Jodie are still to come.'

She asked for a show of hands from the officers canvassing shoppers in the city centre and gave them a pep talk on the likelihood that a tiny detail could crack the case. Then she turned again to Rowan: 'Cassie — you can help Finch with the footwear angle. We've had a development on that — Ian?'

Rowan looked over her shoulder and saw that Ian Chan had slipped in at the back of the room. He weaved through to Warman to the table where she had spread her papers.

'Okay,' he said. 'The good news, first: we've identified several people from blood we found in the eyelets, laces and stitching of the Furman's shoe. One is a known victim of the Furman — Tasha McCorkindale. Three more are victims of unsolved assaults. The bad news: we extracted samples of ingrained blood that we can't identify because they're mixed profiles.'

'How many?' Rowan asked.

'Hard to tell — but several.'

There was a buzz of comment from the gathering, and someone said, 'Bloody hell!'

'Yup. We can't identify them, but the *really* interesting thing is, some of the mixed profiles contain XY alleles.'

'They're males?' Rowan said.

Wicks spoke up: 'It's not just *girls* he likes to kick the shit out of, then.'

'Delicately put,' Chan said with a tart smile. 'No, apparently, our man believes in the equality of the sexes when it come to putting the boot in.'

* * *

Twenty minutes later, Rowan was working through sales records of shoe shops, scanning the lists for sales of a shoe with the unlikely name of 'Fire Rage'. It was the cheaper end of the Clarks range, and sales had apparently been brisk over the past six months. Added to that, there were nine stores or stockists of Clarks shoes in the Liverpool area, and although Finch had already eliminated a few, she still had a four-inch stack of print-outs to wade through for each remaining store.

Roy Wicks was wandering from desk to desk, his hands in his pockets. Nearly everybody else was out on calls — primarily to interview the newly identified victims. All that remained were five telephone operatives and three members of the HOLMES team, working invisibly behind a cordon of screens, with only the rustle of their computer keyboards and the occasional murmured exchange of conversation to indicate their presence.

'Enjoy the warm, while you can, Cassie,' Wicks said, after she gave one particularly deep sigh. 'Looks like you'll be back on Pussy Patrol by the end of the week.'

'Haven't you got some pies that need eating, Roy?' she said, without looking up.

'Must be a sickener for you,' Wicks said, 'putting all that faith in Tasha, and she goes and makes you look like a twat.'

A nerve or blood vessel throbbed behind Rowan's eyes and the columns of figures seemed to bounce with each pulse. Desk space was at a premium since DCS Beesley had brought in his crew, and she and Finch were sharing. She glared at Wicks and was aware of Finch eyeing her uneasily.

'You've got half an hour,' she said, 'why don't you nip down to the Baltic Fleet — see if Osbourne will stand you a pint? After all. He owes you one.'

The smile froze on his face. 'What's that supposed to mean?'

She wasn't in a position to make accusations — not after the disasters of the morning. But she *had* seen them together at the bar that night. 'Jake Osbourne is a bad man, Roy,' she said. 'It's only a matter of time before he's found out.'

'Oh, you *know* that, do you?'

She stared at him without blinking. 'Yes, I do.'

His smile returned and he did a sweep of the room, trying to scoop up an audience. 'The Great Detective. Shirley

Holmes. You were so sure that Osbourne was the Furman, but you were wrong about that an' all. The fact is, Cassie — you had the Furman right in the palm of your hand and you let him go. Sad to think, isn't it — if you'd kept a grip on him, Jodie would be alive today.'

CHAPTER 49

Tasha buzzed her in without a word.

Staring into Wicks's self-satisfied face, Rowan had wanted to punch it. So she'd walked out of the Incident Room before she could act on the impulse.

Tasha looked thin. Her eyes had the haunted, slightly deranged look Rowan had seen on scores of abused women in her police career, and her apartment still looked like a drug-fuelled nightmare.

Rowan hardened her heart — his language might be more colourful than she would have chosen, but for once, Wicks was right — Tasha had made her look a fool.

'You let him go,' Tasha said. The press had been quick to report that Mr Osbourne, the man the police were keen to interview in connection with the rapes, had turned himself in. The police press office must have issued a statement to say that he had been exonerated and released.

'What choice did we have, Tasha?' She stared about her at the frantic array of paintings and pastels, staring into Osbourne's eyes, rendered in crazy, raging colours and thinking, *Was it all a lie?*

'I gave you the sketch.'

'And you sold your story.'

Tasha looked down at her paint-stained fingers. This sullen refusal to talk only enraged Rowan all the more: she'd stuck her neck out for Tasha — she wanted an explanation, a rebuttal, and apology.

'He says he's one of your regulars. You parted on bad terms. He says this is your way of getting payback.'

Tasha spoke so quietly that Rowan had to strain to hear. 'And you believe him.'

'I know you made money out of this. I know he isn't the Furman.'

Tasha glanced up sharply.

'He has alibis for several of the attacks. He says he was one of your regulars — that you concocted the whole story to get back at him for underpaying you.'

'Bastard.'

'Selling your story — it just gives his story credibility. Your testimony is worthless, now.'

'Bastard,' Tasha said, her hands clenched to her sides. She reached for the nearest easel and toppled it. 'Bastard, bastard, *bastard!*' She threw herself at the images of Osbourne, tearing paper, twisting canvases, flinging them, trampling them, her face streaming with tears.

Shocked, Rowan caught her and pulled her into a hug. 'It's okay,' she said. 'It's all right.'

At first she yielded, but then she fought, shoving Rowan away, seizing her by the shoulders. 'It isn't,' she said. 'It *isn't* all right. It can *never be* all right.'

Rowan shook her head, not knowing what to say.

Tasha looked wildly around the room, as if the images might come to life and attack her. 'I can't *do* this anymore, Cassie.'

'Tash—'

'Get out!' she screamed.

'Tasha, listen to me—'

She covered her ears. 'Getoutgetoutget*out!*'

Rowan moved to take her friend in her arms again, but Tasha lashed out, catching Rowan on the cheek. Her head snapped back, and for a moment, they stared at each other in stunned silence.

Then, Tasha's shoulders slumped, she wrapped her arms around herself and turned away. 'Just go,' she said wearily.

CHAPTER 50

When she got back to the station, Rowan met a stream of her colleagues setting out on tasks. She crossed the car park with her head down, car keys in hand.

'Hey, Cassie.'

It was Ian Chan. He disappeared behind an unmarked white van — the standard issue vehicle for Scientific Support. If Rowan hadn't seen Roy Wicks coming out of the side entrance at that moment, she would have kept on walking.

The rain was sheeting down and Chan slid open the side door, hopping in ahead of her. 'Step into my office.' She climbed in after him and he handed her a thumb drive.

'The one that did a David Blaine in your car.'

'Well that sounds faintly obscene,' she said.

He sighed and rolled his eyes. 'Disappeared, and then reappeared,' he said. 'No prints.'

'Could you check the files?'

'Not unless it's logged as evidence.'

'I don't know how I can do that, Ian.'

'Me neither,' he said, in a tone that put an end to further discussion. Then: 'Where the hell've you been? Warman's doing her nut.'

'I had an appointment with the pool guy, remember?'

'Liar.'

'I'm not lying. I had the appointment. I just didn't go.'

He glared at her and she shrugged. 'I was taking a break, okay?'

Chan slid the door to. 'You've hardly *started*, yet. And going AWOL isn't going to help. Face it, girl, you were wrong.'

'I know that, Ian. But Tasha never said Osbourne was the Furman — that was all me.'

'Well, she sold her story — wrecked her credibility all by herself.'

'You saw the medical report — she didn't do those horrible things to herself.'

Chan held up his hands. 'I'm not saying she wasn't raped — but, Cass, you can't take what she told you at face value.'

Rowan looked away.

'Look at the facts,' Chan persisted. 'A couple of hours ago, you'd have sworn that Osbourne was the Furman — look how that turned out.' He folded his arms.

'—And you needn't look at me like that. What about the credit card receipts, the hotel, the car park tickets — all time- and date-stamped? You've got to let it go, Cassie.'

She let her arms fall to her sides, all her anger suddenly drained, replaced by an enfeebling hopelessness. 'I know, but—'

'Will you *listen* to yourself?' Chan said, not bothering to hide his irritation. 'Do you want to be stuck on Operation Kerbwatch till you draw your pension?'

'I just want to get the job done.'

'That's all *any* of us want. But you also want to be known for more than your pink spangly tops and pert little bum.'

Rowan rounded on him, her face aflame. 'Fuck off, Ian.'

Chan raised his hands defensively. 'Hey, I'm only quoting the heteros who give a damn about your physical assets. You know I only lust after your brain.'

He fluttered his eyelids so coquettishly, she almost smiled.

'Jake Osbourne might be a nasty, bullying shithead,' he said. 'But that doesn't make him a rapist and murderer. And

I gotta tell you, hon, all the evidence says he's neither of those things.'

She stared morosely at the trays racked against the internal walls of the van. 'So what am I supposed to do?'

He touched her arm, lightly. 'Cassie. Sweetheart. If you like your job, and you want to be doing it in six months' time, do as you're told, for once.'

'What?' she said, incredulous. 'Try to match a man to a shoe?'

'Cinderella for the modern age,' he said, with a smirk. 'I'd do it for nothing.'

Rowan ignored his attempt to lighten the mood. 'What if he's had his bog-standard brogues for years, and just wears them for best? What if he paid cash?'

Baffled, Chan said, 'Who uses cash, these days?'

Rowan stared at him in disbelief. 'The credit crunch just passed you by, didn't it?'

'Like a massive tornado that sucked up the whole of Kansas and left just my little house standing.'

'The Furman thieves from hookers,' she explained. 'They deal in cash — my guess is, so will he.'

'Well, then you're screwed — and I'm late for a callout.' He seemed to regret the tartness of his reply and taking her hand between his thumb and index finger, he gave it a friendly shake. 'If you want to catch the Furman, all you've got is one shiny shiny shoe, so you'll have to make the best of that.' He slid the door open and waved her out.

Rowan frowned. *One shiny shiny shoe.* She slammed the door closed again.

'Cassie, I'm *late*,' he complained.

'You're right.' Her blood popped and fizzed with excitement. 'Ian Chan, you're a bloody genius.'

'Terrific, wonderful. Glad I could help.' He reached for the door lever again, but she slapped his hand away.

'When I was attacked, the Furman was wearing his shiny shoes and dark trousers. Penny Kominksi said he was wearing black trousers, black shirt, and shiny leather shoes.'

Chan sighed. 'Ye-es, she thought he was a waiter.'

'At *first* she did — then he made out he was a security guy. And you found male DNA on the shoe.'

'True . . .' he said, obviously not following.

She should tell him. But if she did, she would have to tell Warman, and either she'd squash the notion, or give the damn thing to Wicks, and she'd be stuck behind a desk for the rest of the day.

She gave Chan a smacking kiss on the forehead, slid the door open and jumped down.

Chan peered out at her as if she'd gone mad. 'What are you doing?'

Rowan grinned. 'If Warman asks, I'm seeing a man about a pool. But between you and me, I'm making the best of one shiny shoe.'

CHAPTER 51

Saturday, midday

The city centre pubs were packed with lunchtime trade. Rowan reasoned that the Furman was convincing as a security guard because he dressed like one: dark clothing, dress shirts, leather shoes. But also because he carried himself like a man who was easy with himself, commanding, physically. The Furman didn't mind using his fists — and his feet — which made it more likely that he worked security in pubs and clubs, rather than, say, building sites or office blocks. Most of the rapes had been between five and six or midnight and one a.m. — start and end of shift for the mega-pubs in the city centre.

Uniform and plain-clothes police were still canvassing in Liverpool One, and Rowan stole guiltily from one pub to the next, certain she would be spotted. She had locked her phone in her desk drawer, in case Finch — or worse, Warman — rang to find out where the hell she'd got to.

The breweries set up mega-pubs for serious drinking — tables and chairs were considered unnecessary fripperies that reduced footfall through their premises. Happy hours ran from teatime to dinner time, and two-for-ones were offered on everything from cocktails to export ales — which meant that door supervisors earned their ten quid an hour. The majority of managers had been helpful, given that business was brisk, and Rowan was taking bar staff from their work. Even so, she'd had no luck at all.

The rain drove in from the river in relentless sheets and the pavements were awash. By three o' clock, she was too wet and miserable to care if she was seen; she trudged from pub to pub with her head down, determined to keep trying until someone told her to stop.

She slipped into one of the smaller pubs near St John's Precinct at four thirty, just to escape the wind and rain. She sat at the bar, shivering, and asked for a coffee.

The woman who served her was a tall brunette, probably in her late thirties. She combined expensive hair styling with trashy make-up: eyelashes that were so thick you felt the draught when she blinked. Rowan had her pegged as the boss — the hired help could never have afforded the weight of diamonds on her fingers.

'It's shite.'

'What?' Rowan said.

'The coffee. But it's hot.'

'Sounds perfect.'

The landlady reached below the bar and came up with a towel emblazoned with the Stella Artois crest. 'Go on,' she said, thrusting it into Rowan's hands. 'It's clean.'

Rowan towel-dried her hair while the landlady zipped down the bar to take an order and set the coffee spurting from the machine. She joked with the customers, flirting outrageously, but it was clear the men knew exactly how far she was prepared to indulge them.

A minute later, Rowan was sipping hot liquid under the barmaid's curious gaze. 'We don't usually get your sort in here,' she said.

'Coffee drinkers?' Rowan asked.

'Police,' she said.

'That obvious, huh?'

She leaned across the bar, her gold bangles clattering on the wood. 'You checked out the lads as you came in — but not like you were eyeing up the talent.'

Rowan winced. 'That obvious . . .' She reached into her jacket. 'Detective Constable Rowan.'

The landlady's eyes widened with alarm. 'For God's sake, put it away — d'you want to empty the place?'

Rowan tucked her warrant card back in her pocket. 'Sorry. Call me Cassie, then.'

'You can call me Crystal.' She watched Rowan closely, as if waiting for a comment.

Rowan extended her hand. 'Thanks for the towel, Crystal. I take it you're the landlady?'

She tilted her head in acknowledgement. 'I take it you're not here socially?'

'I'm investigating the abductions.'

Crystal tensed, then she gripped Rowan's hand more firmly. 'Sooner you get that perv the better.'

Rowan nodded. 'The guy involved might be working as a doorman.'

'We don't use no doormen, here, love,' Crystal said. 'My Dave's an ex-boxer. If anyone gets out of order, they're out on their arse.'

The answer was intended to disarm, but Rowan had seen a flash of recognition behind her eyes. Crystal knew something. 'Ah, well,' she said, toasting her with the coffee cup. 'It was worth the visit just for the coffee.'

Crystal waved that obvious fib away with a flick of her beringed hand. 'I thought you'd got someone from that drawing in the paper.'

'Turns out he had an alibi.'

Crystal snorted. 'Any self-respecting criminal *would*.' Her eyes narrowed. 'But you know that.'

Rowan kept her expression blank. She had already screwed up by insisting that Osbourne was the Furman, she couldn't afford to start any rumours that the police were convinced they had the rapist and he'd wriggled off the hook.

'We questioned a man,' she said, carefully. 'He left the station with the boss's blessing.'

Crystal said, 'So, you're just a jobsworth, hassling the locals 'cos that's what the boss told you to do.'

That stung. 'She doesn't even know I'm here.'

Crystal stalked off to serve a new arrival, with a dismissive, 'Huh!'

The safest course of action would be to leave while Crystal was busy, but busy as it was, a pub like this couldn't support the landlady's taste in diamonds. Which meant that she, or her doting husband, had a few other irons in the fire. Which, in turn, meant she would almost certainly know most of the villains in the area.

The customer who'd just come in was obviously a regular — he called Crystal by name, and when she commented that he was early, he said, 'I heard that big bruiser of a husband of yours was out Christmas shopping, thought I'd take me chance to propose.'

She pulled his pint and eyed him with a haughty smile. 'Propose what, Gary? He's took himself off to Boodles to find something nice in rubies and diamonds for Chrimbo. Best you could do is a string of placky pearls out the Pound Shop.'

The other men at the bar gave a collective, 'Ooh . . .' followed by laughter. Someone shouted, 'It's her better half you should be courting, Gary.'

'It's not about the money, lads,' Gary said, handing over his cash with a sanctimonious sniff. 'I'd give all me worldly goods for a smile from those luscious lips.'

Crystal prodded the coins in her palm. 'Well, I'm sorry to tell you, Mr Rockefeller — but if this is your worldly goods, you're fifteen pee short.'

Their audience hooted with laughter. 'You've broke me heart,' Gary said, fishing in his pocket for the money owing.

'And that's not all that'll be broke, if you don't behave.' Crystal turned away with a smile and Rowan caught her eye.

She stalked to the end of the bar. 'You still here?'

Rowan said, 'I like the ambience.'

'That'll be the stale beer. It's a bastard to get out the carpets.'

'Could I have another coffee?'

Crystal narrowed her eyes. 'If you promise to go as soon as you've finished.'

'Will you answer a couple of questions?'

She glanced protectively at her clientele. 'That depends.'

'On what?'

'On whether you think your boss let the Furman go.'

'No,' Rowan admitted, in all honesty. 'I don't think she let the Furman go.' She'd come to the realisation that Osbourne was altogether a different kind of animal.

The landlady stared into her face like she could read a lie behind the eyes. 'All right, then. You can ask — but I'm not promising nothing.'

'The man I'm looking for is youngish. He may have been out of the country.'

'Haven't heard a question, yet.' Crystal kept a weather eye on the customers.

'Okay, here's the question: would you know of a doorman or bouncer who has a reputation for being too free with his fists — and his feet?'

Crystal frowned, peering into the darker corners of the pub. After a few moments, she looked again at Rowan. 'You're talking about the kind of hard man who likes to beat up women?' She sounded wary, clearly unwilling to give too much away until she was sure it was relevant.

'Not just women,' Rowan said.

Crystal stared at her thoughtfully for a few moments, and Rowan added, 'We have evidence that he's given a few men a kicking.'

Crystal angled her body to look past Rowan. 'You ready for another, Frank?' she said. Rowan heard a grunt from behind her.

Rowan began to swivel on the bar stool, but the landlady touched her hand to stay her. 'Do us a favour, love, while I do a bit of a tidy up. Take Frank his pint.'

She drew a pint of draught bitter and Rowan carried it to the back of the bar. There was an overhang from the accommodation upstairs which made this rather dingy section darker than the rest, but as she approached, her breath caught in her throat. Frank sat at a table on his own, sucking his pint through a straw. His head was clamped in a contraption of metal rods and bolts, and he had a scar the shape of a crescent moon running from his right eye to the top of his cheek bone. His eye socket was empty.

'Thanks, queen,' he growled. His jaw was clamped tight by the metalwork. Frank looked like he would be sucking his ale through a straw from some time to come.

'No problem, Frank,' she said, forcing herself to look into his one good eye. 'Car accident?' she asked.

He grunted. 'Felt like it.'

She pulled up a chair. 'Doorman?' she asked softly.

He looked quickly into the brightly lit bar area. Crystal was entertaining the men with a story. When he saw that they were safely ignored, he nodded.

'Where?'

'Why?'

Rowan sneaked a look at the bar, lowered her voice. 'I'm after this bastard.'

Frank's good eye darted frantically. 'No.'

'No one will know,' she said.

'*No.*'

'The sooner I get to him, the sooner you'll be able to breathe easy, Frank.'

'You don't understand — he's fucking crazy.'

'I know,' Rowan held his gaze. 'I know.'

He licked his lips and looked away, his eyes searching the table, the floor, as if he'd lost something.

At last, he said, 'You can't tell no one. I—' He winced, the long sentence putting too much strain on the shattered bones of his face.

'I swear,' she said, covering his hand with hers. 'Nobody will know but me.'

He fiddled with the straw in the empty glass.

'I'm gonna find him sooner or later, Frank. But the city will be a hell of a lot safer if you save me some time.'

He shoved the straw into the new pint and took a long pull, flinching with every swallow. Then he set the glass on the table and gave it a twist so that it sat dead centre of his beer mat.

'Theme pub,' he said, without looking at her. 'Hanover Street. McNally's.'

CHAPTER 52

By five p.m., thirty plain-clothes police officers were in place in and around McNally's bar. Lee Maseby was twenty-five. His father had been in the armed forces, stationed in Germany when Lee was in his mid-teens. When the family relocated to the UK, Lee had remained, but was deported in late spring for breaching Germany's strict laws on residency permits.

Rowan was sitting in an unmarked car on Roe Alley, which ran between two side roads off Hanover Street, as far from the action as Warman could put her — punishment for having disobeyed her orders — again. But she'd rationalised it by saying the Furman knew Rowan; her instructions were to stay out of sight unless a direct request for backup was broadcast. She had Finch for company, which wasn't exactly a comfort.

Maseby was expected for the start of his shift at any minute. Rowan should feel excited, vindicated, but what she felt most was cold. She'd had no time for a pit stop at the station and change of clothing, and realising that she'd left her mobile phone in work, she'd made the call from a kiosk on Paradise Street and waited for backup, sheltering in a doorway on School Lane. Finch had picked her up ten minutes later in an unmarked car. It was dark, the temperature had plummeted, and it was still raining. She leaned forward and turned up the heat, thinking if Wicks made the arrest, she might just have to quit the job.

They listened on the agreed radio frequency, Rowan shivering and miserable, Finch worrying at his fingernails. Rowan checked her watch. 'He's late.'

'He'll be here. There's another dozen cops watching his flat. We'll get him.'

Finch's phone rang. He listened for a moment, then he sucked a lungful of air and blew it out. 'Yeah,' he said. 'No kidding.'

Rowan said, 'What?' Something had happened, she could hear it in his voice.

He nodded. 'Yup.'

'For *God's sake*, Finch.'

He cupped a hand over his phone. 'There's been a screw-up,' he said. 'Maseby arrived for work at half-four — the boss just hadn't seen him.'

'Which means he probably saw our lot arrive and slipped out through a side door.' Rowan slammed the heel of her hand against the dashboard. '*Shit*, he'll be long gone.'

Just then, a shadow appeared, clinging to a drainpipe on the side of one of the buildings twenty yards down the road.

'What the hell?' Finch said.

'It's Maseby,' Rowan said. 'He must've got out over the roof.' She reached for the door lever. 'Call it in.'

The figure shinned down a drainpipe and dropped the last few feet to the ground. Rowan launched herself at a run, not bothering to shout, not wanting to give him even that much warning. He saw her, turned, and her shoulder hit the back of his knees almost in the same instant.

'Police!' she yelled belatedly. Maseby's head bounced off the drainpipe and he fell with a grunt of pain.

Five officers came skidding around the corner within seconds. She grappled with the Furman, her knee in the small of his back. He heaved himself on all fours, bucking wildly, and jerked his head back, making contact with her forehead. Her skull boomed and she saw stars, but she didn't let go.

'Not this time,' she yelled. 'Not this time, you fucker!'

Suddenly he collapsed, all the wind gone out of him, and it took a moment before she realised that three other cops had joined her. They gripped his arms, his legs, his head, while she cuffed him and rattled through the words of the caution.

' . . . do you UNDERSTAND?' she finished at a roar, adrenaline surging through her like forty-thousand volts of electrical current.

'FUCK you, you fucking *tart*,' he screamed, fighting all the way.

She grinned in his face, wiping blood off her forehead. 'He understands,' she said.

CHAPTER 53

'You can forget it — I'm not talking to *her*.'

Lee Maseby, AKA the Furman, looked like the kind of man who would have sand kicked in his face. He was average build and height, with a long neck and large Adam's apple. He wasn't particularly well-muscled — you would wonder how he survived weekends as a bar doorman in Liverpool. Until you looked into his eyes. There was a cold hatred in those eyes that said he would maim a man for life and never lose a minute's sleep over it.

Maseby was a Thai boxer and Kung Fu fanatic who had never won at competition because he didn't have the discipline — for Lee Maseby, it was all about inflicting pain. Warman had suggested that Wicks should sit in on the interview, Rowan agreed only after Wicks agreed that she would take the lead.

'My client says you attacked him.' Maseby had been allocated the duty solicitor, Paul Bailey. Rowan had met Bailey a few times in interviews; he was a good brief, and she respected his skill, if not the people he defended.

Rowan fingered the butterfly bandage above her right eye. 'Believing myself to be in imminent danger of physical harm I defended myself with proportionate force,' she said.

Maseby shifted in his seat, folding his arms. 'I'm not saying anything with her in the room,' he said. 'She's a fucking mad dog.'

'My client wishes to make it known that he refuses to cooperate while Constable Rowan remains in the interview room,' Bailey said.

Rowan smiled. 'Thanks for the translation. But you don't need to say anything, Mr Maseby,' she said. 'From the blood on your shoe, we've identified several victims — men and women you attacked *before* you started taking the precaution of hiding your face. I'm sure those victims will identify you.' She had to hope they weren't all as scared as Frank. 'When we match your DNA to the freight yard, where you attacked me, and caused fifty thousand pounds-worth of damage, we'll have you on theft, criminal damage, GBH, rape, abduction, resisting arrest, and murder. Enough to put you away for several lifetimes.'

'*Murder?* Look, if she's on about that girl they found in the river—'

'We'll come to that, Mr Maseby,' Bailey said, and keeping his eyes firmly on Rowan he added. 'I think you'll find the rape charges hard to prove.'

'Really?' Rowan said. 'Well, in the twenty-first century even prostitutes have the right to say no, Mr Bailey.'

'I *said* I don't fucking *want* her here,' Maseby muttered, glaring at his solicitor in a way that made Rowan nervous on his behalf.

But Bailey was an old hand. He leaned back in his chair and said, 'Relax, Lee. For the record, Mr Maseby intends to sue Merseyside Police Authority for excessive use of force in the attempted arrest on the docks.'

'What?' Rowan was so outraged that she didn't take in the fact that Maseby was admitting to being in the freight yard.

'He had a two-inch splinter of glass pulled out of his foot,' Bailey said. 'We have photographs.'

'He lost a shoe when he kicked me in the face,' Rowan said tightly. 'And we took a few for the album, ourselves.'

'My client says you attacked him with a bottle.'

'If I had, it wouldn't be his *feet* I'd go for.'

Wicks snorted in appreciation.

Maseby's gaze fixed on her, and she stared him out.

'I'm requesting a break,' Bailey said, speaking clearly for the tape, and addressing himself to Wicks. 'My client has made serious charges against Constable Rowan. We expect her to be replaced before agreeing to continue this interview.'

* * *

Rowan went to report to DCI Warman, and Wicks shambled into her office a few moments later with a Mars bar in his fist.

Warman looked at the chocolate bar, up to his face, then back to his fist. He muttered an apology, then pulled the wrapper over the remaining third and slipped it into his pocket.

'We seem to have reached a stalemate,' Warman said.

'He's taken a dislike to young Cassie,' Wicks said, with surprising restraint.

Rowan stood elbow to elbow with Wicks, in Warman's narrow office, breathing the sickly-sweet smell of his chocolatey breath, and knowing that his attack of piety was only because he knew she was about to be pulled from the interview team.

'Finch has done some digging,' Warman said. 'The breach of residency regulations was an excuse to get him out of the country. Maseby had been accused of a serious sexual assault on a sixteen-year-old girl outside a nightclub. She dropped the charges, but the German authorities deported him for the residency violation.'

'So, let's go in with that,' Rowan said. 'If he knows the Germans are cooperating, it might rattle him.'

Wicks gave a doubtful, 'Hmm . . .'

A look passed between them, then Warman said, 'You know I can't let you go back in, Cassie.'

'I made the arrest, ma'am,' Rowan said, feeling a bitter knot of anxiety and anger in her chest. 'I know some of the victims. I—'

'Knowing the victims is hardly a recommendation. We've had the discussion about objectivity . . .'

Wicks slid her a sly look and Rowan felt heat creep into her face. Bad enough she'd had that particular bollocking — did she have to bring Wicks in on it?

'We won't get anything out of Maseby while you're in the room,' Warman insisted. 'His accusations—'

'—are bullshit,' Rowan said.

'Of course. But your presence in the interview room would taint any information, any confession he makes. The officer that supposedly brutalized him remaining in the room throughout the interview — I can't allow it.'

Rowan opened her mouth to protest, but Warman raised a finger, and she subsided. 'You have unique insights, I'll grant you, but I'm afraid you're toxic to the interview process.'

She means you think like a whore.

Rowan had worked for months in the freezing cold, parading herself like a piece of meat. She'd been pawed by slimy men who drove around the city with a hand in their pants, looking for women. She'd been kicked in the face and nearly run over by a truck. She had found Maseby when he went to ground. It was her arrest. And now Roy Wicks was being handed the interview on a silver platter.

'You worked alongside the sex workers for a number of months,' Warman continued. 'You've spoken at length to the victims. I would value your input to the next phase of the interview.'

Rowan blinked. *It wasn't just a dig.* Ian Chan's voice popped into her head. *She's holding out an olive branch — for once in your life, take the damn thing.*

Rowan exhaled, letting go of days of tension. 'Okay,' she said. 'I'd like to know why he's admitting to the freight yard.'

'You have a theory?'

'Maybe it puts him in the clear for Emma Hammond.'

'Emma was abducted the night after you chased him down to the freight yard, yes?' Warman asked.

Rowan nodded.

'And by a man on crutches. . . I don't see how that points in any direction but Maseby,' Warman finished.

'Bailey's no fool — he wouldn't give anything away for free,' Rowan countered. 'There has to be an advantage to Maseby. Bailey said they had pictures of the damage to his foot, and the next attack wasn't until Friday — the attempted abduction of Penny Kominski. Maybe he lay low for a few days.'

Wicks grunted. 'And I suppose someone went out and impersonated him just to make him look bad?'

'You want to make yourself look helpless, a pair of crutches'll do the job,' Rowan said. 'The Furman was badly cut — we know that, from the amount of blood in the freight yard — and I'm sure the ME will confirm that Maseby's injuries are what you'd expect to see from standing on broken glass. But Emma was taken only a day after he sustained those injuries. How d'you suppose a man with a badly gashed foot managed to carry an unconscious woman from his car, then drag her down two flights of steps?'

'Now you're saying there's *two* rapists running round the city?' Wicks said. 'Why d'you have to complicate everything, Cass?'

'No, it makes sense,' Warman said. 'Roy — see what you can find out. Cassie — talk to the ID officer, get Maseby set up for a VIPER recording first thing tomorrow. Then contact the witnesses. I want Emma, Jodie, the witness in the car park, all of the sex workers, to view it.'

The Video Identity Parade Electronic Recording — or VIPER — system, a virtual ID parade, had been gradually introduced countrywide since 2002, and had revolutionized the process. A suspect could be recorded, eight lookalikes selected from a database of over twenty-five thousand volunteers, and the virtual parade ready for witnesses to view in just a couple of hours.

'That won't take long,' Rowan said. 'What do I do then?'

'Then, Cassie, you go home.'

Rowan took a breath.

'No arguments,' Warman said, 'You look ready to drop.'

'Ma'am, I could—'

'You've done a good day's work here,' Warman interrupted, 'but there's nothing more you can do tonight.'

A good day's work? *Did Pat Warman just praise me?* Rowan glanced left to Wicks, but he was already on the way out of the door — she must have flipped out for a second — she could hear him, now, slouching down the corridor, whistling. She backed out of Warman's office, feeling a little unsteady, and was smiling to herself as she shouldered open the fire escape door.

'You just can't let it go, can you?'

Startled, Rowan whipped round. Wicks was standing a few steps up the stairwell; he must have been waiting for her.

'What d'you mean?'

'Osbourne. You've had him in your sights since the start.'

'I never mentioned Osbourne,' Rowan said. 'Now why would he be at the forefront of your mind?'

'"Maybe it puts him in the clear for Emma Hammond",' Wicks said in a high falsetto that was meant to mimic her voice. 'And who else *could* it be but Osbourne, am I right, Cassie?'

'Well, you'd know, Roy.'

She caught a glint of hard anger in his eyes. 'Let it go.' It sounded like a threat. He took a step towards her, but Rowan held her ground and he didn't follow through. He eyed her with contempt. 'You've got a lot to learn, girl.'

'I'm young,' she said. 'Teach me.'

He reddened. 'You know why you couldn't arrest the Furman the first time? Because you're a lightweight — in every sense of the word.'

'He got away because you didn't do your job.'

His hands tightened into fists, but she held her ground.

'I've been on the job thirty years,' he spat. 'I've seen this city through the recession, Hatton's mob, the Toxteth riots, drug wars, gun crime and suited thugs looking to make a fast buck, riding on the back of Liverpool One. I was nicking hard men when you were still latched onto your mother's tit.'

'So what went wrong, Wicks?' she said, hearing a matching anger in her own voice. 'What happened to you?'

His eyes flickered, and for a second, he looked confused, uncertain, even. Then he lurched at her. This time she did flinch — but he lumbered past and carried on down the stairwell.

She waited to hear the fire door slam shut after him before she slumped against the stair rail. A trickle of sweat made its way from her neck, down the curve of her spine. *What the hell is he into with Osbourne?* She took out her notebook and thumbed back to the names and addresses she had scribbled down from Wicks's task sheets the day before. Different parts of the city, from plush suburbs to solid working-class areas, all of them women. All of them had recognized Osbourne from Tasha's sketch — he had sold every one of them a security system. *Okay*, she thought. *I'll do as I'm told; I'll organise the VIPER parade and leave. But I might just make a few house calls on my way home.*

CHAPTER 54

The rain had finally stopped, beaten westwards by a scouring north-easterly that rattled the slates on the roof and howled down the chimney. Cassie stared out of her kitchen window, absently drying a coffee mug. The house was empty when she'd arrived home at seven fifty. Alex had left a note: they had waited until seven thirty. *Tried to reach you. Turn on your damn phone!* It said they would be in Ego's on Hope Street, if she wanted to 'touch base'. He'd signed off *Regards, Alex*. Like she was a business contact. There was a PS: *Don't forget to dig something out to wear tomorrow!*

Oh God, the bloody wedding.

She climbed the stairs and forced herself to look through her wardrobe. She would stay an hour — *Two, tops*, she promised herself. Then she would offer her congratulations to the bride and groom and make her excuses. Alex could do the family schmoozing, for a change — 'touch base' with their snooty Scottish relatives. PACE regs barred her from attending Maseby's VIPER ID, but she wanted to be at the station on Sunday when the Furman was charged.

It hadn't taken long to contact the victims and invite them in for the ID parade. That job done, she had tackled the women on Wicks's task list, all of whom had contacted the hotline when Tasha's sketch had gone out to the media. All of them were clients that Jake Osbourne had sold security systems to, all lived alone, all were single women. What surprised her was none of them was under forty.

Her first interviewee had been Lillian Foster; an octogenarian, wrinkled as Methuselah, but she wore court shoes with two-inch heels, a smart tweed suit, and she was freshly powdered and perfumed.

'He came highly recommended,' she said. 'After the burglary.'

'Who recommended him?' she asked, 'Community Support Officer? Victim Support?' Neither of which should recommend firms.

'Oh, they *came*. Gave me some advice: double-bolts and deadlocks, window locks this and five-lever that.' They were drinking tea from matching porcelain mugs in her cosy sitting room, a plate of Mr Kipling Bakewell tarts on a table midway between the two of them. She lifted the plate, urging Rowan to take one. 'But at my age, it's in one ear and out the other. The other chap was much more helpful. It's all right,' she said, seeing Rowan's look of alarm. 'I don't let just *anybody* through my front door. He was a policeman — showed me his card — and before you ask, I made sure he was a match to the photo.'

'D'you remember his name?' Rowan asked.

'Love, I'm eighty-three years old, and this was three months ago.' She paused with her Bakewell tart halfway to her mouth. 'I do recall he was a bit portly — downed four of my French Fancies without taking a breath.'

'Would you know him again if you saw him?'

'I might . . .'

Rowan still had Tasha's sketch of Wicks in her handbag. A flush of hot blood rushed to her face — if she was wrong about this, it could finish her career. Her hands trembling, she retrieved the sketch.

Lillian Foster exclaimed, 'That's him! Roy, or Ray something.'

'Detective Constable Roy Wicks?' Rowan said.

'Yes,' Mrs Foster said, with a satisfied nod. 'That's it — Constable Wicks. He gave me Mr Osbourne's card and everything.'

The others told her exactly the same story. A burglary, a visit from Community Police, another from Roy Wicks — a follow-up courtesy call, he'd said. He'd recommended Jake Osbourne to every one of them.

* * *

Rowan rummaged through her wardrobe and picked out a dark blue trouser suit in defiance of her brothers' disapproval — and a coral pink ruffled blouse in deference to the occasion. She hooked them on the wardrobe door, still mentally working through the evening's interviews.

The women were all impressed by the 'service' Wicks had provided, were grateful for the advice. Before she left, Rowan asked each of them why they had called the hotline — after all, they seemed happy with the security measures Mr Osbourne had put in place.

The sketch of Osbourne in the *Mersey Daily* was a very good likeness, they said. But Lillian, the most forthcoming of them, hesitated as if she wanted to say more.

'Lillian . . .' Rowan prompted.

The old woman fiddled with the cup in her hand. 'You don't like to give a person a bad name.'

'Of course not. But if there's anything you feel you should say . . .'

Lillian touched her arm, suddenly looking frail and anxious. 'You won't tell him I said this?'

Rowan covered the old lady's hand with her own. 'Not in a million years.'

Lillian nodded, making up her mind. 'He made me feel — I don't know.' She looked helplessly at Rowan. 'Like I wasn't safe in my own home.'

* * *

Somewhere in the house, a door closed with a secretive *snick*. Rowan stood still, listening to the old building heating and cooling, straining against the dark torrent of wind that raged about it. The streetlight outside her bedroom window flickered, fading and sparking brighter, as if a giant moth fluttered around it, hypnotized by the faint orange glow. Her heart tripping, she tiptoed out into the hall.

That soft *snick* again, and the blood roared in her ears.

The creaks and sighs of planking and plaster fell silent for a moment. It seemed almost that the walls leaned in to listen. Then—

Snick.

Rowan reached for her Casco baton, discovered that she'd left it on the work surface in the kitchen.

Snick. A movement to her left. She spun, saw the bathroom door open a couple of inches, then begin its shuddering progress to close again.

She took one step. Another. The door gave one last soft *snick*. She swung it fully open, felt the cold night air on her face, and almost laughed with relief.

Bloody Neil! The quarter-light was propped ajar, admitting gusts of blustery wind. She let her breath out in one long rush and, laughing, reached up to secure the window.

She checked the rest of the bedrooms and returned to the kitchen, trying to think if they had anything edible in the fridge. Everything was as she left it: the mug on the drainer, with the tea towel where she had abandoned it, next to Alex's note. Except it didn't *feel* right. It felt like something — some*one* — had been in and disturbed the air, leaving it turbulent, troubled.

Tiredness, she told herself.

A hollow *boom*, somewhere in the darkness beyond the window. *The wind*, she told herself. Probably toppled a watering can in the yard. *That's all.* But it sounded heavier than that — weighty. So maybe a wheelie bin had tipped over. *Or maybe someone blundered into it.*

The windowpane was still spotted with the spattering of the last downpour. She could see nothing in the darkness beyond. She thought about the handprints she had found on the window last Tuesday. The wind shivered the droplets of rainwater on the window, forcing them back, taking them to where they had been two, three, five minutes earlier.

She leaned across the sink and stared into the darkness. Something moved. Something big and monstrously human in the darkness beyond the glass.

Rowan jerked back with a surprised yelp.

The shape retreated and she stared at the door. The wood was old and softened with rot in places; she could see the force of the wind bowing the old wood panels. A sudden gust rattled the key in the lock, and Rowan launched herself forward and slid the bolts home, top and bottom.

For a minute, maybe longer, she stood with her back to the door, feeling the wood flex against her, as if a hand was seeking out its weak spots and testing them. An object skittered past just the other side of the wood panelling, and she shuddered, her arms and legs jangling with the nervous shock.

'To hell with this,' she hissed, and again, shouting, this time. 'To hell with it!' She grabbed her Casco baton from the table and kept going, down the hall to the front door, straight out before she had the chance to think how stupid it was. Osbourne had had it all his own way up to now. Well, screw that. This was her home, and she would not — would *not* — be made to feel afraid in the one place she should feel safe.

Her dad was right: go looking for trouble and you'll find it. But when trouble came looking for you, the best way she knew to deal with it was to meet it head-on.

Whoever was out there, he would expect her to come out of the back door, so instead she made her way to the side entry at the end of her row. This entryway gave access to an alley that ran the full length of the street along the backs of the houses. She'd take him by surprise. The side entry was dark and narrow, and Rowan eyed it with dread; if she had done as Warman told her, she would be eating good food at Alex's expense right now.

Heart hammering, fingertips tingling with adrenaline, she flicked her Casco baton to its full extent.

It was probably just a flapping piece of tarpaulin, she told herself, as she headed down the narrow gap between the houses. *Or a newspaper, blown across the yard*.

Even so, she wished she had a can of pepper spray.

The backyards of the rows were edged by brick walls, six feet high, with a gate to each property. The alley was wet with rain, and the old paving slabs gleamed like new coal, but it was clear. Her neighbours knew better than to leave bins outside — they attracted kids with a fascination for fire, and burglars who used them to boost over the walls. The wind tugged and pummelled her, slowing her progress. As she reached her own back gate, she heard a dull thud. Rowan jumped, almost turned and fled. Something rolled and skipped across a hard surface.

'*My house*,' she muttered quietly. 'I should feel safe in my own damn house.'

She clicked the hasp of the gate and the wind tore it from her, slamming it hard against the brickwork. She could see nothing. She took a few rapid breaths, psyching herself up, then stepped inside, swinging left and right, baton ready.

Her neighbour's security lights flicked on, deepening the shadows, blinding her. Rowan swore. She only hoped that the distorting effect of the light gave her some bulk.

'POLICE! DO NOT MOVE.' She kept her voice in the lower register.

The lights clicked off, and for a second or two all she could see was a pulsing red glow at the centre of her vision. Then something solid in a wedge of shadow by the far wall seemed to shift. Real, or an after-image of the high-wattage lamps?

She yelled again: 'LET ME SEE YOUR HANDS' — although she could see almost nothing. Slowly, a pale oval emerged from the solid patch of dark, shaping itself into a man's face.

'WALK TOWARDS ME — SLOWLY,' she commanded, trying to blink away the corona of red and green colour from her vision. 'DO *NOT* MAKE ANY SUDDEN MOVES.'

The shadow seemed to ripple and pool for a second, diverging so she thought there might be two prowlers, and her heart seemed to lose its rhythm, dancing and skittering in her chest. But as her vision cleared, she saw he was wearing a dark coat that billowed and flapped in the restless wind.

Rowan held her baton over her right shoulder, her elbow bent and tight to her side, the better to get a good swing; letting him know she would use it given the slightest provocation.

She backed away, beckoning him towards her and the man took another step. The pallid haze from the fluorescent tubes in the kitchen caught the side of his face and Rowan stared in disbelief.

'Mr *Palmer*?' He said nothing.

Doubts crowded her mind. 'What the *hell* are you playing at?' He began to speak, but she waved her free hand to silence him. 'Never mind — I don't want to know.'

She worked around to the side of him, aware of his height and bulk, aware that he had the advantage in the small space.

'You're going to walk ahead of me.' The wind caught her words and cast them into the night, so she had to shout. 'Turn right out of the gate.'

He obeyed without quibbling. Over his shoulder, he said, 'I've been trying to reach you all day — your phone was switched off.'

That much was true. Even so, she planted a hand in the flat of his back urging him forward, into the alley. 'Keep moving.' she said.

He turned. 'I was concerned for your safety.'

She took a step back, her heart hammering. They were in the passageway between the houses, with brick walls either side that a determined man might use as weapons to crack a skull.

He raised his hands. 'I'm trying to help—'

'Stop talking,' Rowan said. 'Just shut the f—' *Hold onto yourself, Cassie.* She took a few breaths. *'Please* — just . . . stop talking.'

His shoulders slumped and he went meekly to the front of the house, where he turned again, slowly this time. His hands out to the side, palms up. 'I'm here because I wanted to be sure you were all right.'

'Yeah? So why didn't you knock at the front door — instead of sneaking around the place like a damn stalker?' She gripped the baton, charged with adrenaline, ready to swipe at his vulnerable points: elbows, knees, ankles.

'I was about to when I heard a noise at the back of the house. The gate was open,' he said.

'Unlocked?'

'Open,' he corrected. 'Wide open — banging off its hinges.'

'Why are you here?' Rowan demanded.

He reached inside his coat and the wind caught it, sending the cloth flapping around him like a demented crow.

'Don't make me use this,' she warned, raising her baton.

'A card,' Palmer said, offering it to her between his thumb and index finger. 'Just a business card.'

She plucked it from his fingers. 'Mine. What's this supposed to prove?'

'The break-in I told you about? Someone got into my office files, cancelled all of my appointments. I had the locks changed earlier today. I went out for a time and when I got back, a courier had left a package for me at the reception desk. The cutting from the *Mersey Daily* was inside — and your business card.'

'So what?'

'Flip the card over.'

She glanced down just long enough to get a glimpse of the back of the card. Her address was written on it.

'That's how I knew where to find you. I came to warn you, Constable Rowan.'

She looked into his face and thought again about the handprints on her kitchen window, Tasha's jacket thudding onto the roof of her car, Neil's stolen thumb drive, placed carefully on her passenger seat, outside her home.

'Okay,' she said, 'Come with me.' She grabbed him just above the elbow with her free hand and propelled him towards her neighbour's house.

Bill Grayson answered.

Bill was a six-foot Jamaican. He and his wife, Stella, had helped Rowan through the death of her parents and Stella had looked after Neil while she worked night shift more times than she could count. Bill had the muscle gained from a life of labouring in the building trade, and a slight obsession with bodybuilding. Bill also had an innate distrust of men in suits.

'All right, girl?' He looked at Palmer like he was calculating how far he could throw him.

'I'm fine, Bill. This man's name is Alan Palmer. I'm taking him into my house to talk to him.'

Suspicion deepened to aggression. 'He bothering you, Cassie?'

That was too complicated a question to answer, so she said, 'We're going to have a chat in my house. But you'll remember him, won't you, Bill?'

Grayson thrust his head forward so fast that Palmer jerked back. 'Oh, I'll remember Alan Palmer, all right,' he said softly.

* * *

Rowan directed Palmer through to the small sitting room at the front of the house and made him sit down. She remained standing, between him and the door.

'I'm sorry,' he said. 'It was foolish and rash to come to here. But I didn't know what else to do. Someone carefully cut out a newspaper clipping containing your photograph. Your business card was on my desk, when I last saw it.'

'And you believe this mystery man stole it and wrote my address on it,' she said, thinking *Palmer came to your house, Cassie — Palmer, not some mystery man.* 'The same mystery man who wrote your office number on Jodie Pickersgill's hand?'

Palmer raked his fingers through his hair, and she noticed a tremor in them. He caught the look and clasped his hands together.

'When did you get this delivery?'

'Uh, I don't know the exact time,' he said. 'I was out between three and five this evening.'

'Well, whoever is messing with you, it isn't the serial rapist.'

He blinked, and she saw self-doubt as plain as guilt on his face. 'How can you be so sure?'

'Because we have the rapist in custody.' She watched him closely. 'We have DNA linking him to the victims — it's going to be announced on the late news.'

'Oh.' He frowned at his hands. After a time, he rubbed his hands on the legs of his trousers and stood, looking a little shaky. 'I'm sorry I wasted your time.'

She watched him walk down the path to the gate, thinking, *You haven't been honest with him, Cassie.* But Palmer had come to her house, snuck around her backyard and frightened the living daylights out of her.

Bill's front door opened, and her neighbour glanced across to her.

'All okay?' he asked.

'Fine, thanks, Bill,' she said, although she didn't believe it for one second.

CHAPTER 55

Palmer checked his watch; he was going to be late for dinner with Karl Atherton.

He rang his friend. 'I've been delayed, Karl,' he said. 'I've only just got home.'

'Are you all right?'

'No,' he said, truthfully.

'You sound strained.'

He almost told Karl there and then that he had been right all along, that he wasn't ready to take on a full patient list. That he wasn't fit to manage his own emotional upset, let alone analyse others. But he said, 'I'll tell you all about it when I get there.'

'Ah,' Atherton said. 'A long story. I *like* those.' His friend's measured tones, the hint of humour at the back of his words, were a balm. 'Well, there's no rush. I decided a warming casserole would be just the thing on a night like this.'

'I'll be there in half an hour — I just need to shower and change.'

He closed the phone and moved through to the bedroom, dragged out a clean sweater and a pair of cord trousers, then speed-dialled Elspeth's landline one last time. It was still switched to voicemail. He checked the charge on his handset and slipped it into a dry overcoat — the one he had used all day was hanging on the back of a chair in the kitchen, reeking of damp wool.

The heat of the shower made him realise how cold he had become, and he luxuriated under the stinging spray until every inch of his skin tingled.

By nine p.m., he was out of the door. He walked the distance to Karl Atherton's flat, taking a shortcut through the park, detouring only to pick up a bottle of wine. The cloud cover was low and the air smelled of damp and decay. He kept to the paths, dodging puddles and the offer of company from a sad-looking man sitting on a bench overlooking one of the brimming duck ponds.

Palmer rang the front doorbell to warn his friend of his arrival and made his way to the side of the house. Raindrops gleamed on the black paintwork of the fire escape. He started up the steps, already relaxing, anticipating the warm welcome, the food and conversation.

The kitchen door stood open and the thick, meaty aroma of beef stroganoff wafted down to him, along with the meditative notes of a Chopin étude. His footsteps clanged discordantly on the cast iron and he trod more softly, not wanting to spoil the tranquillity.

A pan bubbled on the stove and the oven light glowed; the smell of the food was maddeningly enticing. Two wine glasses stood ready on the table and Palmer called through to the sitting room, 'Karl? Shall I open the wine?'

The corkscrew lay beside the wine glasses and he stepped further in to the kitchen, ready to pop the cork and get started on the wine, stubbed his toe against something. He looked down, expecting to find that a corner of the rug was rucked, saw something that didn't make sense.

Karl Atherton lay face down on the tiles. For a moment he stared, uncomprehending. Then he was on his knees, next to his friend.

'Karl!'

He set the bottle down, heard the gritty *crack* of glass on tile. Atherton had a small cut just below his hairline. He must have fallen, hit his head on the edge of the table.

Palmer crouched closer, listening for sounds of breathing, could hear none. All he could think was, *I was speaking to him just an hour ago.* He touched Atherton's face. 'Karl,' he said again. The old man's cheek was warm. 'Oh, my dear old friend . . .'

Gently, he loosened Atherton's collar to search for a pulse, and stared, puzzled, at two livid marks, no more than a millimetre across. He opened the top button of Karl's shirt and recoiled at the sight of an angry red line across the lacy skin of his throat.

'No.'

This can't be happening. He eased Atherton onto his back. His eyes were bloodshot, his face swollen and purple.

He hardly knew what he did next. Later he had flashes — trying to rouse Atherton, saying his name over and over, lifting his friend and cradling him in his arms—

A soft *flump* from the next room brought him to. He eased Atherton to the floor. Another muffled thump, like someone moving furniture around. He surged to his feet and was through the door in one furious action.

The long sitting room-office was in darkness; the only light was cast from the fire that crackled merrily in the hearth. It reflected playfully from the gold-embossed volumes of Karl and Millie's collection of classic fiction and glittered on the rows of academic texts shelved from one end of the room to the other.

A humped shadow seemed to crouch menacingly on Atherton's desk, twenty-five feet away in the gloom, and he heard again that furtive sound.

'Come out, you cowardly fuck!'

He flicked the light switch—

—saw a wall of books stacked four feet high around the desk; behind it, a void in the rows of shelving.

Palmer took a couple of steps. A thin hand reached up to add another book onto the stack.

He heard a mumble of disjointed words. *Dylan*.

Corbie sat in the centre of a semicircular barricade that extended from Atherton's desk to the bookshelves. His green eyes shone luminous as a cat's. He was muttering something over and over to himself, his lips moving constantly, but Palmer could barely hear a sound.

'Dylan,' Palmer said.

Palmer almost shrank from the intensity of his. But it wasn't Palmer that Dylan Corbie saw — it was something other. Something that made him look at and through Alan Palmer with no hint of recognition.

'Dylan,' Palmer said again. No response. He moved to the side of the desk and crouched beside his patient.

He seemed to be trying to complete the wall of books, to close the semicircle and create his own castle-keep of words. Palmer removed one of the texts from the pile and Dylan scooted under the desk, folding his long limbs into the confined space of the recess. 'It's all right, Dylan,' Palmer soothed, replacing the book.

Dylan's hands came up, shielding his eyes from Palmer's gaze.

'Tell me what happened, here,' Palmer said.

Dylan stared at him, as if trying to hear the soft whisper of what lay behind the words. 'Lies taste of honey,' he muttered. 'Got to write it down.'

'Dylan . . .' Palmer said, grieving afresh.

'Stick to the facts,' Dylan hissed, his eyes fracturing the light in green shards.

CHAPTER 56

Emergency lights strobed blue and red in the darkness: two marked police cars and an ambulance, the green-clad paramedics scuffing their heels by the open doors of their vehicle.

A crowd had gathered beyond the tape; they craned their necks to see what was happening on the top floor of the brightly lit house. The CSIs had arrived already, their plain white van parked just outside the cordon. Two of them worked on the fire escape; the door at the top of the steps was open, and light spilled out. Every few seconds, the CSIs were frozen in phosphorescent white flashes — Ian Chan must be inside, documenting the scene.

Rowan showed her warrant card and ducked under the tape. Finch stood on the tarmac drive, coatless and shivering, his hands in his pockets and the wind riffling his fair hair.

'They won't let you go up,' he said glumly. 'Preserving the integrity of the scene, they said.'

'Palmer called it in?' she asked. There was no sign of the analyst.

Finch nodded, turning his back on the crowd of onlookers, less than twenty feet away. 'He was supposed to be having dinner with the victim — Karl Atherton — some kind of

310

head doctor. Found Atherton strangled, one of his patients doing his nut in the sitting room.'

'Strangled . . .' Rowan gazed up at the windows on the top floor, the photographic flashes like silent bursts of lightning. The smell of cooking drifted through the open door, and Rowan felt a guilty pang of hunger: she had abandoned a meal of scrambled eggs and toast after Ian Chan had rung to tell her he'd had a call-out to a murder scene, and that Alan Palmer was involved.

'The lad's been following Atherton and Palmer—'

'The lad?'

'Dylan Corbie — the patient.' Finch lowered his voice, although the crowd could not have heard above the beep and chatter of the ambulance's radio and the bluster of the wind that set the police tape buzzing. 'It's all in this notebook they found on him.'

'What does Palmer say?'

Finch shrugged. 'Warhorse is talking to him, now. She reckons Corbie persuaded Atherton to let him in, clobbered him and choked him to death.'

The front door opened, and voices echoed down the stairwell: Palmer's voice, low and reassuring, and something else: something that didn't sound quite human. A keening sound that rose and fell, then abruptly, stopped.

A light came on in the hall and they heard the clatter of footsteps on the stairs. The crowd shuffled and moved forward as one.

'The lad', as Finch had called him, looked no more than eighteen. The emergency vehicle lights highlighted fading bruises on one side of his face. He looked undernourished, and his bony limbs were uncoordinated. He was flanked by Palmer and a female constable in uniform; they seemed to be propping him up, half-carrying him. He stopped, blinking in the light, his eyes swivelling from Rowan to Finch and then past them to the crowd.

One of the paramedics leaned off the ambulance and took a step forward, glad to have something to do, but

Palmer shook his head, turned to the boy and said a few words. There was nothing much in them — all he did was explain to Dylan that the ambulance would take him to hospital and the paramedics would make sure he was safe, looked after — but it was enough to soothe, and Dylan Corbie began to move forward again, this time muttering urgently, as if he had a message to pass on to Palmer that wouldn't wait.

'It's all right, Dylan,' Palmer said.

'No.' He balked at the ambulance steps. 'I should have helped her.' He stared into Palmer's face as the analyst tried to coax him up the steps into the ambulance.

Suddenly, he turned and gripped Palmer's lapel. '*Psych 101*,' he said, as though it was the number of a safety deposit box. 'You just have to look. Can't just fill up an empty hole.'

Rowan caught Palmer's eye and the look he returned was so bleak that she felt she was intruding and had to avert her gaze.

The police constable spoke a few words to Palmer before following Corbie into the ambulance, then the doors closed, and it began its slow progress through the crowd. Palmer stared after it. He seemed unsure where to go or what to do next and someone leaned towards him, microphone in hand.

'Radio Merseyside, Mr Palmer,' the reporter said. 'Can you tell us what happened?'

Palmer stared at the microphone as if it had a life of its own and Rowan stepped up. 'This way, sir,' she said, and gripped his arm just above the elbow, guiding him back towards the house.

'No,' he said, and she heard the horror of what he had seen in that one word. He seemed to gather his strength to say, 'They said I could go.'

Rowan glanced at Finch. He understood: 'I'll call you,' he said.

The greatest press of people was to their right where the glare of the emergency service headlights gave them a good view of the house. Rowan led Alan Palmer to the far side of the cordon and helped him under the tape. His movements were loose, his gaze unfocused.

Shock, Rowan thought.

She led him around the corner and into the long avenue that sloped eastward to the solid terraces of Wavertree and westward, to the contrasting riches and deprivation at the muddled heart of Toxteth.

She guided him into her car, shielding his head as she would a suspect she had arrested, and turned the car towards Sefton Park and his home.

They'd gone less than half a mile when he said, 'Stop.'

Rowan glanced at Palmer. 'Sir, you're in no fit state—'

'Stop the damn car,' he repeated, scrabbling for the door handle. 'I'm going to be sick.'

Rowan pulled in at an angle to the kerb and he practically fell out of the passenger seat and vomited into the gutter. Rowan stepped out of the car and stood by helplessly while he continued to dry-heave over a black puddle of water.

For a minute he bent, bracing both hands on his thighs and gulping air, before easing himself upright.

'Okay?' she said tentatively.

He stared at her. Desperation and despair flashed in his eyes, and finally dull hopelessness. He turned and started walking, his legs jerking like they were on strings.

'Mr Palmer.'

If he heard her, he made no sign.

'Mr Palmer,' she called. '*Alan.*'

He carried on walking and she followed him, caught the sleeve of his coat. He snatched his arm away and turned on her.

'Can't you leave me alone?' His eyes blazed and she took a step back. The light went out of his eyes and he said dully, 'Stay away from me.'

Before she could think of a word of comfort, he staggered off into the darkness.

CHAPTER 57

Word had got around that Warman was going to make an announcement, and virtually all of the inquiry team showed up at the Major Incident Room. There was a definite party atmosphere, despite the grim events of the evening, and the sense of urgency Rowan had felt only this morning was largely absent.

DCI Warman was practically euphoric. 'We could wrap this up in a week,' she said, smiling. 'There's still work to do, but it's only a question of corroboration and consolidation — well done, all of you.'

Rowan couldn't join in the self-congratulatory applause. She didn't even have the consolation of Ian Chan at her side, making sly comments, or the neutral presence of Detective Superintendent Beesley as a moderating influence: Ian was still at the murder scene and probably would be for the rest of the evening; the superintendent was giving a press conference at headquarters.

Wicks sat near the front. Rowan watched his back nervously. He had sold information about the burglary victims to Osbourne, she was sure of that. But what made her sick to the pit of her stomach was the suspicion that he might be in much deeper.

Pat Warman stood with her back to a newly installed whiteboard on which a square of light was projected. A new face sat at the table next to her.

'The murder of Karl Atherton will be assigned to another inquiry team, but it has given us the link between the sex-worker rapes and the Liverpool One abduction-rapes.' She ticked off the points on her fingers: 'Taser used to stun the victim; preliminary examination of the victim suggests strangulation; Dylan Corbie has a history of mental instability, and threats of violence — he spent time in a secure unit.'

She clicked the mouse on the laptop in front of her and an image of a green notebook came up on screen. The next image showed the first page, crammed with small, crabbed handwriting.

'This is a description of a girl Corbie's been stalking,' Warman said. 'One of several — we'll need to trace all of them, make sure they're okay.' She let her gaze flit from face to face. 'He was also stalking Dr Atherton . . .' She moved on a couple more images. 'And Mr Palmer.'

The notebook gave dates, times, locations, descriptions, names — even the weather was catalogued in obsessive detail. The Chief Inspector flicked rapidly though slide after slide. Her inventory stopped at the centre pages of the notebook, both inked with closely written text. There was something off-balance about it, but before Rowan could get a good look at the writing, Warman clicked to the next slide and the screen went blank.

'Ma'am,' Rowan said. 'The witnesses describe a glib, charming, confident, strong man. Corbie's a nerd who keeps notes on the weather. And looks like he couldn't punch a hole in a wet *Echo*.'

'Cassie,' Warman looked more tired than angry.

'Please, ma'am, hear me out.'

Warman sighed and folded her arms.

'The seven attacks we can definitely pin on Maseby were vicious,' Rowan said. 'He used extreme violence — fists and his feet. Tasha nearly lost an eye. Two more I know of had multiple fractures of the jaw and facial bones.' She paused, wondering if she was making the second big mistake of the day. But she had to try at least to make them listen.

'But if you look at the three other attacks — Emma Hammond, Tasha McCorkindale and Jodie Pickersgill, their faces were unmarked. He took them somewhere out of the way. They all described the same place — a vast tiled area, like a swimming bath. He tied them up and played with them.' She flashed to the bruises on Tasha's neck — to Emma, telling her in a whisper how he had strangled and revived her over and over as he forced himself into her. 'He tortured them with a taser. He choked them.'

'Cassie, we've all read the medical reports,' Warman interrupted.

'He took his time,' Rowan pushed on. 'The Furman — Maseby — is impulsive, a smash and grab merchant — literally — the guy who attacked Emma, Tasha and Jodie likes to think he has some kind of finesse.'

'Nobody disputes the facts, Cassie,' Warman said. 'But there are different interpretations that may be put on them. I'd like to introduce Dr Andy Milton.' She nodded to the man seated next to her. 'Andy is a forensic psychologist, specializing in sex crimes. Andy will explain.'

Milton stood. 'It's not uncommon to see alliances between two very different character types in sex crimes, forming what we call a "rape alliance",' he said. 'Typically, a dominant personality joins forces with a weaker type. Dylan Corbie could be the weaker, masochistic half of the rape alliance. He follows girls, keeps tabs on them, but takes a step back when the dominant player — Maseby, in this case — is ready to act.'

'Dylan is subservient to Maseby?' Rowan said.

'Yes.'

'So why did he kill Atherton?'

The psychologist ruminated on this for a few moments. 'Recent entries in his diary have an angry — even violent — tone. Relationships are dynamic, behaviours evolve.'

Wicks shifted in his seat impatiently, swivelled to face her. 'You've been proved right, Cassie — two stalkers, two attackers, we got them both. We found Corbie in Atherton's flat — with the body, for crying out loud!'

'Dylan could well have held a grudge against Mr Palmer,' Warman said. 'New background has come to light, regarding his professional standing.'

Dr Milton spoke up again: 'Mr Palmer was under investigation by the British Psychoanalytic Council earlier in the year.'

'It seems,' Warman said, with fastidious delicacy, 'that Benjamin Kehoe, a troubled fifteen-year-old boy in his care, committed suicide in Mr Palmer's own consulting rooms.'

'Oh, yeah,' Wicks said. 'You can trust a headshrinker who doesn't even notice his patient's about to top himself.'

'That will do, Roy,' Warman said. 'Let's look at this objectively: Dylan Corbie was found at the scene. He was Dr Atherton's patient, he has a history of mental illness — and of threatening violence. We can't change the facts to fit whatever your theory of the moment happens to be, Cassie.'

Rowan kept her mouth shut — she didn't need Ian Chan kicking her ankle to recognize that Warman's slap-down was said for the benefit of the entire team. She had pushed it as far as Warhorse would tolerate.

The Chief Inspector wrapped up with another round of congratulations and the team began to drift off.

* * *

Rowan walked down to the CID office on the floor below, and sat at her desk, sunk in thought, while officers and staff flowed around her, picking up personal belongings, chatting, laughing, making arrangements for what was left of Saturday night.

She was thinking about Palmer. His panic when he'd got the card with her address on it. He had discovered Dr Atherton's body, moments after he'd been murdered. If he

317

hadn't come to her house to warn her, would he have been in time to save his friend? He had been so gentle with Dylan — she was sure he didn't believe the boy was capable of killing Atherton any more than she did.

She became aware that she was being observed. Wicks sat with his back to his desk, slurping a late supper of noodles, watching her with undisguised amusement.

'You know what,' he said. 'I feel sorry for you — worshipping at the high church of misery. You should be off down the pub, celebrating with the rest of us.'

She glanced around the room: they were the only two left. 'Don't let me hold you up,' she said.

He dumped the remains of his meal into the bin. 'If you change your mind, we'll be in the Baltic Fleet.' He hoisted his trousers up and tucked in his shirt, still watching her. 'Still obsessing over Osbourne, are you?'

'I wasn't,' she said, quite truthfully. 'But it seems *you* are.'

His forehead flushed dark red.

'I mean, he's in the clear, isn't he?' Rowan said. 'I checked the evidence myself.'

'Yeah,' he said, 'that's right.' He sounded awkward — maybe even cornered — and the shifty squint of his eyes said he wished he'd kept his mouth shut.

'So why d'you even mention him? Guilty conscience, maybe?'

Wicks shrugged. 'I haven't the foggiest what you're on about.'

'I know you've got a scam running with Osbourne, Wicks.'

'You're out of your tiny mind.' He sounded outraged enough, but he'd hesitated. Only a moment — no more than a stuttered heartbeat — but it was there, and they both knew it.

Her pulse quickened. 'You've been feeding Osbourne leads. The women who recognized Osbourne from Tasha's sketch — I've talked to them.' Her heart thudded hard, now, but she forced herself to go on. 'I know you searched crime reports on burglaries — I *know* you sent Osbourne to middle-aged and elderly women grateful for a personal recommendation on security from a police officer.'

A horrible thought occurred to her. 'Oh, God — is he *blackmailing* you? Is that why he had convenient alibis for the key dates?'

'You've lost it, girl,' he said. 'You've really—'

'I hope you're on a hefty commission, *Roy*,' she interrupted. 'You'll be needing the cash when you're suspended from duty.'

Wicks laughed suddenly. 'Says who?'

She stopped feeling frightened and got angry. 'It's all in the task sheets.'

'What task sheets?' He lifted his in-tray, tipped it upside down to show it was empty.

Rowan felt the ground drop from beneath her.

'Had a bit of a clear-out.' He dropped the wire tray back onto his desk. 'Now if you'll excuse me, I'm going to take a piss.'

She watched his broad back as he sauntered out of the room. She waited until the heavy plod of his footfall had retreated a safe distance down the corridor, then tore through the paperwork on his desk. The task sheets really were gone. With a guilty glance at the door, she slipped behind the screened area, where HOLMES operatives worked, and began sifting through pink flimsies, word-processed reports, memos, scraps of paper. There was no sign of the completed task sheets. She listened for a moment, her heart still tripping. Then she pressed the return key on the nearest computer. It sprang to life — an access screen, with a login and password dialogue box. There was no way she would gain access to those files without authorisation.

'What are you doing?'

She spun to face the questioner. It was the HOLMES team manager.

'Nothing, Sarge.'

His eyes tracked over the desks, as if he had memorized the position of every sheet of paper. His gaze fixed on the monitor; the incriminating login screen was still lit.

'I — I wasn't sure if I'd handed in my task sheets,' she stammered. 'I was just—'

'Well, *just* get your arse the other side of this screen,' he said. 'You know the rules. You can ask a HOLMES operative tomorrow.'

She slunk past him, feeling like a criminal. Wicks was at his desk again, squeezing into his overcoat, grinning like he'd just heard a really funny joke.

She walked towards him, her head down, but he stepped in her path, leaned in close, so the sergeant wouldn't hear. 'Like I said, I've been a long time in this game, girly. Things have been busy the last two weeks. Stuff gets mislaid. And talking about getting laid, I've got a date with a tasty telecoms operator.' He turned his back on her and swaggered out of the door.

CHAPTER 58

Rowan had stood, stupefied and afraid in the Major Incident Room until the sergeant reappeared from behind the screened area in the corner and told her to leave, or he'd have her escorted off the premises.

Her mobile rang as she was leaving, and that call made her feel more desperate and alone than she'd felt since her parents' deaths. She'd driven around for an hour, unwilling to go home, and finally wound up at Palmer's place.

The front room of Palmer's house was lamp-lit, and music pounded hard against the windows. Rowan leaned on the doorbell. She peered through the nearest pane of the bay, shielding her eyes against reflections, then returned to the doorbell and leaned harder.

A shaft of light sliced across the hallway, then the front door flung wide and Palmer stood in jeans and sweater, one hand gripping the frame, the other on the door itself. For a second he seemed suspended with the wind blotting his hair, like a mariner hanging on to ship's rigging for dear life. His eyes were red-rimmed and his grief had hardened into something more dangerous. The music blasted at his back: the angry, insistent drumbeat and the screaming delivery of the lead singer like a howl of fury.

She steadied herself. 'Mr Palmer.'

For a few seconds more, he stared at her, his eyes wild, then the savage light in them dulled and she sensed a dark hollowness beyond the rage. Unexpectedly, he yielded to her, letting his hand fall from the door frame. She walked towards the noise and heard the front door slam behind her.

The front room was sparsely furnished: a high-end music system on a cupboard built into one of the alcoves, an armchair, coffee table and sofa. A small rocking horse stood in one corner with a teddy bear slumped on its dappled back, softening the bachelor-pad ambience. Flames danced erratically in the suck and downdraught of air in the fireplace, while the bass notes of the music blasted her eardrums and resonated in her chest. She went to the player and muted the sound.

The silence throbbed with anguish. Palmer eased himself into the armchair; a bottle of whisky stood open on the coffee table, a third down. Palmer scooped up a tumbler from the floor beside him and took a swallow of tawny liquid. He leaned forward and pushed the bottle to her with his fingertips. 'Help yourself,' he said. 'Glasses are in the cupboard.'

'It's tempting, believe me,' Rowan said, taking a seat on the sofa. 'But I need a clear head tonight.'

'Good for you.' He raised his glass to her in an ironic salute.

She suppressed any sympathy she felt for him — for all she knew, he was everything Warman had accused him of. Hadn't he turned up at her house uninvited; hadn't she found him hiding in the shadows of her back yard? What if the handprints on the kitchen window were his? Her native survival instinct told her to stay wary. He was watching her, and she had the uncomfortable feeling that he was reading her body language.

'What do you want from me, Constable Rowan?'

She wanted to tell him that she was afraid her colleague might be involved in the abduction and rape of women — she wanted his advice — but she wouldn't tell him a damn thing until she was sure of him.

'They're closing the investigation into the rapes.'

'Why do I need to know that?' he said.

'Because my boss thinks Dylan Corbie murdered Doctor Atherton.'

He huffed a breath, looked into his drink for a second, then into her face. 'And what do *you* think?'

'I think you're analysing me instead of having a conversation.'

He smiled, wagged a finger at her. 'Very good.'

'Oh gosh, I'm flattered.' She hardened her voice. 'Tell me about Benjamin Kehoe.'

The smile vanished and his eyes glittered angrily. 'What about him?'

'I've heard the official version,' Rowan said. 'I'm willing to hear what you have to say.'

She'd half-expected sarcasm, but he didn't answer at all; just reached for the whisky bottle and poured himself another shot. After a minute or two, he took a breath, swallowed the whisky in one, wincing at its heat.

'Police . . . analysts,' he said, setting the glass down on the coffee table. 'We're very much alike.'

'Yeah?' she said. 'How's that?'

He looked at her. 'We find answers in silences.' He rubbed his hand over his face, and she heard the rasp of stubble on his chin. After a moment or two longer, he began.

'Ben Kehoe was with me for two years. I won't give you his full history, but his was the kind of childhood that would finish most people.' He leaned forward and clasped his hands together. 'I wanted to help him. I wanted him to be well.'

'You make that sound like a bad thing,' Rowan said.

He tilted his head. 'In analysis, it's not always a good thing.'

'Because?' Rowan prompted.

'It's not easy to explain to a . . .'

'Stuck for a word there, Doc?' she said. 'Don't think a cop would have the brains for it? Look, you're stewed — and you're entitled to be — you've gone through something I hope I never have to face in this or any other lifetime. But that doesn't give you the right to patronize me.'

'You're right,' he said. 'I'm sorry.'

She dipped her head, accepting the apology. '*So* — in analysis — it's not a good thing to want someone to be well because . . . ?'

He leaned his head back against the chair and exhaled in a long, shuddering sigh. 'Because we see what we want to see, instead of what *is*. As an analyst, I failed to see past Ben's show of optimism, the improvement in his affect and sociability.'

The room was silent except for the hiss of coals in the hearth, and the occasional stormy gust, rattling the windowpanes.

'He left his final session smiling,' Palmer said. 'Asked to use the bathroom on his way out — my consultation room was in my home at that time. After a few minutes I went to investigate.' He stopped and she saw his jaw working.

'Ben had—' He stared into the fire as if reliving the horror of it.

'He'd slashed his throat with a Stanley blade,' Rowan said for him.

Palmer swallowed. 'He was still breathing — if you can call it breathing. I tried to . . .' He turned his hands as though he could still see the blood on them. 'But there was nothing I could do.'

'The British Psychoanalytic Council cleared you of any blame.' Rowan said. She'd read the report at her desk, before the sergeant had turfed her out.

He offered the ghost of a smile. 'Surprising how little that helps.' He picked up the whisky glass again and finding it empty, he rolled it between his hands, staring at the facets of the cut glass like he could see the past in the shimmer of light. 'You see, my three-year-old daughter was in the house at the time.'

Rowan stared at him, horrified. 'She saw what happened?'

He closed his eyes briefly. 'I'm thankful she was a least spared that. But she saw *me*, covered in blood.'

He snatched up the whisky bottle and poured another shot. Glass cracked against glass — an ugly sound to finish an ugly story. Now he looked her in the eye. 'So, why do you feel you need a clear head tonight?'

She hesitated. The call she'd taken as she'd left the police station was from Lillian Foster — the ancient widow and client of Jake Osbourne. Her first words were, 'You told me he wouldn't know.' And Rowan felt an icy chill in her gut. Lillian eventually told her that she had had received a threatening call — this must have been minutes after Rowan's confrontation with Wicks. 'He knows,' she'd said. 'Don't contact me again.' If Rowan had entertained any notion that she could take Wicks's little scam to the senior ranks, it was scuppered by that call. Because she had no doubt that Wicks — or Osbourne — had already got to every one of the women.

'Constable Rowan, I've been straight with you,' Palmer's eyes were steady and sharp, and she revised her estimate of how drunk he was.

She wasn't ready to tell Palmer what she planned to do so she side-stepped, remembering how he had guided Dylan into the ambulance as tenderly as a parent would their own child. 'Do you think Dylan murdered Dr Atherton?' she asked.

Palmer looked at her in blank astonishment. 'Dylan never hurt anyone but himself.'

She nodded satisfied. 'I had to ask. But that means someone else murdered Dr Atherton — and Dylan Corbie stumbled onto the scene.'

He watched her closely. 'And you think you know who that someone is?'

'I do,' she said, and it sounded like a solemn vow.

It kept coming back to Osbourne. But Osbourne was careful, and forensically aware, and with Tasha discredited and her bosses patting each other on the back on a case successfully closed, there was no credible evidence.

She broke eye contact, uncomfortable under his intense scrutiny, and focused on a coal pulsing red in the fireplace.

If she did give him Osbourne's name, she knew for sure that Palmer would shut down. After she'd finished the BPC report on Ben Kehoe's suicide, she'd done some background reading. So, now she knew that as a therapist, Palmer had a moral *and* legal duty to protect his patient's privacy — he might even lay himself open to criminal prosecution if he failed in that duty. Unless a third party was in imminent danger, he would be in violation of his professional code if he broke the rules of confidentiality.

And on the subject of professional codes — did she dare tell him about Wicks?

She looked at him for the first time in maybe a full minute. He seemed alert and interested, yet he'd said nothing, waiting for her to think her thoughts and come to a decision.

'You've got to understand, I could lose my job, telling you this,' she said.

'Then we'll call this a preliminary consultation,' he said, matching her weary smile. 'Sanctity of the confessional.'

He was making a joke against himself and she liked him for it.

'The official report on the serial rapes will say there were two men, working together in the city,' she began. Then she explained the very different MO of Maseby and the stalker who had abducted and tortured Tasha, Emma and Jodie.

'It's not my area of expertise,' Palmer said, 'But I think that's sound reasoning.'

'The forensic psychologist called it a "rape alliance" between Lee Maseby — the working girls call him 'the Furman' — and a submissive type.'

He nodded.

'And they think Dylan is his partner in crime.'

His concentration broke and he did a double take. 'They — *what?*'

'You don't think he's capable of rape?'

'It's hard to know that for sure,' he said.

The answer surprised her; she'd expected an outright denial.

'Dylan is a complex and conflicted individual,' Palmer explained. 'But I know for an absolute certainty that he is incapable of forming *any* kind of cooperative alliance with another person — man *or* woman. He simply wouldn't trust them.'

'God, I wish you'd been there at the debrief,' she said, fervently.

'So you think that the man who—' He stopped and cleared his throat. 'That Karl's murderer is Maseby's accomplice?'

'No.'

He flopped back in his chair. 'Then I really don't understand.'

'I think Maseby had *nothing* to do with the abduction-rapes of Tasha McCorkindale, Emma Hammond, and Jodie Pickersgill.' She rubbed a hand nervously over her face. 'Can I trust you with this, Mr Palmer?'

'You know you can,' he said, and she was astonished to realise that she did.

She took a breath and let it go. 'I believe that the man the media is calling the Mall Stalker has had inside help.'

'*Inside*?' he said. 'You mean inside the investigation?'

She didn't answer.

'One of your colleagues is helping a *killer*?'

Her mouth was dry, and she had to work her tongue over her teeth before she could answer.

'I believe someone has been feeding him information — about key times and dates we've been looking into. And tonight—' She ran out of breath and had to suck in more air. 'Evidence of a — a lead I've been following vanished from the incident room. Witnesses have been intimidated.'

He blinked as the full weight of what she'd said sank in. 'Constable, you have to tell someone.'

Rowan allowed herself a tired, bitter smile. 'I've no proof. And I messed up — opened my big mouth before I had it all in the bag — so . . .'

'Who is the man your colleague is helping?'

She wondered why he couldn't put it together himself: the break-in at his office; his work number inked on Jodie's hand; Rowan's own business card, her home address written on the back— it had to be one of his clients — and Osbourne was the only client who had been questioned by police. But she supposed good therapists didn't judge. Maybe his priest analogy was right. Whatever the reason, she couldn't tell him that Osbourne was the man who raped Tasha and the other three women — not until she had evidence. Jake Osbourne had been questioned, provided solid alibis, and been eliminated from the inquiry.

'I can't name him,' she said at last. 'Not without proof.'

'Then I don't see how I can help you,' he said.

'Tell me how to catch him. Tell me what to look for.'

'I'm an analyst, not an investigative psychologist,' he said.

'I don't need an investigator — I already know he's a rapist and a killer. I need to know how he thinks.'

Palmer's eyes were wells of sadness. 'If he's as clever as you think, all you can do is wait.'

'Wait? Until he snatches someone else — until he kills again?'

He fixed her with a look. 'Until he makes a *mistake*. Even bad men are traumatized by murder, constable. You can't take a human life without some psychic consequences. Eventually every killer starts to unravel, and that's when they make mistakes.'

'Yeah, well, I can't think of a single one, so far.'

'You found him out, didn't you?'

'Okay — *one* mistake. But he won't make another. I think that's why he killed Jodie.' The implications of what she'd just said made her feel sick. 'Jesus, what if he changes his MO — I dunno — starts using a different weapon, a different way of killing his victims — I mean, could that happen?'

'It's possible.'

'Then how the hell am I supposed to keep track of him?

'There are some things he *has* to do, in order to fulfil his fantasy,' Palmer said. 'They remain unchanging and unchangeable.'

'He uses a taser,' Rowan said. 'He strangles his victims as he rapes them, reviving them over and over.' Palmer closed his eyes for one weary second.

'Is there a chance he might just . . . stop?' She heard the desperate hope in her voice.

Palmer shook his head tiredly.

'With Jodie's murder, he crossed a line. With Karl's . . .' He couldn't finish that thought, but he picked up again with, 'For him, there's no going back.'

Rivers of iced water ran through her veins. 'So what happens now?'

'The more he acts out, the more his world destabilizes. And the more his world destabilizes, the more dangerous and unpredictable he becomes.'

'And you're asking me to wait until that happens? Well, excuse me, Mr Palmer, but you can screw that *sideways*. There must be *something* we can do. Dylan was there at Dr Atherton's — if he saw—' She stopped herself in time, but she saw pain crease Palmer's features. 'Jeez, I'm sorry.'

Palmer waved away her apology. 'Dylan is experiencing a psychotic break,' he said. 'It could be a while before he's lucid again.'

He edged his drink further from him and sat staring at it for five minutes, before getting unsteadily to his feet.

'Where are you going?' she asked.

'For a walk. I need to clear my head.'

* * *

Once out of the house, he crossed the road and went directly into Sefton Park. She fell in step, leaving him to sift through his thoughts.

For fifteen minutes he walked fast, as if trying to escape a pursuing terror. He walked and she walked on with him, their shadows slinking ahead of them, then pooling at their feet and slipping behind as they passed under lamp after lamp on the curved paths of the park. The wind had abated, but it rippled the puddles and drove sharp, spiteful needles of cold ahead of it.

At last he slowed his pace and glanced down at Rowan. 'Why are your colleagues so convinced that Dylan murdered Karl?'

'You mean aside from the fact he was found cowering under a desk at the murder scene, spouting gibberish, completely off his head?'

'Aside from the *obvious*,' he said, and she heard a sharp waspishness in his tone.

'There I go again. Sometimes I wish my mouth had a five-second delay, so I could bleep out my worst gaffes.'

He gave her a half-smile, and she knew that she was forgiven. The path curved ahead of them, gleaming like wet tar. They carried on in the cold and the dark without speaking for a few moments, their footsteps ringing out in the silence.

'Dylan has been following Dr Atherton,' she said. 'Stalking him. They found a notebook on him — seems he kept a record.'

He showed no surprise and Rowan said, 'You knew about this?'

Palmer rubbed his forehead as if it would make his tired brain work more efficiently. 'I think that Dylan is terrified of losing sections of his life — that his memory plays him false — so he fills up the pages of his notebooks hour by hour with meaningless details of his existence.'

She felt a spark of hope. 'Wait a minute — if he followed Dr Atherton home, it'll be logged in his notebook?'

'Yes . . .'

'And if he saw the killer go into to Atherton's flat, that will be recorded, too.'

'It will.'

A plot began to form in her head. 'You think that Dylan followed Osbourne to Dr Atherton's house, and what he saw sent him over the edge.'

'I do.' Palmer stopped and faced her. 'Karl had been strangled,' he said. 'But there were two other marks on his neck.' He touched his index and middle fingers a couple of centimetres apart to the left side of his own neck.

'Taser burns,' he said. 'We have to stop him.'

'We can't — not without proof.'

'I know,' Palmer said, pain creasing his face. 'I know.' He began walking again.

They needed Dylan's testimony. Rowan remembered the odd exchange between Palmer and his patient as Palmer helped him into the ambulance. 'What did Dylan mean by "Psych 101"?'

'I wish I knew.' Palmer hunched his shoulders against a strong gust of wind.

Rowan replayed the scene in her head. 'And who is "she"?'

Palmer frowned. 'She? I don't—'

'Dylan said, "I should have helped *her*."'

She saw the therapist working through what she had said. As he walked, his shadow seemed to shrink and flatten, as if he drew it back into himself by a thread, then it lengthened behind him, growing thinner and thinner as if the thread connecting them would break and Palmer would lose a part of himself.

He stopped abruptly and stared at her. 'He *did* say *her*, didn't he?'

Rowan felt a burst of excitement. 'Could he have been talking about Jodie Pickersgill? Could he have witnessed her abduction?'

Palmer exhaled, nodding slowly. 'He wanted to help her, but he was afraid.'

'Dylan could—' Rowan stopped, and her shoulders slumped. 'But Dylan might not be able to talk to us for months.' The fizz of excitement left her, and she felt suddenly exhausted.

'We don't need to talk to Dylan,' Palmer said. 'Whatever he knows is in the notebook.'

CHAPTER 59

Sunday, 29 November, 1 a.m.

Rowan should have gone home. The wedding was set for two p.m. and she was desperate for sleep. But she couldn't get Wicks's smug face out of her mind. He had warned Osbourne — she knew it as sure as she knew that the Scottish branch of the Rowans would size her up at the nuptials and swap knowing glances that said, 'Hasn't she let herself *go*?'

'Yeah, well, sod 'em,' she muttered, zapping off a quick text to Alex. It was a two-and-a-half-hour drive to the Lake District. She could be there and back in plenty of time for the wedding.

Osbourne had been alibied by his mother — and by the date-stamped receipts he'd presented when he turned himself in. The Penrith Travel Inn had confirmed he had checked in on two key dates and, apart from a couple of hours each day to see his mother, had stayed in his room until he checked out again. Cumbria Police had checked the hotel's CCTV images and confirmed it. But it was odd that he hadn't stayed at his mother's house. And Rowan couldn't shake the idea that with his knowledge of security systems, Osbourne could have found a way around the hotel's surveillance system.

The village of Threlkeld lay four miles east of Keswick beneath the rugged granite slopes of Blencathra. At Tebay Services, she stopped for coffee and a cookie as big as her head. Checking her watch as she returned to the car, she realised she'd made good time and decided to take a nap before driving on. It was freezing with the broken passenger window still patched in plastic, so she turned on the engine and jammed her hands in her pockets against the cold. Her knuckles grazed something hard in her right pocket. She withdrew the object and placed it on the dashboard. Neil's thumb drive. Ian Chan had returned it to her only twelve hours earlier, and she couldn't believe she had all but forgotten it. Granted, a lot had happened since: Maseby's arrest, Osbourne's exoneration, Dr Atherton's murder — but looking at it now, sitting squat on the dash, she felt a stab of apprehension.

It *was* placed in her car as a message, she sure of that — even Ian Chan, despite his rationalisations and wise counsel against paranoia, had agreed with her on that.

So, if there were no prints on the device, she thought, taking a tremulous breath, the message had to be on the drive itself. She slotted it into the media port on her car stereo with a judder of revulsion and listened with the volume turned low to track after track of grinding, screeching, wailing heavy metal. Then, silence.

She strained her ears, listening.

Was that a whisper? She turned the volume up a notch. *A gasp?* Her fingers trembling, she gave the dial another quarter-turn.

Screams tore through both speakers and she pressed herself back in the seat in an unreasoning attempt to escape the awful sound. Every nerve in her body seemed shot through with electric charge. She fumbled the dial the wrong way, and for a second, she thought her eardrums would burst.

The screaming stopped, abruptly, and Rowan heard a soft sobbing, followed by a whisper, close to the microphone: 'Well, Jodie, aren't we having fun?' *Osbourne?* She couldn't tell. The sound of breathing, a whimper, then: 'What d'you want to say to Constable Rowan?'

Rowan's scalp prickled, and she looked around her, fearful that she was being watched. The car park was almost empty, the cars in darkness.

A sob, an intake of breath, then, 'Please . . . please, *please* help me . . .'

The next she was aware, Rowan was standing on the tarmac next to her car, her heart rattling in her chest. 'Jesus,' she murmured. 'Jesus . . .'

* * *

She drove the last forty minutes of her journey in silence, irrationally afraid even to turn on the radio in case those terrible sounds invaded her ears again, and arrived into Threlkeld at four thirty. It had rained on and off during the drive north, but now the clouds parted, and moonlight silvered the rooftops, setting the mist that crept down from the crags a-shimmer.

Mrs Osbourne's house was a grey nineteenth-century stone-built cottage on a street lined with neat cottages, some in the local granite, others rendered and limewashed so that they glowed in the moonlight. The house next door had been converted to a teashop, now tightly shuttered against the winter winds. Hers was bigger than the rest, set further back from the road in a walled garden. In summer it must be filled with the scent of roses, but in late November the ramblers over the door were as brown and thorny as briars, and the silvery light of the moon gleaming on the windows gave it a chilly, unwelcoming cast. Rowan parked in a bus stop bay opposite and prepared to wait for an hour or so, before venturing to the house. Then a light went on in the front room and the curtain was lifted. Rowan locked the car and crossed the street.

Climbing the steps, she felt her hackles rise, glanced right and saw a figure, partly obscured by the reflections on the windowpane, watching from the front room. Shocked, she took a step back. The woman in the window did not withdraw her gaze and was slow to respond when Rowan rang the doorbell.

Mrs Osbourne could not have been much over fifty. Her hair was the same sandy brown as Osbourne's, her eyes the same unsettling aquamarine. She was dressed neatly, a cardigan over skirt and blouse, and she wore a light powdering of make-up, even at this early hour.

She listened while Rowan explained who she was, her gaze never leaving her face, her attention so acute that Rowan wondered if she might be deaf and reading her lips.

'I know about the nonsense in Liverpool,' she said. 'Cumbria police were here.'

'May I come in?'

'No.'

'Then, may I talk with you?'

She raised her eyebrows. 'Why would I want to talk to you about my son?'

'A young woman is dead, Mrs Osbourne,' she said quietly.

'My son had nothing to do with that,' she said. 'He was with me. *Caring* for me. The police have the receipts and — so on.' She waved a hand as if the details were too tiresome to discuss.

No expression of concern for Jodie, no real emotion at all behind the blank denial of responsibility. Rowan tried to gauge if Osbourne's mother was anxious — or if she had perhaps provided alibis because she was afraid of her son.

'You see, I'm wondering if *you* might have given him the receipts — just to help him out of a tight spot.'

'You can wonder all you like.' Mrs Osbourne stared at Rowan with icy disdain.

'Sometimes people *do* cover for the people they love—'

'Love doesn't come into it,' Mrs Osbourne said, as though Rowan had suggested something slightly obscene.

'—Or out of loyalty or guilt, or a sense of duty.' None of which had an effect on the woman, so Rowan added, 'Or because they like to feel needed.'

'How *dare* you.'

Why would she be so shocked by the idea that her son might need her? Rowan wished that Palmer was listening to this.

'You see, I know he didn't stay here all the time he claimed he was here,' she pushed on. 'My *guess* is you helped out, buying a car park ticket, or maybe holding onto a few grocery receipts. Did he leave one of his credit cards with you, so you could pay for a few items?'

Mrs Osbourne's mouth twisted into a smile. 'Do you *really* imagine I would involve myself in such an elaborate conspiracy?'

'I don't know,' Rowan said, honestly. 'Let's say you didn't know you were part of it. Let's speculate that he left his card and suggested you treat yourself. Maybe he asked you to dig into your purse and find a few receipts he might use for his tax return.'

Doubt stirred in the woman's liquid blue eyes.

Rowan dipped into her pocket and brought out the small, black thumb drive that had tormented the remaining miles of her journey, replaying over and over in her head.

'There's an audio recording on here, of one of the victims — I think it's Jodie Pickersgill, though I can't be sure. She's being tortured — there's a man's voice, too. Tormenting her. I don't recognize it, but you would know your own son's voice, wouldn't you? Will you listen to it?'

Mrs Osbourne pushed her hand away. 'Get that thing out of my face.' There was no flicker of empathy, only an entrenched contempt.

'You won't listen? If you're so sure your son is innocent, wouldn't you want to prove it — at least to yourself?'

Rowan recalled Mrs Osbourne standing at the window, fully dressed, at four thirty on a Sunday morning. *She's expecting him,* she thought with a shiver of anxiety.

'I think you *know* what he's done,' Rowan said. 'What he's capable of doing.'

Mrs Osbourne's gaze darted away, but only for a second. 'Aye, well, I've no interest in your opinion. Now, you'd best be on your way. Go on — get off my property, or I shall call the police.' She slammed the front door and Rowan heard her footsteps retreating down the hall.

A moment later, she caught a movement through the glass of the window to her right. Osbourne's mother had taken up station once more. Her face, expressionless and as pale as the moon's reflection.

* * *

Rowan reached the outskirts of Liverpool just before eight, blasting rap through the speakers to keep her awake on the last leg of the journey. The wind had dropped abruptly, leaving the city preternaturally quiet and still, and she let herself into the house with a grateful sigh.

She would log the thumb drive into the exhibit room as soon as the team rolled in, but she didn't expect that to be anytime soon. Most of team regarded the case as wrapped up with the arrests of Lee Maseby and Dylan Corbie, and she suspected that the Baltic Fleet would have been crowded out with elated cops till the early hours. She would have time to snatch a few hours' sleep. And once she'd got the wedding over with, she would try to gain access to Dylan Corbie's notebook, but right now, she craved rest. She bolted the front door and dragged herself up the stairs, hearing Alex's soft snore in the spare room, and fantasizing about a warm duvet, soft pillows, and oblivion.

She dumped her handbag on the floor by her bed and peeled off her jacket, her eyes closed, still standing, but already halfway to sleep.

Something prickled at the back of her nose. The musky scent of men's cologne. She'd swear that in the twenty-four hours Alex had been home, the house had started smelling like the cosmetics counter of a department store.

Her eyes flew open. Something came out of the dark. She raised her arm in a defensive reflex. An electrical flash lit up the air like a lightning bolt, freezing her attacker for an instant. *No face.* The darkness seemed to intensify after the brief flash of light. She smelled ozone.

She grabbed his arm and twisted, yelling for help, trying to gain some leverage. He was too strong. She stumbled backwards; her feet became entangled in the strap of her handbag. She fell, dragging him with her. Something bounced out of the door and clattered through the stair rails onto the stairs.

He was on top of her, his eyes wide, lit from within by a freaky light — *not faceless, masked.* The weight of him crushed her, the stench of his breath in her face was nauseating. She rolled and he cracked his head against the door frame. A second thud from the next room sounded like a distant echo. She pushed away from him with her feet, but he launched himself at her, trapping her against her bed.

His hands were around her neck, his thumbs pressing her throat. She punched the side of his head, already weakening, flailing helplessly. She saw red, then the edges of her vision began to close in.

A loud *crack!* And she could breathe again. She dug in with her heels and levered herself onto the bed, sucking air into her lungs. Another *thwack!* And she heard plaster crack.

'Bastard! You leave her ALONE!'

Neil!

She rolled onto her side and staggered to her feet. Saw Neil swinging wildly with a baseball bat, the attacker backing for the stairs. Neil raised the bat again. The man stepped in with a slashing movement and Neil dropped his weapon, clutching his right arm.

The attacker turned and fled as Alex stepped out of his room, still full of sleep. 'What the f—?'

Neil held his arm, a look of wild surprise on his face. Blood trickled between his fingers and dripped on the carpet. 'He cut me,' he said, his face white with shock.

Rowan pulled Alex from where he was standing, a stupefied look on his face. Took both his hands and clamped them over Neil's forearm. 'Lift his arm over his head,' she said. 'Squeeze tight.'

She swept up the bat and threw herself at the stairs.

The attacker was struggling with the bolt on the front door. He rammed the bolt back, giving a yell of pain, then, with one crazed look over his shoulder, he had the door open.

Rowan yelled, 'Hey!' and flung the bat, hitting him squarely between the shoulder blades. He stumbled, fell over the threshold into the street, but was up and running almost without pause. She leapt the last few steps and was through the door.

The cold tore at her bruised larynx; she couldn't find her rhythm. He gained ten yards. She kept going, though her legs felt boneless. He reached a car further down the street and was in it before she'd run three more paces. Her knees gave way and she sank to the ground. The engine roared, and he was gone in a flare of tail-lights.

CHAPTER 60

Sunday morning

By the time Rowan had been checked over by the paramedics, made her statement and provided a practically useless description of her attacker, Neil was in surgery. Scientific Support had taken her clothing for trace analysis, barring her from her own bedroom, but conceding that she needed something to wear, they sent one of the female CSIs to root out a few items from her wardrobe.

Now, she sat in DCI Warman's office. Warman had turned up and whisked Rowan off to St Anne Street.

Warman dragged her chair around her desk to sit next to Rowan. 'We'll get a DNA profile — I'll fast-track it. The CSU found small samples of tissue in the bolt rack of the front door and on the pavement where he fell.'

Rowan nodded. 'Did they find a taser?'

Warman avoided her eye. 'Yes — but Cassie, you shouldn't jump to conclusions.'

They found a taser. Thinking about the possibilities that presented sickened her.

Warman reached across and patted her hand. Rowan moved a fraction — it was unintentional, a reflex, but undeniable — and Warman removed her hand, her manner instantly cooling.

'It was Osbourne,' Rowan said.

'Cassie, we've been over this—'

'Maseby is locked up. Corbie is locked up — who else *could* it be?'

'I'm sorry about your brother. It's a horrible thing — but it's not unique. Burglaries happen all the time in—'

'In a house occupied by two men and a cop?' Rowan said. *Oh, you nearly said it, You nearly said, 'in your neighbourhood'.*

'And since when did burglars start carrying tasers?' Warman made no answer. 'It was Osbourne,' she repeated.

Warman fell back on her favourite phrase: 'Yes, well, let's not theorize ahead of the evidence.'

Rowan stood; if she stayed, she would say something she would regret. She found the thumb drive in her pocket and handed it over.

'What's this?'

'I believe it's a recording of Jodie Pickersgill,' she said. 'There's a man's voice on there, too. I think it's Osbourne.'

Warman's lips parted and she looked uncertainly at the device. 'Dear God. How did you—?'

'I — I can't do this, right now. I need to check on Neil,' Rowan said. 'I have to see if —'

'Of course.' Warman seemed flustered. 'Take a few days.'

Rowan nodded dumbly, shuffled to the door feeling dizzy with confusion.

'Cassie,' Warman said. 'The press and TV are hanging around your house and the hospital. Best to avoid them.'

It wasn't advice. It was a warning.

Rowan held Warman's gaze. 'Understood,' she said.

Rowan edged through the crowd of reporters huddled around the entrance of the A&E department at the Royal with her head down. She was spotted almost immediately, and cameras and microphones were thrust at her.

'—Can you comment on the attack, Constable Rowan?'

341

'—Is it true the attacker used a taser?'

'—Is your brother all right?'

'—The police made arrests, yesterday — is the killer still out there?'

That one, she nearly answered.

Grateful that officers in uniform prevented the media contingent from following her through the doors, she escaped inside.

The waiting room was still busy with Saturday night casualties. She saw head wounds and twisted ankles, bloody noses and split lips — the perfect end to a night out on the lash. The few who weren't drunk or stoned seemed out of place: a middle-aged couple, the woman nursing her arm in a sling, an elderly man with a racking cough.

Alex leapt to his feet when he saw her. 'Are you okay?' He had gone ahead in the ambulance with Neil.

'I'm fine. How's Neil?'

'Jesus, Cassie.' He turned down the collar of her jacket to inspect the bruising.

She shrugged him off, moving him away from the doors and the camera flashes. 'Is he still in surgery?'

'The bastard severed a tendon. They're trying to repair it.' He ran his hands through his hair. 'There could be nerve damage, Cass.'

She felt suddenly cold. 'When will they know?'

He shrugged helplessly. 'What are we going to *do*?'

At that moment, she wanted somebody else to take the burden, somebody to comfort her, to take care of her, to tell her that everything would be all right. But since her parents died, Rowan had unintentionally, and in small increments, stepped into her mother's role. She took Alex's hand.

'We're going to wait.' She led him back to the chairs on the far side of the room, where there were more spaces and fewer drunks.

Her mobile rang and she shot a guilty look at the reception desk. They were fully occupied with a new arrival, wearing a tiara and a wedding veil, an L-plate tacked to the back of her dress. She was crying, bleeding from a cut over her eye — and she seemed to have brought her entire hen party with her. Rowan turned her back and hit 'answer'.

'Constable Rowan — is that you?'

'Mr Palmer?'

'Thank God.' His voice cracked on the second word.

'Mr Palmer, I can't talk right n—'

'He has someone. The phone woke me — she was screaming.'

Adrenaline flooded Rowan's brain like a double shot of espresso. The waiting room lights seemed suddenly too bright and her fingers tingled.

'He said everything that's happened — all of this — is my fault.' She could hear him hyperventilating. 'I think he's going to—'

'Sir,' she said. 'I've seen first-hand what he does to women. I don't need to hear what the crazy fucker has planned.'

'I'm sorry,' he said quietly.

'Did you recognize the voice?' she asked, thinking, *It's Osbourne.*

'No. He sounded local.'

'Did you get a number?'

'It was withheld.' He sounded close to tears.

Alex was watching her anxiously. He mouthed '*What?*' and she lifted a finger, asking him to wait. The time for caution was past; she needed to stop Osbourne and she couldn't do it alone.

She moved away from her brother and cupped her hand over the phone. 'Mr Palmer, could it be Jake Osbourne?'

'I — no, I don't think so,' he said. 'As I told you, he sounded local—' He broke off, and all she heard for a few seconds was his ragged breathing.

'Mr Palmer?'

'Oh, God . . . The man who cancelled my appointments. My clients were convinced it was *my* voice they heard — that it was me who rang to cancel. But Osbourne was exonerated — didn't he have alibis?'

'I think his mother gave him his alibis for the key dates.'

'So why would he implicate himself all over again?'

She sighed. 'I think I might have triggered this,' she said. His breathing stilled and the line went so quiet that she almost asked if he was still there. But she recognized the change for what it was: this was Palmer in listening mode, his whole mind and body straining to hear what she had to say.

Rowan glanced at her brother. More irritated than anxious now, he raised his eyebrows and spread his hands as if to say, 'What the hell?'

She turned her back on him. 'After I spoke to you last night, I drove up to the Lakes to see Osbourne's mother. I thought that maybe he'd duped her into covering for him, or she was protecting him out of a misguided sense of loyalty — I don't know. Anyway, I was wrong. She was hostile, and when I got back, I was attacked in my home.'

'Are you all right?'

'I'm okay,' she said, 'but my brother—' She choked, and Palmer began to speak, but she cut across him, hardening her voice, using anger to fight back her tears. 'He's injured — but he'll survive. Look, Mr Palmer, I'm going to talk to my superintendent and my immediate boss, DCI Warman. They'll want to speak to you.'

'I'll keep my mobile switched on.'

'Okay. Just sit tight.'

She hung up and glanced towards the main entrance. Alex got to his feet, a look of alarm on his face.

'You're not thinking of leaving?'

'I have to, Alex. That call — it was—'

'I don't *care* what it was, Cassie. This is your little *brother*.'

A bubble of anger burst in her like a blister. 'I've looked after *our* little brother on my own for *six years*, Alex — don't try and play the guilt card with me.'

He opened his mouth and shut it again without speaking. She saw a deep, lacerating hurt behind his eyes.

'I didn't mean—' she began.

'No, it's okay,' he said bitterly. 'You're right. You've been there for him and I haven't. You're a saint, and I'm the selfish bastard who let you both down. But you can't just stop, now, Cassie — not when he needs you most.' He pushed his fingers through his hair; he was shaking. 'I don't know how to *do* this. I don't know how to get through this.'

'Minute by agonizing minute, Alex,' she said, not unkindly. She took a breath and it hitched like a spasm in her chest. For a minute they just looked at each other, neither knowing what to say. At last, Rowan shook herself, angry that his need was robbing her of decision. 'I can't just sit here,' she said roughly.

Alex stared at her as though he couldn't believe she was actually going to abandon him, and she had to look away. 'Call me when he's out of surgery.'

'But where are you going?' He sounded plaintive, like a lost boy.

Jesus, Rowan thought. *Brothers.*

She ran to the main entrance, and out into the gathering mist, skirting the press, running up the hill to the taxi rank. She didn't care who followed her: she was heading back to the station.

Inside the taxi, her phone buzzed in her hand. It was Palmer.

'Give me something to do,' he said.

'There's nothing you *can* do,' she said. 'Except let me do my job.'

'He *wants* me to be a part of this — don't you see? The calls, the threats, Karl—'

'This is police business, Mr Palmer,' she warned.

'Osbourne has made it my business.'

She couldn't think of an argument against that.

'At least let me talk to my boss,' she said. 'Promise me you'll wait to hear from me.'

He didn't promise, and she didn't blame him. She just hoped he didn't do anything stupid.

CHAPTER 61

Palmer didn't wait. Whether what he did was stupid, only time would tell.

He tried Osbourne's number, and when it went to voicemail, he left a message, and backed that up with a text: 'Jake, I know it was you who phoned me. Please, don't hurt the woman. Call me, and we'll talk. Or give me a location and I'll come — alone — I promise. No tricks, just you and me. We can work this out.'

He was trying to give Rowan extra time, but he was also giving Osbourne a reason to let the woman go: with his identity known, there was no cause to kill her.

Five minutes later, his phone rang.

'You really put the anal in analysis, Palmer.' Osbourne laughed softly. 'Recognize my voice, did you? What about *hers*? You should have.'

'Jake, listen—'

'No — *you* listen. It's supposed to be what you're good at. Actions have consequences, Alan. Remember I said that.' The line went dead.

Palmer tried again, but the phone disconnected before it even rang — Osbourne must have blocked his number.

Why should I recognize her voice?

Actions have consequences.

The air seemed to chill by ten degrees. *Elspeth.*

In a brief moment of dislocation, his world tilted, its landscape seemed alien and threatening, the horizons skewed so that he did not know how to orientate himself.

He rang Elspeth's landline. It was engaged.

He tried her mobile. It was switched off.

He hung up and ran for the door.

The wind tugged and buffeted him, fighting him all the way. He ran the short distance with his head down, staggering in the fiercer gusts, frantic to reach Elspeth's house.

* * *

In her street, knotty calluses on the trunks of the pollarded trees stood out like the twisted joints of an arthritic. Elspeth's house was by the third poplar   Lucy had incorporated this fact into one of her counting games. Palmer counted them now, as though conjuring his daughter's presence in his mind might keep her safe. His breath burned in his lungs, the muscles of his legs tearing with the strain. Fifty yards. Twenty. He saw Osbourne as a tall shadow beside the third poplar.

'No!' He tried to shout, but his voice was trapped in his chest and he could barely breathe. His legs gave way and he stumbled against a garden wall, leaning heavily, staring at the shadow as it thinned and vanished, merging with the rain-blackened tree trunks.

A shadow. Only a shadow.

He lurched on till he reached the third tree, willing danger away from his wife and child.

The front door stood open. It swung in the wind, slammed shut as if by some mischievous hand. Opened again. *He left it on the latch. He wants me to see this.*

The house was dark. Palmer hurled himself down the path, yelling their names, knowing it could be a trap. Not caring. Blasted through the door and bounced from one side of the hallway to the other, calling, calling, as if he could call them back to him. Sitting room, dining room, kitchen — all empty. Phone off the hook. Back to the stairs. The front door slammed, then the wind pushed it wide again.

He slingshotted around the stair newel, launching himself upward, stumbled on the fifth riser, fell, dragged himself up the last few steps, searched bedrooms, bathroom, attic. Nobody. Nothing.

He stood at the top of the stairs, arms hanging at his sides, body shaking. Osbourne had them.

A jangling ring. His heart leapt, beating fiercely, painfully against his ribs. He pulled his mobile from his pocket, his hand shaking so badly he nearly dropped it.

'Alan?'

'Oh, *Elspeth*.' He almost sobbed her name.

'I got your messages.' Elspeth at her coldest and most distant. And he had never been so glad.

'I've been so worried.'

'Alan, have you been drinking? Has something happened?'

He lost his footing and sat down hard on the top step, clamped a hand over his mouth to stifle — what? A sob? A laugh? Maybe both.

'I'm stone-cold sober,' he said, 'and everything is fine — it's just that I've been trying to reach you all day.' Already hiding the truth, not wanting to frighten her. More selfishly, not wanting her to know that he had put them all in danger. Again.

'We've been in transit.' She paused. Elspeth might despise what she termed 'theatrics' in others, but she wasn't above allowing herself some dramatic licence. 'I'll be staying with my parents for a few days.'

He exhaled in a rush. 'Good,' he said. 'That's great.'

'There's no call for sarcasm, Alan.'

He *should* be angry: Elspeth's parents lived on the northerly edge of Northumberland, near Hadrian's Wall — four-and-a-half-hour drive from Liverpool, but that meant four and a half hours from danger, and he wanted Lucy and Elspeth as far away from that as possible.

'No, really,' he wiped sweat and tears from his face. 'It'll be good for you and for Lucy — she hardly ever gets to see her grandparents. Just let me know when you plan to come back,' he said. 'We need to talk.'

'I think the time for talking is over,' she said.

'Even so,' he said. 'You will—' He had been about to say, *You will warn me*, but he modified this to, 'You will call me before you set off?'

'Alan, what on earth—?'

'Can I talk to Lucy?' he interrupted, evading her question, needing to hear his little girl's voice, to have aural proof that she really was safe.

'She's in bed,' Elspeth said.

'Elspeth, what are you trying to do?' In all the four years and two months of his daughter's life, Alan Palmer has never missed saying goodnight to Lucy.

She sighed. 'Don't be melodramatic, Alan. She's had a long day. She was tired, I put her to bed early.'

Someone called Elspeth's name — her father, by the sound of it.

'Look,' she said, 'I have to go.' She cut the connection, and when he redialled, her phone was once more switched off.

The next number he dialled was Detective Constable Rowan's.

'He's been in my wife's house.'

He heard her breath catch.

'She's all right,' he said. 'They're away.' Even so, he felt a fresh stab of cold fear. 'But he was *in my wife's house.*' The repetition increased the horror of it — of what might have been. He heard the rising panic in his voice and stopped. 'He rang me. Said I should recognize the woman's voice. He warned of consequences—'

There was a pause, and he cursed himself for having blurted it out so clumsily.

'We'll get somebody to come over and take a statement. Check your wife's house for fingerprints.'

'He's too clever to leave fingerprints. It doesn't even look like the lock's been forced,' Palmer said, feeling frightened and helpless.

'All right. Just hang on in there,' she said. 'I'm doing everything I can — and if you can think who he might have taken, call me.'

CHAPTER 62

No bells, no whooping sirens, but Palmer knew he had only minutes before somebody showed up.

He moved swiftly from room to room, his heart thudding hard and fast. Osbourne's sitting room was even more Spartan than his own: just a top-of-the-range Bose music system, a huge wall-mounted TV, and a sofa. This wasn't the place to find what he came for.

Too public, Palmer thought. *Too vulnerable to prying eyes*. On to the bedroom, then, no time to waste. He had broken the kitchen window to gain entry. If the sound of shattering glass hadn't alerted the neighbours — if he found what he was looking for fast — he might just get away without being challenged.

If.

One wall was given over to built-in wardrobes, divided into rails and shelving and shoe racks and drawers that maximized every square inch of space; the suits and overcoats weight-graded, the shirts and ties colour-matched as fastidiously as the racks of a Jermyn Street tailor.

On the floor of one of the wardrobes, a large square plastic box. No labels: Osbourne wouldn't need any reminder of its contents. This was what Palmer had come for.

He snapped the handles from their stays and opened the lid, releasing a whiff of old paper, dust and ageing leatherette. The odour of memories.

He unpacked photocopies of cheques, certificates proclaiming Osbourne Salesman of the Year, clients' letters of commendation, a university degree, A-level certificates. He worked down through the strata of Jake Osbourne's life, and at the bottom of the box, he found a red leatherette photograph album and a shoebox, greyed with age.

A thump overhead.

He froze: somewhere above, a door slammed; sirens wailed in the distance.

He seized the album and hid it under his overcoat, hesitated, reached in again, snatching up the shoebox. Then he ran, aware of a clatter on the stairs outside the flat echoing his own footsteps. He was halfway down the hall, almost in the kitchen.

A sudden clamour of noise in the outer hall. Palmer jerked, his heart leaping into his throat, and he fumbled the box, almost dropping it.

'You get out of there, you thieving bastard!' The neighbour. 'You get your scabby arse out of there!' The front door handle rattled.

The sirens were closer; he heard the whoop and throb of two — maybe more — vehicles. He kept moving, into the kitchen, where tendrils of mist had stolen in through the broken window, coating every smooth surface like a night sweat.

He boosted himself onto the sink drainer, slipped and felt a slash of burning pain. He cried out, dropping the shoebox, examined his right hand. A gash two inches long dripped blood onto the drainer and the wool of his coat. A sliver of glass showed just under the skin.

He took a breath, pinched the glass between his thumb and forefinger and closing his eyes, pulled it from the cut. 'Shit!' It was an inch long and viciously sharp. He grabbed a tea towel from the sink taps and wrapped it tight around the wound.

The neighbour started kicking the hell out of the flat door. 'I've called the police!' he yelled.

Palmer swung round, feet first to the window and eased through, lowering himself to the ground. Blood soaked through his makeshift bandage and he twisted it tighter, wincing at a hot stab of pain.

The shoe box. It was still on the work surface near the drainer. A stretch even for him. He tried, reaching through the window, and his fingertips just brushed one corner. Sirens reverberated down the streets, like a howling of wolves converging on their prey.

He made one last desperate grab for the box. The lid flipped and spun, landing in the sink and the box tipped towards him, spilling its contents onto the drainer. Cursing, he grabbed a fistful of papers with his good left hand and stuffed them in his coat pocket.

He ran   down the side passage of the house with sirens screaming in his ears like a lynch mob — reached the gate.

The front door flung wide. 'Hey!'

Fog hung thick in the air. *Use it — keep going. Keep your head down and don't look back.*

'Hey, *you*!'

He couldn't help it. He glanced sideways — just for a second — but it was enough.

'I *know* you,' the man shouted. But he made no move and Palmer belted down the deserted street, nursing his injured hand across his chest. Inside his car, he fumbled the key in the ignition, tried to turn it with his damaged hand. A police vehicle blasted past, creating twin vortices of vapour in its slipstream. He ducked, tried the ignition again, yelling against the pain that sliced through the torn flesh of his palm. The engine caught and he coaxed the car into the thickening murk.

CHAPTER 63

Rowan sat at her desk and stared blindly at an evidence bag she had just signed out of the exhibits room. She'd had to play on Hoff's sympathies to get it, but it was all she had to go on.

DCI Warman had been preparing to go home when Rowan got back from the hospital. She listened patiently enough while Rowan told her the details of the call from Palmer.

'What are you proposing, Cassie?' she asked.

'That we find Osbourne.'

'You yourself looked into Osbourne,' she said. 'He's in the clear.' She paused. '*Isn't* he?'

Rowan dithered. *Tell her about Osbourne's mother?* But she'd said nothing that might implicate Osbourne or implicate herself. All Rowan could honestly say was that she'd seemed cold and shifty.

'Palmer's not lying, ma'am,' she said, knowing it sounded weak.

'I didn't say he *was*, Cassie,' Warman said, more kindly than Rowan would have expected. 'I'm telling you that he's not *rational*, right now. Palmer just found his close friend murdered. He'd been drinking. Half out of his mind, he woke in the middle of the night and *thought* he heard a woman's screams.'

'The audio recording on the thumb drive—'

'—Will be examined by an audio forensic specialist, and compared with Osbourne's interview recordings,' Warman said. 'But that takes time. There's really nothing more you can do, right now, Cassie.'

Rowan had to concede defeat, but she couldn't rest; the screams Palmer had heard down the phone echoed with the screams she'd been forced to listen to on that vile recording. So, she waited until she was sure Warman had left for home, then called Hoff, told him what had happened — even told him her suspicions that the man who attacked her was Osbourne.

Hoff had arrived fifteen minutes later, wheezing and coughing and cursing the fog for his bad chest, even though he had his cigarettes and lighter in his hand and reeked of Benson's extra strength. Phlegm rattling in his chest, he'd unlocked the exhibits room and handed over evidence bag 20/C2/7546.

'It's your responsibility, now,' he said. 'Carry it with you if you leave the office. Stick it in your handbag if you nip to the ladies. Sleep with the bloody thing under your *pillow* — just don't let it out of your sight till you sign it back in — the boss reckons it's gonna make the case against Corbie.'

As designated Exhibits Officer, it would be his neck on the line if the chain of custody was broken, so Rowan had promised solemnly.

He rubbed a hand over his face. 'Right. I'm going home. I'm sorry about your Neil and that, but it's Sunday and I need some kip, so I'm going back to bed — and I don't expect to be disturbed again. Right?'

'Right, Hoff.'

He shuffled off, chuffing like a steam train, a cigarette already out of the pack, ready to light up as soon as he was off the premises.

Rowan broke the tamper-evident seal and began leafing through Dylan Corbie's notebook. Corbie had recorded names of streets, people, brief descriptions, occasional sketches, times, places — even weather reports. She scoured every page, hoping to find something about Osbourne, some clue to his whereabouts.

'Why don't you go home, Cass?' She gave a start; she had thought she was alone. It was Finch, looking unhappy and concerned.

'I can't go home, Finch. Scientific Support are crawling all over it.'

'Go to the hospital then.'

'Neil is still in the operating room. Alex is at the hospital — he'll ring me when there's news.'

Finch shuffled from foot to foot but didn't seem ready to leave.

'Don't feel you have to stick around on my account,' she said.

'I don't.' Finch jammed his hands into his pockets and angled his head. 'What you looking at?'

Rowan remembered Warman's encyclopaedic knowledge of her unpaid overtime and wondered if Finch was the DCI's eyes and ears.

She gave a mental shrug. If she could convince Finch, maybe he could convince her boss. 'Palmer says Dylan Corbie writes down everything that happens to him. It's all here.' She held up the notebook for him to see. 'What he ate for breakfast, how many minutes he waited for a bus, who he sat next to in lectures. Oh, and those creepy details of who he followed, where they went, what they were wearing.'

Finch frowned. 'So — he's a perv. We already knew that.'

'So, if he killed Dr Atherton, why isn't that factoid logged in this little green book, alongside the mind-numbing trivia of his day?'

Finch shrugged. 'Cassie, someone saw Dylan Corbie on the late news and called the hotline, yesterday. Said he followed her around Liverpool city centre a week ago. Cornered her in an alley at the back of M&S.'

356

'Did he attack her?'

'No — but only because she got on the phone to her mates. They arrived just in time.'

'The bruising on his face?' Rowan asked, remembering the fading marks she had seen as Dylan was taken into the ambulance.

'Can you blame them?' Finch said.

Rowan didn't blame them. But she didn't believe that Dylan Corbie was the Furman's accomplice, either. Palmer was certain that the notebook was the key. She leafed through the notebook again, from front to back and found nothing significant.

Then she remembered that when Warman had shown them the images on the whiteboard, something had jarred. She turned once more to the centre and looked at the numbers inked in tiny numerals at the bottom corners of the pages. 'Well, that's not right,' she murmured.

'What?' Finch asked.

'Some pages are missing. The numbering's off . . . See — it jumps from thirty-six to forty-five.'

'And?'

'Palmer said Dylan's obsessed with writing everything down. Why would our space cowboy rip eight pages out of his Captain's Log?'

Finch stepped closer, intrigued now. 'Like you said, he's a space cowboy. He must've got the numbers wrong.'

'No — Look. See that?' She fingered the staple. 'Bent. And look at this—' A tiny shred of paper was caught behind it. 'He writes the time and date for every entry — no exceptions. The last entry' — she turned the page to check — 'is at four thirty-seven, yesterday. Finch, there's virtually a whole day missing.'

'Well, that just goes to prove it, doesn't it? He killed Dr Atherton and destroyed the pages so he didn't incriminate himself.'

'If that's the case, where are the missing sheets?' Rowan demanded. 'He was arrested in Atherton's flat, Scientific

Support took his clothes. They would've said if they found anything.'

'It's what we *didn't* find that's interesting.' They turned as one. Ian Chan sauntered into the room, looking fresh and sharp. He set his camera case and CSI kit on the floor and perched on Rowan's desk. 'Any news on Neil?'

Rowan shook her head, not trusting her voice.

'All right — let's see if this little snippet will brighten your day.' He eyed Finch, his expression speculative. 'Can he be trusted?'

Finch looked pained.

'Ian, *please*,' Rowan said.

Chan opened his mouth and closed it again, staring past them to the door. Rowan swung her chair and saw Pat Warman.

For a second she seemed flustered, as though embarrassed to be caught eavesdropping, but she recovered quickly. 'Cassie, I thought you'd gone.'

Snap, Rowan thought, slipping the notebook into her jacket pocket.

Warman handed Finch a sheet of paper. 'I got a call as I was driving out of the car park. There's been a break-in at Jake Osbourne's flat. A neighbour saw Alan Palmer leaving the house. Recognized him from press photos.'

'The bloody idiot,' Rowan muttered.

Warman narrowed her eyes. 'Did you know about this?'

'No, ma'am.'

Warman glared at her.

'I knew he was desperate, but I didn't think he'd do anything so—'

'Cracked?'

Wicks.

'At least Palmer's out looking for Osbourne, instead of faffing around arresting innocent people,' Rowan said.

'*Faffing?*' Warman's eyes bugged.

'I didn't mean you, ma'am,' Rowan said. 'What I meant was—' Wicks smirked at her and she stammered to a halt.

'What you meant was . . .' Warman prompted.

Oh, crap . . . She didn't want to go over it all again — not with Wicks in earshot. 'The city would be a safer place with Osbourne off the streets.'

Wicks snorted, but Warman gave him a sharp look and he clamped his jaws shut, shaking his head in exasperation.

'We're all sympathetic to you, Cassie,' Warman said, with the careful articulation of an angry woman who sees the need for sensitivity. 'But we already have forensic evidence linking Lee Maseby to multiple assaults. And we have Dylan Corbie at the scene of Dr Atherton's murder.'

'Actually, Chief Inspector—' Chan tried to interrupt, but Warman waved him away.

'Osbourne has solid alibis for the abductions,' she went on. 'There isn't *one shred* of evidence against him.'

'Yeah, well, alibis can be fixed, can't they?' Rowan said, her eyes on Wicks.

Wicks stared her out. 'It does your head in, being proved wrong, doesn't it Cassie?'

'This isn't about scoring points, you *prick*.'

'Cassie.'

Rowan's throat ached and her eyes burned with unshed tears. 'Jake Osbourne attacked my brother.' She dragged the collar of her shirt from her neck. 'He broke into my house and attacked me.'

'You said yourself,' Warman said, still trying to be the mediator, the mentor, 'the man who attacked you wore a mask — you can't be sure who it was.'

Rowan was feverish with exhaustion and frustration and the terror that Osbourne was out there playing with a new victim. 'I *am* sure,' she said. 'I just can't prove it.'

'And if the DNA evidence points towards Osbourne, I promise you, we'll bring him in,' Warman said.

'By then it'll be *too late*.'

'Look,' Warman said, 'I know how you must be feeling right now — but you must see there's nothing we can do.'

When she thought about it later, Rowan realised that Warman was genuinely trying to help. But with her kid brother undergoing surgery, the stink of Osbourne's breath still rank in her nostrils, and Wicks rocking on his heels, enjoying the spectacle of her trying to convince the boss, all Rowan heard was that word, "feelings".

'Men have instincts, women have "feelings", is that it, ma'am?'

There was a shocked silence. Rowan wished she could take it back, but she wouldn't — *couldn't* — apologise while Wicks was standing there with that malicious look of glee on his face.

'I've given you a great deal of latitude, up to now, Constable Rowan.' Warman spoke quietly, but they all heard a quiver of fury in her voice. 'I suggested earlier that you should take a few days' compassionate leave. Now I'm telling you.' Her grey eyes flashed like honed steel. 'Go home: you are suspended from duty until further notice.'

* * *

Ian Chan was waiting for her outside the locker room.

'What the hell was *that?*' he demanded.

Rowan shouldered her rucksack and carried on walking. 'I'm sick of playing politics, Ian.'

He snorted. 'You couldn't play politics with loaded dice and a twenty-point lead. You practically called her incompetent in front of half a dozen witnesses.'

'She's so damn sure Dylan Corbie is her killer, she just won't listen.'

Rowan headed towards the rear exit and the car park, storming through one door after another, with Chan hard on her heels.

'If you'd just held off — I told you we found — or rather didn't find — something interesting at the scene.'

Rowan stopped. 'What do you mean?'

'We've completed the search of Atherton's flat. He was tasered and then garrotted, but there's no sign of a taser, no garrotte.'

'No taser?' she repeated stupidly.

'And no garrotte.' Chan watched her, and she began walking again, her legs suddenly heavy and clumsy.

'So we have proof the killer's still out there.'

'Well, who d'you think tried to zap you with enough electricity to power Blackpool Illuminations?'

She glanced sharply into his face. 'I think it was Osbourne — but I didn't think *you* believed that.'

Chan rolled his eyes. 'You may be a fashion disaster; you've got a gob on you like the Mersey Tunnel, but you're not stupid, and you're not paranoid — of course I *believed* you. But we need proof — and here's the shitty part — we *still* don't have it.'

She turned around and started heading back the way she came.

'Woah . . .' Chan said. 'Where d'you think you're going?'

'We have to tell Warman.'

'No-no-no-ooo,' he said gripping her firmly by the elbows and steering her the last few yards to the exit. '*I* have to tell Warman. *You* have to go home.'

Rowan resisted. 'Ian, she may be a bitch, but she's not petty.'

Chan snorted. 'High praise, indeed.' He turned her to face him, still gripping her elbows, as if he feared she might bolt for freedom. 'You've called her judgement into question God knows how many times — and you don't play nice, you just come *right* out and say it. You've made her look a fool in front of the media—'

'That wasn't me.'

'You, Tasha, who cares? Warman went all out on the sketch, and then had to backtrack because Tasha — *your friend* — sold out to the media. And you *will* keep on defending her.'

'Well, what am I supposed to—'

He shushed her. 'You caught the Furman, which won you back a few Brownie points — but it also pissed her off, because while you were out catching him, you weren't doing

361

what she told you to do. And just when you have the chance to build a few bridges, you drag out the flamethrower and burn the lot down.' He gave a bark of exasperated laughter. 'Cassie, you're a frigging nightmare.'

Rowan let her arms go limp. 'You're right. I fucked up. Again. But Wicks—' She broke off.

'Wicks?'

She shook her head. Wicks was just one more bad man she had no proof against. 'Doesn't matter,' she said.

Chan slowly released his grip of her, watching her as though she might suddenly sprint back up the stairs for one last confrontation with Warman.

'She will go after Osbourne, won't she, Ian? Tell me she'll go after him, and I swear, I'll trot off home and sit this out.'

He took a breath, exhaled. 'Osbourne will stay in the clear until we can find evidence against him. You know Warman — she'll go by the book, like she always does. She'll work within protocols, keep him in mind, wait for the audio analysis and the DNA results from your house.'

Chan's voice faded to a distant echo and Rowan felt pressure piling up and up until her chest tightened, and she wanted to punch someone. She reached for the door lever.

Chan put his hand on her arm. 'For God's sake, take a few days off — get your head together. When Warman's got this in the bag, she'll be in a more forgiving mood.'

'By that time, another woman could be dead.' Rowan opened the door to the car park and the inward draught sucked foggy air into the corridor. 'Shit.'

'What?'

'My car — it's at home.'

'Jump in a taxi.'

'I need wheels, Ian.' She held out her hand.

'Nuh-uh. Not a chance.'

'Okay, you won't loan me yours, I'll have to take a fleet car — and since I'm on suspension, that's theft.'

He narrowed his eyes, trying to gauge how serious she was.

'You want to see your friend on a TWOC charge?'

'You're just mad enough to do it, aren't you?' he said.

She looked him in the eye. 'You know I am.'

He dipped in his trouser pocket and handed her the keys to his Audi A4 and she turned to go. He made to follow her, but Rowan stopped him.

'Trust me, Ian,' she said. 'You don't want to be party to this.'

CHAPTER 64

Palmer gingerly unwrapped the tea towel and plunged his hand under the freezing stream of tap water, hoping it would numb the pain. It didn't. But at least it flushed out any remaining splinters of glass.

Ten minutes later the cut was clean and freshly dressed — Elspeth had insisted that he have a good-quality first-aid kit in the new house — as if Ben Kehoe might have been saved with a lint-free pad and a sterile bandage.

He tried to block out the pain and concentrate instead on the fading detritus of Jake Osbourne's life laid out on his kitchen table. The album was neatly compiled: Jake as an infant, a toddler, a schoolboy, all dated and the occasions carefully recorded in copperplate script: *Jacob Gareth Osbourne, DOB 23.10.93*, *Jake on his second birthday*, *Jakey on his trike, Christmas Day 1996*. Only two of the father — both in the earlier section — unsmiling, gripping the young Jake's shoulder as if he was trying to prevent the boy from running away. A gap of two years, then his mother with a succession of men. Sometimes young Jake was in the picture, sometimes not. The later labels were all written in a neat, childish print; Jake's, no doubt.

All the time, Palmer's hand throbbed, pulsing in time with the beat of his heart; a constant reminder that time was short.

He retrieved the letters and scraps of paper that he had salvaged from the shoe box, flattening them out with his good hand, then moving them around, trying to make sense of the chronology. In amongst the brittle sheets of paper and crumpled envelopes he found a dozen Polaroids of Jake's mother with more of her men-friends. She was dressed in bright, clashing colours, her blue eyes wide and startlingly beautiful; she struck pouting sexual poses for the camera, kissing her partner, nibbling an earlobe — nothing explicit, but intimate. Uncomfortably so, given that they must have been taken as a keepsake for her son.

The envelopes — five of them, though Palmer had seen more in the shoe box — were all sealed. Each was addressed to Mr K Osbourne, and the writer had taken great care with the lettering: Palmer could see the faint impression of pencil-lines drawn and then erased, to guide the hand of the child and keep the laboriously joined-up script even and neat. He picked one up and squinted at the postmark. It was franked nineteen ninety-nine; Jake Osbourne would have been nine or ten years old. The fragment of a rubber band adhered to the back of the envelope, perished with age, but stubbornly clinging to it, the slight tackiness holding a piece of paper in place.

Palmer carefully peeled it away and saw that it was a compliment slip from a business address in Jersey. The hand-written message read, '*Enc. Fourteen letters, unopened. Please don't encourage the boy in this Marian.*' The signature was an unreadable squiggle, except for the initials, *K* and *O*, which stood two centimetres taller than the rest.

Keith Osbourne had returned his nine-year-old son's letters unopened.

Holding it clumsily in his injured right hand, Palmer sliced the envelope open with a vegetable knife. The page inside was neatly folded, unruled, but again he saw the faint remnants of lines drawn in pencil.

Jake had written in his best joined-up writing that he had passed his cycling proficiency test and was to be allowed a paper round. The boy confided his ambition to save up and buy a business when he was big, just like his daddy. He finished with a plea for his father to come home.

Don't encourage the boy in this Marian. Palmer felt sick.

The phone in the hall began to ring, its tone querulous and insistent. Palmer went to it reluctantly, his mind still working through the significance of the photographs and the letters.

'Alan Palmer.'

'You've got a damn nerve.' Osbourne. Of course, he would have state-of-the-art security on his flat — he must know about the break-in.

'*Quid pro quo*, Jake.' Palmer strained for sounds in the background. Was the woman there — was she still alive? He could hear nothing but the ragged grating of Osbourne's breathing.

'I'm *warning* you.' Osbourne's voice cracked — a sure sign he was on the edge.

'You already screwed up my life, Jake,' Palmer said. 'What else can you do?'

'I could have a chat with Elspeth and Lucy.' Behind the crack in his voice, rocks seemed to shift, screed to skitter. 'See if we can find a way between the three of us to screw you a bit more.'

Palmer clamped down hard on the memory of gut-liquefying fear when he had found Elspeth's house open and empty. 'You'd have to find them, first.'

'Oh, I know where they live. I can wait.'

Another stab of terror. He stamped on it, squashed it flat — he couldn't deal with Osbourne if he was afraid of him.

'No, Jake — you can't wait — for you, it's all about instant gratification. But I'm *trained* to wait. And in my professional opinion — mental fuck-up that you are — I won't have to wait long.'

Palmer thought he heard a sound in the background. *A whimper?*

'You've no fucking *right* to talk to me like that.'

'And you have the right to torture and kill? You have the right to threaten my *wife and daughter?*'

'I haven't even started, yet. When I'm done with you, you'll beg me to rip your fucking *heart* out.'

The adrenaline tore through him, and Palmer felt sharp and reckless and dizzy. 'Like your mother ripped *your* heart out? Held it, bleeding, in her hands?'

'You leave my mother *out* of this.'

'I know you've read up on this, Jake. You know very well that analysis *never* leaves the mother out.' Palmer heard a yelp of fear, then a woman's terrified breathing on the other end of the line.

'Are you listening, Alan?' Osbourne rasped. 'I hope you're listening, because you're about to hear me choke the fucking life out of her.' The woman screamed, then Osbourne was on the line again, and Palmer heard her sobbing quietly. 'You hear her, *Doc?*'

Palmer felt a crushing panic. He wanted to take back every word, to beg Osbourne not to hurt her, but instead set about deliberately baiting him. 'Looking at those quease-making snapshots of a dysfunctional childhood, I can see why you'd want to lash out,' he said, forcing control into his voice.

'Shut the fuck up.'

'I mean, just how many men were there?'

'I'm gonna gut you like a rabbit, Palmer. I'm going to feed your liver to you slice by slice.' Osbourne sounded almost drunk with emotion. 'I'll skin you and nail your hide to your wife's front door as a welcome home present.'

'You know where I am. We could be having this conversation in person. Come and get me.' *Come and get me and stay the hell away from her.*

No answer.

'What are you waiting for, Jake?'

'No,' Osbourne said, his voice grating with emotion. 'I set the rules of the game. I'm going to—'

'Give it a rest, for *once*, will you?' Palmer kept talking, creating white noise that allowed Osbourne no space for thought. 'I've seen the pictures, I've read your pathetic, *whiny* little notes to your father. Jeez — it's no wonder he sent them back unopened!'

'You bastard!' There were oceans of hate and hurt in Jake Osbourne's voice.

In a child's voice Palmer recited: '"When I'm big, I'm going to have a business just like you." Did you think if you tried hard enough, you could *be* him, Jake?' He stopped, heard only Osbourne's breathing, choked, maybe even tearful. 'Is that why you came into analysis — looking for a surrogate father?'

His mobile began to ring in the kitchen. He said slowly, with a serenity he did not feel, 'Kill her, if you feel you have to, but I think I'll pass on the ringside seat.'

Breaking the connection was the hardest thing he'd ever done.

He stared at the phone until the jangling ring of his mobile jarred him out of his horrified paralysis. He ran through to the kitchen and wrestled the phone from his over-coat pocket. 'Rowan?' She was gone. He was about to hit the speed dial to call her back, when it rang again.

'We don't have much time,' he said, breathless with anxiety.

'Are you at home?' she said.

'He just called again.'

'Palmer, if you're at home, you have to get out of there.'

'He's losing control, Rowan.'

'Okay,' she said. 'I heard you. But you've got to get out — two officers are on their way to arrest you.'

He barely heard her. 'I think I bought her a little more time. But—'

'Mr Palmer—'

'Cassie,' Palmer interrupted. 'He'll kill her if you don't find her — *fast*.'

'Okay,' she said again. 'All right, I'll find her. But will you *please* get out of there? What the hell were you doing in his flat, anyway?'

He stared helplessly at the array of papers and letters. 'Trying to find answers.'

'Yeah? And how's that going?' she asked dryly.

'Was there anything in Dylan's notebook?' he countered.

'Nothing useful. Just a lot of stalker stuff. But some pages are missing.'

For a moment, Palmer was stunned. 'That's not possible.'

'Four double sheets,' Rowan insisted. 'Eight sides. I'm thinking Osbourne took them,' Rowan went on.

'No. That can't be. They found the notebook on Dylan, didn't they?'

'Yes, but—'

'Dylan has a pathological need to keep his notes safe,' Palmer said. 'Why would he tear out four double sheets?' A thought struck him with the force of a freight train. 'Dylan said, "I should have helped her." D'you remember? At Karl's flat.'

'Yes,' she said. 'We talked about this. You thought he meant Jodie Pickersgill.'

'That was before we knew Osbourne had taken another woman.'

'Look,' Rowan said. 'I don't know where you're going with this, but can't you *please* do your thinking on the hoof?'

'Was Dylan talking about *her?*' Palmer interrupted. 'About the new victim — what if Dylan saw Osbourne abduct her? He said, "I should have helped her" because he felt guilty that he didn't try to stop the abduction.'

'All right — *okay*,' she said. 'But we still don't have the missing sheets, and Dylan is still away with the fairies, so it's not going to do us a whole lot of *good*, is it?'

She was right — without the missing pages, it was no use to them at all. But there was something else Dylan said. *What was it?* His hand throbbed and his head ached. *He grabbed my lapel and—*

'—Psych 101.' Palmer almost shouted it, feeling a sudden fizz of excitement.

'What?'

'Dylan said "Psych 101".' He patted the pockets of his overcoat. *No keys.* 'It was a clue.'

'*Jeez*, Alan, they're going to *be* there any second.'

Palmer lifted papers, photographs, letters, finally locating his car keys under the bloody tea towel by the kitchen sink. 'Dylan is an English student, but he reads a lot of psychology. Karl Atherton teaches psychology courses.' He spoke rapidly, the words tumbling from his mouth. 'When Dylan said Psych 101, it was a coded reference to Karl. Osbourne didn't tear out those pages, *Dylan* did. Cassie, he's hidden them in Karl's flat.'

Rowan said, 'Oh, hell . . .'

He paused in the action of struggling into his overcoat — it wasn't the reaction he had expected.

'The place is sealed, Mr Palmer. And I'm on suspension. I can't get you in there.'

'I have a key,' he said. 'Meet me there, if anyone challenges us, you can flash your warrant card.' She hesitated, and it took all Palmer's years of training to keep quiet, to let her come to her own decision.

'Ten minutes,' she said, exhaling in a rush.

He headed for the door.

CHAPTER 65

Rowan broke every speed limit on the route to Karl Atherton's flat. There was no sign of Palmer's car. She ran up the front steps. The door was locked. She rang the bell and stood back to get a look at the top-floor windows. The upper floors were obscured by the fog, floating like drifts of gauze above her. Police tape was wrapped around the black paintwork of the fire escape. It ascended like a mythical stairway to the clouds. She checked her watch. *He should be here by now.*

Her mobile rang. It was Finch.

'Cass, where are you?'

'Breaking into a crime scene.'

'*What?*'

'Nothing. What d'you want, Finch?'

'I thought you should know. We're at Palmer's house; there's no sign of him.'

'Good.' She went to the kerbside and peered toward the main road expecting to see him tearing through the mist.

'No, Cass — it's not good. The front door is wide open and there are signs of a struggle. Cassie, there's blood.'

For a second she couldn't move — couldn't even speak. *I was only talking to him a few minutes ago . . .*

'Cass?'

'Finch, I'm at Karl Atherton's flat. Palmer is convinced Dylan left some clue to Osbourne's whereabouts.' She went to the side of the house. 'I'll call you back if I find anything. You need to trace Palmer's phone — but do it fast, because this bastard is slick — he's not going to hold onto it for long.'

The silence on the line made her say, 'Talk to me, Finch.'

'Cassie,' he said, 'Palmer's mobile — we found it on the path near his house.'

'Shit,' Rowan said. 'Shit, shit, *shit*.' She broke the connection, ducked under the police tape, and started up the steps.

CHAPTER 66

Pain sliced behind his right eye, and Palmer smelled burning candle wax, mossy water and the faint, metallic whiff of urine. He opened his eyes and saw only a blur. He blinked to clear his vision, but the haze remained. He lay still, trying to make sense of his surroundings: he was lying on a tiled floor; tall pillars rose out of a mist that swirled and thickened around him. A hundred candles flickered to his right — he could almost feel the heat of them.

Jake Osbourne stood a short distance away, his back turned. Palmer heard the repeated *snick* of a blade. Osbourne dropped something with a clatter, then turned around. He was holding lengths of blue cord.

Palmer closed his eyes, willed his muscles to relax. Was the woman here? In the cold empty space sounds were magnified and distorted. Yet beyond the gritty slip of Osbourne's shoes on the floor he thought he could hear breathing.

He focused on the sound of Osbourne's footsteps, waiting for him to come closer. *Wait . . . wait . . .*

Another step. Another.

—Now!

He grabbed Osbourne's ankle, followed through, sweeping sideways. Osbourne yelled, lost his balance, fell. Palmer levered himself forward on his hands, ignoring the shout of pain from his injured palm, butted Osbourne in the midriff as he tried to rise.

Osbourne fell backwards with a grunt and Palmer scrambled to his knees. Osbourne kicked out, clipping him with the tip of his shoe. His head snapped back and sparks of white light burst across his vision. The knifing pain behind his eye flared, he felt the skin over his eyebrow give and blood dripped into his eye. He blinked furiously, heard Osbourne coming at him, began to surge to his feet, but his legs gave way and he crashed to his knees again.

Osbourne grinned down at him. Wisps of vapour seemed to rise from his hair and clothes like smoke. He held a small black object in his hand.

Move, Alan — for God's sake, move!

Palmer lunged — *slow, too slow*. Osbourne parried him easily, landing a kick to his ribs.

'Say g'night, Doc,' he said.

A second of agony, like a net of fire thrown over him, coursing through every nerve, every muscle, every cell. His brain seemed to boil with pain.

Then, nothing.

* * *

It was cold. He tasted the bromide tang of foggy air on his tongue, in his throat. His skin felt burned. Narrow ribbons of mist stratified the air in drifts of grey and phosphorescent green. The shift and shimmer of light from above confused him and for a second he was back in the aquatunnel at Blue Planet, Lucy's hand in his, gazing at her face as she stared rapt at the flicker and dance of light through the water.

Then his hands were pulled roughly behind him and, despairing, he realised where he was.

He tried to make sense of the space, but in the capricious ebb and flow of air currents shifting the vapour, he could make out little detail. The candles were a shimmering haze, some five or six yards distant; they seemed to be arranged in an arc around one of the pillars. The vapour shifted and thinned, and he saw a woman: fair-haired, small, her arms pulled so tightly behind her it seemed they must be dragged from their sockets. Her head lolled on her chest and her hair, cut into a short bob, fell forward across her face. He knew her immediately.

'Amy . . .'

Amy Sefton slowly raised her head and stared at him, her eyes wide with shock.

'Yep,' Osbourne said. 'Thought we might have a group therapy session.' He slapped Palmer on the chest, like he expected him to appreciate the joke.

A flash of blue, then Palmer was choking. He hitched and gagged, straining against the cord binding his wrists, but the pressure increased, and dark smoky clusters gathered at the edges of his vision.

'Stop, *please*, *stop*,' Amy screamed, 'You're *killing* him.'

He fought for air, the smoky darkness crowding in — red and black — tumbling over and curling, smothering.

Then—

—Air. Light.

Palmer sucked the clammy air into his bruised trachea, coughing, gasping, retching.

'Sorry, Doc,' Osbourne said, patting him again on the chest. 'Was that a bit snug?'

He finished tying the cord around Palmer's neck, and Palmer rested his head gratefully against the pillar, tilting his head back to drink in the dank air.

'You bastard,' Amy sobbed. 'You absolute *bastard*.'

Osbourne was on his feet and covered the distance so fast the candle flames seemed to duck in anticipation of an imminent onslaught.

Amy screamed, squirming from his touch, fighting her bonds.

'Will you *look* at that?' Osbourne said, pleasantly. 'I haven't hardly touched her, yet. That's not to say I won't expect a farewell shag, for "Auld Lang Syne" . . .' He winked at Palmer. 'Now let's get to business.' He dug in his pocket, brought out another short length of rope.

Amy sobbed, 'No . . .'

'What about the group session?' Palmer asked, his voice hoarse, the rasp in it echoing Osbourne's. He stared into Amy's eyes, desperate for her to understand that she had to stay calm.

'If you two were any good, you wouldn't be here today. So, no offence, Alan, but I'll pass on the analysis.'

'Is that why we're here?' Palmer asked. 'Because we're incompetent?' *Keep him talking; give Rowan time to find us.*

Osbourne strode to him and Palmer willed himself not to flinch.

'If you were just *incompetent*, I'd have moved on, found someone worth the consultation fee.'

He moved restlessly back to Amy, punching a hole in the mist and making the candle flames gutter with an audible growl. 'We had a deal. She reneged on it.' He crouched beside the terrified woman and she whimpered. 'You had to blurt it all out to Alan, didn't you, Amy?'

'I didn't tell him anything — I *swear*.' Amy Sefton watched the rope in Osbourne's hand as if it was a snake about to strike.

'She's telling the truth, Jake,' Palmer said.

'You expect me to believe you? *You*—' He was on his feet again, tearing the gathering veils of fog and sending spiralling threads upwards, like lost souls seeking the light. '*You* promised confidentiality, Alan — I mean, isn't that some kind of sacred *vow* for you people?' He raised his arms and let them fall, and the cord, still in his hand, struck the side of his trousers like a whip.

Blood ran into Palmer's eye, stinging and burning, and he blinked rapidly. 'Sadistic, murdering bastards don't deserve the privilege of confidentiality, Jake.'

Osbourne stared at him, his face scarcely three inches from Palmer's. In the unreal light, Osbourne's irises seemed to glow — darker blue at the edges and turquoise at the centre — making Palmer think of the deceptive cool glow of a gas flame. Heat radiated off him in waves.

Osbourne stared a while longer as though there was something he had seen in Palmer's face that he couldn't quite make out, then his free hand flicked up and, God help him, Palmer couldn't help flinching this time. Osbourne bared his teeth again, pressed his thumb just above Palmer's eye and Palmer jerked his head back, grunting in pain. He came up hard against the pillar and Osbourne rubbed his thumb from left to right above Palmer's eye.

'Wouldn't want you to only get half the show.' He rose smoothly to his feet.

CHAPTER 67

Rowan eased the door shut behind her. She had knocked out just one small pane of the latticework of the door to gain entry and with the fog thickening, the damage shouldn't be obvious from the street. She tiptoed through the kitchen, aware that Karl Atherton's neighbours might well be at home on a Sunday morning.

They had found Dylan in the sitting room — that would be the place to start.

The curtains were drawn and she hesitated in the doorway, uncertain if she should risk turning on the light. The room had the seasoned smell of pipe tobacco and something slightly musty. As her eyes adjusted to the gloom she saw that the place was stuffed with as many books as a public library: bookcase after bookcase of textbooks and paperbacks and journals, some stacked two deep.

'Great, Palmer,' she muttered. 'And exactly where am I supposed to start looking for the needle in this damn haystack?'

She saw an anomaly at the far end of the room — a humped form, and a darker patch of shadow. She felt a thud of anxiety, until she remembered that Dylan had been found hiding behind a barrier of textbooks he'd built on and around one of the desks. As she walked towards it, the deeper shadow resolved into a section of empty shelving.

She turned on the desk lamp and went through the drawers, emptying one at a time and sifting through letters and scribbled notes and scraps of paper, finding nothing. She rummaged through the bin, picked up book after book, holding each by the spine and fanning the pages. A railway ticket fell from one, but there was no sign of the missing sheets from Dylan's notebook. *He could have tossed the sheets on the fire, dropped them out of the window onto the street.* But Palmer said the notebook was Dylan's way of making sense of the world — *he wouldn't just chuck that out the window, would he?*

She sighed, continuing the search, because it was better than doing nothing, picked up the next textbook, and the next, riffling the pages and stacking the books behind her on one of the empty shelves as she checked them, turning again and again to the semicircular wall of books, willing herself to take it slowly rather than miss the one crucial clue that might help her find Osbourne. She reached for the next book on the pile, lifted it—

—Her phone rang. She jumped, fumbled the book, dropped it, broke its fall with the toe of her shoe. She wrenched the phone from her inside pocket. Finch's name showed up on the display.

'Cassie, we've had a missing person report.'

She let the book lie.

'Amy Sefton. She was Osbourne's therapist for a few months.'

'Does Warman know?'

'Of *course* she knows.'

'Well how much more proof does she need?' Rowan asked, irritated by his defensive tone.

'We're officially looking for Osbourne now, okay?'

'Yeah, well, good luck with that.'

'Look,' Finch said hotly, 'I didn't *have* to call you.'

'I know. But my brother is in *hospital*, Finch—' She broke off: this wasn't Finch's fault. 'When did this Amy go missing?'

'A friend called round to her house at seven this morning. They were supposed to head off early to Manchester on a shopping trip. She was already gone by then — the house was wide open. But it could've happened anytime after two o'clock, yesterday afternoon, which was the last time her friend saw her,' Finch went on. 'She's not answering her mobile phone, but we should have a fix on it, soon. The boss is looking into it now.'

'You'll call me back if you get a location?'

'I don't know,' he said. 'I shouldn't even be talking to you.'

'Oh, for *crying out loud*, Finch.'

'It's all right for you,' he said, suddenly huffy. 'You've got nothing to lose.'

'Wow,' she said, too stunned to think of a sharp response. 'Thanks.'

He muttered an apology and she extracted a promise that he would keep her informed.

Osbourne now had both therapists. Rowan set down her phone and stared dismayed at the columns of books she had still to search.

She tore into them, shaking them so hard that the spines of some of the older tomes ripped away from the boards.

Finch rang ten minutes later and she snatched the phone up eagerly.

'Cass.' He sounded excited. 'We've got a location — a disused warehouse at the north end of the docks.'

'A warehouse? That doesn't sound right. Has it got a cellar or basement?'

'I don't know — look, Cassie, I've got to go.'

'Finch, wait — I thought we were looking for a swimming pool.' She picked up another book and shook it. The binding gave with a nasty tearing sound, but it yielded nothing of use.

'It's brick-built, like Tasha said,' Finch told her. 'Maybe the damp was just water damage. Emma and Tasha were blindfolded, weren't they?'

'Finch, I was speaking to Palmer minutes before you got to his house. Minutes before that, Osbourne was with Amy, threatening to kill her. He must be somewhere close by—'

'Cassie, we're moving. I've got to go.' He hung up.

'Finch!' She stared at the blank screen for a second.

Tasha isn't stupid — she can tell the difference between a roof leak and a space designed to hold water. They're looking in the wrong place.

Her stomach did a guilty flip: if she had followed through on the swimming baths, she might have discovered the kill site.

Kill site. Her guilt was supplanted by a queasy terror — Osbourne planned to kill both Amy Sefton and Alan Palmer.

The pile of books seemed to have got bigger. Hundreds to search through, and no time. Palmer had said Psych 101 was a clue. She googled Psych 101 on her phone. Was faced with millions of results.

She stood for a full minute, with her thumb over the speed-dial key for Ian Chan's mobile, broke into a sweat thinking about the possible repercussions for her moribund career and for Chan if he got dragged into a disciplinary hearing. Then she dialled. And hung up. And redialled — and hung up again.

Her phone rang, and she was so on edge she almost dropped it.

'Cassie?'

'Alex?'

'I've been trying to get through.'

'God, Alex, I'm sorry. How is he?'

'He's in recovery. The surgeon seems pleased, but he said it'll be a while before we're sure there's no lasting damage.'

'Oh.' She'd wanted better news, a happy ending.

'Where are you?'

'I'm working.'

'You can't be working, Cassie.'

'I told you — I'm no good sitting still, I—'

'No, I mean you *can't* be working: Charlie Inghams came in to check on Neil. He said you'd been suspended.'

Rowan closed her eyes. *Good old Charlie.* 'Let me know when Neil wakes up,' she said. 'I'll be right there.'

'No, I'm not going to help you wreck your career. You want to know how Neil is, come and see for yourself.'

She felt anger flare like a migraine behind her eyes. 'Listen, you sanctimonious bastard — there are people who might not make it through the night if I don't find them.'

'You should listen to *yourself*,' he shot back. 'You *have* to be the one, don't you? Saint Cassie — always the martyr. Go ahead, Cass — fix the world.'

For a moment, she was too shocked to speak. Then her survival instinct kicked in and she got mad.

'Here's the thing,' she said, putting a measure of cop toughness into her tone. 'A sadistic headcase is out there with two people, and some very sick ideas about how to enliven a dull Sunday morning. So I haven't got time to go on a point-scoring mission with you, and I haven't got time to hold your hand.' After a second's hesitation, she thought, *What the hell.* 'Now, you can help me, or you can hang up and let me get on with it.'

There was a stunned silence at the other end of the line.

'Are you there?' she asked.

'I'm here. But I think I'm hallucinating. Did you just say *you* needed *my* help?'

'Don't let it go your head. I've just broken into a murder scene, and since I've told you, that makes you an accessory.'

'Are you *crazy*?' he hissed.

'The psych who was murdered — he taught psychology at the university.' She outlined her discussion with Alan Palmer about Dylan Corbie. 'He's an English student, reads a lot of psychology,' she said, repeating what Palmer had told her. 'Palmer thinks the reference to Psych 101 was a hint that he'd left the missing pages in Atherton's flat.'

'So what d'you want from me?' he asked.

Rowan stared at the stacks of books, feeling totally helpless. 'I'm looking at a literary Great Wall of China here, Alex. I just need something to narrow the search. Is there such a thing as a Psych 101 textbook, for instance?' Rowan picked up one of the texts one-handed and gave it a half-hearted shake.

Alex laughed. 'The 101 is just shorthand for basic level, Cass,' he said.

'Okay, smart arse—'

'Hang on, though,' Alex said. 'If Doctor Atherton taught psychology, he might have written on the subject. Lemme try a search on Amazon.'

A few moments later he said, 'Nothing on Psych 101.'

Rowan switched her phone to speaker and tapped in the same search term. 'But he's written a few textbooks on psychoanalysis and psychotherapy.'

'Are any of them in front of you now?'

He waited while she scanned the spines of the texts.

'No.'

'I'm typing in "basic psychology" as a search term.' He groaned when the results came up. 'There's about a *thousand* texts on basic psychology.'

'This is bloody hopeless!' Rowan said.

'Wait a minute — did you say Dylan Corbie studied English?'

'English and psychology,' she said. 'Why?'

'What about *Room* 101?'

'The TV programme?'

'The novel,' he corrected. 'Orwell? *Nineteen Eighty-Four*?' He gave an exasperated sigh. 'Never mind. Google "Room 101", and the psychologist's name.'

'No good,' she said, a few seconds later. 'Maybe I should just go back to the books.'

'No — Cass — wait.' She heard excitement in his voice. 'Try "Room 101 psychology journal".'

Rowan typed again, waited agonized seconds while the search engine on her phone loaded. She scrolled down the screen fast. 'This is a waste of time, Al—' Something had caught her eye. She scrolled back three entries.

'Do you see it?' Alex asked.

'Dr K. Atherton, "From Nineteen Eighty-Four to Room 101, a psychological study of the uses and abuses of memory." '

'It's in *Clinical Psychology and Psychotherapy*,' Alex said. 'Well, what are you waiting for?'

Rowan could have wept with frustration. 'It's a magazine — a journal. These are all books in front of me, Alex.'

'It could be in bound format — you know, a collection,' Alex said.

His excitement was infectious. She tilted her head, reading the spines with new enthusiasm. 'What am I looking for?'

'Probably dark leatherette with gold lettering.'

She dropped her phone on the desk and began the search in earnest. Found it near the bottom of the last pile: a volume in bound black leatherette.

Bookmarking the article were the four double sheets Dylan Corbie had torn from his notebook.

CHAPTER 68

Alan Palmer gritted his teeth against the pain, fixing his gaze on Amy Sefton, willing her to be strong. Begging Osbourne would not help. Begging would only feed his fantasy and hasten the end. *Please, Amy — show me you understand.*

'All this because his star pupil was promoted over him,' Amy said. Her voice was weak, but she made eye contact with Palmer.

She understands.

'I taught her everything she knows,' Osbourne said. 'All the moves, the sales patter, when to use stats and when to turn on the charm — and they promoted *her* to the board.' He stared at Palmer, his hands limp by his sides.

'What hurt more, Jake — her betrayal, or being passed over for a woman?' Palmer asked.

'Don't you dare analyse *me.*' Osbourne slammed the pillar above Amy Sefton's head and her whole body jerked.

'We're trying to help you "come to terms with the natural conflicts arising from the promotion of one of your mentees to a senior position in the firm".' Palmer was paraphrasing from Amy's initial, fudged handover notes. 'Did he *dictate* that twaddle to you, Amy?'

She smiled. 'I should have known you'd see through it. The deal was he wouldn't bother me if I kept quiet, omitted certain *details* from my referral notes.

'I read about your suspension from the BPC register,' she explained. 'I'm afraid I approached you to take Jake on as a patient because I thought you wouldn't ask any difficult questions.'

'See — even she thinks you're a hopeless case,' Osbourne said with a crooked grin.

'But he isn't, is he?' Amy said. 'He knew I was hiding something from him. Shall I tell him what that is?'

Osbourne paced to her and leaned on the pillar, leaving a bloody thumbprint on the glazed bricks.

She blanked him. 'He raped me,' Amy said, her voice toneless, her face expressionless. 'During a therapy session.'

'Women,' Osbourne rasped. 'You ovulate like fucking bunnies at a whiff of testosterone — then scream rape.'

'Bunnies,' Palmer said. 'Classic regression.'

'Shut it.'

'You know why you want me to watch you kill her?' Palmer asked.

'To punish your father who abandoned you,' Amy said.

'The father who left you to watch helplessly while all those men fucked your mother,' Palmer added.

'You shut your filthy mouth.' The words echoed and skittered around the vast empty space and Osbourne stood with his fists clenched, ready to fight with an enemy who was bound and helpless.

'You kill,' Palmer said, '*because you are afraid.*'

'I kill because they can't identify me if they're dead.' The rope in Osbourne's right hand twitched.

'But you've already been identified, Jake — by Tasha McCorkindale.' Palmer forced power into his voice, when he could have wept with fear. 'Your mother gave you an alibi — you could've walked away a free man — gone back to your old life. Instead, you went after the two people who will put you right back at the centre of the investigation.'

'You're giving me bellyache, Doc.' Osbourne took a step forward and Palmer braced himself.

'Somatisation,' Amy said. *Now* they were working together: distracting, disorientating, pounding Osbourne's emotions so that he didn't know how to act.

'Psychobabble,' Osbourne said. 'Word-wank.'

Amy pushed harder. 'Your body is surging with adrenalin now, but you couldn't identify the emotions behind that surge if your life depended on it.'

'*Shut* it.' He aimed a kick, landed hard at the top of her thigh and she screamed.

Abruptly, the blind rage left him, replaced by something colder and Osbourne stood still for some time, while the mist gathered around him, shrouding him so that he seemed almost to *fade* into it. His breathing, laboured at first, slowly returned to something like normal.

'You fucked up *my life*. Now I'm going to fuck you up.' He swivelled his head to look at Amy and raised the rope, pulling it tight between his hands.

Amy gasped, but didn't speak.

Palmer's heart pounded, sending shooting pains through his head. *Say something — anything.*

'All — those — men.'

Osbourne swung to face him. '*What* did you say?' For the moment, he had forgotten Amy.

Her eyes were closed, her lips pressed tightly together as she fought the pain.

'You wanted to make your mother happy,' Palmer said. 'But here's the paradox: you knew that you couldn't be what she *wanted* you to be.'

Osbourne stood over Palmer, scuffing the tiled floor with his heel, like a bull about to charge.

Palmer's mouth dried but he made himself go on: 'In the end, you began identifying with your hated father — but that only made you despise yourself even more.'

'You think you know me?' Osbourne yelled. 'Arrogant prick!' He lashed out with the cord, cutting Palmer across the cheek. Palmer grunted with pain.

Osbourne struck again and again, his eyes liquid blue fire. Palmer turned his head, screwing his eyes tight, unable to defend himself.

'You don't even know *yourself*,' Osbourne said, standing back at last, so breathless with exertion he could barely speak.

Palmer saw one last flash of blue and felt again the terrible choking pressure on this throat.

CHAPTER 69

It wasn't much to look at. A dumpy sandstone building behind spiked fencing at the south-eastern corner of a playing field near Princes Park. Currents and draughts worked on the fog, attenuating it here and there to allow feeble sunlight to penetrate the murk. The cold was so intense Rowan's fingers hurt. The building was overgrown with brambles and gorse, and in the shifting vapour she could see that the structure was no more than twelve feet high. *But Tasha said it was a cathedral-like space . . .*

She checked Dylan Corbie's close-written notes. The shape was right — a 'lopped-off pyramid, like a ziggurat' — he'd even given dimensions and from what she could see he was bang on. But the place where Tasha had been held was twenty or thirty times bigger. She recalled Dylan's desperate, gabbled words to Palmer as he was taken into the ambulance, the look of terror on his face.

Dylan never set foot inside this building, Cassie. He was too frightened.

She remembered, too, that Tasha had said Osbourne forced her down a set of steps. *Okay*, she thought, what Dylan had described was an *entrance* — which meant that the bulk of the structure must be underground.

She had rung Finch to give him the location as she drove from Karl Atherton's flat; they had already stormed the warehouse, but it was empty, as she'd known it would be. Osbourne had sent them to the wrong side of town.

The gate was chained and padlocked. But when she lifted the hasp it fell open: it had been looped through a couple of links to make it look like it was clasped. She swung the gate open just wide enough to slip through and worked carefully around the perimeter of the building. Gang tags overlaid older graffiti: love messages and names and obscene sketches scored crudely in the rock. At the northern face she found a second gate. On the lintel above, fading in and out of the mist, a date: 1889. The gate was rusted to a dull brown and only the odd flake of black hinted at the original colour of the paintwork. *That'll scream like a banshee*, she told herself. Even so, she tested it lightly with her fingertips.

It swung easily, soundlessly outwards.

Hardly daring to breathe, she stepped inside the recessed entrance. A steel door of more modern construction was set three feet deep into the wall. It stood slightly ajar and she moved towards it, step by careful step.

Grey tendrils of vapour stole through the gap, oozing past her, as if drawn to it, and Rowan felt a shimmer of dread. She peered through the opening and saw flickering light.

Voices skittered and echoed from below like bats' wings in a cave.

Rowan shivered — something was happening inside. She heard shouting. Then a scream.

For a few seconds there was silence, then a bellow of rage.

She edged out of the entrance and around to one of the blank walls of the structure, before dialling Finch's number. 'Finch, where the hell are you guys?' She could hear the whoop of sirens through the earpiece.

'We're doing our best, Cassie, but the fog is bloody awful by the river — and there's been an incident on the Dock Road—'

While Finch bitched about the traffic and the difficult driving conditions, Rowan crept back to listen at the flat, steel door. She heard heavy thuds, the grunts of a man in pain; punctuating it, a woman, her voice high-pitched, begging the attacker to stop.

'Finch,' Rowan whispered. 'I think they're both in there and something *really bad* is happening. I'm going for a closer look.'

'*Cassie*,' Finch said. 'Stay out of there. Are you listening to me? Cassie, you *can't* go in — you're suspended.'

'Like you said — I've got nothing to lose.' She ended the call and pocketed the phone, then slipped her Casco baton from her belt.

Another hard *thwack* made her flinch. A man's voice, breathless with exertion, the sibilant sounds magnified and distorted so that she couldn't hear the words. Then a horrible wet choking echoed and flittered from below her, electrifying every nerve in her body.

* * *

A steep stone staircase led down. Rowan gripped her Casco baton tightly and descended a few steps. The fog lay, veil upon veil; in the swirling vapour she could make out brick and tiles. It was deep — maybe thirty feet deep — *like a swimming bath* — Tasha had said. The space was divided by pillars.

A reservoir, Rowan realised. *It's an underground reservoir.*

A blaze of candles formed a corona of buttery yellow towards the centre of the space. The mist reflected and scattered the light, casting grotesque shadows. Amy Sefton was tied fast to one of the pillars, Palmer to another, facing Amy. Rowan could see his hands tied behind him, a rope knotted tightly at neck height around the pillar.

He was choking. She couldn't see Osbourne.

Amy Sefton screamed again, 'Stop! Please, stop it!'

Osbourne loomed from behind one of the pillars and Rowan held her breath. In the misty atmosphere, he seemed momentarily insubstantial, but he gathered solidity and form as he emerged into the blurred light of the candle flames.

He rushed Amy, roaring like an animal. His shadow swelled, distorted by the candlelight, growing to monstrous proportions, slipping along the wall and climbing towards Rowan. She felt a superstitious horror of the shadow's reach and pressed her body flat against the wall.

Palmer choked, fighting for breath, pushing with his heels, driving himself backward, trying to relieve the pressure on his throat — to make the solid brick and tile give a fraction to allow him a precious sip of air.

Jesus . . . Jesus . . .

Osbourne's back was turned to her, and Rowan slunk to the bottom of the stairs, edging right, using the pillar Palmer was bound to as cover.

Osbourne screamed in Amy Sefton's face, 'Adrenaline ripping through you and you can't do *fuck all* about it. But you can feel superior, can't you, Amy — because you can *identify* the emotion.'

'Stop it,' she sobbed. '*Please*, Jake.'

Palmer's head was bleeding. An angry weal ran diagonally across his face and a bandage wrapped around his right hand had come loose, unravelling in a bloody ribbon. Rowan kept her gaze on Osbourne's back as she worked to free the analyst. But the rope was knotted too tight — she couldn't loosen it. She put her baton down, her heart hammering so hard in her chest she thought Osbourne would surely hear it.

Palmer, aware of her now, rolled his eyes toward her. They were bloodshot and his face almost purple. *Dear God — he's dying!* She pulled a penknife from her pocket. She couldn't even slip the thinness of the blade under the rope.

'Where do you *feel* it, Amy?' Osbourne yelled. 'Where do you *feel* your pain?'

Frantic, now, Rowan turned the knife blade around and sawed through the rope, hacking and slicing, driven half-mad by Palmer's desperate choking.

Amy sobbed, then her voice was raised in fresh alarm, 'No, please . . . no more . . .'

Osbourne had something in his hand. 'Tell me where it hurts, I'll make the pain stop,' he said. 'Head? Or heart? Or guts. Or here—' He jabbed Amy.

Suddenly the air seemed to buzz and crackle, Rowan got a whiff of ozone, and Amy went limp.

Shit. Rowan slashed at the rope till it frayed, ripped through the last threads with sweat stinging her eyes. It gave.

Palmer fell forward, coughing and choking, taking air in huge whistling gasps. Osbourne wheeled round in the act of slipping the taser back into his pocket. His eyes widened and Rowan rose to her full height, stepping away from the pillar. He threw himself at her — no warning. She side-stepped, slashed his forearm with her penknife. He parried and the blade flew into the shadows.

Osbourne clamped a hand over the cut. On his pinky finger, he wore a sapphire-and-diamond ring.

'Bitch,' he snarled.

For a moment she froze, almost hypnotized by the weird blue-green of his eyes, the hatred in them. Then she darted left, crouched to scoop up the baton. He ran forward and she surged to her feet, putting herself between Palmer and Osbourne, the baton trembling in her fist.

'What d'you think you can do with that feeble weapon, Constable?'

'Come near me, you'll find out.' Her breathing was harsh, and she felt her heart pounding in her throat.

The fog had been torn apart in the struggle, but now it wrapped around him, welding to him as though it recognized a confederate force.

He smiled. 'Think you can take me, little girl?'

Her legs liquefied beneath her but she forced aggression into her voice. 'I've put you down twice already, Jake. This time, I won't be playing.'

'The first time, you had the element of surprise — the second, you had help — how is young Neil, by the way?'

She wavered for a fraction of a second, and he made a feint for her. Rowan swung the baton down hard onto his injured arm and he yelled, staggered left, came at her again. Palmer flicked one leg out, and Osbourne tripped, fell, sending candles flying left and right. He rolled and was on his feet in seconds, ten feet from Palmer. Too close to Amy.

Osbourne kept his eyes on her, bending just for a second to pick something up. At first she thought he was righting one of the candles, but too late she realised he had a knife in his hand — and no penknife, either. This had the sharp, evil blade of a butcher's boning knife.

Before Rowan could work out which way to move, Osbourne was standing behind Amy, using the pillar as cover, holding the knife to her neck.

* * *

Palmer drank air, stretching his neck, his Adam's apple bobbing as if he was swallowing long, cool draughts of water. His throat was livid with rope burns and every breath seemed painful. 'This isn't your fantasy, Jake.' His voice, a hoarse whisper, sounded unlike him.

Osbourne adjusted his grip on the hasp of the knife and glanced toward the lengths of cord a short distance from him.

'He needs to—' The fog-laden air caught in Palmer's throat and he began a racking cough.

Rowan said it for him: 'I know,' she said. 'He needs to choke his victims.' She bent, as if to show Palmer the bruising on her neck, using the gesture to cover her real intention.

'Why so surprised to see me?' she asked, her eyes fixed on Osbourne, while she tugged at the knots that bound Palmer's hands. 'You wanted me here, right? You did plan to take us all in one day, didn't you, Jake? Except you fucked up at my house.'

'Like I said, you had help.'

'Yeah, well, help is on the way now. So, feel free to leave whenever the mood takes you.' In the distance, a distant siren wailed. 'Only I wouldn't leave it too long.'

For a moment, it looked like he was seriously considering it. Then Osbourne grabbed a handful of Amy's hair and pulled her head back, exposing the pale flesh of her neck. 'Step away from him, bitch,' he rasped, pressing the blade into Amy's flesh, bringing a beading of blood to the surface.

Rowan stood and moved a step to the right. The hand holding the baton was rock steady now.

'Drop the baton.'

She gripped it tighter.

'I *said*—' He began to draw the knife across Amy's throat.

'Okay!' Rowan yelled. 'All right.' She held the baton away from her. 'I'm putting it down — okay?'

'Kick it.'

In the gloom, she couldn't see where her penknife had ended up, but she was sure it flew right, so she hoofed the baton left, hearing it roll, jingling, into a dark corner. 'It's gone. Now ease up.'

He thought about it for a few seconds, while Rowan held her breath. Blood spilt down Amy Sefton's neck, soaking into the wool of her sweater. Slowly, Osbourne released his grip of Amy's hair, and stood.

Rowan glanced right, searching for her knife — any weapon was better than none — but he caught the look and followed her gaze, instantly suspicious.

She switched her focus to the ruined votary, the remnants of which flickered in an untidy arc ahead of her. 'What *is* this big obsession with candles, anyway? Didn't you get enough birthday cake when you were a kid?'

Palmer coughed and spat blood. 'You don't know how close you are, Constable.' It sounded like something had torn in his throat.

'Shut the fuck up, Palmer.' Osbourne barely glanced at the analyst. 'Did he tell you about Ben Kehoe, Cassie? And his wife and daughter — where are they? Some analyst — he can't even keep his *family* together.'

'You should see the photographs in his childhood album,' Palmer's voice was barely a whisper, now.

Darkness shifted behind Osbourne's eyes, as if something dangerous and hidden had stirred in the mud of a lagoon.

'A willowy hermaphrodite posed next to all those big, strong men.' Palmer took a breath on each of the last three words, his voice almost giving out. 'Mummy definitely went for the macho type.' He looked half-dead, but he was still fighting, using words as weapons.

Rowan listened to the tick and crackle of heat from Osbourne. Palmer was getting to him. He moved to the right of the pillar, balancing on the balls of his feet, extending his arm like a fencer about to thrust. 'I *said* shut up.'

Rowan shifted her weight, ready to take him down if she got the chance.

'You know why he works in security?' Palmer asked. 'The alarm systems and sensors and triple locks — they're a metaphor for what he's done all his life — lock down and sound the alarm bells when anyone gets too close.' He laughed, and Rowan heard a frightening wetness in it. 'You're as scared as your victims, Jake.'

'So, this is all a front for a frightened little boy?' Rowan asked.

'He fears his mother and loves her and hates her and wants to destroy her. Each woman he hurts represents the mother he wants to kill.'

'Bullshit,' Osbourne spat.

Rowan watched him move closer, inch by inch, as Palmer baited him. *That's it, Jake. Just a bit further —*

'She gave me an alibi for *murder.*'

'That was control.' Palmer continued to address Rowan, not even looking at Osbourne. 'Not love. His mother's alibi re-established his dependency on her.'

Rowan stared at Osbourne in wonder. 'He's damaged goods. I almost feel sorry for you, Jake.'

'Pity the child.' Palmer's words fluttered up into the vast space like a whispered prayer. 'But despise the man.'

Amy's eyes began to flutter open, and Rowan willed her to be still.

They heard revving car engines, caught a flicker of red and blue light, but she knew it would be up to her: the only access a narrow door, a steep drop to the theatre of action, and poor visibility. The Matrix team would be stymied. Nevertheless, she said, 'The police are outside, Jake. Just waiting their chance. You're going to prison.' She saw a flicker of doubt in Osbourne's eyes.

He wiped the sweat from his brow with his forearm, smearing blood onto his face. 'Okay. I'm going to prison — what have I got to lose?' Suddenly, he swung back to Amy.

He's too far away, Rowan thought. *I'll never reach him in time*. For a moment of blind panic, all she felt was paralysing fear—

Then she got spitting mad. *Why should the Osbournes of this world always have things their own way?*

'What was it like,' she demanded, 'playing the eunuch in your mother's male harem?'

Osbourne brandished the knife. 'I'll fucking *kill* you.'

'You could try,' she scoffed. 'But since I'm not tied up and tasered, that won't be so easy.' He took a step towards her. *Keep coming Jake — I'll knock you flat on your arse . . .* Rowan could almost *hear* the rising tension in him — like a violin string bowed at the upper limits of hearing.

'*How* many lovers *did* she have? Fifteen? Twenty? More?'

She edged right — at least then if he rushed her, Palmer would be out of the line of fire.

'How did it feel,' she went on, forcing a Judas tremor out of her voice, 'knowing they'd been with her, had put their hands all over her?' She would side-step, sweep round to grab his knife hand and use his momentum to carry him forward — smash him into one of the pillars. *Great in theory — but Jesus, that's a big ugly knife.* 'Could you *smell* the sweat and stink of sex on them?'

He came at her, screaming. 'You shut your filthy mouth!'

She froze. At the last moment, she brought her arm up and the knife blade tore through her jacket into the flesh, glancing off the bones of her lower arm. Fiery pain ripped through her. Then his fingers closed around her good arm and he shoved her back into a pillar. Her skull hit the tiles with a dull crack.

Osbourne spun her round to face Palmer, his left arm around her neck, his right holding the knife.

Rowan fought against nausea and stark, blank terror.

'D'you like to watch, Alan?' he said, squeezing her throat in the crook of his elbow. 'You've got a grandstand ticket for this one.'

Palmer tried to shout, but he choked and spat more blood. His head slumped to his chest and Osbourne kicked his foot. 'Hey — don't you die on me. Wake up.'

Rowan tried to prise Osbourne's arm from her throat, he was too strong.

'Stop struggling,' he warned.

She felt the tip of the blade puncture the skin of her stomach, just below her ribcage.

Osbourne kicked Palmer hard, and this time, the analyst raised his head, slowly.

'There are some things he *has* to do, in order to . . . fulfil his fantasy.' Palmer spoke so softly that she could barely hear him above the pounding of her blood in her ears.

'He's telling you I'll choke you to death, rather than disembowel you, Cassie.' Osbourne laughed, kissed her cheek. 'Isn't that a comfort?'

Palmer looked into her face, his eyes pleading with her to make sense of what he'd said.

She tried to think against the fear and the throbbing pain in her arm, and the suffocating pressure of Osbourne's forearm on her throat. Palmer had told her that some things within the fantasy were unchanging and unchangeable, and she had told him what Osbourne had done to Emma, and Tasha, and Jodie.

Suddenly, she knew.

Rowan held Palmer's gaze and let her arms go limp. Osbourne tensed.

She reached back with her good arm and touched his leg with her hand.

'What the fuck?' he said.

'Is this how you like it?' she asked, brushing the tips of her fingers along the length of his thigh.

'What the fuck are you *doing*?' Osbourne demanded.

'Is *this* how you like it?' she said again, using the words he had used to torment his victims. She slipped her hand into his trouser pocket. Her fingers closed around a plastic casing, about the size and shape of an electric razor.

At the last moment, Osbourne roared, 'No!' and tried to shove her away. But he was too slow. Rowan pressed the tip of the taser into the muscle of his thigh and squeezed the trigger.

He fell to the ground, and she tore the taser from his pocket, shocked him again in the shoulder.

'Is THIS how you like it?' she yelled, tasering him in the chest as the first armed Matrix officers burst through the door.

EPILOGUE

Rowan walked with Palmer across the car park of the Beechwood Clinic. Dylan Corbie had asked if he could meet her. It was December, Christmas only a few days away, and bitterly cold. A few dry flurries of snow had fallen in the short journey out to the suburbs of the city, but the ground was so cold that it blew like torn paper, collecting in gutters and outlining the paving stones, leaving the paths clear.

Rowan matched his long stride, feeling comfortable with him, companionable. She had come to look forward to her daily visits during Palmer's stay in hospital, and to a degree, her growing friendship with Palmer had dulled the pain of losing Tasha as a friend.

'Are you all right?' Palmer had become eerily attuned to her changes in mood.

'Yeah,' she said — an automatic response — but then she shrugged, sighed. 'No — not really. I saw Tasha today.' They had got into the habit of honesty on her visits to the hospital. She had shared with Palmer her disappointment that Alex had stayed in England only long enough to see his younger brother home.

Palmer looked at her now, expecting more, and she said reluctantly, 'She's not doing so well.'

'I'm sorry.'

'Her studio was stripped bare. All her sketches and watercolours and acrylics — everything she's worked on for the last two years. Tasha's a messy sod — but there's a joy in it, you know? The clutter of brushes and pots and dirty rags — the splashes of paint on the floor, the smell of linseed oil and turpentine.'

'And now?'

She shrugged. 'Now it smells like a hospital. There was just one blank canvas mounted on an easel in front of the picture window. It felt like that meant something — I dunno — something significant.'

She pictured the pristine white surface, stark against the sweep of grey snow clouds over the Mersey.

'Perhaps it means she needs to start again,' Palmer said.

'I think it means she's empty. She doesn't *know* how to start again.' Rowan shook herself. Now was not the time for morbid thoughts. 'How about you? Any news on the divorce?'

Palmer's jaw tightened.

Tactful, Cassie. She held up her hands. 'Don't answer that.'

'It's okay. I suppose I just never thought I'd hear that question addressed to me.' He slowed his pace. 'Elspeth held off while I was in hospital, but now I'm out of danger . . .' He winced. 'That sounded bitter, didn't it? She has agreed to joint custody, though.'

'Well, isn't that a good sign?' Rowan asked. 'She didn't argue that your job put her and Lucy in danger?'

Palmer avoided her eye. 'I didn't actually tell her that Osbourne had been inside her house.'

Rowan knew that he would have agonized over that decision: Alan Palmer had a strong sense of right and wrong. 'What happened wasn't your fault,' she said. 'And you've a right to see your daughter. Osbourne's well out of the picture. The CSIs found Emma's, Tasha's and Jodie's DNA in the underground reservoir, along with his. And there was a fourth woman — we don't even know what happened to her. Osbourne's mother is still claiming she had no idea what was going on, but it turns out it was her car Osbourne parked in the hotel car park in Penrith to give himself an alibi. He's covering for her. Says he told her it needed work doing — he used his own car for the abductions.'

'Did you find evidence of that?'

'He'd had it professionally steam-cleaned, but the CSIs took it apart — literally. And they found evidence of all three in the nooks and niches that even the professionals miss. Jake Osbourne is going nowhere.'

He nodded, his mood sombre. 'It might not heal them, but at least Tasha and those other women will get the justice they deserve.'

She could have hugged him for that. 'Part of me wishes I'd never seen that damn hospital report. I look at Tasha and *know* what he did to her, how she suffered. Now I've got all that vile stuff in my head and I know I'll never shift it. It'll haunt my dreams and poison our friendship until we can't stand the sight of each other.'

She saw a fleeting spasm of pain crease his brow and she winced. 'Me and my big mouth, again. That's how it's been for you and Elspeth, hasn't it?'

'I can never be with Elspeth without the spectre of Ben Kehoe's death coming between us,' he said. 'It's taken me a while to accept that.'

* * *

Dylan was waiting for them in one of the consulting rooms. He had been looking out for them at the window and now he turned to face the door. He had gained a little weight, but he was still achingly thin, and he retained an ethereal quality. His movements were slowed by medication.

He squared his shoulders and said, 'Hi, Alan.'

He's practised that welcome, Rowan thought, liking him for it.

'It's good to see you, Dylan,' Palmer said with real warmth.

'You sound different,' Dylan said.

The scar over Palmer's right eye was healing well and the rope welts on his face and body were almost gone, but the bruises on his neck had been slower to fade, and he still had to speak softly to protect his voice. 'I think perhaps I am.'

Dylan laughed.

'Was that a psychoanalytic joke?' Rowan asked.

Dylan glanced with shy curiosity at her.

'This is Cassie Rowan,' Palmer said. 'Cassie is the police officer who found the pages from your notebook in Karl's flat.'

'Thanks for coming,' Dylan said, offering his hand. He tried for eye contact but didn't quite make it.

'Man of the match,' Rowan said, taking his thin hand and holding it in hers. 'You should be proud.'

Dylan glanced up at Palmer, his green eyes bright with astonishment and pleasure.

'Psych 101,' Palmer said. 'Without your directions, Cassie would never have found us.'

Dylan lifted his chin, digesting the significance of what they had said. He took a seat in an armchair and they followed his example. 'It's all a bit fuzzy.' He sat for a few moments, surreptitiously inscribing something on his left palm with the index finger of his right hand.

Rowan said, 'Oh—' and dipped into her jacket pocket, then handed him a crisp new green notebook and pen. 'I didn't have time to wrap it,' she apologised.

'Thanks.' Dylan turned the notebook over in his hands as if marvelling at it. 'I have eidetic recall.' He glanced at Palmer.

'Yes,' Palmer said.

'I'm not so good on feelings, though.' Dylan smiled shyly at Rowan. 'We had a few talks about the relative importance of feelings and facts.' He shrugged. 'Hence the notebook, full of facts. Easier than thinking or feeling.'

'I'm such an idiot,' Rowan said, cursing herself again for a clumsy fool. 'I just smuggled a flask of whisky into an AA meeting, didn't I?'

Dylan looked in astonishment at Palmer and the corners of Palmer's mouth turned up into the beginnings of a smile. 'Yes,' he said. 'She's always this direct.'

* * *

On the way back to the car, she said, 'I didn't mean he should be proud of the stalking — he does *know* that, doesn't he?'

'He has mental health problems — but he has an IQ of 160 — he's not stupid.' Palmer smiled, softening the sharpness of his response. 'And since you brought it up, you should be proud, too.'

She quirked an eyebrow at him. 'You reckon?'

'You went against orders, risked your career — even your life.'

She blew air between her lips. 'Tell that to my boss.'

'I did, Cassie. She told me you've been exonerated — I told her you deserve a commendation.'

It gave her an unexpected shiver of pleasure to hear him say her name, but she flashed him a cynical cop smile. 'Nice of you to say it, Alan, but the modern police force doesn't reward insubordination with medals.'

'So, no commendation?'

'Finch got that — for leading the team to the kill site.'

'And Wicks?'

She shrugged. 'Like he told me, he's an old hand — used to covering his tracks. I'm just grateful I didn't have to watch him pick up a medal.'

They walked on in silence.

'What about you?' she asked at last. 'How do you feel?'

'Bruises are healing,' Palmer fingered the scar over his eye.

She stopped at the car, keys in hand, and pierced him with a look. 'We had a deal — no macho bullshit.'

'Okay.' He exhaled in a long, shaky rush. 'Here's the truth: I wanted him dead. I wanted revenge for Karl and Tasha and Jodie Pickersgill and Amy Sefton — for all of the people he hurt. I misused my professional training and judgement in an effort to destroy him. I wanted his vile presence effaced from the earth.'

Rowan leaned with her back to the car and stared at the tiny crystals — more ice than snow — chasing in circles across the tarmac. 'If I'd had a gun, I'd have shot him like a rabid dog.'

Palmer stared at her, and for once, she was glad of her inability to stop what came into her head from coming out of her mouth. Because he looked *lighter*, somehow. 'But he didn't die,' she said. 'And neither did you, or Amy. From where I'm standing, that's a result.'

THE END

FREE KINDLE BOOKS

Please join our mailing list for free Kindle books
and new releases, including crime thrillers, mysteries,
romance and more, as well as news on the next book
by Margaret Murphy!

Thank you for reading this book. If you enjoyed it please
leave feedback on Amazon or Goodreads, and if there is
anything we missed or you have a question about then
please get in touch. The author and publishing team
appreciate your feedback and time reading this book.

We're very grateful to eagle-eyed readers who take the
time to contact us. Please send any errors you find to
corrections@joffebooks.com

Follow us on Facebook, Twitter and Instagram
@joffebooks

Made in the USA
Coppell, TX
05 August 2020

32463741R20240